It came out before he had a chance to think,
but in retrospect it was the most truthful thing he could
have said.

She was here . . . at the crux of his past and future . . . at
the heart of all that had been his hopes and expectations . . .
with her curvy frame and sun-polished cheeks and big
green eyes that flashed her emotions like semaphores.
So easy to read.

So easy to want.

Before she could respond, he bent to touch her lips
with his.

Her lips were warm and sweet, and there was a hint of
exploration in the way she fitted them to his. In his travels
he'd kissed a number of women, usually ones with considerable experience. Their eagerness had a measured, practiced feel that was nothing like her earnest response.

The world around him fell away as her arms circled his
waist and she met his embrace. He didn't hear the movement, the quick thud of paws on the path, or the growl until
it was too late.

It was probably no accident that he took the brunt of the
impact . . .

Also by Betina Krahn

The Sin & Sensibility romances

A Good Day to Marry a Duke

The Girl With the Sweetest Secret

Three Nights With the Princess

Behind Closed Doors

Published by Kensington Publishing Corporation

Anyone But A Duke

BETINA KRAHN

ZEBRA BOOKS
KENSINGTON PUBLISHING CORP.
www.kensingtonbooks.com

ZEBRA BOOKS are published by

Kensington Publishing Corp.
119 West 40th Street
New York, NY 10018

All Kensington titles, imprints, and distributed lines are available at special quantity discounts for bulk purchases for sales promotion, premiums, fund-raising, educational, or institutional use.

Special book excerpts or customized printings can also be created to fit specific needs. For details, write or phone the office of the Kensington Sales Manager: Attn.: Sales Department. Kensington Publishing Corp., 119 West 40th Street, New York, NY 10018. Phone: 1-800-221-2647.

Zebra and the Z logo Reg. U.S. Pat. & TM Off.

First Printing: December 2019
ISBN-13: 978-1-4201-4351-5
ISBN-10: 1-4201-4351-4

ISBN-13: 978-1-4201-4352-2 (eBook)
ISBN-10: 1-4201-4352-2 (eBook)

10 9 8 7 6 5 4 3 2 1

Printed in the United States of America

For my beloved Rex,
the partner of my "second half"

Prologue

London

"Our family has never had much luck with dukes," Elizabeth Bumgarten declared, smoothing her already impeccable skirts and staring out the window of the darkened carriage into the chilled September night.

"He's not a duke." Sarah Bumgarten countered her mother's observation, sitting straighter so as not to crumple her costly blue satin. "He's an earl. A new one at that . . . three months . . . mostly spent in Italy garnering family support and alliances." She smiled, thinking of his handsome face and irreverent wit. "But he's finally home."

"I am only saying, he could have found time in his busy schedule to call on you." Her mother sniffed. "In London for days and not even a word."

"He is now responsible for his family's businesses." Sarah thought of his previous devil-may-care attitude toward those weighty concerns. No doubt it was a huge adjustment for him to have to contend constantly with directors, ledgers, and lawyers. "I'm certain that after tonight you'll be complaining that his lordship is always underfoot."

She glanced down at her smartly gloved hands and the

package they held. She couldn't wait to see him open the birthday present she had chosen.

"At least he's not a duke," her mother muttered. "One in the family is quite enough."

Sarah expected her mother to recount again the unfortunate way that her son-in-law had become the Duke of Meridian . . . his older brother, Arthur, had died abroad under unknown circumstances. It was just one of several unfortunate happenings involving their family and men of ducal rank. It was almost enough to put Elizabeth off noblemen altogether. Except, of course, that she had one more daughter to see married. And for once, Sarah found herself in sympathy with her mother's fondest hopes.

For the early part of the season Terrence Tyrell had talked and teased, walked and waltzed with her under the gaze of London society, raising both eyebrows and expectations. She was hardly the most eligible young woman in the marriage hunt, despite her considerable wealth. Always with her nose in a book, dogging some ghastly physician's footsteps, picking up stray animals, or riding hellbent on her demon horse through London's outer boroughs. She made him laugh, he said when questioned by his cohorts. But in private he called her "pretty" and gently touched her hair.

Then, just over three months ago, he'd inherited the title of Earl of Kelling and was whisked away to Italy by the family elders. Now he was back and was undoubtedly expected to settle down, take a wife, and produce an heir. What better time than the final grand ball of the season to take the next prescribed step in the life of a nobleman?

Before he left London he had dropped hints that the family council would meet in Florence, and he made references to the exquisite ring that every earl's bride had worn. Tonight could be the night. If he proposed, by next Monday the *Times* would share the news with all of England, and her mother would be over the moon with delight.

The grand Palladian-style mansion glowed with candlelight reflected by gilt furnishings, French satin, and family jewels. No garish gaslight would intrude on this grand gathering. They paused in the doorway as their names were announced, and Sarah took a deep breath. Her mother's hand on her elbow reminded her of decorum's demands, but she couldn't help scanning the faces, looking for *him* as they moved forward.

She had to greet their host and hostess, the Earl of Sunderland and his countess, Lady Maribel, and then to acknowledge sundry others of rank and precedence before she would be free to join him. It was the final major event of an unusually long season and, coincidentally, his birthday. She held the flat, ribbon-wrapped box at her side, now wishing she had waited to give it to him . . . or at least had chosen less conspicuous wrappings.

Smiles, continental kisses, and handshakes distracted her as she paid duty to all the proper people. Mercifully, her mother absorbed most of the attention, answering queries about married daughters and a forthcoming grandchild. She managed to steal away and enter the ballroom proper, smoothing her rich blue gown and her long kidskin gloves.

Heads turned and whispers began as she made her way around the room, scanning the glittering crowd until she spotted him.

It would be crass, under so many searching eyes, to rush to his side. She had to let him come to her. As she paused to exchange greetings with an older couple, he turned slowly toward her.

That dark hair, those aquiline features, that easy smile . . . *were attached by an arm to a dark-haired woman in a pale yellow gown*. She was a sloe-eyed beauty with olive skin and a demure smile that seemed oddly knowing. As the pair turned, his gaze swept across the ballroom and passed over Sarah without the slightest glint of recognition.

She stood with leaden limbs and a racing heart as one of the earl's boisterous dark-haired companions pointed to her and asked the earl something. He turned with a half smile and replied in Italian before escorting the woman on his arm across the ballroom toward her.

"There you are," he said a bit too loudly, before speaking in what she recognized as Italian to his voluptuous companion. "*Mi amore, vi presento* Signorina Sarah Bumgarten." The woman said something in a dry tone that sounded like "*Sono, in effetti, incantata*" to her, which might have meant either "enchanted" or "eat grass, you cow" in her language. He nodded before turning to Sarah. "My dear girl, I would have you meet Signorina Ava Marie Lombardi, of Florence . . . soon to be my countess."

Words—always her obliging servants—utterly failed her.

She looked between them and forced a brittle smile, hoping to hide the fact that her heart was shattering into a million pieces. She managed a sociable lie about the pleasure of making the woman's acquaintance, and watched helplessly as Terrence's Italian bride turned to him and said something that set the Italians around them smirking. She caught two words that were appallingly similar in English: *dollaro* and *principessa*.

She backed a step and brought her hands up defensively—realizing too late that they held the gift she had brought.

"Ahhh." The Lombardi creature pounced on that mistake with icy amusement, focusing on that pretty blue paper and brilliant yellow bow. "*E così per lui? Eri una **bambina** tanto dolce.*"

Bambina. She had read enough of Dante and other Italian classics to know she had just been called a child. When she looked up in disbelief and caught Terrence's gaze, he quickly looked away. He might be uncomfortable, but he clearly did not value her enough to intervene in such rude and degrading treatment.

She glanced away, only to find a quarter of the ballroom watching that unthinkable exchange. Standing at the front of the onlookers was her mother, and the horror on Elizabeth's face jolted her wits back into action.

"I believe you have mistaken me for someone else," she said, throwing the gift on the floor near his feet and hearing the satisfying tinkle of breaking glass. "I am not now, nor have I ever been a 'sweet child.' And it appears that I have mistaken you, sir"—she looked at the earl through a prism of hot tears—"for a gentleman of character and worth."

She turned on her heel and strode for the door, spine straight and head held high, ignoring the slither of gossip trailing her through the crowd.

Moments later, as she donned her wrap near the front doors, her mother came rushing down the stairs from the ballroom to pull her aside.

"What did that beast say to you?" she demanded.

"Nothing I shouldn't have seen coming," she answered bitterly.

"Where are you going? You cannot run from this, Sarah. You must stay and hold your head up and brave it through. The Richardsons are here and the Spencers. They will see us through."

She pulled the hood of her cloak up over her hair and looked around the grand entry hall, watching the faces of the people staring at them while pretending not to stare.

"I don't want to be seen through. I don't want to have to bow and scrape and pretend I give a flying fig about these awful people. They think I'm odd and eccentric because I read so many books and help stray animals and study medicine. Well, they can all bloody well die on the privy, for all I care."

As she turned to the door, her mother grabbed her wrist and held her until Sarah turned a scalding look on her. She loosened her grip and then, reading the pain and fury in her daughter's gaze, released her.

"Wait, I'll get my cloak—"

"No. You stay and gut it out with the Spencers and Richardsons." Banked tears finally slipped down her cheeks. "You'll want a life here after I've gone."

"Gone? What are you talking about? Where are you going?"

"*Anywhere*"—Sarah forced the words past the constriction in her throat—"*but London.*"

Chapter One

Months later
The English countryside

"**B**lasted animal," Sarah Bumgarten muttered as she strode down the tree-lined country lane. She had started this search near the main house, and ventured farther and farther—until she now found herself almost to the village, still on foot in unsuitable shoes. It was an exceptionally warm day, and she was annoyed to have to spend it looking for her dog when there was so much to be done at Betancourt. Every footfall on the gravel of the road sounded like teeth grinding.

Consarned dog. She pushed her hair back from her face. *Running off to hell and gone, again.* The last two times, she had found him in Betany terrifying the locals. Nero was more dog than most of the villagers had ever seen . . . Irish wolfhound with a bit of heft that probably came from a mastiff somewhere in the line. He was tall and gray and had red-brown eyes as bright as copper pennies. He was stunning. And intimidating. And he had a grin that could melt an iceberg. All of which had combined to lure her into rescuing him from London's mean streets. She had no idea how an Irish wolfhound pup came to be running free in London's West End, but she wasn't one to pass up a hungry, frightened animal when it came her way.

It wasn't long before the Iron Penny Inn and Tavern came into view. The rambling stone and half-timber structure had served as the social center of the village of Betany for generations. If anyone had seen Nero in the vicinity, it would be Bascom, the sturdy, taciturn innkeeper. He kept an eye on the village as well as his own property. If he hadn't seen Nero, there was a good chance she could get him or his son William to help her search.

Raucous male voices and harsh laughter from the far side of the tavern caught her ear as she approached the inn. That low, wicked rumble was punctuated by a yelp of surprise . . . anger . . . pain.

Damn and blast!

"Bascom!" she shouted as she ran past the open tavern door. "Bascom, I need help!"

A dog was in trouble, and she would have bet her best riding boots which dog it would be. Her heart gave a furious thump as another yelp and then some snarling reached her.

Around the corner, in the side yard of the Iron Penny, four men surrounded her wolfhound. Nero was growling and showing teeth as he crouched defensively and looked for a way out. But the men were steadily closing the gaps between them, hefting rocks and taking turns taunting Nero. As she caught her breath, one of the four lobbed a rock at her dog, who dodged, but only into the path of another missile hurled at him. He yelped and shrank for an instant, then came back growling and baring teeth.

She bolted toward the fray, yelling, "Stop! This instant!"

The men turned on her, surprised—by her appearance as much as her demand. She had dressed for a day of visiting the local vicar and a few tradesmen: a yellow cotton day dress printed with blue flowers, made with French-blue piping, and satin ribbon laced through the bodice. She had meant to present a ladylike appearance to the people of Betany—to reassure them that someone was upholding Betancourt standards. However, her hair was down and windblown—she hadn't had time to put it up when housemaid Mazie stumbled up the stairs to tell her that Nero was missing again.

"Well . . . look wot we got 'ere," one of the men said, turning to her with an ugly grin filled with dark gaps and yellowed teeth.

"That's my dog." Her anxiety rose as two of the others closed on Nero. "You leave him alone!"

"Ooh, hear that? *Orders*. We got us a duchess, boys," another, taller fellow declared before giving an enormous belch. Fumes from spent liquor wafted in her direction as he made a sloppy bow of deference.

Drunk, she realized. At this hour of the morning.

"Yer mutt near took my leg off when I went out back to take a piss," the farthest wretch snarled, glaring at Nero as he removed his belt. "He needs teachin'." He drew back with the strap and found his arm stopped—held. His wrist was caught in the grip of a man with long hair, hands like iron bands, and eyes filled with heat like forge flames.

"Lemme go." He turned and swung at the stranger with his free hand, but his ale-sodden reflexes were no match for the stranger's quickness. The blow was deflected and the next minute, the stranger's fist rammed into his gut and all hell broke loose.

The wretch nearest Sarah lunged for her and she slammed a fist straight into the middle of his face. There was a crunching sound and a howl that might have come from her as pain shot up her hand and arm. Suddenly there was a storm of scuffling and growling and the sound of fists smacking flesh all around the tavern yard.

She got in several solid kicks and at least one more good face punch before a shotgun blast jarred the scene and the frantic conflict froze. Bascom charged into their midst, his formidable double-barrel shotgun leveled at the miscreants.

"I told you lot to get out," he ordered. "You ain't welcome in my tavern nor the rest o' Betany." He gave the closest fellow—the one cradling a bloody face—a shove.

"She broke my damned nose!" the rogue howled, stumbling to the side.

"Out. Now." Bascom stalked closer and shoved again, harder. "Pick up yer friends, an' clear out."

For a moment it looked as if he might turn on Bascom, but instead he looked past the innkeeper to Sarah, with eyes burning.

"Ye'll be sorry, *duchess*. You an' yer mangy mutt."

Sarah's heart hammered. She gulped a breath as the ruffian stumbled over to his closest comrade, helped him to his feet and braced him upright as they staggered off together. She looked around to find Nero sitting primly between two figures sprawled and motionless on the ground.

Behind him stood a man in shirtsleeves, vest, and riding breeches, with his booted legs spread and his arms crossed. His hair was long enough to brush his shoulders and his face was sun-bronzed. But his eyes—for a moment, across that space, she could have sworn there were white-hot sparks in his eyes. She looked away and blinked to clear her vision. When she looked back, he had turned and was disappearing down the bend in the village road.

Trembling, she turned to Bascom.

"Who are those men?"

"The same lot wot's been around this past month or two. Always trouble. Drunk half the time, fightin' the other half. Tearin' up shops and market stalls. Jus' plain mean, the lot of 'em."

"Ugh." She made a face and stuck out her tongue. "I think I might have bit one of them. I have an awful taste in my—" She headed straight for the pump at the nearby trough, gave the handle a few pumps and flushed her mouth out with cool water. Looking up, she found Bascom cradling his gun and watching her with a wry expression.

"Well, Lord knows where they've been," she said defensively.

He chuckled and gave her injured hand a nod.

"Better see to that."

She winced as she gave her throbbing fingers a couple of exploratory touches that made her draw a sharp breath. "Nothing seems broken. A soak in some Epsom salts and some willow bark tea will fix it up."

"You know best. Jimmy Donner tells one and all how you saved his arm after he got it broke in the thresher." He frowned as he watched her wrap her hand in a handkerchief. "But, now, will ye take a bit o' advice and chain up that beast o' yours?"

She cradled her injured hand against her middle, reluctantly considering that advice and wishing there were another alternative. She looked around for Nero, and caught sight of his rump escaping around the corner of the tavern.

Annoyance ignited to full anger as she took off after him. Bascom wasn't far behind as she raced to catch Nero. The dog ran pell-mell to the rustic stable behind the inn that served the guests' horses. She lifted her skirts and ran faster, muttering between breaths when she saw him dart inside the shedlike stable. She stepped inside and found it darker than expected and she had to pause a moment to let her eyes adjust. She called for Nero, but there was no response.

In a far corner, she found him braced in a guarding stance—body taut, ears up—beside one of the empty stalls. He watched her approach with a wariness he had never displayed toward her before.

"What the devil?" She moved cautiously forward. She

knew Nero wouldn't harm her, but clearly he intended to keep them from—

She stopped beside the stall. There was something dark on the straw . . . another dog. Something beside it was squirming. Soft mews reached her.

Puppies.

In the stall lay a female dog with a young litter, no more than a week or two old. Sarah grinned and gave Nero a stroke down his back as she edged past him, into the stall. At her gentle touch he relaxed visibly, then hurried to the mother dog and nosed her as if assuring her that this human meant no harm to her and her babies.

The mother lifted her nose to Nero's muzzle in acceptance of his presence. It struck Sarah as she watched her troublesome pet settle beside the female's head that this was what Nero had been doing these last few days: visiting this dog and her puppies. There was probably only one reason he would do so.

"You rascal," she muttered as she bent to look at the little ones. Their eyes were just open and their bellies bulged as they rooted for more milk. They were mostly black or gray, like their parents, and it was hard to say which parent they would favor as they grew. A soft chuckle made her look up. Bascom was leaning against a roof post, wagging his head and grinning.

"Looks like yer boy's got hisself a family."

"Looks like."

"That's a sheep dog—one o' them borderland collies. From up north country. Ain't much work for a sheep dog if there ain't no sheep."

Sarah scowled. "No sheep? The farmers up there are selling off their flocks?"

He nodded and frowned. "These are bad times, milady. Price o' wool is so low. Not much work, but plenty o' mischief about these days. Strangers ramblin' here and yon. It's got so ye don't know who to trust."

A flash of memory brought one specific stranger's face to mind: the man with the sparks in his eyes. She recalled a blur of motion and the sound of struggle behind her while she was dealing out a nose-breaker. After Bascom's warning shot, there were two bodies on the ground and the man stood over them, chest heaving, as he watched her. He wasn't part of the group that had abused her dog—he'd somehow rendered two of the wretches unconscious.

"That other man—the one with the long hair and steely eyes—who is he?" she asked Bascom.

"No idea," Bascom said on a heavy breath. "Like I said, lots o' strangers about in these parts."

She took in that response and then looked back at the dogs. Nero was licking the mother dog's ears and muzzle with surprising tenderness. "Any guess where we might find her owner?"

"Aw, she's a stray. Some sheep herder couldn't feed her no more, so he turned her out . . . or she run off."

She nodded at his logic.

"Well, I can't have Nero coming here to see her every day and getting into trouble." She pursed one corner of her mouth. "I'll send Young Eddie back with the pony cart to pick them up and bring them to Betancourt."

She looked down at the now sated and drowsy puppies.

"We always have room for a few more babies at Betancourt." She smiled in spite of the pain throbbing in her fingers. "I can't wait to get my hands on them."

"How much for a room tonight?" the long-haired stranger asked as Bascom placed a tankard of ale on the tavern table in front of him that evening.

It was just past sunset and the taproom was barely half

full. It was planting season, and folk from surrounding farms were too tired to go into the village after a day's hard labor. The rains and spring storms were past, and village folk were taxed by planting gardens and repairing winter damage to houses, barns, and shops. Bascom had greeted the few patrons by name and served most without having to take an order.

There was one patron in particular that drew his attention: the stranger from earlier in the day, the one who helped deal with the wretches baiting the duchess's dog. He had stabled his horse at the inn and had spent the better part of the day strolling the village and hiking the rolling hills around Betany and Betancourt.

The man had returned not long ago and chosen a seat at a table in the corner by the cold fireplace. He ordered some dinner and ate like it might be snatched away at any moment, and then propped his feet on the stone hearth beside him. Bascom, like a good tavern keeper, remembered his choice of drink and after a while brought him a fresh tankard of stout.

"Two shillings, even." Bascom answered the query, studying the man and his deep voice. "Two an' six if ye be wantin' a bath."

"Just the room will be fine," the stranger said with a wry twist to his mouth as he pulled coins from his pocket, sorted out two, and handed them over. The slight rasp to his voice piqued Bascom's curiosity. "But answer me a question, if you will." The innkeeper's pause and the way he adjusted the towel hanging over one shoulder encouraged the man to continue.

"Who was that woman this morning . . . with the dog? They called her 'duchess.'"

"The duchess? She come from Betancourt—th' Duke of Meridian's seat." He glanced around the taproom and lowered his voice. "House folk up there say she's th' duke's sister."

"She could hardly be the duchess, then," the stranger said, taking a sip of his ale. "Being the sister of a duke." His angular face tightened into a scowl. "And . . . I wasn't aware the duke had a sister. I understood there were just a pair of brothers in the Graham family."

"All I know is wot I heard. Whatever she is, she runs the place." Bascom chuckled. "Ain't much that gets by her. Knows healin', she does—as good as a city doctor. Gets called for tendin' man and beast alike." The innkeeper lowered his head and his voice. "The duke took off. Up and left. Ain't been seen in years. So, when she come to look after the place, folk were right flummoxed. But she's takin' the place in hand an' helped with the house an' the stock an' tenants, so—"

"Oy—barkeep!" A loud, rough voice split the peace of the taproom. A moment later, a big, roughly dressed man ducked through the open doorway and paused just inside the peaceful taproom. "We'll have ale—plenty of it!"

With him were two men with split lips and swollen eyes—familiar injuries. They were the two the "duchess" had bashed in the side yard earlier, during the dustup over the dog. They were back, glowering, and they had brought a big, ugly friend.

Bascom picked up the empty tankard and made his way toward the men, eyeing the bar and the shotgun behind it.

"You gents"—he addressed the smaller two—"ain't welcome at th' Iron Penny. I told you that this morning. You an' yer kind keep away from my inn and my village. Folk in Betany don't stand for bullyin' and brawlin'."

Two of the locals lowered their heads and abandoned their table to make for the door. Those who were left clutched their tankards anxiously and slid chairs back from their table to make way for a quick exit. The stranger took a sip of ale and watched Bascom edge toward the bar.

"That ain't sociable," the big fellow declared without even a pretense of good humor. "We come fer a drink an' we're gonna get one."

"Or a dozen." That came from one of the worse-for-wear dog baiters behind the big fellow. The narrowing of their eyes and grim set of their faces made clear that they intended to make good on the old saying, "Down twelve pints an' start a fight."

"I believe you gents have been warned."

Arthur Graham, now a stranger on his own lands, rose quietly and moved toward Bascom's back. He curled his hands into fists and felt every muscle in his body tighten with expectation. The threesome hadn't come to drink, they'd come to get revenge.

"You should leave. Now."

"An' who's gonna make us?" the big one snarled, looking him over, assessing and dismissing the threat he presented. "You, pretty boy?"

Pretty boy? Arthur's eyebrows rose.

There was only one way this would end, he thought: with those two lowlifes in a heap and their beefy friend on top. Three against one . . . not the worst odds he'd faced. But then, maybe he could make it one-on-one if he picked the right one.

The two returning miscreants' eyes shone with a lust for revenge and an expectation that it would soon be forthcoming. Bascom took one measured pace to the side, glancing at the shotgun behind his bar, and Arthur slid into his place, facing the three. His hand brushed a chair as he moved, then he opened it to slide his palm down the back of the chair. He casually dipped a shoulder to maneuver his hand to grip the back of the seat and the two finally read a threat in his move and growled, "Get 'im, Steig!"

Arthur came up swinging the heavy oak chair, but not at the pair he had bested earlier—at the brute with the ugly sneer instead. The big man's reflexes surprised Arthur. The man staggered under the blow, but managed to grab the chair's leg and yanked hard, trying to wrest the seat from his opponent.

Arthur had chosen well; once the brute "Steig" was engaged, the others hung back, content to snarl encouragement. When the big fellow couldn't take the chair from Arthur, he seemed to take it personally. With a roar, he shoved the chair—and with it, Arthur—away. Then out came the knife, a good-sized blade with a bright edge that spoke of devoted sharpening. No doubt that knife had seen and ended many such disputes. The tavern's remaining patrons, those who hadn't already fled, scrambled for places against the walls.

Arthur pulled the seat of the chair to his chest and used it like a shield as the big man attacked. Steig's moves— short, focused jabs and low, fast arcs of the blade—were classic knife-fighting technique. Arthur was surprised to find himself facing a brute who owned some skill. But in his experience there were disadvantages to concentrating all of your power on an edge of steel. A knife fighter, crouched and braced, was essentially a one-armed man. Very few were as strong and agile as a bare-knuckle fighter who knew how to use his fists, his feet, and his core strength in explosive bursts.

Bascom had made for his shotgun the minute the big man lunged at Arthur, but didn't reach it before one of the two miscreants caught him and slammed a shoulder into his side, pinning him against the bar. The other bully joined him, and Bascom, now held fiercely between the two, could do nothing but watch as Arthur battled the brute who came to punish the innkeeper for daring to oppose them.

Several swings of that big knife told Arthur all he needed to know. He slammed the chair against a post, broke off a couple of legs, and then wheeled and attacked. His feet were his weapons at first and with the chair bottom shielding his chest, he braved the knife to deliver a crushing kick to one of the big fellow's knees. The joint buckled and wrenched a roar of pain from Steig as he lurched and stumbled aside. He returned seconds later, limping badly and bent on a more personal kind of revenge. His increasingly wicked slashes and jabs were parried by that broken chair and Arthur's quick reflexes.

The tavern filled with growls and thuds and encouragement from villagers. Onlookers shouted "Look out!" and "Get 'im, lad!"

The odds changed when the big man's blade tip grazed a nearby post and stuck long enough for Arthur to bring the chair down on his arm like a hammer. The big man howled and the knife went flying. Another of Arthur's punches hit home, and it was suddenly hand to hand. They came together in a flurry of staggering blows that ended when a chair was swung at Steig's back by an intrepid villager. That second front of attack, though far from powerful, was enough to break the big man's concentration. Arthur exploded upward with a blow to his chin that snapped Steig's head back and dropped him like a wet sack of grain.

Shocked silence was followed by a cheer, a tussle at the bar, and a roar of anger as the remaining villagers descended on the less-imposing miscreants. The pair was dragged outside and, from the sound of it, given their second thrashing of the day.

Someone ran for the constable and the big man was soon dragged down the street and locked up in a secure stone room in a nearby barn. A bit of ale-fueled fisticuffs could be overlooked by the law, but adding a knife to a brawl took it to a potentially deadly level.

Arthur stood in the taproom panting, his limbs twitching with the aftermath of the action coursing through them. His heart pounded as his senses cleared to resume their normal function. As he took stock of his surroundings and injuries—a scratch here and there, a bruised jaw and a sore rib or two—he counted himself lucky indeed. The brute had more skill with that blade than he'd expected.

He lumbered to the bar where Bascom stood breathing heavily from his belated bout with the two who had held him. The innkeeper held out something to Arthur, who frowned, but then extended his hand palm-up. The innkeeper deposited the two shillings Arthur had given him earlier for a room.

"On the house."

Arthur smiled, then put one back on the bar, sliding it across.

"I think I need another pint. Or ten."

Bascom poured a pint from the tap and set it before him. "Yer money's no good here, stranger. Wot do I call you?"

There was a slight hesitation in the answer. "Art."

"Well, Art, welcome to Betany."

The next morning, Arthur rose before dawn, grabbed a piece of bread and a hunk of cheese from the cold kitchen, and resumed his rambling exploration of the surrounding area as he breakfasted. Predawn mist clung to the trees as he sauntered along the wooded lane that he remembered well. It led to Betancourt, the Meridians' seat, and didn't seem to have changed much in the years since he'd seen it last. He recalled walking that same path one night . . . in the dark . . . his life in turmoil. But, a more recent memory eclipsed that thought and caused a hitch in his gait.

There she stood in his mind's eye . . . *the duchess* . . . wrapped in yellow, looking pure as sunshine . . . sun-kissed hair loose and hugging her shoulders . . . eyes hot with anger. She had stopped him dead in his tracks with her similarity to . . . when they called her "duchess" his heart had quivered for a moment. But her voice, her actions weren't Daisy's.

She claimed to be the duke's sister, but he knew full well that was a lie. He gave a huff of a laugh. If the Grahams had produced a female, she would have been a strapping specimen with broad shoulders, an aquiline nose, and a voice like a foghorn. Certainly not that curvy bundle of dynamite that broke a man's nose in defense of—

He was so focused on that memorable little figure that he didn't notice the rustle of leaves or the crunch of a fallen branch behind him. The bark of the gun and the punch to his shoulder surprised him, but it was an instant before he felt the white-hot sear of pain from the bullet that entered his body. He managed to look back over his shoulder and take three more steps before his legs gave out and he collapsed on the grass beside the lane.

Chapter Two

"Another coal-black one. Not a speck of white," Sarah said, looking down at the foal struggling to gain its feet only minutes after being born. She stood in the door to the box stall in Betancourt's stable, watching as the mare that had given birth hovered nearby, overseeing her offspring's efforts. "Dancer blood breeds true." She turned to Eddie, the young hand recruited from a local farm to assist the aging horse master with Betancourt's growing stable of horses. "How many does that make?"

"Twelve, milady," Eddie said, gazing fondly at the newborn. "Twelve coal black. Never heard of such a thing."

The mare, whom Sarah had dubbed Lady Maker, snorted and nudged her foal to try for his feet again. When his wobbly legs steadied and held his sturdy little body upright, Sarah laughed and was so desperate to hug somebody that she threw her arms around Eddie. The young stable hand stood wide-eyed and motionless in her embrace until she released him.

"Our father was a heckuva horse breeder," she said, gazing fondly at the foal again. "Brought in Friesian and Arabian stock to combine with our western saddle horses and improved confirmation and endurance in Silver River stock. Midnight Dancer was probably the best stallion that ever came from our ranch. Of course, *Daisy* claimed him straightaway and brought him across the pond with her."

"Daisy, milady?" Eddie looked down, struggling with embarrassment.

"My oldest sister. She married Ashton Graham, the old duke's younger brother . . . who may be . . . who *is* the current duke."

"I thought you was th' duchess. Ain't that what Mister Edgar says?"

"Edgar has me confused with my sister, and I gave up on correcting him." She smiled tightly. "Edgar is confused a lot these days."

"Ain't that th' truth." Eddie winced, clearly familiar with the aged butler who rambled the great house, forgetting where he was each time he turned a corner.

Sarah headed down the alley between rows of box stalls filled with mares and foals that came to the gates of their stalls to greet her. Eddie followed, drawn by her vivacious presence and her uncanny way with beasts.

"Our spread in Nevada was called the Silver River Ranch. I was just a young girl, ten years old, when we left there." She paused to pet a few velvety noses. "But already I had to saddle my own horse and curry and feed her and see to it she met with the farrier regularly."

"You, milady?" Eddie seemed genuinely astonished. "They made ye haul yer own tack an' feed yer own horse?"

"Of course." She smiled at his dismay. "Westerners pride themselves on self-sufficiency. Out West, you have to be able to do things for yourself or you don't survive. My sisters and I were each assigned chores on the ranch, to teach us the value of work. I learned from the ranch hands how to drive cattle, find water for the herd, and build a fire at night. Then there were orphaned calves to feed, and dogs to train, and chickens and ducks to tend. That was the start of my love for animals."

But it was not the start of their love for her. From the day she was born she had seemed to have a remarkable effect on animals of all kinds. They recognized something in her and accepted her presence and attention as if she were one of their own.

They reached the cross alley outside the tack room, and there, in a large wooden box on the floor, lined with straw and old blankets, were Nero's mate and puppies.

"Look! They're climbing all over each other. They'll be walking soon and then running." She rushed to the box, but tempered her enthusiasm as the mother sat up anxiously. "It's all right, mama, I'm not going to bother your little ones."

She knelt by the box and cooed to the puppies, who responded by turning in her direction. With each soft and musical word the mother relaxed more and before long was stretching her nose toward Sarah. She let the dog sniff and then stroked the collie's head and massaged her ears, sensing that a relationship had just been born.

"We're going to have to give you a name, girl," she said with a chuckle. "How about . . . Nell? Nero and Nellie. Sound good to you?" Another lick of her hand sealed it.

When she exited the stable, there were four dogs, two young goats, and a pair of escaped piglets waiting for her. They had heard her voice and were waiting by the door for her. Each pat and fond word left tails wagging, twitching, or curling. She made sure each animal got some attention, and then handed the piglets off to a surprised Eddie with instructions to return them to their pen. As she struck off up the drive for the main doors of the great house, she could see Eddie holding the piglets and shaking his head at the four-legged parade she led.

The front court had seen some changes in the months since she arrived. She paused with her arms folded to examine the impressive face of the venerable brick and stone

mansion. She'd had the beautiful long windows re-glazed
and cleaned; they sparkled in the morning sun. The weathered front doors had been sanded and painted a dignified
black, with new brass fittings applied. On each side of the
entry were topiary shrubs in large stone planters that she
had found under the dovecote and restored to use. Tidy
new gravel paved the front court and trailed off toward the
stables and barns. It looked like someone lived here now.
Someone important.

Her first glimpse of Betancourt, as a fourteen-year-old
girl fresh from New York, had struck her speechless. She
was awed by the thought of being connected, even tangen-
tially, to such a place. Daisy was there, dressed like a
princess, and there were the duke and his handsome brother
Ashton, who became her brother-in-law.

She and her sisters had been treated like royalty. The
duke even took her hand for a dance as her sister Cece
played the violin one evening. A real duke, but he was kind
and mannerly and a little funny, though he didn't seem to
know it. She was saddened to think that his gentle presence
was gone from the world. No one had heard a word from
him since he set off on his travels. After five years—by the
duke's own decree—the Meridian title and property had
reverted to his younger brother, Ashton. She was now
sister to a duke, albeit by marriage.

A low rumble from the village road set the dogs barking, and she turned to find a pony cart racing up the long
drive, headed straight for the doors of Betancourt. The
driver's shoulders were hunched forward as he slapped
the reins and the pony dug in with determination. The pair
were clearly on a mission. Sarah waded through the excited animals to meet the driver at the front doors.

"Duchess!" It was Thomas Wrenn, a tenant who farmed
Betancourt land, down by the river. To augment his
income, he delivered flour and feed from the local mill to

he village, and his route took him by Betancourt's front
gates on a daily basis. As he halted the cart near the front
doors and jumped down, it was clear he had more than
flour in his cart.

A man lay sprawled atop the sacks packed into the
wooden bed of the vehicle. Thomas beckoned, out of breath,
and looked frantic as he rushed to the rear of his cart. She
picked up her skirts and bounded up onto the wheel spoke
to see what had happened.

"Found him on the road a ways back and brung him as
fast as I could," Thomas declared, breathing hard. "I think
he's been shot."

Had he ever. Thomas lifted the old blanket he'd covered
the fellow with to reveal a nasty hole in the man's left
shoulder. The front of his shirt was wet with fresh blood,
but there was older, dried blood on his sleeve and down
his side. Her gaze swept to his face and for an instant she
froze. It was the long-haired stranger who had helped
defend her dog the day before.

Again and again, the previous evening, she'd found
herself wondering who he was and telling herself it was
the shock of the unthinkable incident that etched him so
deeply in her thoughts. But, clearly, she hadn't just imagined that chiseled, sun-burnished face, or those broad
shoulders and neatly shaped frame. She looked up to find
Thomas staring strangely at her, and she blushed and made
a show of feeling for a pulse in the stranger's neck.

Thankfully he had one, though it was slow, and she realized with a start that it was up to her to make sure that
stalwart heart kept beating.

"He needs tending right away," she muttered, then
jumped down to run to the door and call for help.

There wasn't much help to be had. Edgar and another
aging houseman by the ironic name of Young Ned, tried to
lift the wounded stranger from the cart, but even with

Thomas Wrenn's help, they had difficulty moving him. Sarah growled, hiked her skirt to climb up onto the bags of grain, and had the men turn him onto his side while she rolled the blanket and shoved it beneath his back. When they rolled him back toward her and unrolled the rest of the blanket beneath him, the blanket became a makeshift stretcher.

The poor man was carried, bumped over the sill of the front entry, and then lugged through a pack of curious dogs to the stairs. Mazie and Deidre, two house women in mob-caps and aprons, were pressed into service and the six of them managed to get him up the main stairs without doing too much additional damage to his body.

By the time they reached the head of the stairs, Edgar looked ready to faint and Young Ned, who had always had a touch of the asthma, was wheezing like a leaky bellows.

"Let's just . . . get him . . . to the nearest bed," Sarah ordered, spotting a nearby pair of ornate doors. "In there," she declared, nodding toward them.

"But that's . . . that's . . ." Edgar stammered, looking horrified.

"The nearest bed," she answered with a finality that even Old Edgar understood.

It was in fact the duke's bedchamber, which had lain abandoned for more than three years . . . since Daisy and her husband, Ashton, returned to New York. The group half carried, half dragged the man across the room and with heroic effort hoisted him up and onto the bed. Fortunately, the blanket remained between his bloody clothes and the elegant silk counterpane Daisy had chosen when refurbishing the duke's chambers.

Sarah's back was aching and her sore hand was throbbing as she lifted his shoulder enough to find the other bullet hole. In one side and out the other, she realized, and forced herself to focus on that bit of luck. According to her medical books, "through and through" was the best kind of bullet wound. At least she wouldn't be doing more damage by fishing around in his flesh for a hunk of lead.

She sent Mazie and Deidre for her medicine chest, boiling water, and bandages, and then opened his ruined shirt to inspect the wound. She winced. Thomas's good deed and all of the jostling had started the poor man bleeding again. But the fact that the bleeding had slowed or stopped before said there was hope. She pressed the wound with her own bandaged hand and asked Edgar and Young Ned to remove the man's shirt.

"Really, mi-milady . . . should you be . . ." Edgar looked to Young Ned, seeming shocked to indecision. Or incapacity. Neither of which took much.

"I-I can help, milady." Thomas had retreated toward the door, gripping the hat he had doffed in deference to his opulent surroundings, but he came forward now.

"Please," Sarah said, nodding to him. He hurried to the bed and as he began to remove the man's shirt, she turned away to give Young Ned orders. "I'll need more light. Pull the drapes all the way. And get his boots off."

When the sunlight bloomed around them and she heard boots hit the floor, she turned back to her patient and gasped aloud. The stranger's uninjured shoulder was covered by an intricate pattern inked into his skin.

A *tattoo*.

She had read about them—she read about *everything*—but had never expected to see one in person. On impulse she ran her fingers over that ornate skin, expecting to feel a difference in texture. But his tattooed shoulder was as sleek and smooth as the rest of him. From what she'd read, sailors got tattoos in exotic ports of call—the Far East, the Spice Islands, Indonesia, New Zealand—cultures where men reportedly wore them as badges of honor and experience.

She blinked. He didn't look like an exotic islander. He looked like an Englishman who had been left out in the sun too long. His skin was baked to a turn beneath his shirt . . . the same color as his face and arms. Clearly, he'd spent time outdoors. Shirtless. She picked up his bruised left hand and on his knuckles found fresh scratches and bruises, and on his palm some calluses that spoke of manual labor. But there was a knob near the tip of the middle finger of his right hand. A writer's bump . . . he had also spent time with a pen in his hand.

Her exploration was cut short by Mazie's and Deidre's arrival with her medicine chest, hot water, and bandages. After removing her own now bloody bandage and washing her hands, she donned an apron and cleaned his wound. Her own special honey and herb plaster came next, and then she bandaged it as tightly as she dared.

"It's fairly neat, as bullet wounds go," she told Thomas and Young Ned, who helped her lift and position her patient for binding. In truth, she had little to compare it to outside of books. This was her first real bullet wound. "The bleeding has almost stopped. We'll watch him round the clock for the next day or two and see he gets nourishment when he wakes up."

She grabbed a bar of strong soap and had Mazie pour the last of the hot water over her hands. Hand washing, she had read recently, was key to avoiding putrefaction. As she dried her hands, she turned back to her patient and studied his strong profile and finely honed muscularity.

"It's up to his constitution to do the rest."

That afternoon she assigned household staff to sit with him and watch for signs of pain or rising consciousness. She took the evening shift herself, bringing a book and four dogs with her into the duke's precious sanctum.

She moved a table and lamp close to the bed, and snuggled into a large stuffed chair beside it with Gwenny, a small terrier, and Lancelot, a mixed-breed hound, vying for space on her lap. Nero, as usual, was at her feet, and curly-eared Morgana—ever the sly and naughty spaniel—climbed right up on the foot of the bed to nestle against the stranger's feet. Three times Sarah ordered her down, but three times she waited for Sarah to be absorbed in her book and climbed back up again. In the end, Sarah sighed and let the vixen stay there.

Twice, her patient moaned and moved restlessly. She got up to check, and he seemed to grow warmer each time. She prayed there wouldn't be an infection and fever. She wetted a cloth for his forehead, allowing her fingers to linger on his hair for a moment, which produced a curious feeling of familiarity in her. Had she seen him before somewhere? Bascom said he was a stranger in these parts, and no one in the household seemed to recognize him. Could she have seen him in London, before she fled—retreated—*relocated*—to the country?

No, she told herself, she would remember him. That hair, those neatly carved features, and that intense stare were unforgettable . . . though, her attention *had* been otherwise occupied in those last days in London. She had been so caught up in—a surge of potent memories blindsided her, sending her spirits plummeting. Tall, dark, and refined . . . infectious smile and wicked wit . . . the heir to the Earl of Kelling, had listened to her and talked to her . . . shared her enthusiasm for books and nature. She came to hope—

She yanked her thoughts back from that precipice and away from the events of that party—that awful moment when—

She took a deep, furious breath, appalled by the still tender emotions that, she had consoled herself, would fade.

Well, they weren't fading quickly enough. She had left all of that behind, and *behind* was where it belonged. She was making a fresh start, making her own way, making a difference. She intended to have a life that was worthwhile, no matter what London's malicious wags said.

Propping her hands on her waist, she stood studying her mysterious patient, distancing herself, steeling her reserve. Her fascination with his unusual appearance and curiosity about his story had somehow roused those memories in her. That had to be it. He was utterly masculine; that in and of itself was enough to make him exotic.

She had been raised in a house full of females, so males of the species were alien to her in nearly every respect. They were puzzles, and—Heaven help her—she never could resist a good puzzle.

That was it, she decided; he was a tantalizing unknown.

Having that settled in her mind was reassuring.

"Whoever you are," she said to her enigmatic patient, "don't get used to this." She gestured to the large, regally draped bed he had landed in. "Because you're headed upstairs to the old nursery as soon as you're well enough to move."

Chapter Three

By the next morning, Sarah had a crick in her neck from dozing in the chair and her curled-up legs were full of pins and needles. Her patient seemed to still be sleeping, so she called Mazie upstairs and installed her in the bedside chair with a pile of linens to mend, so Sarah could return to her daily rounds of the house and estate.

As always, she was accompanied by Nero, Gwenny, Lancelot, and Morgana. The minute she stepped out the kitchen door, their troupe was joined by a number of ducks, a pair of feisty goats, and sundry barn cats that crept along in the shadows with a wary eye on the dogs.

She was halfway through the stable, petting the noses extended to her as she passed, on her way to check on Nero's puppies, when a rider reined up at the stable door and called out.

"Milady?" She heard boots hit gravel as a man called, "Duchess?"

She winced at the misapplied title and grumbled. "How many times do I have to say it: I am not a bloody *duchess*."

Lifting her skirts, she hurried back down the alley. "Who is calling?"

At the door, peering into the dimmer stables was a figure

she knew. Samuel Arnett—tall, lean, and sun-weathered—was a tenant from the west road who had heard of her medical acumen and twice before had prevailed upon her to come and treat his ailing mother, Old Bec.

"It's Ma, yer ladyship," Samuel said, snatching his cap from his balding head as she approached. "Got it bad this time. Can ye come?"

The old woman hadn't seemed all that ill the last time they called for her, but that didn't mean she wasn't in a bad way now. Elders could take sharp turns for the worse in very little time.

"Of course I'll come, Samuel." She glanced up at his mount and was surprised to see a saddle strapped precariously on the back of a very large and unhappy-looking plow horse.

She started to ask what had happened to the sweet little mare he had ridden before, but he craned his neck to look past her into the stable and said in a rush, "Ye'll be wantin' to bring yer own horse, duchess. Old Gus here, he ain't trained proper to a saddle. He's not fer a lady like yerself." He gave her a pained look. "I barely hung on long enough to make it here."

Moments later, Eddie was saddling Sarah's horse, the striking and powerful Fancy Boy, and one of the stable lads was running full tilt to the main house to fetch her medicine bag. She looked down at her blue cotton day dress and judged her full skirt suitable and her tall, side-button leather boots durable enough for the short ride. She would need a hat, however, and located an old straw hat hanging in the tack room.

In less than ten minutes, they were riding briskly down the drive and turning in the direction of Samuel's farm. He seemed relieved that his mother would soon be tended, and he relaxed visibly as he answered her queries about his wife, Young Bec, and their five children.

"Doin' fine," he said. "Young Bec's growin' her sixth, and th' oldest two boys 'as been a real help with th' plantin' this spring. The lambin' went well, an' we got a number of first-time heifers that'll be comin' fresh soon."

It was a heartening if somewhat vague report, Sarah thought, trying to recall just how many heifers the Arnetts had. "And your mare? What happened to her?"

The question seemed to surprise Samuel. "She's . . . um . . . out o' sorts, lately. Jus' not herself. I figured to give 'er a rest and see how she comes out of it." A moment later, he pointed out a neighbor's farm. "That's Clyde Ralston's place. He lost half a dozen sheep, a fortnight ago." His brow furrowed as he turned to her.

"Lost? What do you mean?"

"Stole. Right out of the pen. Slick as grease on a axle."

Sarah looked over her shoulder at the distant cluster of simple stone and frame buildings, surrounded by a patch-work of kitchen gardens. "That's Betancourt land," she said, frowning.

"Aye," Samuel agreed. "I've took to sittin' up on moon-less nights with my shotgun." He bent toward her and low-ered his voice. "That's when they come—curse their thievin' hides. Th' dark o' the moon."

"Who comes?" She bent closer, to match his confiden-tial mood.

"Thieves. Been slippin' around these last few weeks. Didn't take much at first—a couple of head here an' there—but lately it's been more. Bold as brass, they are. Walk right in barns and coops and pens in th' dead of night. Took ever' piglet on Jess Croton's farm last week . . . near two dozen." He wagged his head, looking angry. "It totals up."

Sarah frowned and searched the countryside that glowed lush and verdant in the late morning sun. It was hard to believe that somewhere in that calm, picturesque landscape lay forces bent on thievery.

"What about the authorities?" she asked. "Surely the constables have attempted to catch the thieves."

Samuel wagged his head, looking as doleful as his big, slow-moving mount. "We got just a brace o' constables in th' whole county, an' they're busy in the villages. They ain't got time for farm folk." As she settled into thoughtful silence, he surprised her by adding: "Time was . . . th' duke at Balleycourt kept th' roads and farms safe. Always had a few strong arms about to keep the peace on Meridian land. But we ain't got no duke now."

"But you do." Sarah felt spurred to her brother-in-law's defense. "Duke Arthur left the title and estate to his brother, Ashton. He's duke now."

"Yeah?" He pushed his cap back and scratched his head vigorously. "Where is he?"

"New York," Sarah said, unsettled by that admission. Her sister Daisy, no great lover of British aristocracy, had made Ashton promise to see that their children would be born in the United States. And she seemed constantly to be on the brink of birthing another lusty little American. The pair had returned to England only once—for the weddings of her two middle sisters, Frankie and Cece, nearly three years ago. But since the deadline for Duke Arthur's return had passed, nearly a year ago, Ashton had shown no interest in returning to claim the title and estates.

Her spirits sank. Where was the duke, indeed? Clearly Betancourt needed more than just a refurbished house and a full stable. Try as she might, she couldn't be everywhere help was required. She would have to look into this ring of thieves.

As they approached the Arnetts' cottage, her exotic Fancy Boy began to shy, arch his neck, and dance anxiously, but Sarah was too occupied with Samuel's revelations to do more than give him a knee and a curt word. They were met at the cottage door by Young Bec, and Samuel offered to walk Fancy Boy to cool him off and give him some water. Sarah gave her beloved mount a pat and handed him over.

Old Bec was lying on a cot in the cottage, moaning softly, looking pale and pitiable. Sarah pulled out her thermometer and reminded the old woman what it was and how she had to hold it in her mouth, under her tongue. Young Bec produced a constant stream of chatter, while the children crowded around to see what the fancy lady would do this time. When she took out her stethoscope, they clearly remembered what it was, from the last time she visited. It was for listening to a heart, and every single one of them begged to listen.

The old woman's heart sounds were steady, and her lungs sounded clear, despite a somewhat forced cough. It was her back and hip, Old Bec said, that troubled her most. Some poking, prodding, and moving the old girl's limbs decided it: lumbago. The same as last time. And the remedy was the same: medicine powders and rest. After measuring out a packet of medicine and showing Old Bec how to stretch and sit with a pillow against her lower back, Sarah was entreated to stay for a cup of tea and freshly baked biscuits.

She emerged later, surrounded by children begging to show her their rabbits. It was an invitation she could not refuse. They led her around the cottage to a row of hutches and she soon had an armful of gorgeous long-eared bunnies. The girls were especially proud of their newest crop of baby bunnies. For a few moments she reveled in the memory of her own childhood fascination with rabbits.

The sun was well overhead when she took her leave, saying she had a patient at Betancourt to tend. Samuel brought Fancy Boy around and helped her mount. She bade the Arnetts goodbye and headed back down the wagon road before she realized Fancy Boy seemed calmer, almost . . . mellow. It seemed Samuel had taken good care of him while she saw to his mother.

As she rode into the stable yard of Betancourt, she saw another horse tied at the post ring by the front doors. She handed off Fancy to Young Eddie with orders for a carrot and plenty of hay. At the house she found Constable Andrew Jolly enjoying a cup of tea in the parlor, with Mazie and Deidre attending his every word. At the sight of her, the housemaids shot up, and the constable set his cup down with a clack, lurched to his feet, and straightened his jacket over his ample middle.

"Duchess," he said with a nod, moving away from the settee.

"It's Miss Bumgarten, Constable," she corrected, though with a smile. "What brings you to Betancourt?"

"I been riding this day, warnin' folk that a fellow got shot last night. Right on the road. 'Twixt here an' Betany."

"Then surely you have also heard that it was Thomas Wrenn who found him early this morning and that he brought the man here. He's upstairs, recovering, right now."

"That's why I come. Could I talk to him, duch—ma'am—miss?"

She looked to the parlor maids, who lowered their gazes and shook their heads.

"Apparently he hasn't awakened yet." She shot a dark look at the pair to remind them that they had abandoned their post at his bedside.

"Dolly's with 'im," Mazie said, blushing. Dolly was the earnest young house girl recently promoted from the scullery. The older housemaids shamelessly took advantage of her youth and inexperience to lighten their duties whenever possible.

She addressed the constable. "I'll send word when he comes around."

Jolly looked unsettled and fingered his bucket-shaped constable's hat. "We never had such goings-on in these parts." He scowled. "It ain't safe, milady, you bein' here all alone."

"I'm hardly alone, Constable. I have a house full of people."

He glanced at the pair of aging housemaids with a rueful smile.

"Aye, then, you'd do well to have a couple of yer menfolk break out the bird guns an' keep an eye out. Mebee keep yer horses and stock in the barns and stables of a night."

She thought of Samuel Arnett's nightly vigil.

"Is that really necessary?"

"Constables can't be everywhere," Jolly declared, shifting his feet and fingering the weighted nightstick at his side. "Folk got to look to their own safety. Ain't been a shootin' here for . . . well, I don't remember when was the last. But now, somebody's usin' *guns*."

"I'll take your warning seriously, Constable. We'll keep an eye out. And you may want to talk to Bascom at the Iron Penny. There was a dustup there yesterday with some rowdy sorts. It wouldn't surprise me to hear they've been involved in other criminal activities . . . maybe even this shooting."

She watched from the parlor window as the constable rode away. She recalled the men who attacked Nero and might have done much worse if it hadn't been for Bascom and the man lying upstairs with a hole in his shoulder. The drunken bullies had vowed revenge and may have taken some measure of it last night. Who else would have shot an unarmed man—especially that man—in the dark of night?

She shooed Mazie and Deidre back to work and headed

upstairs. After peering into the duke's bedchamber to find Dolly diligently stitching linen by her patient's bedside, she headed for her room down the east hall.

It was the very room she and her sisters had occupied years ago when they first arrived at Betancourt, decorated with paper covered in climbing ivy. The soft furnishings, drapes, and linens were all soothing shades of green, and the posts of the tester bed were carved with twining vines that supported a quilted canopy made to resemble a forest sky. Since she arrived, she had lain under that canopy feeling secure and very much at home. She looked around at the place she had claimed in the heart of Betancourt. How secure would she feel this night when she climbed into bed?

From a cherrywood chest at the foot of her bed she pulled a pair of ebony-handled revolvers rolled in a leather holster. Uncle Red had left them at her mother's house in London when he married the countess and went to live in Sussex. In her storm of humiliation and anger, she had seen them in his study, grabbed them, and carried them with her to Betancourt.

Red had taught her to shoot, albeit covertly. Her lady mother would have fainted dead away at the thought of her daughter handling, much less practicing with, guns.

But Red had indulged her desire to know all kinds of things, including how firearms worked. When he married and moved away, he said he would feel better if he knew Sarah could defend herself against London's "low down, kipper-suckin' sidewinders" . . . meaning the randy upper-crust male population. He had even thrown in a couple of lessons on landing a punch, which had come in handy just yesterday. Rubbing her hand, she felt a residual soreness, then flexed her fingers and repeatedly made a fist. It would have to do.

She pulled one of the heavy Colt revolvers from the

holster, looked it over, and sighted down the barrel. The steel felt oddly foreign in her hand. She frowned. She had to do something about that.

Arthur awakened slowly from a dream that he was being shot again and again and again in the shoulder, only to find that very shoulder was bound in bandages and hurt like the devil. A *host* of devils. He groaned, raised his head, and took stock of the soft bed, large room, fancy hangings, and excess of light.

Holy thunder, his very eyeballs hurt. He shut his eyes, hoping it would help him think where he was and remember how he came to be here, but came up with nothing. His head was foggy and his body ached like it was all one monstrous bruise. He turned his head and discovered a large stuffed chair, and a table holding various medicine bottles beside the bed.

Explosive retorts tore through the room and brought him upright in bed with his head swimming. That could only be gunshots! That was what had awakened him; he hadn't been dreaming. Alarmed, he threw back the fancy covers and was relieved to find he was at least wearing breeches.

Every part of him protested as he slid his bare feet to the floor and braced for a moment on the bedside. The floor seemed to tilt strangely beneath him. Hand over hand, he staggered to the end of the bed and clung to the foot post for a moment, blinking. Then came another quick volley of gunfire. Somebody was waging war out there.

He stumbled to the double doors and out into a hall he recognized. He looked back at the room where he'd spent the night and gave a huff of surprise that roused another pain in his shoulder. How the hell did he get there, of all

places? The staircase was just where he remembered and
the railing and balusters felt strong and familiar as he
leaned on them. The next thing he knew he was on the
worn marble floor of the center hall and lurching toward
the front doors.

The afternoon sunlight struck him like a lightning bolt
to the brain. He shielded his eyes with an arm and swayed,
listening for the gunfire. It had stopped, but he sensed it
had come from the rear of the house, the back lawn. He
made his way around the corner, surprised at how kind
the small river gravel was to his bare feet and only now
wondering where his boots might have gone. He kept a
hand on the brick of the house until he reached what he
assumed was still the kitchen door. Produce crates and old
flour barrels stacked beside the aged door confirmed his
assessment, and by the time he let go of the wall he felt
himself standing fairly straight.

Someone was shooting, and he had to find out who
and why.

He turned the final corner and stopped dead. There, in
a short buckskin skirt, simple white shirt, and riding boots
stood a young woman with a sizeable revolver in her hand,
taking aim at a rank of old bottles and cans set up along the
top of a shoulder-high brick fence. She squeezed off four
or five shots in quick succession and glass shattered and
tin rang as her targets flew off the wall.

He stiffened, unsure if he'd made that strangled gasp
aloud, but she wheeled on him with the gun pointed and he
realized he had. Shocked by her sweetly fringed eyes and
lovely face and by the long-barreled gun she was pointing
at him, he staggered back. As he tried to make sense of it,
there was only one thing that came to mind.

"D-did you shoot me?"

"What?" she said, eyes widening as she approached.

"Did you shoot me?" He managed a bit more volume.

"Don't be ridiculous—I don't know you well enough to shoot you." She advanced on him with the gun still in her hand. "What are you doing out here?"

"It sounded like a battle was going on—I had to find out what was happening." He widened his stance, summoning all the energy he could.

"You should be in bed," she declared, eyeing his bandaged shoulder.

"And you should be . . . crocheting some damned thing or other . . . but here you are, shooting the hell out of the place."

"Old cans and a few wine bottles nobody will miss." She holstered the big revolver and propped her hands on her waist, assessing him.

"Who did shoot me?" he demanded, thinking it the most logical of questions.

"That is a very good question. I haven't a clue."

His gaze dropped and he finally registered what she'd just done. His jaw dropped at the sight of a six-gun holstered on each of her hips. The holster ties around each thigh disappeared through a provocative crease in her skirt. *What the hell?*

"But I do know you've lost blood and need bed rest and nourishment." She walked right up to him, seized his good arm, and turned him toward the house as if he were a recalcitrant child. She barely reached his shoulder, but she turned him easily.

He stared at her, transfixed by the shining streaks of blonde in her sandy-colored hair and he inhaled deeply. She smelled of warmth and sunshine, with a hint of roses. Her cheeks were flushed and her lips were . . . perfect Cupid's bows with . . . *what the hell was he doing staring at her lips? He really was out of his head.*

She gave him a nudge and when that didn't move him

forward, she put her arm through his good one and pulled him toward the front doors.

"Who are you?" he demanded, pulling her to a halt and focusing on her face. Big eyes—startling sea green—rimmed by those decadently long lashes. She was the one he'd seen at the inn—the one with the dog.

The duchess.

"Sarah Bumgarten," she said, trying to move him along. He resisted and she looked up at him to clarify: "Sister-in-law to the Duke of Meridian."

Mystery solved! A *Bumgarten.* The name resonated in memories that took him back to another lifetime. Sarah. The littlest one. The one who loved horses and was curious about his butterflies and had descended on Betancourt's library like a hungry hawk. His recollection of her from those days was of her with ribbons in her hair and books tucked under her arm. Now she was the duke's—

The impact of it hit him like a haymaker: *My brother is now the duke.*

"Where is—the duke?" His throat was so dry he could barely speak.

"In New York. With his family."

"He has a family?"

"Of course. A wife—who is my sister—and two children. Boys." She looked up. "Who are you?"

"I kn-new him"—it tumbled out without much thought—"at school."

With that, his legs began to wobble. She noticed and yanked his arm up and across her shoulders. "Don't you dare fall," she ordered irritably. "We had a terrible time getting you to bed." A second later she clasped him around the waist and ushered him toward the doors.

"What is your name?" she demanded, breathing hard.

"M-Michael." He managed to provide a reasonable

half-truth, despite the way his attention was glued to the nubile young form against him.

Any other time, he might have been embarrassed to have to lean on a female for support, but this was no ordinary female, and right now he was getting light-headed and felt like he weighed a bloody . . .

The man weighed a ton, she thought as she struggled with him up the stairs. "I could use a little help, here, Michael."

He moaned and threatened to sink—she had to finish getting him up the stairs or they would both take a nasty fall.

"No, no—stay awake." She struggled to keep his half-naked body upright. "We have to get you into bed."

By the time they reached the top of the main stairs, she knew she would never get him up another flight of steps to the bed waiting in the nursery. Where the devil were the servants? She called out for Dolly, Mazie, Deidre, Ned, and even Edgar . . . there was no response. Her patient was tottering determinedly toward the duke's chambers—groaning "bed"—and there was only one course open.

She steered him toward the duke's grand repose, and it was all she could do to get him close enough, quickly enough, for him to collapse onto the bed. Fortunately, he fell on his uninjured side. Breathing heavily, she rolled him onto his back and spotted fresh blood on the binding of his shoulder.

"Dang it. You've made it bleed again," she said irritably.

"Water," he croaked with a sandpapery rasp.

Muttering about headstrong fools, she poured water from a pitcher lurking behind the medicine bottles and lifted his head, ordering him to drink. He obeyed and downed the entire glass before melting back onto her arm and closing his eyes. She stood holding him for a moment, cradling his head, staring at his face and thinking of that voice. Deep, with a hint of a rasp. He claimed to be an old school chum of Ashton's. Was he here for a reunion? A job? A handout?

It was then that she noticed the scar around his neck, paler than the rest of his sun-bronzed skin. She ran her fingers over it lightly. How on earth did an old school chum of Ashton's acquire a scar like—

"Tickles," he said thickly, startling her.

He had opened those piercing eyes partway and was staring at her. She jerked her arm from under his head, dropping it onto the pillow, and propped her fists on her waist, above her holstered guns.

"Just checking your health," she said, her cheeks warming. "It appears you've had other injuries."

"A few," he said, eyeing her from beneath half-closed lids. "This is my second gunshot."

"Really?" She sounded skeptical in her own ears as she looked over his bare chest, thinking that she hadn't seen that sort of scar.

"Leg," he said, pointing to his left. "Old sea battle."

"And you managed to survive," she concluded.

"Seems to be my fate, surviving."

"The navy, then," she said. "You served aboard a British ship?"

His half smile was tainted by pain. "Not exactly."

"American?" She pressed for an answer, though it betrayed an unseemly interest in him. "Canadian?" He must have figured she would continue guessing through the list of the world's naval forces, for he sighed.

"It wasn't naval. Or voluntary."

"Oh?" She scowled, trying to make sense of it.

"Shanghaied."

"Ah." She had heard of the press gangs that operated in port cities and weren't picky about how they filled "recruitment" orders for able-bodied seamen. Her infamous appetite for reading had led her to a few seagoing memoirs that she had found shocking but fascinating.

"Food," he said, meeting her gaze again and grabbing her hand. "Don't let me starve to death."

There was a hint of—desperation? teasing?—in his expression and a warmth in his touch that confused her. She was suddenly jittery. She pulled her hand back and his fell to the bed beside him. When she looked up, his eyes were closing and his lips were settling into a what might have been a grimace or a smile. Whatever it was, it sent a trickle of warmth through her.

This growing interest in him was not healthy, she told herself. Who knew what kind of man he was or what he was doing here? She scowled. She had to get him well enough to travel and send him on his way, pronto.

"You'd better heal quickly, friend-of-Ashton's," she said as she headed for the door, the stairs, and the kitchen. "Not even an old school chum should be sleeping in the duke's bed."

Arthur heard that last bit through a deepening haze and smiled groggily to himself. In the duke's bed. He'd never had a chance to sleep in it when he was the duke. Uncle Bertram had occupied it throughout his tenure as guardian and long after Arthur came of age. His own room was down the hall. He couldn't help wondering what had become of it and of the collection of butterflies and other insects he had amassed and displayed upstairs in his old schoolroom.

Fatigue and discomfort from the exertion combined to overwhelm him. His last disjointed thought as darkness claimed him was of Sarah Bumgarten's arresting green eyes as she pointed a gun at him.

Chapter Four

"You have to sit up," Sarah commanded the next morning. She had stacked pillows at the head of the bed and now urged him to move up and onto them while Young Ned drew back the drapes and opened the windows. "We've brought you some nourishment."

"Food?" he managed to croak. She could have sworn she heard his stomach rumble.

Watching him struggle to reposition himself with one arm, she gave a "tsk" of annoyance and put her arms around his shoulders to help him. He turned his head toward the lock of hair that fell over her shoulder and inhaled. Slowly. Deeply.

Alarmed, she yanked her arms from him as if he had scalded her, and pushed her hair back behind her shoulder. She was definitely putting it up today, no matter how much time it took.

"I'm starved," he uttered in a whisper that gave her a shiver.

Then his lidded eyes fastened on her and her breath caught. A second later, she blinked and turned away. He was either well enough for double entendres or she was imagining things.

He groaned as he lay back on the pillows, and she took a steadying breath and retrieved a bowl from the tray. Settling on the edge of the bed, she spooned some broth and held it out to him. He sniffed, then opened his mouth and a second later pushed up enough to peer into the bowl.

"Broth?" He was clearly taken aback.

"It's beef and bone broth. You need simple nourishment so your body can begin to repair itself."

"What I need is beef. Good, honest, British beef." He took the bowl from her hands and tilted it up to drink it down in several gulps. Then he wiped his mouth with the back of his hand and thrust the empty bowl back at her. "Potatoes . . . sides of bacon, fried good and crisp . . . a pan of scones . . . jam . . . coffee . . ."

She sprang to her feet. "Well, you're getting broth. Until you're ready for something more solid."

"I'm ready now," he declared, scowling.

"Well, I'm the doctor and I say you're not." She crossed her arms.

"You're a doctor?" He seemed genuinely surprised.

"Why do you think Thomas brought you here?"

"Where did you study?" he demanded, his color deepening. She could have sworn his chest broadened. She had to find the wretch a shirt, and soon.

"With Dr. Everett Millhorn. In London. And I've read widely . . . all the latest journals and findings." Then it struck her. "Where did *you* study?"

He gave a snort. "The school of hard knocks. Years of experience. And it's taught me that patients need to eat when they're ready, not on some nannyish regimen of sops and pablum."

"Nannyish?" She was taken aback by his ungrateful attitude. How dare he criticize the quality of her care? She scowled and uncrossed her arms. "Very well. We'll feed you normal fare . . . when you're able to make it down the stairs to the dining room under your own steam." She dropped the bowl on the nearby tray for a servant to collect, and headed for the door. "Luncheon is served at twelve o'clock sharp."

The wall reverberated with the force of the door slamming behind her, and he stared at it for a moment before realizing that his heart was pounding. She acted like an imperious old dowager—laying down orders and conditions as if he were a servant instead of—what? What was he here? Besides comfortable and unwilling to abandon his sumptuous surroundings. He hadn't slept in a bed this good since the maharaja's palace in Bombay.

He looked around at the rich tapestry bed hangings and the velvet paper on the walls. Whoever refurbished the duke's chamber had deep pockets and an artist's eye. Wine-red backgrounds hosted delicate tracings of gold and green leaf motifs in the heavy satin hangings and drapes. The gold fringe, wine and gold pillows, forest green upholstery, and rich Persian carpet contained every jeweled hue known to humankind. On the walls freshly gilded frames surrounded portraits of the first Meridian to bear the title of duke, along with one of his lady wives and numerous children.

Curiosity drove him from the bed to peruse the paintings more closely. He didn't recall them being so bright and vividly detailed—had they been cleaned somehow? But then, he was never really allowed in the chamber; he'd only gotten distant glimpses of his prime forebear.

He thought of the portraits of the other Meridians in the great hall and parlor. Most were hung so high it was hard to tell what the faces truly looked like. He shook his head. It had never occurred to him to have a portrait painted of himself—the sixth Duke of Meridian—to place among them. His thieving, penny-pinching uncles certainly would never have suggested it.

A hollow feeling grew in his chest as he realized that his short tenure as titled master of this house and these estates would scarcely rate a footnote in the annals of Britain's nobility. He had produced nothing, introduced nothing, increased nothing . . . left nothing for posterity but a void. An empty title his brother now had to fill.

He steadied himself on the backs of chairs, a lowboy, and a writing desk as he made his way around the chamber and paused at an open door to peer at the marble bathing fixtures that had been installed in what was once an attached dressing room. Marble. Lots of it. There was a sense of permanence now, a subtle grandeur in this renewed heart of Betancourt. No doubt Daisy's doing. The heiress he had courted and almost married. The first woman he had ever kissed. The one he traveled the world to forget.

Now he had come home to find her younger sister—the very image of Bumgarten energy and vitality—had taken up residence in the heart of his lost inheritance. He didn't know whether to laugh at Fate's wicked sense of humor or despair at its heartless jest.

He stood in the middle of the room, feeling out of touch and out of place . . . grappling for footing in this new and unexpected version of home.

How long he stood there, stuck in a quicksand of memory and regrets, he couldn't later say. A thump at the door and the turn of the handle, startled him and set him staggering for the bed.

"Cursed beast—git—go away!" A rotund woman in servant gray, a mobcap, and an apron struggled to keep something from entering with her. She shut the door with a bang, turned, and spotted him. "Oh, sarr—ye dasn't try to get up by yerself. Ye still got wickle-foot. Ye'll be landin' on yer nethers, like as not."

He stared at her as if she spoke Chinese, but allowed her to bustle him back under the covers.

"Mazie, sarr." She introduced herself and managed something approximating a curtsy. No one had curtsied to him in years.

"Mazie." He nodded to her, thinking she hadn't been here during his time as duke, and then looked to the door, which was rattling again. Something thumped against it and it sounded for all the world like claws were raking the wood. "What the devil is that?"

"*Devil* be right, sarr. That beast's Old Scratch in disguise. Or his hellhound, sure as the sun rises."

"A hell—?" He looked from her back to the door. "Oh, a *dog*. Big and gray, I suppose. And hers."

Mazie knew just which "her" he referenced. "Daft over that beast, th' duchess is. An' he'd chew nails fer her. Ye should see the pair of 'em." She abruptly changed course, squared her shoulders and smoothed her apron.

"I come to give ye a warshin'. Part o' nursin', she says. Keepin' a body clean." She shook her head as if it made little sense to her.

Between fending off the determined housemaid and making good his insistence that he could bathe himself, he all but forgot the noise at the door. Through his soreness and aches, he managed to wash most of himself and had to admit that he felt better for it. Then came a dose of "powders" mixed with water, which tasted slightly astringent and reassuringly medicinal. Afterward, he stretched out under the cover, ready for a rest, and smiled to himself. Lord, he could get used to this.

Mazie, who had retreated to a chair drawn up to the open window and dozed while he washed, finally roused

herself to check on her mistress's patient. Finding him
nodding off, she picked up the water basin and toweling
and headed for the door.

Her cry, the splash of water, and the crash of the china
basin, brought him rudely awake . . . in time to see several
blurry shapes streaking through the door that had finally
been jarred open. He sat up with a start, and a spear of pain
made him realize he had used his injured shoulder. His
next thought was that he was being attacked by wolves.

A huge gray beast climbed the side of the bed and two
smaller fiends launched themselves onto the bench at the
foot of the bed and sprang at him from there. A fourth
bounded up on the far side and came to stand over him,
panting hot breath one moment, sniffing every exposed
part of him the next.

"Out! Get away, get off the bed!" he growled, pushing
one inquisitive muzzle after another away from him, only
to have it return immediately to poke, sniff and—*ye
gods*—lick.

He was in danger of being consumed, literally, by their
curiosity when *she* came rushing through the door.

"What on earth?" She paused for a moment, taking in
the broken basin, Mazie's drenched apron, and the dogs all
over her patient. Her eyes narrowed and she stalked to the
bed with her hands on her waist . . . just above those
blessed revolvers. The woman was wearing guns again.

The nosing and licking stopped. The dogs froze in
place, watching her.

"These beasts belong to you?" he demanded irritably.

"They do." She snapped her fingers in a summons, but
the dogs remained standing on his stomach and lying across
his legs, watching her. "They're usually better behaved."

"Oh, I'm sure." He had never told such a lie in his life.

"Nero," she said sharply and pointed to the floor beside

her feet. The big lug dropped from the side of the bed and lumbered over to the place she had apparently assigned him. "Gwenny." She pointed to Nero's side and the small wire-haired dog jumped from the bed to take a seat by the giant Nero. Next was "Lancelot." And when he hesitated, she pointed again and spoke his name in a lower register that carried unmistakable threat.

The hound lowered his head and climbed across Arthur's feet to drop from the bed and take his place beside the others. Then she looked at the final miscreant, a spaniel of some sort, who showed no signs of moving. She pointed emphatically to the final place in the line of dogs. "Morgie," she said, "*now*." And the dog didn't move.

"Morgana!" she barked, eyes hot with irritation. "Don't make me come over there."

If dogs could look insulted, this one did. She looked away, then back at Sarah, then at him. She gave his arm one last, defiant lick, then walked calmly up and over him to drop to the floor. The seat she assumed was farther from the others than expected, but technically she had obeyed.

"I regret the intrusion," Sarah said, bracing for comment. When none came, she continued, "They're just curious." Then she pointed emphatically to the door. "Out."

He watched the dogs, led by a chastened Nero, trail out of the room.

"Well, that was a shock," he said, wondering at the control she exerted over them. He'd never seen the like. "I thought I was going to be eaten alive."

"They prefer more tender meat," she said archly, folding her arms. "Now that you're awake, we should move you upstairs to the nursery."

"I was just falling asleep when your pack pounced on me." He couldn't resist engaging her eyes. "I can't move just yet." He grimaced and touched his injured shoulder. "I need to regain some strength."

She considered that for a moment, and then looked away.

"As I said, luncheon is at twelve."

"There is just one problem," he said. "Unless you dine regularly with half-naked men." He threw back the covers to display his chest and bare stomach. "What have you done with my clothes?"

Her eyes crackled with angry lights and she folded her arms.

"Your shirt was ruined." She turned away with a tightened mouth. Was that outraged modesty in her expression or an attempt at righteous scorn? "Fine. Stay where you are today. I'll see you are left alone."

She stalked for the door and motioned Mazie—who stood watching between her mistress and their patient—to continue cleaning up the mess on the floor. The maid nodded as Sarah sailed out, then with a soft whistle, bent to retrieve the broken china.

Moments later, the door closed behind Mazie, and Arthur took a deep breath and pulled the decadently soft covers back over him. He grinned as he recalled Sarah Bumgarten's visceral reaction when he bared his body.

"Half-naked men at luncheon it is, then."

Cook's famous cottage pie was on the menu for luncheon, which was the fashionable name for what had always been called dinner at Betancourt. It would be accompanied by roast root vegetables and freshly baked rolls with butter . . . preceded, of course, by a fine nutritious broth . . . followed, in deference to Sarah's penchant for sweets, by a fruit compote with honey-almond biscuits.

When she entered the long, oak-paneled dining room, Sarah found the great table set at one end with a cloth, candelabra, and full china and silver service. She scowled. Most of the time she took a simple luncheon in the breakfast room, which she'd had wainscoted and repainted a cheerful yellow. Better for the digestion, she told the staff.

She was on her way to the door leading down to the kitchen to learn why this table was set, when her patient appeared in the arched doorway to the great hall, clinging to the doorframe. To her horror, he was wearing only breeches and bandages.

His chest and lower legs were bare as birthing day, and he wore a wry smile that was the very picture of insouciance.

"H-how dare you—wh-where is your shirt?" she sputtered, unable to take her gaze from his chest and that cursed tattoo.

"I believe you said it was ruined," he said, his voice raspier than usual. The exertion of coming downstairs had clearly taken a toll. "But you did say luncheon at twelve sharp." And as if on the dot, the great clock in the front hall struck twelve. "And I'm starved." He rubbed his belly and her gaze fastened helplessly on that movement until she tore it away and headed for the bellpull.

She rang several times, furious that he had called her bluff and made it downstairs without assistance. Or clothes. It took a moment for Young Ned and Deidre to come lumbering up the stairs.

"Where is the shirt you were to find him?" Sarah demanded.

Deidre looked to the floorboards for help. "I . . . wus . . . um . . . in the kitchen an' I told Dolly to find one." She looked up and her jaw dropped at the sight of the half-naked man in the dining room archway. "She didn't?"

"Obviously not," Sarah said irritably. It was one more instance of Mazie and Deidre pawning off their duties on others. "Find Dolly and find out what happened to the—hell's bells—never mind! I'll do it myself."

She stalked to her flagrantly exposed patient, pointed to a chair, and ordered, "Sit down before you fall down." The moment he made it to the table, she headed for the upstairs hall, muttering, "If you want something done right, you have to do it yourself."

She glowered as she tromped up the steps. Some days she feared she was turning into her mother, and Heaven knew, one Elizabeth Strait Bumgarten in the world was enough.

She turned left at the top of the steps and soon was in the old duke's bedchamber in the west wing, going through the highboy that contained his long-abandoned wardrobe.

With every drawer she opened her irritation mounted. The old duke's shirts were gone. She hadn't packed much when she left London, and found when she arrived at Betancourt that she needed clothing that allowed her to move in ways her ladyish clothes didn't permit. Those shirts had lain for years in drawers—she had felt safe in assuming they wouldn't be needed by His Grace. And she hadn't taken them all, only two or—

With a nudge from events half remembered, she rushed down the hall to her room in the east wing and continued her search. A folded shirt lay in the bottom of her sewing basket. Success. Clasping it to her, she hurried back down the stairs to the dining room, where her patient was seated at the table . . . with Ned, Deidre, and Old Edgar gathered across the table from him, watching him groan with pleasure as he devoured a warm, fragrant dinner roll. The sight of her sent the servants scurrying back to their stations by the sideboard and dumbwaiter.

He looked up with a roll in one hand and a mug of cider in the other. "You're back. Thank the Almighty. I'm starved!"

"I found you one of the old duke's shirts," she declared, holding it out to him. "We will not lunch until you are decently clothed."

He might have reddened a bit beneath his tan. He swallowed hard and deposited the rest of the roll on his bread-and-butter plate. He wiped his hands on his breeches and for a long moment, stared at the shirt she offered.

"A duke's shirt?" he said, his voice lower and raspier than usual.

"The old duke," she said. "Arthur."

He looked like he'd been punched. She could have sworn he paled, but after an increasingly charged moment, he broke the silence.

"Well, if it's good enough for a duke . . ." He rose and, bracing his side against the table, took the garment and unbuttoned it. As he opened it, he frowned, which became a scowl, and then a glower as he forced his arms into the sleeves and found they fit like a sausage casing. The shirt barely covered his shoulders and bandages, and the front wouldn't close across his chest. He looked at her in confusion. "The duke—wasn't a small man. Are you certain this was his shirt?"

She stepped around him, staring at the strained fabric, and found darts in the back and extra seams taken on the sides of the shirt.

"It appears someone took a few tucks in it." She felt heat rising in her face to betray who had done the "tucking," but she refused to give him the satisfaction of learning she was responsible. She looked away and, in doing so, spotted the perfect solution. She went to the window and removed one of the tasseled crimson cords that held back the drapes.

"This will do in a pinch."

He staggered back a step when she came at him with the drapery cord and uttered an involuntary "Agh" when she wrapped the drapery cord around him and tied it in a great, droopy bow.

"There." She tugged the sides of the shirt closer together and then nodded. "Nothing a bit of Yankee ingenuity couldn't fix." She turned to the wide-eyed servants who were clearly trying not to laugh at the picture he made in a too-small shirt tied with a bold red drapery accessory with tassels that dangled between his nethers and his knees.

"Ned, you may begin serving."

The next time she looked at him he was back in his seat and slathering another roll with butter. He accepted his new fashion accessory with abominable aplomb. Nothing, it seemed, could dampen his appetite. He bit into the roll like a starving man, and groaned and closed his eyes as he chewed. She had never seen a man affected by food in such a drastic way. He made it seem appallingly pleasurable and slightly indecent. Her throat tightened as she watched his jaw muscles flex and the butter glisten on his lips.

"So, Michael, where are you from?" She claimed the silence, determined to impose some decorum on the meal despite its disastrous start. "What is your surname?"

"From here," he responded, reaching for a third roll—not that she was counting.

"Where, here?" She sipped her lemon water. "Do you mean Betany?"

"Nearby," he responded, washing the roll down with a mouthful of cider.

"And your surname?"

"Gr—ant."

She considered that for a moment.

"So, Michael Gr-ant. You say you were at Eton with the

duke." An expensive undertaking, a public school education. One needed noble or high social connections, she had learned, to even be considered for admission. If he had such connections to a prominent local family, surely he would reveal them when questioned. But he just continued doggedly chewing. "Would that be the old or the new duke?"

"Both," he said, leaning back to allow Young Ned to ladle soup into his bowl. Then he bent forward with an appreciative sniff, picked up a soup spoon, and dug in with a vengeance.

"So you knew both Ashton and Arthur. What can you tell me about Ashton?" She was determined to test his claim of being an old school chum and hoped that food would distract him enough to let her get at the truth.

"A scrapper." He spoke between spoonfuls of soup and was half through the bowl in record time. "Used his fists as much as his head. Wasn't much for book work. That changed when Master Cleese got hold of 'im."

"Master Cleese?" she echoed, urging him on.

"History master. Had a way with stories. Nobody fell asleep in his recitations."

"So he liked this Master Cleese and began to study?"

He nodded, then raked the bottom of his bowl with the spoon.

"Went on to university, I heard," he added. "Oxford."

"And did you go to university, too?"

"Nah. After school, I mostly had to teach myself."

"And yet, you managed to become a 'medic' of sorts."

"In practice." He turned to Young Ned, who stood nearby. "More rolls, please." He noticed her staring and grinned. "Great rolls. The best I've ever tasted, and I've tasted plenty."

"I imagine," she responded, forcing a neutral tone.

When the cottage pie and roast vegetables were served,

his eyes widened and he motioned for larger portions as he was served. There was a gleeful, almost defiant appreciation to his consumption that made Sarah want to order him to behave. But then, she didn't want to reveal just how closely she scrutinized him, or how unsettling she found his appearance and behavior. To eat like this, he must have gone without food or even starved at times.

"So tell me about your travels abroad," she said, sitting back primly, watching him stuff himself. He was going to burst if he kept this up.

"Travels?" he said around a mouthful of new carrots, parsnips, and pearl onions. "How do you know I've been abroad?"

"You said you were aboard a ship and wounded in a sea battle. That would hardly be on the Thames or the Mersey."

He chewed thoughtfully for a moment, then nodded.

"I've been a lot of places. Egypt. India. Cape Town in South Africa. Morocco. Italy, of course. And the South Seas."

"The United States?" she asked, watching keenly for a reaction.

"Not yet. Always wanted to go out west. Met a few folk from—" He halted and beckoned for another piece of the cottage pie, beaming as a great slice was deposited on his plate. "It's been a while since I had a proper cottage pie. The sausage and cheeses, and the onion and garlic are perfect. I need to meet this cook of yours."

"What are you doing here?" She sat forward, sensing that now was the time to be more direct. "In Betany."

Another thoughtful pause came before he answered.

"I thought it might be time to visit and see what the old place is like."

"And see your family?" she prodded.

"Don't have much left." Both elbows were on the table and his cheeks bulged with pie. "My parents died. I had a brother, but I haven't seen him in years. A few stray aunts and uncles—none I'd care to keep up with."

"So you basically came to Betany for the scenery?"

He gave a huff of amusement. "You could say that."

She could say a lot of things, she thought, including the fact that she didn't believe a word of his story. He was holding things back, important things. And though he seemed to know a few things about Ashton, she wouldn't bet that he knew either duke personally. Heaven knew, his manners were not the sort that came out of an English public school. And there was that tattoo. She considered asking about it—

"My turn. I heard you practicing again." He paused, gesturing with an empty fork to the guns she hadn't bothered to remove. "What are you practicing for? Not a pheasant shoot—those are strictly long guns. A contest?" He chuckled. "A killing maybe?"

She looked down at her gun belt as if surprised to see herself still wearing it, then reddened.

"Protection," she said, lifting her chin. "There are unsavory sorts about, and I was advised to make sure Betancourt could defend itself."

His smile faded as he studied her face.

"You're serious," he said. "And you propose to be that defense?"

At that moment Edgar shuffled into the dining room.

"A caller, milady." His jowls wobbled. "I said you were lunching—"

Chapter Five

"I don't mean to intrude," came a man's voice, "but I could not pass Betancourt without stopping to see if everything is all right."

In the doorway behind Edgar stood a man in a trim riding coat, breeches, and boots, holding a crop and an expensive topper. He was on the tall side of average, had brown hair and sharp brown eyes, and was in every respect an attractive and gentlemanly looking sort, which made this breach of etiquette all the more surprising.

"Whom do we have the pleasure of greeting, sir? And why have you come?" Sarah laid her napkin aside and rose to meet the intruder. Her demand for an explanation must have set the fellow back on his heels . . . either that or the fact that she was wearing firearms. He stared, slack-jawed, for a moment, then seemed to recover himself enough to give a polite nod.

"A thousand pardons for the interruption, but I was told in the village that there was trouble about and the duke is not here to see to the security of the estate."

"Betancourt is perfectly secure and all is well, as you can plainly see." Sarah waved a hand to indicate the placid air of the great house, then drew herself straighter. She had supposed the day would come that someone would arrive to challenge her presence at Betancourt and her care of her brother-in-law's inheritance. She was all too aware that her role as steward here was self-appointed. And, dearest Heaven, he'd caught her wearing Uncle Red's guns! She refused to blush. "You have not answered the question, sir. Who are you?"

"I am the duke's cousin, George Parker Graham." This time the deferring nod came paired with a smile so intense that she could almost feel it touching her. "And who, if I may inquire, do I have the honor of addressing?"

"I am the duke's sister-in-law, Sarah Bumgarten. I am here at his request to watch over the estate while he is away."

"Truly? I wasn't aware the duke had a sister-in-law—or, indeed, that he was ever married." A moment later his attention slid down her figure—lingering for a second on those guns—and on to the man still seated at the table. His gaze narrowed on her patient's broad back and long hair. "In fact, I have been reliably informed that the duke has been missing for some time and that his brother has failed to investigate or even put in an appearance."

Sarah followed his gaze to Michael Grant and watched her patient go rigid and turn slowly in his chair. When he looked up there was an intensity to his expression that reminded her of his face outside the Iron Penny.

"And who is this?" George moved toward Michael with an open look of appraisal. The sight of her patient's ill-fitting shirt and bizarre crimson belt brought a scowl that quickly became incredulity.

"My patient, Michael Grant. A local fellow who was shot near Betancourt's gates." She hoped her embarrassment didn't show. A gentleman arrives—quite possibly family to Ashton—and finds her wearing six-shooters and lunching with a half-naked man. Dear Lord. And the big red drapery tassels . . . whatever had possessed her? "He is recovering here."

Michael rose, wiped his mouth with his napkin, and turned to face George Graham fully. The silence, as the men took each other's measure, prickled with tension. George took in Michael's exposed slice of chest, worn riding breeches, and bare feet.

"I am surprised to see . . . so much of him." George raised an eyebrow. "Where are your proper garments, sir?"

Michael's response sounded an octave lower than usual.

"My clothes were ruined in the attack. Miss Bumgarten was kind enough to find me something to wear." He straightened, emphasizing his height and muscularity, but keeping his face a slate of determination. "She is something of a physician in these parts."

"Indeed." George turned to Sarah, pointedly giving Michael his back. "Charitable to a fault, as women of worth and refinement are wont to be. But kindness, sweet lady," he addressed her, "must always be tempered with caution. Especially in these hazardous times."

Sarah saw Michael's face harden and his eyes narrow on George's back. The men had taken an instant dislike to each other, and she had no idea why or which was being truthful about his identity and reason for being here.

"We were about to finish our luncheon," she said, hoping to defuse the volatile atmosphere. "I could have the servants lay another plate if you would stay and join us." She saw the way Michael's nostrils flared and his eyes started to burn with anger. Not such a good idea, that invitation, but it was too late to rescind it.

"A most hospitable offer, Miss Bumgarten, but I must be on my way. I am expected elsewhere. Perhaps you will see me to the door." He held out his arm and she had no choice but to graciously accept.

Once they were in the main hall, George slowed his step and put his hand over hers on his arm. His expression glowed with warm regard that grew into a smile.

"I confess, I did not expect to find so lovely and amicable a hostess here. I feared, from things I had heard, that I would find Meridian's venerable seat in a terrible state. Fortunately my supposition was wrong." He looked around the great center hall with undisguised admiration. "I have always loved this place. It does my heart good to see it in capable hands."

"I did not know the old duke had such a cousin, sir," she responded, relieved to find he accepted her presence and role there in such a complimentary way. His response had a rueful ring.

"I spent my youth on the Continent—at boarding school and then at university in Paris. I came home some time ago, but have been occupied with business in London until now. I confess I was alarmed to hear talk that the duke is missing and the estate was left untended."

"Perhaps you do not know, then, that Duke Arthur left instructions in the event he was unable to return to England and Betancourt."

"I have heard nothing of such arrangements."

"Arthur has now vacated the title in favor of his younger brother. Ashton Graham is now Duke of Meridian."

That seemed to unsettle him.

"And where is Duke Ashton now? Why is he not here?"

"He is traveling . . . in New York with his wife and children."

"For how long?" George's increasing grip on her hand became uncomfortable. "How long has it been since he was here?"

"Some time," she hedged, withdrawing from his arm. "I was appointed steward several months ago and am seeing to affairs here."

He glanced over his shoulder toward the dining room.

"I see that you are earnest in that charge." He glanced down at her armament. "And formidably equipped." Stepping closer, he brought his hands up as if to clasp her shoulders, but something in her face stopped him and his hands retreated to his sides. "However, you are quite young to shoulder such a burden. You must guard against being too tenderhearted. With the best of intentions, I am certain, you have taken a man into your household and to your table who doesn't know how to comport himself decently in a gentlewoman's company. What do you know about that man?"

"Not much," she admitted. "But the hole in his shoulder was quite genuine. I assure you, I am more experienced and discerning than I may appear."

He gazed into her determined face for a moment, then smiled. "I am relieved to hear it. I am intrigued by your capability, Miss Bumgarten, as by your lovely presence. If I may be so bold as to ask, may I call on you from time to time? I would love to get to know you. As family, I feel honor-bound to see that you are safe and Betancourt is secure."

"You may certainly visit, Mister Graham. Family is always welcome here. But I believe your concern is unnecessary."

She told herself that his forwardness was the result of interest in her presence and his concern for the family seat. She could understand that things might look quite disturbing from an outsider's viewpoint, especially since she was found wearing guns and dining with a half-naked man tied up in a crimson bow.

And if he had heard stories . . . Heaven knew what gossips in London were saying about the duke. It hadn't occurred to her that word of his absence had spread that far. Apparently, it was unknown outside the family that he had made plans for Ashton's succession to the title if he didn't return.

"Until later, my dear Miss Bumgarten." He reached for her hand and placed a kiss on it that was the essence of courtliness.

"Until later, Mister Graham," she responded as he strode for the door.

He reached it before Edgar was close, opened it himself, and flashed a disarming smile as he stepped out and closed it behind him.

She probably should have been pleased with his admiration and bold approach, but it felt more like flattery to her. And she had vowed that she would never again trust empty compliments, or mistake flirtation and amusement for something of worth.

Turning back to the dining room, she mulled over George's visit and her cool reaction to him. When she looked up, Michael Grant was leaning against the frame of the dining room doorway, munching a sweet biscuit and watching her. She halted, feeling oddly exposed under his scrutiny.

"Charming fellow, George." His tone was laden with insincerity.

"Well-mannered, at least," she responded.

"And you hold to the notion that 'manners maketh the man,' do you?"

"A man's manners are telling," she said, teetering on the edge of scolding him for his lack of table etiquette and courtesy toward another gentleman. Wait—she was thinking of him as a gentleman?

"He came here out of concern for Betancourt," she said. "That is an honorable and worthy concern. He left reassured that it is in good hands."

"He'll be back." Michael looked past her, toward the front doors.

"I should think so. He was invited to return," she said, puzzled by her patient's animosity toward a man he had just met, though she had to admit that she hadn't invited George, he had boldly invited himself. "He is family, after all."

"Is he indeed?" The question didn't beg a response, but she gave one.

"I believe so. And he seems to be a proper gentleman."

"He did dress the part. There is another saying: 'Clothes maketh the man.' But I can tell you, Miss Bumgarten, that there is always much, *much* more to a man than clothes and manners. And the truly important parts are never easily seen."

She had paused near him in the doorway, and for a moment met his gaze. Certainty stared back at her without a hint of dissembling or evasion. He let her search him, as if saying *here I am . . . see what there is . . . look your fill.*

Gazing into a man's eyes was not only improper, it was dangerous. Experience had taught her that what she saw might be as much a reflection of her own longings as of the reality of another's heart. She looked away, struggling for composure and trying to remember where they were before they were interrupted.

"You should go back to bed," she said, surveying the table.

"I agree." He yawned, stretched with his good arm, and then patted his half-bare belly with outrageous contentment. Then he stepped back to snatch a handful of biscuits from the tiered server on the table, and lumbered back to her. "I think I may need some help getting up those stairs."

"Ned," she called, thinking he couldn't have gone far. "Deidre?"

No one answered and—of course—they would have forgotten to set out the table bell. When she turned back, he was walking gingerly toward the stairs while holding on to the wall. Muttering to herself, she met him at the foot of the stairs and inserted herself under his good arm. They were both breathing heavily by the time they reached the top of the stairs.

She helped him to the duke's bed and ordered him to remove the shirt, saying she would see it altered to fit him better. He handed her the biscuits first, which she deposited with a huff on the bedside table, then he peeled the shirt from his body. She found herself staring at that tattoo on his shoulder when he handed her the garment.

He settled back on the bed with a sigh and closed his eyes. He looked exhausted.

She was halfway to the door, irritated by her own excitable impulses, when he stopped her with a request.

"Perhaps, Miss Bumgarten, you could see what they've done with my boots. I was wearing them when I was shot and I'm kind of partial to them."

Later that afternoon Sarah sat by the open window in her bedchamber, ripping stitches out of the shirt she had assigned to her troublesome patient. Every thread that popped was accompanied by a word that would have sent her mother for smelling salts.

How dare the man take such liberties with her . . . her . . . imagination?

She reddened at her errant thought. It was her own cursed fascination with his exposed body that started this inappropriate dwelling on him. But after he awakened, his combination of confidence, aura of mystery, and unmistakable interest in *her* had deepened her curiosity. He was a puzzle; rough and demanding one minute, restrained and thoughtful the next.

Or was she imagining such things?

She huffed. It was not her imagination that he ate like a starving ranch hand and afterward paused to offer her worldly advice on the content of men's character.

Her scissors snipped and fingers tugged threads until the altered sides of the shirt were back to their original dimensions. Fortunately she hadn't had a chance to finish the alterations she had started. Admittedly, they had been a bit slapdash. She held it up in the afternoon light. A good pressing and it would probably fit him.

She rang for Mazie and then strode down the upstairs hall, intending to hand off the business of freshening the shirt to the housemaid. Then she should check on her patient's boots. She had finally remembered Ned and Thomas Wrenn pulling them from him in the duke's bedchamber. They had to be somewhere in the house.

She stood at the head of the stairs in the great hall, waiting for Mazie, when the sound of a door opening came from the hallway in the opposite wing. She saw nothing amiss until a familiar figure stepped into the hallway from Duke Arthur's old room. She clasped the shirt to her as she watched the man who called himself Michael Grant disappear into a stairwell that he shouldn't have known was there.

"What are you . . ." she muttered, just as Mazie came puffing up the main stairs.

"Yea, mum?" the rotund housemaid said, leaning on the railing with one hand and fanning herself with the other. "I heated up th' irons, like ye said, an' when the shirt's done, I be fixin' to work on polishin' th' silver. No time fer lollygaggin,' I alwus say."

Sarah looked at the wrinkles her fist was pressing into the shirt, then up at the door where he had disappeared. Her eyes narrowed.

"Oh, I think the shirt is fine just as it is. And tell Ned to lock up the silver. There won't be any polishing today."

Arthur climbed the narrow servants' stairs, contemplating what he had seen in his old room. Everything was the same as the day he left it. A bit of dust here and there; it looked as if care had been taken to leave his possessions undisturbed. His books still filled the shelves, with his natural curiosities still tucked in around them. His writing desk still wobbled from one short leg, but looked like it was ready for him to sit down at any moment to pen notes on his "finds." The bed was narrower than he recalled and the highboy that held his clothes didn't seem as massive, but his mounted and framed butterflies still covered much of one wall. Above his bed hung the sketches and water-colors he had made of insects and flowers.

It pleased him to see it all, but he found it hard to produce a smile. The young man who belonged in this place was no more. He had been content here amid his studies and small treasures, despite the isolation his uncles and aunt had imposed on him. Until he met Daisy Bumgarten. She had barreled into his life like a transcontinental express . . .

He headed out the door and turned right, trying to remember the nearest passage to the third floor. The door he found creaked on its hinges, but he was so intent on mounting those stairs and seeing what had happened to the rest of his world that it didn't occur to him to be stealthy.

By the time he reached the next landing, he was pulling himself up by the rope railing and gritting his teeth. His injured shoulder was on fire. Clearly, another dose of Sarah Bumgarten's mysterious powders was in order, but not before he saw what had become of his collections.

The door to his schoolroom-cum-laboratory was closed

but, thankfully, not locked. Inside, the floors had been swept and someone had had a go at dusting, but there was still a light film of disuse on the tables and specimen cases. He rolled up one of the window shades and stood watching the shaft of sunlight stretch across the room to his display cases. It was the blues that drew his eyes first: the Adonis blue butterflies he had been so proud to collect and display.

In truth very few others ever saw his beloved collection. He had never had friends at Betancourt—anywhere, really. And his uncles and aunt had always behaved as if he were the village idiot when he tried to share his enthusiasm for the beautiful creatures he found in—

"What in blazes do you think you're doing?"

He started at her voice and turned to find Sarah just inside the doorway. Her hands were fisted at her sides and she was breathing heavily from the climb. He was so surprised that the truth was all that came to mind.

"I wanted to see what was up here." He waved a hand at the collection around him. "You were so keen to have me on this level, I wondered why. And I found this." Before she could reply, he turned aside and strolled around the room, examining the butterflies and insects on display. "So this is where Arthur spent his youth."

"There's nothing pawnable in here, if that's what you're after." She crossed her arms and braced, watching his reaction to being caught—what? snooping? plundering? outright thieving?

"I suppose you're right," he answered, seeming remarkably calm for having been caught searching for valuables. "Not that they wouldn't fetch a pretty penny in some markets. Unless I miss my guess, there are some rare specimens here. Look at this." He pointed to a darker butterfly with white markings, then went to roll up the shade beside it for a better look.

"Really, this is outrageous. I insist you come downstairs immediately"—she hurried to him and tugged his arm—"or I will be forced to call the law on you."

"For what? Looking at a collection that should be displayed proudly and seen by all and sundry?" He looked down at her and she experienced a shiver that had to do with the hardness of an arm under her hands and an expanse of bare chest at close range. "Have you seen what's here?"

"Of course, I have," she said, feeling her irritation starting to waver under an onslaught of *interest*. She thrust the shirt she carried into his hands. "Be so good as to put that on, and spare us the sight of your—"

There was no way she could finish that sentence and retain her dignity.

He scowled at the garment, shook it out, and slipped his arms into it. To prevent herself from staring, she turned to inspect the shelves and collection cases that ringed the room. But she could see from the corner of her eye that it fit well enough. Annoyingly well, in fact.

"How do you know these things are valuable?" she demanded.

"I may lack university degrees, but I have been a student of nature all my life," he said as he buttoned the shirt and tested the fit by flexing his good shoulder and arm. Satisfied, he looked over at the specimens glowing—practically iridescent—in the sunlight. "Even if I hadn't studied such things, who could miss how beautiful these creatures are? The old boy had quite the eye, if I do say so. You must admit"—he nodded to a particularly striking specimen—"the coloring of that purple emperor is nothing short of extraordinary."

She hesitated, then stepped to the window and examined the butterfly. Rich, velvety purple, with black and white borders and spots that seemed to have been painted with the skill of an old master.

"It is . . . lovely," she admitted, the last scraps of her indignation deserting her. He didn't display the slightest guilt at being accused of thievery, and in fact, seemed oblivious to it. She told herself he could just be very clever and slyly calculating the worth of the duke's collection.

"People should see these things . . . appreciate them . . . learn from them. There are rambling clubs and birding societies and naturalist associations . . . all kinds of people who would give their eye teeth for a chance to see and study this collection."

Rambling clubs? Birding societies? She looked up and caught an expression that gave her a strange sense of having seen his face like that before . . . alight with pleasure and wonder.

"I confess, I am partial to the blue ones over there." He took her hand and pulled her to a large case with a host of blue butterflies. There, he felt along the edges of the case, saying, "There's usually a way to—" And he came up with a hexagonal key that fit in the lock. She gasped and would have stopped him from opening the case, but her impulses to protect the display and to see what he intended, somehow canceled each other out.

When she saw that he didn't touch the sky-blue wings, she was glad to have held her tongue. In fact, he tucked his good arm behind him as he bent to study the specimens at close range.

"Wait—" He hurried to the worktable and came back with a circular glass encased in a ring of wood. He rubbed dust from it with the tail of his shirt, used it to look at the butterfly. Every muscle in his body seemed to relax. He studied the largest blue one for a moment longer, then offered her the lens. "A gossamer-winged blue. They glow in the light."

As she bent to look through the glass, her breath escaped on an "ahhh." It looked like tiny rainbows had been captured and fitted together around lush, living tiles of color.

He watched her reaction, then bent beside her to share the view. The warmth radiating from him gave her gooseflesh.

"They're amazing creatures," he said, as much to himself as to her. "More than we know."

She looked up, straight into his gaze, and felt a sudden connection that drew her to him in a way she couldn't explain. The next moment she sensed that he had a similar reaction as his eyes widened.

"It looks like there are plenty more," he said softly, the rasp in his voice an ear-tingling whisper. He took her hand and pulled her to another case filled with brilliant yellow and orange butterflies. He opened that case, too, and then another with black and white specimens, some of which had eye-like dots on their wings that made it seem the creatures were looking back at them. Owl butterflies, he called them, and they did look like owls.

As they explored the collection, she marveled at the care the duke had taken with each and every creature. Even the mundane gray moth was accorded a dignified mounting and label. The specimen drawers were set on gimbals that allowed them to be pulled out for examination and made vertical for display. The worktable held a pile of research books and a journal with handwritten entries and drawings depicting what the duke had seen under his microscope. Every aspect of the collection bore evidence of methodical use and care.

By the time they came back to the cabinet near the window, containing the purple emperor, his insights had convinced Sarah he was truthful when he spoke about his study of nature. So, he was a battle-hardened sailor, a self-taught naturalist, and—if he were to be believed—

a physician of sorts. He was a puzzle wrapped inside a riddle, wrapped inside an enigma . . . which made her itch to know about him all the more difficult to dismiss.

"Of all of these creatures, I think the 'emperor' would be my favorite," she said, gazing at it.

He smiled. "The beasties worm their way into your heart. Each species has its own life cycle, mating rituals, favorite flowers and other foods, and there are hundreds of species . . . perhaps thousands. Taken in total, that's a variety that boggles the mind. And that's just the butterflies and moths. Think of all the other insects . . . birds . . . animals."

Her surprise must have shown in her face, for he laughed softly and brought a hand up to run the back of his fingers down the curve of her cheek. She held her breath as the sensation spread through her, magnified by her awareness of his closeness, muscular frame, and haunting gray eyes.

"Such beautiful but benighted creatures." His voice was so deep and full that her skin seemed to vibrate in response.

"Benighted?" She feared saying more would disrupt the moment.

"They spend so much time growing, preparing, spinning substance into possibility . . . only to spend their final beauty and vitality in a few short weeks. Their lives as mature creatures are heartbreakingly brief."

"That's all they live? A few weeks?"

"Sometimes just days," he said. "But they manage to feed and meet and mate . . . make offspring . . . pollinate flowers . . . inspire awe . . ." Standing close, gazing down at her, he seemed to be searching for something.

His head lowered and she felt a trill of expectation along her spine. He paused, his gaze suddenly focused beyond her, on the window beside them, and he straightened abruptly.

"What is that?" he asked, his voice no longer low or soft.

"What?" Surprised by his sudden change, she shook herself mentally and prayed her face wasn't as red as it was hot. She turned to the window and steadied herself on the sill. She heard him say "that" and saw he was pointing to the floral plantings in the center of the rear lawn.

"The butterfly garden," she answered, puzzled by his reaction and ridiculously disappointed at what hadn't happened just now.

Men always have other motives, other things on their minds.

"But a butterfly garden there?" he said, shaking his head. "When I was here before, it was . . ."

"Moved." She tried to hide her annoyance. "When the old duke was here, he wanted to move his butterfly garden to a place with better drainage. So Daisy and Ash saw to it after Duke Arthur left. They wanted it to be a surprise for him when he came home. Only . . ."

He finished her thought and his own.

"He never came."

Chapter Six

Arthur felt his way down the steeply pitched servants' stairs and went straight to the duke's chamber. The windows were open and a breeze was moving the gauzy inner curtains like an invitation.

He braced himself on the sill and stared at the flowers blooming in the large circular garden below. Anchoring the plantings was a paved circle at the center, set with benches and surrounded by flowering shrubs and simple topiaries. At the heart of it all were two central arches draped with what looked like climbing roses. Footpaths meandered through the eye-pleasing palette of color.

From his window—the *duke's* window—he could see it all. Even now, after years away, he could name most of the plants. The local butterflies loved buddleia and oxeye daisies, hyacinth and lavender, showy lupines and geraniums. But other plants he saw were new to him. Where had they gotten additional varieties? How would they know which ones were good for food and nectar? As he watched, a cloud of butterflies rose from the shrubs, spiraled the arch, and then settled—one by one—on other flowers.

He sank onto his elbows in the window, suddenly feeling weak in the knees.

This was for him. They had done this for *him*. Ash and Daisy—the two people he cared most about in the world—had cared enough for him, even in his absence, to create something that would delight his heart. Clearly, they had expected him to return.

Something in his chest swelled at the thought that he hadn't been forgotten. He closed his eyes tightly against the waves of feeling that battered his self-control. It surprised him that, after all he had been through, he was still capable of such powerful emotion.

That evening, Sarah paced the old duke's study, thinking about what had happened in Arthur's laboratory. She had convinced herself that she was fortunate a kiss hadn't happened. She needed to get him well and on his way as quickly as possible. But, thinking of his departure, she experienced a sense of loss she knew meant he had already made a worrisome impact on her. He lurked on the edge of her mind, waiting to insert himself into every thought, each situation. And worse, every time she was with him, she had a nagging sense that there was something more . . . she should be seeing him . . . differently.

After their encounter he had confined himself to the duke's bedchamber, and when she peeked in he seemed to be sleeping. Later, she sent Mazie in with a dose of her special medicinal powders, and had the kitchen send a tray of food up for dinner. The food, Mazie reported, was devoured so completely that it looked like he'd licked the plates clean. At least his robust appetite hadn't been affected.

Something about the location of the butterfly garden had disturbed him. Going over his reaction, she realized it had to do with the garden being moved. He had slipped and said he had been to Betancourt before.

Abandoning the account books she was working on, she exited the study and was soon on her way to the rear lawn. She needed to see the garden and figure out why its location meant something to him.

It was sliding past dusk; shades of purple and blue were creeping over the landscape. As she rounded the last corner, she stopped dead. There, in the middle of the garden, stood her patient, booted feet spread, face raised to the oncoming night. Somebody had found his boots and, from the looks of it, had polished them for him.

She studied his broad shoulders and relaxed stance, wondering what he was seeing and feeling. Something about the darkness and the blended fragrances of the flowers, created a hum in her blood that she didn't trust. But, this was her chance to get answers, and if she turned back now she might never know the truth.

She walked quietly along the path to the center, and halted a few steps behind him, sharing for a moment the sounds and scents of the night garden. He showed no sign of knowing she was there until he spoke in a low, quiet voice.

"It's beautiful, isn't it."

"It is." She stepped to his side, looking around the garden that was drowsy with moon shadows. "A feast for the senses."

"Strange how the night can seem so different around the world. It's the same stars, the same moon, the same dark, velvet sky." He took a deep breath and then quietly let it out. "It's the scents, I think, that change it. Sand, dust, and hints of spice some places . . . jungle vegetation, crops in full season, or animal musk in others. Even at sea there are smells . . . the salty air . . . wet and swollen ropes, the tang of oil and steel . . . sulphur-tainted smoke from ship engines."

"You've been a lot of places." She ran her hand through

some spires of lavender, releasing their fragrance and savoring that sweetness.

"I have."

"Which place do you like best?" She recalled the places he'd named. "Egypt? India? Italy?"

He thought for a moment, then bent to pick a daisy that was nodding in the light breeze, near his feet. "America, I think."

"But you said you've never been there." She frowned.

"Exactly. That's what I like best about it." His voice made it seem his thoughts were miles away. "The next place is always the *best* place. The one where hopes and dreams and happiness are all still possible."

The undercurrent of pain in those words went straight to her heart. As she grappled with how to respond, he tucked the daisy he held into her hair, just above her ear. That gesture unraveled what was left of her defenses. For good or for ill, she had to speak what was in her heart.

"Who are you, Michael?"

He studied her and her question for a long moment. "A man, long gone from home, now returned." He straightened to a near military posture and nodded as if introducing himself. "Sailor . . . traveler . . . sometimes scribe . . . student of nature . . . psychic when needed . . ."

"Defender of dogs," she whispered.

He chuckled. "That too, I suppose." His gaze settled on her as if memorizing how she looked at that moment. "I am what you see, what you experience. My manners are rusty because living has not been easy for me. But I hold fast to my convictions and am not afraid of much."

Those words resonated with her intuition. Still, she needed more.

"What are you doing here?"

He thought a bit too long before he answered.

He was being careful.

"I believe I said: visiting my home. Sometime or other, we all go home. At least, we want to." He stroked her cheek as he had earlier in the laboratory. "And invariably, we find that 'home' has changed."

"So, how has your home changed?" she said, feeling her attraction to him deepening.

"You." It came out before he had a chance to think about it, but in retrospect it was the most truthful thing he could have said.

She was here . . . at the crux of his past and future . . . at the heart of all that had been his hopes and expectations . . . with her curvy frame and sun-polished cheeks and big green eyes that flashed her emotions like semaphores. So easy to read.

So easy to want.

Before she could respond, he bent to touch her lips with his.

At the instant of contact, a rush of warmth came over him unlike anything he'd ever experienced. Inside him something loosened; something, long bound, was set free. He took her by the shoulders and kissed her gently, relishing the lush contours of her mouth and the way she softened under his touch. Pleasure poured through him and for a moment he tried to capture it all. But sensations kept coming, overflowing his senses and overpowering his ability to store or categorize them. He finally abandoned that battle and simply immersed himself in that kiss.

Her lips were warm and sweet, and there was a hint of exploration in the way she fitted them to his. In his travels he'd kissed a number of women, usually ones with considerable experience. Their eagerness had a measured, practiced feel that was nothing like her earnest response.

The world around him fell away as her arms circled

his waist and she met his embrace. He didn't hear the movement, the quick thud of paws on the path, or the growl until it was too late.

It was probably no accident that he took the brunt of the impact . . .

Somewhere in that potent mix of sensation, the sound of a dog's approach had registered in Sarah's senses, but not as a threat. Nero's growl and lunge shocked her as much as it did Michael. They both staggered.

"Dammit, dog!" he roared as he tried to shove her behind him as Nero growled and barked furiously.

She pulled free and bolted around Michael.

"No, Nero—*stop!* You know better than this!" She faced the big dog with her chest heaving. "What's gotten into you?" She turned to Michael, whose fists were clenched, prepared. "He didn't bite you?"

Michael eased and looked himself over. "No new holes, I think."

The barking stopped, but it was clear the dog wasn't ready to back down. He growled, even as he lowered his head to Sarah's approach. She could feel tension radiating from his body and kept her voice calm and manner controlled.

"That's enough. I'm fine."

Nero raised his nose to her, giving her a good sniffing, as if verifying what she'd just said. Then he gave Michael a glare that spoke of unfinished business. "Go back to the house." He didn't move and she pointed. "Go. *Now!*"

Nero turned away and she could have sworn he scuffed his paws on the brick path as he went. She looked back at Michael, her face hot and her lips feeling thick and conspicuous, even in the dim light.

"I'm sorry. He's always been protective," she said. "He's not used to seeing me . . . he probably thought I was being attacked."

"Mazie calls him a hellhound," he said. "Now I see why." He took a deep breath, then nodded to indicate something behind her.

She turned and found Nero had stopped at the edge of the garden. He sat with his ears erect and eyes glowing. She took two steps toward him and pointed to the house again. "Go!"

He rose and took a couple of steps, then sat down again. Waiting. His obedience, apparently, had limits.

"I have to take him in," she said, telling herself it was probably just as well. She looked at Michael, wishing she could bring herself to ask even a small part of what was in her mind. In the end, she gave him a simple: "Good night."

"Good night, Sarah Bumgarten."

She grabbed Nero's collar and steered him to the house. A glimpse over her shoulder showed Michael standing in the garden, still, savoring the night. It was that image of him that stayed with her after she settled into her ivy-canopied bed and relived that soul-drenching kiss.

What was wrong with her? He was a stranger with secrets, and secrets held that tightly were almost always about disagreeable, dishonorable, or outright terrible things. Then, why did she have this feeling of knowing him, of having met him before? She had no business risking her slow-healing heart in a flirtation with a man she couldn't trust to tell her where he lived. She had an estate to run, a title to guard, a living to procure for the people of Betancourt. She knew only the barest bits of his background, and nothing of his purpose in being here.

By dawn, she had decided firmly that no matter how pleasant it was, or how potent its lure, that kissing business would never happen again. As Uncle Red was wont to say, "No sense stickin' yer toe in the water if you ain't fixin' to go swimmin'."

"Damned inconvenient, her turning up."

That same night, George Parker Graham lounged in a weathered chair with his polished boots propped on a scarred table and his pricey top hat resting on his knees. The ramshackle stone-and-timber cottage not far beyond Betancourt's borders was one large room that smelled of old sweat, spent ale, and the bad habits of the men who sheltered there. He winced and brought his handkerchief to his nose.

"On the other hand, she's a tasty little thing, all light hair and big, bold eyes . . . once you get past the firearms, of course. Fresh and far too willful for her own good. American through and through." He looked at the rough-clad men in various stages of consciousness—some with heads on the tabletop, others sprawled and nodding off around the room. The ale and whiskey he provided kept them occupied and kept their presence in the area a secret. "If I play my cards right, it could be a bit of a bonus, claiming that juicy bit."

He frowned, thinking of yesterday's encounter with Sarah Bumgarten, then picked his gentlemanly hat off his knees, and placed it on his head. The one wretch at the table with eyes still open sat straighter, watching him.

"Wot next, yer lor-sship?" the fellow asked.

Your lordship. George rose and smoothed his vest. He liked the sound of that. His father, the old baron, had kicked off just in time. *Your Grace* would sound better, but realistically, that would never happen. He would have to be content with controlling Betancourt's assets.

"You lot stay put while I check into this business of Arthur handing off the title to his younger brother. Damned nonsense. Nobody abandons a dukedom, even an impoverished one. The only way that could happen is if the heir is dead." He froze for a moment. "Is that what they've done . . . declared him dead? The courts have to wait seven years to declare a person dead. This could work to my advantage. I have a connection or two in the Inns of Court. If he's been declared dead and the new duke is absent and neglectful . . . we could claim it's a special circumstance . . . the title and estate in dire straits . . . desperate for a proper steward. Which of course would have to be a devoted family member." He looked at the man, whose eyes were rum-glazed and whose head was sinking. "The *dire straits* is where you lot come in."

Moments later he grinned as he stepped out into the night, thinking again of that magnificent old house, those rich and productive lands, and the curvy little spitfire he would claim along with them.

After a sleepless night on the rack of unrelenting logic, Sarah rose early, saddled Fancy Boy herself, and rode into Betany straightaway. Mazie had revealed that their patient claimed to have stayed at the Iron Penny and said he had a valise and a horse there. Rather than send Eddie to fetch his things, she decided to go herself and spend a few moments with Bascom.

The innkeeper was glad to hear his guest was found. He answered her questions as best he could while he collected the man's belongings.

Sarah's heart sank when she learned her patient had given the name "Art" when he hired a room at the inn.

Michael? Art? Which name was really his? Maybe neither. She'd never been so unhappy to be right.

According to Bascom, the ruffians that threatened her dog had appeared that same night in his tavern, and they brought with them a big, nasty brute of a friend. When they started trouble, "Art" stepped in and saved the innkeeper from damage to his tavern and his person.

"Fought like the devil, he did," Bascom said, leaning an elbow on his bar. "That big feller had a knife half as long as my arm. Never seen the like. They traded blows that'd knock a bull to its knees. But Art laid 'im out flat, an' sent fer th' constable. Got that big bloke locked up in Pankhurst's barn even now, waiting for th' magistrate." He rubbed his chin thoughtfully. "My guess? It was them cursed dog-baiters that lay in wait an' shot 'im."

Sarah returned to Betancourt with just as many misgivings as she had when she left. He seemed to have spoken the truth when he said he wasn't afraid of much and he certainly had proved that he would fight to set things right. But he had used two names, at least one of which was false. Only a man with something important to hide would do such a thing.

Chapter Seven

Arthur stood atop the roof of Betancourt as the sun came up that same morning. The roof had been restored recently—at least sometime within the last year. He toed the edge of several pieces of slate with his boot and found them firmly secured. It should last another century or two. With a deep breath, he walked the front wall of the house and squatted at the southwest corner to watch the estate begin the day.

The land was laid out before him like Joseph's multi-colored coat. Planted fields and pastures rolled as far as he could see, rimmed with hedgerows, dotted with old haystacks, and broken up by ponds and acres upon acres of woods. The pastures were populated with cows and sheep, and it looked like most of the cottages were occupied and the barns were in use. Smoke curled from chimneys and barn doors were being thrown open for morning chores.

Near the main house, he saw that fresh planks had replaced weathered siding on the barns. The stables had a new roof and had been freshly painted, complete with window boxes filled with flowers. The pastures and pens contained horses with foals, cows with calves, and goats with kids. There had been an explosion of births on the estate.

He recalled with a wince the way he had wandered through the barns and stables as a young man, oblivious to the empty stalls, the musty smell of moldering hay, and the stench of abandoned pens. Over time, the dairy was closed and the cows were sent for meat. Fewer workers tended fewer and fewer animals, and he hadn't even noticed. He noticed now . . . the resurgence of life here . . . the pleasure of seeing it coming back to its potential.

He remembered the day that change had begun. It was the day Daisy's uncle, Redmond Strait, a tough-talking, hard-drinking old Westerner, rode in with a herd of cattle he had purchased to replace some of Betancourt's missing stock. Clearly, more had been added over time.

While he watched, people began to appear, coming from the far side of the barns. He squinted and moved to another corner to make out the old cottages the farm hands had once used. They had new roofs and glass windows and proper doors to make them secure. People lived there now, and were stirring and heading to work on the estate. He watched them go into the barns, release animals into pastures, and begin shifting milk pails, bags of grain, and barrows of feed for the animals.

As he watched, Sarah exited the house, dressed in a riding habit, and headed to the stable. After a few minutes, she came out again leading a big horse with stunning coloring—dappled white with a flowing black mane and tail. She led the horse to the drive and mounted with that American "hop" he'd seen Daisy use. She set off down the drive and at the end of it, turned in the direction of the village. He watched the sunny river of hair down her back and her perfect seat on her horse until she disappeared beyond the estate gates.

How much of Betancourt's revival was her doing? How

long had she been here, tending to his brother's holdings?
Where was her mother? Where were her sisters? And what
the devil had possessed Ash to hand such a massive responsibility to a young girl?

A young woman.

All right, a *capable* young woman.

The sun warmed his shoulders as it rose in the sky
and he sat down in the shade of a chimney stack, his arms
dangling across upraised knees. A breeze came up and he
lifted his face to it, recalling the last time he'd been on the
roof. He had caught Daisy and Ash together, and escaped
to the roof to think things over. He shook his head to dispel
those dog-eared memories.

He should have written Ash to let him know where he
was and how he was. But how could he have written
while being held for surety in a raja's palace, imprisoned
in Cairo, shanghaied and forced to work on a ship out of
Algiers, or living as a captive scribe for a fiercely acquis-
itive sea captain?

How long Arthur stayed on the roof, he had no idea, but
the sound of hoofbeats roused him from his reverie. It was
Sarah returning, and she was leading his horse. He rose
and stood with his hands on his hips, watching as she
handed off his mare to a groom and untied his valise, dropping it just outside the stable door. She led her horse into
the stable and didn't reemerge.

With an urgency he didn't want to examine, he headed
for the hatch and the ladder that led down into the attic. He
felt his way down two steep flights of stairs, negotiated the
upstairs hall, and was soon lumbering across the yard
toward the stables.

There he found her with her gloves off and a brush in
her hand, giving her fancy mount a thorough grooming.

He watched for a moment with the strange sense of having seen that very thing before.

"That must be some piece of horseflesh," he said, leaning his arm on the top board of the stall, "to rate grooming by a duchess."

She started and turned, her cheeks reddening. "He's my horse. Out West you learn to—"

"Take care of your horse and he'll take care of you," he finished for her. She stared at him for a moment, clearly surprised by his familiarity with that saying, then went back to currying her horse.

"And just to keep things straight," she continued, "I've never claimed to be a duchess. In fact, *duchess* is the last thing I want to be."

"Really?" He couldn't help the half smile that came over him. "Then you'd be one of only two women in all of England to feel that way . . . the other being the Queen herself." He looked her over with a hint of skepticism. "Most well-born women covet a life of luxury and prestige."

"Luxury . . . had it. Prestige . . . more prison than pleasure. Titles . . . not worth handing over your freedom to be called something that's not your name. Not to mention all the rest . . . cranky old husbands . . . the business of making heirs . . . and putting up with in-laws and their gossipy, condescending friends." She gave a shudder and went back to brushing her horse.

"That's quite a list. But 'methinks the lady protests too much,'" he said. "Look me in the eye and tell me you wouldn't love to be a duchess."

"Fine." She turned to him with a show of conviction. "I would not love to be a duchess." The tilt of her head spoke of determination, but he noted that she did not quite meet his eyes. "One in the family is quite enough."

"Ah, yes. Your sister. Married to a duke now." A thousand

questions bubbled up concerning the handover of his former title to his younger brother, but just now he couldn't find a way to start that inquiry without revealing too much about himself. His gaze fastened on the long, sinuous strokes of her brush and the graceful movement of her hands as she went back to grooming—practically caressing—the beast. *Lucky animal.*

Annoyed, he shifted his train of thought.

"What are you doing here, Sarah Bumgarten? You're wealthy, I presume . . . young and spry . . . and . . . reasonably attractive."

She turned to him with narrowed eyes. "Goodness. I can die a happy woman now, knowing I have achieved *spry* and *reasonably attractive.*"

He swallowed a chuckle. She had a few feminine sensibilities after all. "From what I hear, you're well-read and not afraid to get your hands dirty." When she looked confused, he explained. "Mazie said you worked like a fiend to revive the butterfly garden."

"Listening to servant talk, are you? Be careful. Some of what you hear may be totally false."

"So you didn't dig and replant and weed on your knees so much that you had to have the old girl rub you down with liniment?"

She paused for a moment, looking truly annoyed.

"It had gone to seed. I simply put it back to the way it was." She turned fully to him, fingering the curry brush, looking as if she were deciding how much to reveal. "And I wanted to do it myself. There is pleasure to be had in setting things right with your own hands and getting things to grow and thrive. A satisfaction not permitted to duchesses. *Dirty hands?*" She gave a haughty, duchess-worthy imitation. "*Horrors.*"

He grinned.

"Is that why you're here? Indulging in forbidden pleasures?"

She considered her response as she returned to her work.

"I am here at the duke's request, overseeing the estate. A good thing, too. The house needed securing from the elements; the stables, barns, and outbuildings were falling apart; and the staff had dwindled to nothing."

"And are you responsible for the amazing fertility around the place as well? I noticed a number of offspring . . . foals, calves, kids . . ."

She tossed the brush into a bucket hanging on the side of the stall, and crossed her arms, fixing him with a look.

"Surely a man as well-traveled as yourself knows that animals manage all the time to produce offspring without help from humans."

"Of course, but . . . there are often obstacles of location and opportunity. To mate, animals must be in close proximity. That is something we humans can and do affect." He stepped into the stall and edged toward her. "Proximity." His voice lowered as he approached her and she didn't move. When she looked up he felt himself drawn into those beautiful sea-green eyes. Proximity indeed. His voice softened to a whisper. "Opportunity."

He could have sworn her eyes were darkening, pupils reacting.

"It started with Daisy's horse," she said, matching his whisper. "Dancer was something of a . . . ladies' man. His offspring are pure black, like him. Three generations later . . . his bloodline is . . . still . . . visible."

A hot blast of air hit his ear and he looked up to find her horse mere inches from his head. The beast's nose was twitching as it inhaled his scent, and after a moment, he could have sworn its lip curled in judgment.

"We have a few mares and newborns here in the stable,

but you really should see the horses at pasture," she said, slipping away from both him and her inquisitive horse to head into the stable alley. "This way."

He hesitated a moment, staring at the handsome beast that seemed to be glaring at him.

"You and I," he said, pointing between them, "have to come to an understanding."

She led him out of the stable and down the lane to the pasture where horses grazed and foals gamboled. He watched the sway of her skirt and the way the breeze teased her hair. Her hem was raised enough for him to see her riding boots and it took him a moment to realize her skirt was split to allow her to ride astride. He pictured her on her horse, body moving, thighs gripping—he swallowed hard. He shouldn't be having such thoughts about her. She was more than ten years younger than he was, and he was Daisy's—

He scowled as he watched her climb up onto a white-washed fence board and clap her hands. He felt a strange stirring deep in his core . . . something akin to sexual desire, but different in a way he couldn't quite define. This was something he'd never felt around Daisy or any of the other women he'd known. This was different, and he wasn't sure he liked that it was occurring just now and with her. He'd almost kissed her again, back there in the stable, and he was fairly sure she would have kissed him back.

What would getting romantic with her do, besides set him up for disappointment later, when she found out who he was . . . what he was?

"You see that?" she said as he came to lean on the fence beside her. "All of those coal-black foals, yearlings, and three- and four-year-olds are Midnight Dancer's line. Twelve, as of a few days ago. Still breeding true." Moments later, she climbed over the fence and dropped into the middle of some young horses that had come to greet her.

They stretched their noses to her and she gave each a pet and a small piece of carrot.

He watched her walk out into the pasture, her arms draped across the younger foals while the older ones trailed behind. The mature horses gravitated to her and nuzzled and greeted her as if they knew her. He climbed the fence himself and followed her at a distance, watching her talk to the horses as if they were people. Some shook their heads, nodded, or pawed the ground in response. Most were patient, waiting their turn with her, though some of the youngest foals butted through to demand attention. They were quickly nipped and turned aside by their older "aunties." She laughed at that lesson in manners and hugged and stroked the mares. He had never seen anything like it.

That, he soon learned, was just the beginning. From there, they went to the dairy barn where the cows were being milked, and then the pen where the calves waited for their mothers. Here, too, her touch seemed golden. Half a dozen calves gathered around her, clamoring for affection, and as she petted the smallest one she gave it two of her fingers. The calf sucked on them for a minute and she laughed. "Here—give her your fingers," she ordered, seizing his hand.

"No, no—really—that's just—" The oddest sensation he had ever experienced, having the calf suck his fingers. Though the beast had teeth, it was careful not to bite. It just felt—strangely—*Good God!* He pulled his hand back and stared at his tingling fingers in horror.

"Never in all my years—" He halted before saying something daft.

She laughed. "So, Michael Grant, world traveler, seagoing warrior, self-taught naturalist . . . you've never had your fingers suckled by a calf? Your people didn't have animals?"

"Not many. And I was never involved with the ones we had."

There was something in his expression, a shock, a blunt admission of inexperience that seemed out of character for a man who—until this very moment—had seemed so worldly and confident.

As he strode out of the pen, the little calf went running off and jumped and kicked happily, as if she'd just been blessed by Mother Nature herself.

"Sixteen cows fresh, now," she called as she exited and closed the gate behind her. "So much milk we're having to make cheese."

"What kind of cheese?" he asked.

"Cheddar, of course." Her laugh was pure music. Saucy thing, she was enjoying his discomfort. "What else would good English cows make?"

He could think of several other kinds, but decided against listing them.

The goats were next and he had to admit, the kids were adorable. They came to greet her and investigate him while jumping around like they had springs in their legs. She dragged him over to a wooden crate they apparently loved to climb on and gave it a pat. The little things scrambled up on it, competing for space on the top and some even putting their hooves up on her in a bid for attention. One by one, she introduced him to them.

"Posey, this is Michael, a guest at Betancourt." Then she leaned her head toward him and spoke out of the side of her mouth as if she didn't want Posey to hear: "She eats fast, finishes first, then snatches the others' food right out from under their noses."

"Thus, the bulging sides," he said, copying her confidential air.

She nodded. "We have to feed her separately."

Posey sniffed him, made a bleating sound, then hopped down to continue jumping and playing around his feet.

"I think she likes you," she said, and then picked up a little brown and white goat, sharing another confidence as she handed the kid off to Michael. "This is Violet. She's shy around people."

Little Violet snuggled against him, sniffed, and promptly bit his shirt—right above a nipple on his chest. "The hell she's shy." Before he could pull her away, she took a more serious nibble and caught a sensitive bit of skin in the process.

"Aghhh!" He thrust the little beast out to arm's length and plopped her back into Sarah's hands. A moment later, he was striding through the gate, red-faced and stunned by his own reaction. You'd think he was . . . he was . . . *the old Arthur* . . . easily embarrassed, and achingly aware of his inexperience with anything that didn't have six legs.

These were farm animals, for God's sake. Simple creatures doing what came naturally. Not a malicious bone in their bodies. He took a deep breath and forced himself to calm.

Sarah appeared at his side with a worried look.

"Are you all right? She didn't hurt you?" She made to touch the wet circle Violet had left on his shirt and he fended her off like a nervous virgin.

"No, no . . . she just surprised me." He straightened and smoothed his shirt. "Danged goats will eat—" He changed direction and pinned her with a look. "Do you know every blessed animal on the place by name?"

"Only the special ones. But you can see that they're all well-tended and well-fed." She studied him with concern. "I think you've seen enough of Betancourt for this morning. You should probably rest before luncheon. And we need to change the dressing on your shoulder. You know, your face is a bit red." She reached up to feel his cheek and forehead with the back of her hand. "You feel warm."

"I'm perfectly fine," he said, collecting the scraps of his dignity.

At that moment, a commotion arose from between the cow barn and the dairy. The sound of wings flapping, and quacking and honking, announced a mixed flock of ducks and geese being driven by three young girls with switches. The ducks seemed content to rush along under their escorts' guidance, but the geese clearly took exception to being ordered about by three undersized humans. They honked, flapped wings at their minders, and generally made quite a fuss . . . until they spotted Sarah.

"Good God," he muttered as the flock turned toward her, and—since he stood beside her—toward him. Soon they were engulfed by geese and ducks quacking and flapping wings and nipping at their boots.

"Stop that." Sarah waved her arms to keep them back, and then told the goose girls, "Run to the kitchen and get some old bread from Cook."

Arthur stood like a statue, dismayed by the throng of agitated fowl flogging his feet. Sarah intervened, stooping by the birds and speaking calmly to those closest to her. She stroked feathery heads and sleek necks and cooed, telling them how pretty and how special they were. The geese's down and feathers made the softest pillows and warmest featherbeds, she told them, and the ducks' babies were so cute and were the best swimmers in the county. The ones within her reach quieted and stood watching, listening to her voice. After a few moments she began to hum, then sing.

*"Oh my darlin', oh my darlin', oh my darlin', Clementine . . .
you are lost and gone forever . . . dreadful sorrr-ry,
Clementine . . ."*

The remaining goose girl grinned and joined in. The
fractious geese were the last to succumb to Sarah's win-
some spell, but soon, even they quit contending with each
other to listen. She rose and began to sway, extending her
movements with her arms, and to his astonishment, the
birds' heads seemed to move with her. She laughed and
sang a bit louder, motioning him to join in the serenade.

"It's their favorite song," she called, and started another
round. *"Drove she ducklings to the water . . . every
mooorning just at nine . . ."*

"That's just ducky," he muttered, declining.

Two more voices were added as the other goose girls
returned with a couple of crusty loaves a bit past their
prime. He heard a husky voice behind him and looked
over his shoulder to find the rotund cook standing in the
kitchen door, belting out the song. A couple of brawny
farmers had paused in passing, and leaned on their shovels to listen, then to sing along. Two kitchen helpers, a
young footman, and a groom who poked his head out of a
stable window added to the songfest. Apparently everyone
on the place knew this duck-loving "Clementine" and delighted in singing about her demise to a flock of entranced
barnyard fowl.

What the hell kind of insanity is this?

The next thing he knew, he was holding a handful of
bread and being told to break off pieces to throw to the
upraised beaks. A group of pushy ganders apparently
saw him as an easy mark and rushed to be first for a
treat. He braced, refusing to be intimidated by a handful
of greedy geese. For a moment, his strategy worked; he
held his ground and fed the less aggressive birds first.
But a determined gander soon flapped and jumped at

the bread he held . . . catching both the treat and the hand dispensing it.

"Owwww!" He jerked back, appalled by the sight of blood on his finger. The damned thing bit him!

Sarah handed off her bread to one of the goose girls and insisted on seeing his injury. "It's not that bad," she announced. "Just needs cleaning and a wrap. You'll be fine." She produced a handkerchief to wind around his finger.

"It jumped up and bit me," he said, still hardly able to believe it.

"They're usually better behaved," she said, turning him bodily toward the house. "Especially if we sing. If it's any consolation, I doubt it was your finger he was aiming for."

"That's not a consolation," he declared flatly.

She caught his irritable expression and paused for a moment, staring at him. Her green eyes seemed to darken, becoming mirrors in which he glimpsed his own petulance. He was bleeding, true, but it was hardly a major wound.

"Fortunately, you've got nine others," she said, cheerily wiggling her fingers as she pulled him toward the front doors. "Next time, *sing*."

Sarah watched him take a deep breath and brace as she dabbed alcohol on his cut. He was determined to be manly and stoic, but his jaw muscles hadn't gotten the message. She lifted his hand and blew on his finger.

"What are you doing?" He looked at her as if she'd lost her wits.

"If you blow on it, it relieves the sting. Didn't your mother teach you that when you skinned a knee or scraped an elbow?"

He looked between her and his injured digit, and made a face of grudging acceptance. "Didn't have a mother for long. And, in my medical duty, alcohol was considered more desirable inside the body than out."

"I suppose there is something to be said for the anesthetic effect of imbibing alcohol," she said wryly, "especially if you have a difficult patient." Then she fixed him with a tart look. "How about a belt of whiskey?"

Just then, Dolly arrived with Sarah's medical bag and bandages, and was quickly sent for hot water. Sarah rolled up her sleeves and had him take off his shirt and sit in a chair she placed in the sun streaming through the windows. She had been dreading this dressing change . . . had already put it off a day or two and was surprised that he hadn't called her on it. She could hardly admit to avoiding it because she didn't want to deal with his hard, shirtless body at close range.

She cut the bandage, unwound it, and dropped it in a nearby dustbin. He bent to look at the wound at the same moment she bent to look closer at it. Their heads bumped and both froze in place. His exotically tanned skin, the musky scent of him, the warmth he radiated . . . for a moment she was caught off balance.

"It looks good," she murmured. "Pink. Healthy. It's already closed."

"What is that you put on it?" he said, his voice low and thick.

"A plaster of honey and herbs."

"You put *honey* on a bullet wound?"

"It has been reported that . . . direct concentrations of sugar . . . like those in honey . . . keep the germs that cause infection from growing."

Her knees were going weak. All she could think about was that kiss last night in the garden and how she couldn't allow it to happen again.

"Germs?" He tilted his head in an excessively handsome way. That was a kissing angle, if she'd ever seen one.

She should straighten, should start cleaning the blasted wound, should back away—far away from him—now!

"Animals so tiny you can hardly see them with a microscope—like the one Duke Arthur had in his laboratory." Apparently she was incapable of doing any of the sensible things she had just enumerated, because she stayed where she was and licked her lip instead. "That's the latest theory on sickness. Miasmas are outmoded. Germs are all the thing, these days."

"How very *current* of you."

He took a deep breath and pulled his gaze from her, breaking the connection that held her spellbound. She was both relieved and annoyed.

"I do try to keep up." She wetted a cloth, dipped it in the hot water, and began to carefully clean the wound. But her disappointment came out in one final snap. "Let me know if you want a leather strap to bite on. I'll have Ned fetch something from the barn."

Chapter Eight

S he was just tying the last knot on his bandage when voices came from the hallway, approaching the breakfast room. The sputtering one was Ned's. The other one sounded less familiar, until it reached the doorway to the breakfast room, and came paired with a gentlemanly form and entitled manner.

George Parker Graham stopped just inside the door, holding his hat and riding crop, still wearing his gloves and an expression of concern. He looked between Sarah and Michael, seeming genuinely shocked. A heartbeat later, his eyes lit with determination.

"I pray you will forgive the intrusion, Miss Bumgarten, but since our last meeting, I have been deeply concerned for your safety." He swept the room with a look. "I have concern for *all* of Betancourt." His gaze settled on Michael. "I have heard from a reliable source that there are unsavory elements in the neighborhood. I can see now, I was right to be concerned for your well-being and good name."

Color drained from Sarah's face. She was caught again, by the same gentleman, in an even more compromising situation. With a half-naked man. She drew herself up straight and stepped between them, blocking his view.

"I assure you, sir, that all is well." With every second that passed, she recovered more of her self-possession. "I am tending to Mr. Grant's shoulder. If you would be so good as to wait in the parlor." She looked to the anxious underbutler behind him. "Ned, please show Mr. Graham the way."

Ned was more than happy to do so, although he bent, spread his arms, and waved them at George as if he were shooing chickens. George looked at him as if he were a raving mental case, turned on his heel and strode out . . . drawing Ned—still shooing—in his wake.

She turned to Michael, who had risen and stood like a solid block of stone, staring at the door where George had disappeared.

"I believe it's best if I handle this alone," she said. "You should go to your room and rest a while." She pulled his shirt from the back of a nearby chair and held it out to him. "You'll need this."

George Graham was back. She rolled her sleeves down and headed to the parlor. His presence again, so soon, wasn't a good sign. But at least he hadn't caught her wearing Uncle Red's guns this time.

She paused for a moment and drew a deep breath. Her only course was to banish embarrassment and behave as if all were normal and expected. Answer every question, assume authority in all cases . . . and the minute he left, sit down and write Ashton a letter—a telegram—demanding he return to England immediately. Betancourt needed a duke, even a reluctant one.

"Please forgive my earlier tone, Miss Bumgarten," George began the moment she entered the great receiving room. "It was something of a shock to see you with that . . .

unclothed man. I understand, from others in the area, that you are indeed considered a healer of sorts and that this man was brought to you injured. But surely you can understand my concern for your reputation upon seeing you exposed to such an indelicate display."

"You should know, Mr. Graham, that I am not and never have been missish about such things. I am not a sheltered London deb, nor am I easily intimidated by society's rules or those who would press them upon me."

He stared at her for a moment, then affected a smile that didn't quite reach his eyes. "I see that, Miss Bumgarten. Clearly the American in you. All the more reason to be circumspect in your dealings here. You must be aware that your feelings are quite the exception and you must remain above all suspicion."

"And just what would I be *suspected* of, Mister Graham?" she said, thinking quickly. By his own admission he had been investigating her presence here and asking about her in the county . . . gathering evidence . . . but for what? What could he possibly gain from learning she was what she claimed? And if he hoped to discover otherwise, what would he gain then?

"You are a lovely young woman, alone in a great house without chaperonage . . . in company with a strange man who shows not the slightest trepidation about parading his unclothed body before you. Surely you know how that may be interpreted by the less charitable elements of society."

"He is my patient, Mr. Graham." She lifted her chin and clasped her hands harder. Maybe she should have worn Red's guns. "Our encounters have been witnessed by Betancourt's staff."

"Staff? Like the fellow who shooed me into the parlor like a dotty old goatherd? If so, they are hardly in a position to vouch for his behavior. Or, I am sorry to say, for *yours.*" He set his hat and riding crop on the card table near the windows. "I have no doubt of the higher purpose in your dealings and nature, Miss Bumgarten, but what about him? What do you know about him? Where is he from? Are you certain he is not a thief or confidence man? Do you even know his true name?"

That last charge struck a nerve and it must have shown in her face. He moved closer and captured her gaze for a moment before she looked away. A moment later, she could have kicked herself for that small retreat.

"He seems able to move unaided," he said, his voice more intimate, almost lulling. "Surely it is time that he removed himself to a less compromising location. For your sake." He edged closer, pausing as if to judge the effect of his presence. "If you cannot see to his removal, perhaps someone else should."

"And would that someone be you, George?" Michael's commanding voice came from the doorway.

Sarah and George Graham turned at the same time to find Michael standing in the archway with both fists propped on his waist. He was using his injured shoulder. His gray gaze was cool and flinty.

"Michael, please," she said, moving between them. "This is not your concern. I have asked that you return to your room—"

"It appears that *George* has made my presence here a point of contention." His use of George's first name was nothing less than a provocation and he knew it. His posture said he was prepared for George's response, however heated or confrontational it proved. "I believe I am entitled to defend myself and, in so doing, defend your kindness to me."

"It is not her kindness that is objectionable," George declared, stalking to the side to face Michael directly. "It is the way her higher nature is being taken advantage of." He drew himself up. "Who are you, sir, and what are you doing in these parts?"

"I have said. I was born and raised in *these parts*, and I've come home to visit," Michael said tautly. "None of which is your concern. Your continuing challenge of Miss Bumgarten's presence here and her care of Betancourt is more an affront to decency than my occasional lack of a shirt."

"How dare you question my right to see to my family's good name and welfare?" George reddened. "Who do you think you are?"

"Who I am is not important," Michael said, his voice dropping and acquiring that rasp that always sent a shiver through Sarah. "What I am is the issue . . . a man grateful for the mercy Miss Bumgarten has shown me and the effort she has put into bringing this gracious home back to life."

"I have searched the county, made inquiries, and can find no trace of a family of Grants having lived hereabouts," George declared. "That is who you claim to be, is it not? Michael Grant. Born and raised near Meridian land." He turned to Sarah, fists clenched. "He lies, Miss Bumgarten. I will bring affidavits, if you require them. This man is a brawler, a bully, a purveyor of deceptions. I can provide witnesses, should it come to that." He stalked still closer to Michael, raising his voice. "I ask again, who are you? What is your real name and what are you doing here?"

Michael took a deep breath, realizing that the time had come . . . as he knew it would. He looked to Sarah, seeing the doubt in her eyes, hoping that she would forgive him—

at least give him a chance to explain. But for now, his most pressing desire was putting George Parker Graham in his place.

"My full name is Arthur Michael Randolph Graham." He paused for a moment, allowing the impact of that to be felt. "I was not born near Meridian lands, but on them, in this very house. I was named the sixth Duke of Meridian at the age of twelve, and for years afterward was the ward of my uncles, Bertram and Seward . . . Bertram being, through another family connection, the Baron Beesock."

"P-preposterous," George declared, jerking his chin back. "You? A duke of the realm?"

"I was." Michael stepped forward. "And you, George Graham, are the son of Bertram Graham. Which makes any claim you put forward or action you take regarding Betancourt or myself . . . suspect."

"That is the most outrageous thing I have ever heard!" George declared, turning to Sarah. "Did you know of this ridiculous claim? Is this why you allowed him to stay in this house and besmirch your good name? His claim to be Arthur, Duke of Meridian? Can you not see him for the liar and opportunist he is?"

Sarah stared at Michael in shock. Arthur and Michael, both? Graham, not Grant? He was *that* Arthur? When he looked at her, locked gazes with her, she felt a jolt of recognition that took her breath. Was that why she had those fleeting feelings of familiarity with him? Pieces of the puzzle dropped into place: sailor, adventurer, self-taught naturalist, sometime physic . . . he had traveled . . . just as Duke Arthur had. The way he seemed to know about Betancourt and Ashton at school . . . did he know about them because he truly had been there? And the butterflies and insects in the collections . . . he knew about those because he had collected them?

Her face flamed. How had she not recognized him? She tried to conjure a memory of the old Arthur for comparison and got only a soft, indistinct image that might have fit half of the gentlemen in London. But she did remember dancing with him . . . the stiff way he held her . . . the softness of his hands . . . the awkwardness of his movement. If he truly was Arthur, he had changed so much that none of the staff still doddering about could recognize him. Not even Bascom could tell who he was, and she was fairly certain he had seen Arthur numerous times, years ago.

Why would he claim such a thing? How did he think he would get by with it?

"I-I don't know what to say, except . . . I shall have to research this."

"Dearest Heaven, Miss Bumgarten, can you not see what he is? He wishes to insinuate himself into your good graces . . . to lower your guard . . . while plotting to get his hands on Betancourt's riches."

"Riches?" Michael laughed angrily. "There are precious few here now, thanks to your father. He and Uncle Seward and Aunt Sylvia drained, sold off, and outright stole nearly everything of worth at Betancourt. And it would appear the apple hasn't fallen far from the tree." He advanced on George, who stepped back, and then farther back. His voice dropped to that low, raspy register that made it sound like a pronouncement of Fate itself.

"What are you doing here, Cousin? Why are you suddenly so concerned for the noble house your father beggared and the title he tried to usurp?"

George stumbled back against the table where his hat and riding crop lay. He grabbed them and dragged them before him like a shield.

"I will not abide such loathsome charges against my

ather's memory." His voice grew strained. "If you truly were Arthur, you would know that my father spent the best years of his life caring for you and seeing that you had the finest education and the most comfortable life possible. He worked his fingers to the bone to care for his estate . . . neglected his own offspring to cater to your very whim . . . such was his devotion to Betancourt and the precious Meridian heir."

Michael towered over George, forcing the smaller man to look up into his fierce gaze. "My uncle is dead?" His fists clenched. "Then he has already received his just reward . . . in Heaven . . . or the other realm."

Sarah gasped and would have intervened, had George not bolted to the side, out of Michael's reach. With the threat of violence lessened he became once again the aggrieved relation bent on purging the estate.

"Beware, Miss Bumgarten. You do not know whom you are dealing with. I intend to see this imposter exposed and removed from Betancourt as quickly as possible."

Both Sarah and Arthur Michael Graham watched in charged silence as George strode furiously out of the parlor, through the hall, and out the front door . . . leaving the latter standing open. After a long moment a panicked nanny goat came racing into the hall, followed closely by Nero and Gwenny.

Startled, Sarah jolted into motion and herded them back outside. She closed the door and leaned back against it, searching for mental footing. Much of what she had assumed and counted on these last months, had just been knocked into a cocked hat. She looked over at the parlor archway and found Michael standing with his feet spread and arms crossed, watching her.

Arthur. Back from the dead.

She swallowed hard, straightened, and faced him.

"You, sir, have some explaining to do," she said, feeling

strangely numb and unsure of her course. Was she going to give a duke of the realm a dressing down? If he really was Arthur Graham, she told herself, he damn well deserved it. "Come with me."

The study was full of bookshelves, sunshine, and dust motes suspended in still air, until she entered and set it all swirling. He had followed her and stopped just inside, surveying the fireplace, stuffed bookshelves, and worn leather chairs as if reconciling memory with fresh perception. His face bore a strange combination of reluctance and determination.

Instinctively, she took control by planting herself in the great leather chair behind the desk. Pointing to one of the barrel chairs that sat before the desk, she ordered, "Sit."

He studied her position and disposition before complying.

"I want the truth," she declared, folding her hands on the blotter and papers before her. "Now."

"So, this is where I have to recall dates and names and events to prove my identity?" he said. He rubbed the worn leather arm of the chair, betraying his tension.

"No, this is where you explain why you didn't just announce yourself as Arthur when you arrived, instead of engaging in this prolonged deception." She glared, though with less heat than she would have liked. "Assuming you *are* Arthur Graham, sixth Duke of Meridian."

"I'd rather do names and dates," he said with a wince.

"We'll get to that. First, I want an explanation for this"—she waved, indicating his hair and garments—"masquerade." When he hesitated, she insisted, "Now, please."

He rubbed his chin, eyes narrowing, collecting his thoughts.

"I arrived in England six weeks ago with no coin and

no contacts, outside of a salty old fellow who had jumped ship with me off the coast of Portugal." He bent forward and clasped his hands between his knees. "He had family in Portsmouth and we stayed with them while working at the docks unloading cargo. I saved what money I could and was finally able to take a train north. I traded some work, and most of the money I had, for a horse at a way station and made my way to Betany." He looked down at his clothes. "This is no costume." Every word seemed to cost a piece of his pride. "It is—what I have had to wear for a very long time."

She sat back in her chair watching him closely, sensing truth in his words. This seemed difficult for him, this recounting. If he truly was Arthur, it was an admission that his grand plan of exploring the world had proved more arduous and costly than he could have imagined. No funds . . . stuck aboard a ship . . . *shanghaied*, he said. Had that really happened?

"If you are Arthur, you were gone for years. Why didn't you come home before this? You knew the terms of the agreement with Ashton, that he would assume the title if you didn't return in the given time."

"I had what you might call *adventures* . . . the last of which was aboard a ship I was shanghaied onto. The captain was a right bastard, and when he learned I could write and cipher, he set me to keeping his records in addition to my regular sea duties . . . and he . . . made me read him stories each night to put him to sleep. Whenever we put in to port, he locked me up below. My literacy apparently made me an asset he refused to lose." He gave a humorless smile. "After more than a year, he made the mistake of getting drunk one night near Lisbon and forgetting to lock me up. That's when Mack Dowd and I slipped overboard and swam for it."

"So, you arrived here with little money and just the clothes on your back. But you didn't come to Betancourt. You went instead to Betany, took a room at the Iron Penny, and kept your identity a secret. If this was truly your home, why wouldn't you come directly here?"

The look on his face made her wish she hadn't used such a prickly tone. He took a deep breath and scanned the study for a moment as he chose his words.

"I thought Ash was here."

"All the more reason to—" She halted, realizing from his lowered gaze and uneasy posture that he was reluctant to see Ashton. But Ashton would have welcomed him with open arms, *if he had been here*. For the hundredth time since she arrived at Betancourt she wondered why Ashton hadn't returned to England to fully assume the role of master of his estate.

"You must have known he would welcome you, that all of Betancourt would welcome you."

"Betancourt doesn't know me from Adam." He shoved to his feet, hands clenched with frustration. "It never did. I left to see the world and find myself before they had a chance to know me. I thought Ash would have taken my place, but he's not here and the folk don't even know they have a duke anymore. They think you're their duchess, for God's sake."

"I told you, I've never made such a claim," she declared, feeling oddly wounded. Was the prospect of her being taken for a noblewoman so unthinkable?

"I'm not saying you did." He paced away, then back, pushing his long hair back as if it annoyed him. "I'm just saying . . . I never was a real Duke of Meridian . . . not like I could have been." His features tightened and voice lowered to a pain-laden whisper. "Not like I should have been."

For a moment he stood staring at the floor, his chiseled

face a study in loss. There was nothing she could say to relieve his regret. She saw clearly the conflict he felt in returning to a home he believed he had deserted. The fact that he felt such guilt seemed potent evidence of his identity.

She took a deep breath and prayed her raging attraction to him hadn't overtaken her common sense.

"I believe I could use some of those names and dates, now."

Chapter Nine

He looked up with a strange expression that might have contained a trace of hope. With a deep breath, he propped his hands on his waist.

"The year 1618, the title Duke of Meridian was created. Jacob Makepeace Dennison Graham was the first . . . half English, half Scottish—more borderland raider and hot-headed warrior than gentleman noble. History has lost the tale of whatever deed or deeds convinced King James to award him land and title. It was probably something of a bribe and definitely meant to get him away from the unruly borderlands, since the lands granted him were well south. But old Jacob made the most of it . . . tamed the unruly inhabitants of his granted lands, enforced his own brand of justice, and managed to sire a dozen children on three long-suffering wives."

"Which explains the streak of *contrariness* in the present generation," she murmured. "Go on."

"The second duke, Cornelius Graham, was a canny sort who managed to support both sides during England's civil war. One minute a Roundhead through and through, the next a flaming loyalist determined to avenge the king's beheading. He wore a Puritan collar during Cromwell's rule, but silks and ostrich feathers when welcoming the Restoration and the king's return."

"A man of flexible convictions," she observed.

"And wardrobe. The third duke, Eustice Graham, built this house in 1716, and added on to it in 1723, which accounts for the interesting mix of brick and stone in the architecture." He gestured to the study and the house beyond. "He seems to have been something of a stay-at-home, content to see to his estate and tenants. He replanted the decimated forest and saw proper wells dug . . . funded the building of the church in Betany . . . started a proper forge and a grain mill in the area. It was his wife, Ann, who insisted on the checkered marble in the front hall. It seems she got her way a lot. She tired of cold food coming from the outside kitchens and insisted hearths and pantries be installed inside the main house. Her last improvement was a dumbwaiter, installed to prevent accidents on the stairs from the kitchen."

"Thank you, Duchess Ann," she said with a small smile.

He paused, studying her, seeming more composed.

"I have them all," he said quietly. "The dates, the names, the glorious history of the great House of Meridian. Though I'm sure it all sounds more grand and exciting than it really was. Some of my predecessors were little more than fancy-dressed tax collectors who required people to bow and pull their forelocks as they handed over their hard-earned goods and money. If you want, I will set them to paper and you can hold them as evidence."

"That might be a good idea," she said, drumming her fingers on the leather desktop. "You know, there are some family photographs. It wouldn't hurt to see if there might be something in them to . . ." She rose and searched the drawers of an antique chest near the door. She brought a large pasteboard box back to the desk and opened it to reveal a stack of photographs wrapped in tissue.

"How did you know about these?" he asked as he helped her unwrap the photos and lay them out on the desk.

"When I first came, I had to locate documents and go through the accounts to learn what had to be paid. There was quite a bit owing. I searched every drawer and cabinet in the study and library. I found these, but didn't look at them."

Some images were fixed on heavy pasteboard, others were thick paper that was now brittle and had to be handled gently. As they were laid out, they seemed to be mostly photographs of babies and young children. It was hard to tell if the babies were boys or girls at first, since they all wore dresses. But on the backs of the photos someone had thoughtfully penned names and years in ink that was now faded.

She asked Arthur his birthdate and checked it against the dates. A surprising number seemed to be of him. Then came a few photos of him with infant Ashton; Arthur appeared in short pants and a jacket with a velvet bow and Ashton wore an elaborate gown. A christening photo, it seemed. Similar images in succeeding years documented the boys' growth.

She checked the cabinet again and the doors beneath the bookcases, hoping she had missed something. She returned holding her forehead.

"I'm fairly certain there aren't any other photographs," she said, coming to stand beside him and look at the picture of a plump boy in short pants and bowl-cut hair. He looked nothing like Michael or even Arthur.

"Who in blazes takes a dozen photographs of the heir to a dukedom as a baby and a young child," she said, "but doesn't bother to document any other stage of his life?"

He stared fixedly at the photo. When she looked up, she wished she could take back those words of frustration.

"I remember this. It was my eighth birthday." His voice was little more than a whisper. "A short while after my mother died. My father was sick with grief . . . my uncles came to stay . . . insisted I must be sent away to school. In the end they waited, so they could send Ashton and me together. He was six and I was nine when they sent us off. I saw my father only twice after that. From the day I went to school until I met your sister Daisy, my uncles ran my life." He paused and swallowed hard before continuing.

"Your sister changed all of that. When I saw how good she was and how mean they were to her—the same disdain they had always shown me—I began to realize what they had done and the limitations they had placed on my life. I knew I had to change things and to find out who and what I was."

"And did you?" she asked, touching his hand. When he looked at her, into her, she had the sudden, awful feeling that he was seeing Daisy. The tenderness in his voice as he spoke of her sister was hard to witness.

"*Yes*," he said with a determination that surprised her.

For one charged moment he met her gaze with fierce, silvering eyes, then turned and strode out of the study.

She watched him go with an ache in her heart. She remembered the wedding, the shocking events at the altar, the joy of seeing Daisy and Ashton finally united in love and marriage. It hadn't occurred to her that when Arthur disappeared that same night—leaving behind a message about wanting to travel—that it might have been because he couldn't bear to see Ashton with the woman they both loved.

Her heart seemed to deflate and sink, leaving a void in her core.

She pressed a hand over that emptiness, realizing that she wanted to believe him. She wanted him to be Arthur Graham, former Duke of Meridian, who was once betrothed to her sister Daisy. But if he was, then he was also the young man so devastated to lose her sister that he fled his home and country and roamed the world for years.

Daisy had chosen Ashton instead of the duke, but by a twist of fate, she had become a duchess after all. She was

now the wife of the current Duke of Meridian, Ashton . . .
who hadn't come home or shown any interest in fulfilling
his obligations or even reveling in his new title and standing. She couldn't help contrasting his neglect to Michael's
desire to return home. He had crossed oceans and escaped
captivity and swam for his life . . .

The realization of what that meant took the strength
from her legs. She dropped into the grand chair, wondering
if demanding Ash return to Betancourt was the right thing
to do. Whatever happened, she saw with miserable clarity,
it had to be done. With trembling hands, she reached for
paper and pen.

And when Ashton came home, what would happen to
Arthur?

The next afternoon, in a fashionable London town-
house, Elizabeth Bumgarten greeted a caller who claimed
to have urgent information concerning her daughter. The
Bumgarten matriarch hurried to her elegant parlor as her
butler, Jonas, admitted the man.

A well-dressed gentleman of middling height and pleasant features entered the parlor with an air of urgency. He
introduced himself with perfect manners: "George Parker
Graham, Baron Beesock, at your service, Mrs. Bumgarten.
I must apologize for this intrusion, but I bear news of your
daughter that cannot wait."

"Baron? Goodness, this is a pleasant—oh! Frances! The
baby is coming!" Alarmed, she went for the bell.

"No, no." He quickly corrected her impression. "I refer
to Miss Sarah Bumgarten."

"Oh. Great Heavens, I thought—" Elizabeth pressed a
hand to her heart in relief, motioned the man to a chair.
She tensed again as she realized a strange baron with

urgent news of her daughter . . . would not be bringing good tidings. She took a seat opposite him in front of the great fireplace. "What news do you have of my Sarah?"

"She is even now residing on an estate in Wiltshire called Betancourt, the seat of the Duke of Meridian."

"I know my daughter is there, Baron. She has written me about her circumstances, and it is a great comfort to me that she is sheltered by that venerable house. In fact, I intend to visit her there, as soon as my other daughter, the Viscountess Tannehill, is delivered safely. The child may come any day now, and I am on pins and needles."

The baron came to the edge of his seat, looking grave indeed.

"I would urge you to spare some concern for your other daughter. She is at this moment, trapped in Betancourt with a man posing as Arthur, the former Duke of Meridian. I have taken it upon myself, as a close relation of the real duke, to investigate this man and his claim, and am convinced that he is a fraud. Worse, this imposter has no compunctions about involving your innocent daughter in scandalous encounters where he . . . dare I say it . . . is sometimes disrobed."

At her gasp, he halted and transferred to the settee beside her, his demeanor one of grave concern.

"I see that to say more would be too distressing. I will only caution that her safety and reputation are both in peril. Something must be done."

"Sweet Heaven. How could this happen?" Elizabeth's eyes had widened during his speech. Now she fanned herself with her handkerchief and found it hard to catch her breath. "My poor, dear child! These blasted 'dukes' will be the death of me, yet."

"I urge you to act quickly, Mrs. Bumgarten. The imposter even now works to insinuate himself into your daughter's confidence. I tried to convince her of his deceptive and venial nature, but she is too pure of heart to believe the worst of anyone. I can only appeal to your more discerning nature and hope that you will take my warning seriously."

"I shall indeed, Baron. And you say you are a kinsman of Duke Ashton?"

"I am. My father was his closest counselor and aide. It breaks my heart to think of how that man may work his greedy plan to gain control of the estate in the duke's absence." He paused and with the hesitation of a true gentleman, put his hand upon hers for reassurance. "I was devastated to hear of the old duke's, Arthur's, disappearance. But I am certain the new duke, Ashton, will take the situation in hand, when he learns of it."

George Parker Graham exited the Bumgarten home with a smug expression. *Mothers*. The woman was thrown into a tizzy at the thought of her daughter's reputation being sullied. She had practically run to her writing desk as he departed . . . was probably already penning letters to all and sundry, demanding action. It probably wouldn't cross her mind that a telegram would reach her titled son-in-law much sooner. And he wasn't about to suggest it.

His expression warmed to a full smile as he struck off for the heart of English jurisprudence, the Inns of Court. He had a few more cages to rattle before the day was through.

That wretch at Betancourt had no idea of the trouble he was in for.

Chapter Ten

After sending Eddie to Betany's small rail station with the text of a telegram for Ashton and Daisy, Sarah had spent the rest of the afternoon secluded in the study going over documents. She read what little information was in the library on the legalities of the peerage of Britain . . . dug out the folio of documents laying down the conditions under which Ashton would assume Meridian's title . . . and mastered some of the legal jargon in the paperwork regarding the title and property attached to it.

By evening, all she had to show for her search were burning eyes, fuzzy notions of Parliament issuing writs, and a lot of verbiage about which lands and properties were entailed by the original grant and which were not. The "witness" signatures provided the name of the lawyer who had drawn up the documents, but some of what had been written made no sense to her. She wrote a letter to the solicitor, asking him to clarify matters and sent poor Eddie shuttling back to Betany to post it.

Later that night as she dragged herself up the stairs, she caught Mazie scurrying along the upper hall with an armful of damp towels, having just come from Michael's room.

"'E wanted a bath an' I had to light the heater an' show

'im th' whizgizzies in th' closet room." She jerked her head toward the north side of the house. "He be in th' garden now, I expect. Goes there ever' night."

"He does?" Sarah headed back down the east hallway and opened the door to an unused guest room. The moonlight was bright enough to let her see the butterfly garden clearly, and there he was . . . legs spread in a determined stance, looking up at the star-littered sky, no doubt enjoying the sweet scent of the night around him.

If he truly was Arthur—and she felt oddly guilty that she wanted him to be—those sensations would be a balm for his soul. She watched for a long time as he moved around the garden, touching flowers and plants, bending to enjoy fragrances. He did seem to love the garden, was drawn to it in a way that said good things about his heart. Then as she watched he stooped and did something among the flowers. Was he picking some to bring inside?

When he rose, he had something long and stringy in his hand, and he tossed it out of the garden. A weed. He'd tossed it away and then bent for another. She felt a catch in her throat. It was a small action, a simple thing, weeding a garden. But it was also telling, in ways that tugged at her heart. She closed her eyes for a moment, battling a rush of emotion, then turned and fled through the darkened hallway to the safety of her room.

Ladyish trays in bed had never been Sarah's custom. The next morning, she descended the stairs as usual, peered out the parlor windows to gauge the weather, and made her way toward breakfast. Voices and laughter wafted up the kitchen stairs and she slowed, surprised. The staff were hardly a jovial lot. She rarely saw a smile out of the house folk, much less a giggle or an outright laugh.

Frowning, she entered the breakfast room and rang the

kitchen bell to let the cook and servants know she had arrived and they could begin serving. Seated at the largest table, she drummed her fingers on the polished wood and waited. And waited. More trickles of laughter came up through the dumbwaiter and the bellpulls. Her stomach growled and after several more minutes, she rose irritably and headed down the stairs.

In the servants' dining room, one end of the long table was cluttered with dishes containing dried egg, odd bits of sausage, and the remains of leftover toast. Cook spotted her and bustled in to stand with hands on ample hips, looking pleased at the destroyed table.

"He's not here, ma'am."

"Who?" Sarah asked, knowing the answer.

"That fellow o' yours." She grinned broadly. "That man does love his food. An' got a tongue that turns to pure silver when a cook's about."

"Where is this 'fellow o' mine' now?" she asked with an edge that totally escaped Cook.

"Th' stables." Cook gave a satisfied smile. "Said he wanted to see to some horse or other."

But when she arrived there, she found he wasn't in the stable either. Eddie and the stable master, Old Harley, met her outside the tack room with news that Jess Croton's boy, Miles, had ridden up in a lather and said his pa was hurt badly and needed tending right away. Michael had saddled his mare, demanded the bottle of whiskey Harley used to medicate his sciatica, and rode off with the boy.

"You didn't think of calling me first?" she demanded, glaring at the pair. "Fine. Saddle Fancy Boy—fast." She ran back to the house for her medical bag and some bandages, and was soon mounted and riding down the cart road that wound through Betancourt's tenant farms.

Jess Croton's farm, if she recalled properly, was upriver from Thomas Wrenn's and was considered a prime bit of bottom land. She struggled to recall what Samuel Arnett had said about Croton the day she treated Old Bec . . . a loss of some kind . . . pigs stolen. Now there was an injury and Michael had taken it upon himself to ride out and see to it.

"How dare he?" she muttered, tightening the tie of her hat under her chin to keep it from blowing off. "He should have sent for me. Who does he think he is?"

Besides the *former* Duke of Meridian.

The Croton farm was picturesque from a distance; stone and half-timber buildings nestled between the Old Meriton Forest and the river. But as she grew closer, it became clear the place was in disarray. Pens and fences had been knocked down, a hay wagon lay on its side in the middle of the yard, the hay it carried now scattered. A pony cart had been smashed; it lay splintered and collapsed on its broken axle in the middle of a field of debris. The barn doors stood agape, one hanging from a single bottom hinge and the other with splintery holes that looked like they'd been made by an axe. Several dead chickens lay outside a demolished chicken coop and pigs were squealing over a dead sow in their pens.

In the distance, she could see animals loose in rye and oat fields that were just about ready for harvest. Goats had climbed onto the roof of the shed closest to the house, and there was a young child—still in nappies—wandering barefoot among the wreckage.

She pulled up beside the cottage, swung down beside Michael's horse, and grabbed the child's hand. The young one began to flail and cry, so she had to pick him up and carry him inside the open cottage door. There she found a woman in tears, a man on a bed, moaning, and children collected around each, asking if their "pa" would be all right. In the middle of it all stood broad-shouldered Michael with one hand on his narrow hip and the other tilting a whiskey bottle that was draining slowly into the injured Jess Croton.

"What the devil are you doing?" she demanded, thrusting the child into his mother's arms and rushing to the bedside.

"Loosening him up so I can put his arm back in the socket," Michael said without even bothering to look at her. "It would be best if he passed out first—there would be less resistance. But I could only get a quarter bottle from Old Harley. Just as well . . . Jess, here, isn't much of a drinker."

She scowled. "How do you know it's out of joint?"

"I've set a number of shoulders. Happens aboard ship sometimes in bad weather. Have a feel yourself, if you don't believe me."

She stared at Jess Croton, who looked up through a swollen, blackened eye with a half-corked smile. He'd taken a walloping, all right. Bending to investigate, she felt the mushiness of the joint and the misplaced bone.

"It is out of joint," she had to admit. "What do you intend to do for it?"

"First, I have to ask him some questions." He straightened Jess's arm as he held it gently by the wrist. "What happened here, Jess?"

"Bastards come jus' b'fore dawn. Got ever' bleedin' piglet I had lassss time." He was clearly feeling the effects of the whiskey. "Thisss time I wus ready. Had my pa's gun . . ."

"I begged him not to go out there." Jess's wife, Alice, joined them, shifting her youngest to her hip. "They're bad men—terrible bad. He wouldn't listen," she said, choking back tears. "Stubborn ox could've got hisself killed. Then where'd we be?"

"Th' powder wus bad," Jess continued. "Ain't fired it in

years. But, I had to try—they was tearin' up jack—fer the pure devil of it."

"Took most o' my hens," Alice said. "Killed the ones they didn't take . . . stinkin' buzzards."

"Tried to stop 'em, but one had fists like hams an' got in a blow on me. I fell 'ginst the wagon," Jess continued. "Must've blacked out. When I come to, I couldn't get up— my arm wouldn' move." He licked his swollen lips and let his damaged eye droop closed. "Next thing I knew . . ."

"Don't go to sleep, Jess," Michael said, giving him a shake. "I need details. How many were there? What did they look like?"

Sarah couldn't believe he was demanding answers from a man he'd just addled with whiskey. He was slowly straightening Jess's injured arm. She was surprised the poor man wasn't howling.

"F-f-four," Jess mumbled, struggling to stay awake. "Big louts—taller'n me. The one what hit me—he'd been drinkin'. Smelt it on 'im."

"What else? Come on, Jess, what else did you see?" He gave Jess a shake. "Did they ride in? Did you see horses? A wagon?"

"Can't that wait until he's—" Sarah interrupted.

In a flash, Michael put his boot against Jess's side, just beneath his shoulder, and gave the arm a jerk.

"Argh!" Jess forced his eyes open, looking shocked. "What th' . . ."

"Try moving your arm," Michael ordered, releasing him.

Reluctantly, Jess moved it and then sagged with relief. "Ye f-fixed me." And he promptly passed out.

Alice tearfully thanked them and then ushered the children outside to begin rescuing the mess in the yard. The sound of her issuing orders floated back inside the cottage.

"That's some treatment regimen," Sarah said irritably as she helped bind Jess's shoulder. "Get the man liquored up, talk him blue in the face, then put your foot on his ribs and yank. I can't wait to see what you do for the cut on his head. A hot poker, maybe?"

"Head cuts require needlework," he said, looking her over with a grin of such wicked delight it would have given an angel pause. "What are the odds *the duchess* knows how to take a stitch as well as remove one?"

She had trouble looking away from that intriguing expression.

"If by *duchess* you are referring to me, you can lay money on it." She reddened as she opened her bag, selected a needle and a length of suture, and seized the unfinished whiskey to pour over the needle. "I have this in hand." She dabbed Jess's cut with some whiskey and knelt by his head to begin stitching. "Feel free to see if Alice and the children need help outside." She waved a hand. "Go on."

Arthur watched as she set to work—*bossy female*. It took a minute for the image of her vivid green eyes to fade from his vision when he stepped outside. The yard was a mess. He surveyed the damage as Alice ordered the children to look for any chickens that might have escaped the thieves. Righting the wagon, fixing the fences and doors, and moving the shattered cart required more power than he could provide with his injury, but there had to be help nearby. He asked Miles for the location of the nearest neighbor, climbed on his horse, and headed out to recruit some labor for the Crotons.

As luck would have it, Samuel Arnett's place was closest, and another farmer named Ralston had brought some horses to Arnett's farm to have them re-shod by a traveling farrier. When Arthur told them what happened, it didn't take much to convince them to lend the Crotons a hand. Arnett's wife, Young Bec, immediately set about collecting food to carry to the family. The men hitched up a cart, set Young Bec on it along with the food and some tools, and were soon on their way.

"Wot did ye say yer name was?" Samuel Arnett asked as they went.

"Arthur. Graham."

"Ye don't say. We had a duke by name of Arthur." He squinted, looking Arthur over. "You any kin?"

Arthur thought for a moment. His secret was out and what difference would it make to tell the truth? Still . . .

"You could say that."

"Then, you be the duchess's brother?"

"Not exactly. Miss Bumgarten, whom you call 'duchess,' is my brother's sister-in-law." The confusion in Samuel's face forced him to elaborate. "My brother Ashton married her sister Daisy."

"But that would make you . . ." Arnett frowned, trying to puzzle it out.

"Arthur Graham." Arthur gave his mount a heel and surged ahead, anxious to escape the questioning and to get back to the Crotons' farmstead. Thus, he didn't see the grin that spread slowly over Samuel's face or hear the exchange between him and Ralston.

"It's him. Duke Arthur. He's back," Samuel said, eyes wide.

"You sure?" Ralston looked unconvinced. "He don't look nuthin' like that time I saw 'im riding by my place. All that hair, an' he looks like he could wrestle an ox. That ain't the boy I remember."

"Well, fer sure, he ain't a boy anymore." Samuel nodded.

When Arthur's rescue party arrived, they found the young Crotons standing at the end of a field where cows and oxen had trampled grain that was close to harvesting.

Out in the field, Sarah had a milk cow by its rope halter and was talking to it. Arthur stopped to watch as she led the animal out of the field and handed it over to Miles, who ferried it back to the barn. She lifted her skirts and waded back into the grain to retrieve another cow. Once again she began to talk and stroke. The beast tilted its head for her to scratch its neck, and Arthur saw her smile as she obliged.

A couple of young heifers came next and the last cow and calf were still being charmed into compliance when Arthur realized the cart had stopped behind him and Samuel Arnett, Young Bec, and Ralston were watching Sarah weave her peculiar spell over the Crotons' bovines.

"She got the gift," Samuel said, with clear admiration. "Ain't never seen a noble lady with the *touch* before."

"It's a woman's thing," Young Bec declared with a grin. "Animals know when a body's good in th' heart. An' the duchess, she's good as gold."

Good in the heart. Those words lodged in Arthur's core and resonated perfectly with what he had learned about her. The animals knew it. The tenants knew it. Truth be told, *he* knew it. And it was just one more reason he found her both irresistible and untouchable.

Alice rushed to greet her neighbors and fell into Young Bec's open arms while the men surveyed the damage. Most of it was repairable, they declared. With a bit of effort, they'd have the damage fixed and the debris cleared away before sunset. But the first order of business was getting the fences up and those animals out of the grain field.

While Arnett worked on securing the pen by the barn, Ralston waded out into the field with a yoke, hitched up two oxen that Miles called Lou and Lightning, and soon had the pair moving out of the field in lumbering partnership. Young Miles appeared beside Arthur, dragging a yoke intended for the second pair. Arthur hurried to help him carry it, but found himself relying on Miles for direction on how the heavy animals should be harnessed.

Oxen, Miles instructed, worked in pairs: always the same two yoked together, always in the same positions. There was a tradition about their names, too—one was always short, the other longer, but in the same vein. The short name, like Lou, always got the left side and the long name, like Lightning, got the right. The second pair were Flo and Foxglove. Hook them up wrong and they wouldn't move an inch. But yoked right and proper, they would answer a drover's orders of "get up," "gee," and "haw" like they were born to it.

It was a humbling experience, being educated in the temperament and handling of oxen by a twelve-year-old boy. Fortunately for Arthur, he was used to being humbled. The world was full of things he hadn't known and had to learn in order to survive. In truth, he enjoyed learning about the beasts and taking them in hand. Soon he was bellowing orders like a natural-born drover and watching Miles's eyes light with accomplishment.

With the oxen safely stowed and the barn door well on the way to hanging properly, the men and Arthur righted the hay wagon and reloaded what hay they could for transfer into the loft. He caught Samuel staring at his shoulder and the way he favored one arm as he helped with the lifting, and he gestured to his shoulder. "Had a little accident a few days back."

"What kind o' accident?"

"Ran into a bullet with my shoulder."

"Did ye now?" Samuel said, clearly impressed. "Seems we heard 'bout that. Constable Jolly come around tellin' folk. So, that was you."

Samuel tossed a covert look at Ralston.

"Ye couldn'ta landed in better hands," Ralston said,

pushing his hat back to wipe his forehead. "The duchess, she's got a healin' way about 'er."

He looked across the yard to where Sarah was taking a splinter out of one of the Croton kids' fingers and the child was staring up at her in pure fascination as she worked. He knew that feeling in her presence, had felt that same sense of being somehow made better by her touch. For a moment his knees weakened.

She was something rare, Sarah Bumgarten.

"Yeah." Samuel jolted him back to reality. "Yer in good hands, there." He realized the men were watching him watch her and felt his face heat.

For the next hour, Arthur covertly tracked her with his gaze, watching her with the women and children, watching her with the animals left in the pigpens and in the barn. He couldn't stop himself and, strangely, it didn't seem to matter to him that Arnett and Ralston chuckled at his distraction.

Sarah truly cared about these people—his people—about their lives and welfare. She involved herself in their problems and used her knowledge to help them. In a few short months, the folk had come to admire her abilities and appreciate her determination to help them.

He thought of his own relationship to the people of the estate. He had been young and purposefully isolated, in his years here, but he had never really considered what the rest of Betancourt wanted or needed . . . until he had lost it. He saw the way Arnett and Ralston worked and he thought of the precious time they took away from their own duties to help a neighbor. There was a whole community of farmers and herdsmen on Betancourt lands who knew and depended on each other, a community he knew nothing about.

But he was learning. He listened to Arnett's and Ralston's shared concern over the security of their farms and asked questions about their families and their local society. He sweated and strained and, despite his still healing shoulder, met them board for board and pitchfork for pitchfork. He had been forced to work hard physically during his travels, but had never felt good doing it. Oddly, now—on Betancourt—he liked the exertion, the purposeful use of his strength, the feeling that he was doing something good.

By midafternoon, the yard was mostly set to rights and the food brought by Young Bec had been consumed. Sarah promised to send some chickens and ducks from Betancourt to restock the Crotons' coops, and Ralston volunteered to stay at the Crotons' place that night, to watch over things until Jess was on his feet again.

Arthur entered the cottage to check on Jess and told Alice that he would have to keep his arm bound for a few days to give it time to heal. Then he spoke with Miles, telling the boy to come and fetch him if his father needed help or if those men returned. He looked around for Sarah, but Miles said she had just left, taking the shortcut through the forest to Betancourt.

He thought of the woodland that one of his ancestors had replanted and protected more than a century ago. It was now a dense wood full of snags and hollows . . . a perfect place for thieves to hide during daylight.

Rattled by the thought of her alone in that forbidding passage, he stepped outside to look down the little-used forest road. Whatever possessed her to take such a route? He mounted his horse and headed out on that same narrow, overgrown path, trying not to think about what would happen to her if she ran afoul of the gang that wreaked havoc on the Crotons' farm.

Chapter Eleven

Sarah felt the stone in Fancy Boy's hoof almost as soon as he did. The change in his honey-smooth gait was small, but attuned as she was to his movement, she caught it right away and dismounted. She checked his hoof and judged him able to make it home without her weight on his back.

Walking beside Fancy, she savored the light breeze and dappled light coming through the thick leaf canopy overhead. Her thoughts were occupied with the events of the last few days. Today she'd seen Michael—*Arthur*—work hard physically, pure manual labor, to get the Crotons' place set to rights. Clearly that was how he'd acquired the muscular frame that fascinated her so. She frowned as she recalled the way Samuel Arnett and Clyde Ralston instinctively deferred to him and how he seemed to lead even when he was asking questions and learning from them about their work.

Honestly, she couldn't imagine the Arthur she remembered doing any of that. That afternoon, her Michael/Arthur had proved that he was no longer a sheltered heir that had been manipulated by greedy guardians. Every time she thought she had her mind settled about him, something happened to expose a different side of him and she was forced to rethink her feelings about him.

He was strong and forceful at times, tender and thoughtful at others. Lord knew he was handsome in an elemental, skin tingling, joint loosening kind of way. And he didn't rattle or spook easily; his reaction to Cousin George was proof of that. She had the feeling there were depths to the man she hadn't begun to plumb, and—blast her infernal curiosity—she wanted to explore every one of them.

Alerted by the muffled thuds of hooves on the damp earth, she whirled to find Michael on horseback coming up behind her. She blushed, wondering if her thoughts had somehow summoned him.

"What the devil do you think you're doing?" He dismounted and came to stand over her, breathing hard.

"Fancy's got a stone." Her pulse picked up at his air of urgency. "You wouldn't happen to have a hoof knife on you, would you?"

"You know there are thieves and outlaws about, and you've just seen what they can do. What better place for them to hide than a dense and little-traveled forest?"

She glanced around her with a dawning recognition of the potential menace in the snarled undergrowth and looming shadows. Lord, that hadn't even occurred to her.

"It isn't a long distance through." Uneasiness crept into her voice.

"Long enough for men with no scruples and even fewer morals to find you. Then where would you be?"

She thought about that for a moment, trying not to meet his gaze. "Battling my way free." She straightened. "I'm not exactly helpless, you know."

"Imprisoned and held for ransom, more likely. Or ravished and made to suffer the wretches' vile demands." He studied her face. "If something should happen to you, the whole of Meridian would come for my head. Not to mention your family and my stubborn brother."

"Who appointed you my protector?" she demanded.

He propped his fists on his hips, looking her over.

"You've never been held captive."

"True." She swallowed hard. "I understand that you have, but—"

"More than once," he declared, his face hardening. "I was held captive in India as surety in negotiations between the provincial government and a fiercely independent maharaja. And for eight months in a Cairo prison . . . caught up in a brawl that became a rebellious mob. I narrowly missed being beheaded. Later, as I headed back to England, I was shanghaied in Algiers. I know what it is to be captive and powerless, and I am fairly certain you would not do well under such circumstances."

He was probably right, infernal man. But her potential peril suddenly seemed less important than what he had just revealed about his adventures. Holy buckets, the man had been through difficult times.

"So, you really could not have come back to Betancourt before now," she said, watching the play of emotions in his face.

"Correct." His stance softened as he sought her eyes again. "Throughout my travels I seemed to stumble into chaos and upheaval wherever I went." His expression darkened. "Now it seems I've brought it home with me to Betancourt."

She studied him, seeing that sense of abandoned responsibility and guilt she had glimpsed in him before. "I think you're taking this too personally. This band of thieves was roaming the countryside well before you came back to Betancourt. You could hardly be responsible."

He gave her a rueful smile. "But I did leave Betancourt untended and unguarded for years."

"No more than Ashton has." She realized the implications of speaking her thoughts aloud and bit her lip.

"Yes." Michael frowned. "He hasn't lived up to his responsibilities either." A moment passed as he searched her upturned face. "You, however, have more than met *our* obligation to the estate . . . setting the house to rights, rebuilding the stables, tending to peoples' ills and complaints. Including mine."

He reached up to stroke her cheek and she shivered.

"You are a wonder, Sarah Bumgarten. What are you doing here?"

The searching question in his eyes pulled every heartstring she possessed. She had the most compelling urge to tell him.

"I . . . I . . . couldn't stay in London and I needed a place to go. I knew Ash wasn't here, so I figured no one would object. When I got here, winter was coming on and the house was cold and leaky; there were missing slates on the roof and missing glazing in some windows that let in the elements. I needed something to do to take my mind off . . ."

"Off what?" He reached for her hands.

She recoiled from that contact, but he held her fast.

"Tell me."

She braced internally, realizing that she could no longer shrink from the truth behind her presence at Betancourt.

"I was involved with someone. At least, I thought I was. He came back from Italy with a fiancée and I had to learn of his blasted engagement in front of my mother and half of London." She struggled with the feelings that clung to that memory. "I never really fit in there, so I left London, hoping to find a place where no one knew or cared that I was a bluestocking 'jilt.' Betancourt was empty and in need of attention. And I had *attention* to give."

"And the name of this paragon of arrogance and self-ishness?"

She couldn't bring herself to say his name, shamed by the emotion the earl's betrayal still had the power to stir in her.

"It doesn't matter." She forced a smile that felt more like a wince.

"But it does," he said, lifting her face with his finger-tips. His gaze slid into hers, probing, seeking the bruises on her heart. "I need to know who to flatten when I set eyes on him. Callous, trifling bastard."

It was said in an almost teasing tone, but she heard underneath it the flintiness that hardship and misfortune had shaped in him. He spoke the truth when he said he was not afraid of much. In that moment she realized he very likely would throw a punch at an earl.

"Any man who doesn't recognize how bright and en-gaging and desirable you are is either blind or stupid. Or both." He inched closer to her. "So, I'll keep an eye out for an arrogant dolt wearing thick spectacles."

She couldn't help the laugh that bubbled up in her.

"You say the most outrageous things."

"Just the truth, actually. I've never been quick enough to come up with sharp ripostes. It just happens that the truth is often more outrageous than we realize."

He leaned toward her upturned face and his voice low-ered to the nerve-tingling vibration that sent gooseflesh over her shoulders. "The truth about your eyes, for in-stance. They're the color of a South Sea island lagoon. A beautiful blue-green that would make butterflies jealous. And your skin is so smooth and warm, so sweetly freckled."

She would have covered her nose, but he refused to

release her hand. Sweet Heaven, did he intend to itemize every flaw she possessed?

"Your hair—sun-kissed and streaks of gold—is soft to the touch and smells of rose oil." He twirled a finger in a wisp of hair that had escaped her chignon. "You leave every room you enter smelling of your passage."

"So . . . my complexion is ruined and I reek of too much scent?" she said, her throat tight and words a bit forced.

"What I am saying is, you're utterly delectable, Sarah Bumgarten."

"Oh?" She could hardly breathe. "So . . . I'm . . . edible?"

"I'm having a devil of a time here—"

"Not insulting me?" she said, staring helplessly at his mouth.

"Controlling an urge to—*aww, hell.*"

He met her lips with his and completed a circuit of desire that had been charging between them for days. This electrical connection was hot, urgent, and totally overdue. She wrapped her arms around him and rose onto her toes to meet his kiss.

His lips felt hard and demanding at first, but softened as they blended with hers. Her heart beat recklessly; she could hardly take a breath as she fitted her mouth to his and learned the pleasure of tasting him fully. Salty, faintly sweet, he was as delectable as he claimed she was. More, she wanted more of these powerful sensations . . . more and deeper kisses, more and deeper contact . . . she wanted to climb inside his skin and touch every bone and sinew . . . wanted to discover every little known, never shown part of him.

She didn't hear the rustle of leaves, the snap of dried branches on the forest floor, footfalls—clumsy in their haste and growing closer. But Michael heard them. He was breathing heavily as he jerked his head up and looked around. His body tensed against hers.

"Go for my horse—now!" As he backed away, he thrust her toward his mare and growled, "Now, Sarah!"

Confused, but trusting his instinct more than her own pleasure-dulled senses, she wheeled and made it to his horse before it struck her that Fancy was lame and needed help. She hopped up into the stirrup and swung into the saddle.

"Get Fancy!" She held out a hand to him and after an instant of indecision, he grabbed her horse's reins.

As he swung up behind her and they took off, rough-looking men emerged out of the forest and demanded they halt. Threats weren't enough to keep Sarah from kicking Michael's mare into a run.

The road was narrow and overgrown in places, but their direction was clear and they managed to hang on to each other long enough to lose sight of the bandits. Fancy tried valiantly to keep up, but was limping badly and clearly in pain. He finally stumbled to a halt, ripping the reins from Michael's hand as they rode on.

"I've lost him!" he called to Sarah.

She slowed and started to turn back to help her beloved mount. Two men on horseback came roaring up behind Fancy, pointing something at them. There was a crack, then another. The first shot went wide.

"They're *shooting* at us!" Michael pulled her back against him to grab the reins and turn them back toward Betancourt.

In desperation, she leaned to peer around him, and saw Fancy rearing, pawing at the bandits trying to take him under control. She kept looking back, heartbreak blurring the image, until Fancy's struggle was out of sight.

Sunshine warmed their shoulders as they left the woods behind, but nothing could erase the stunning visual of Fancy fighting for his freedom.

"We should have gone back for him—he's worth a stable full of other horses," she said, swallowing tears.

He slowed the horse to a walk. "No amount of bravery can beat a gun. If I've learned anything in the last six years, it's that you have to know when to fight and when to withdraw to fight another day."

It was hard-won wisdom, she sensed, and probably the right thing to do. But she was still devastated by the knowledge that her beloved horse was now in the hands of brutal men who had killed stock at the Crotons simply because they couldn't take it with them.

"He has such spirit," she said softly. "And he's injured. They won't take care of him . . . and if they think they can't use him . . ."

"We'll find him, Sarah." He took a deep breath and pulled her back against his chest. She melted against him, needing the warmth and security of his hard body supporting hers. "He's one of a kind. They won't be able to sell him off without somebody noticing." She closed her eyes and tried to believe him. "I'll search the whole county, inch by inch if I have to. I'll find him, I swear it."

Michael lifted her down at the stable door, stroked her damp cheeks with his thumbs, and then sent her into the house ahead of him. Every footstep cost her precious energy, but the moment she entered the great hall she felt something was different. Voices came from the parlor and she hurried to the archway to find her beloved uncle seated in the center of a knot of household staff, relating one of his Nevada stories.

"Uncle Red?" She could hardly believe her eyes. His face was ruddier, his hair was whiter, and she could have sworn he'd added an inch or two to his barrel of a chest. But he was still every bit the beloved old Westerner who had been her father figure, teacher, and occasional accomplice for as long as she could remember.

"Sarah!" He struggled to the edge of the settee and then to his feet, sending the servants scattering back to their duties. She ran to hug him, and saw him wince as he opened his arms to her. Instinctively, she gentled her customary bear hug for the old prospector, but his embrace was every bit the hearty squeeze she had come to expect.

"Are you all right, Uncle Red?" She pulled back in his arms to look him over with concern. "You look like you're in pain."

"Aww, just saddle sore. Fancy livin' is makin' me soft. I took the train from Suffolk to London to see Lizzie, an' then mounted up an' rode straight—" He halted and scowled at her. "You been cryin'."

Tears welled again.

"It's Fancy—he's been taken by some men who—" She saw alarm building in him and tried to explain. "There are a bunch of thieves—outlaws—who've been stealing and tearing up property on our tenants' lands and we went to help a farmer who got injured. They caught us in some woods on the way home. I was walking Fancy because he picked up a stone and they came up quickly on us and they had guns—"

"Guns?" Red's alarm changed to outrage. "In England? Hell, the coppers don't even have guns here."

"Fancy couldn't run and we had to get out of there."

"Yellow-bellied bastards," Red growled, pulling her against him and patting her. "We'll get 'im back, Sarah. I promise you."

"Damned straight we will," came a deep voice from outside the parlor doorway. Sarah looked up to find Michael stopping just inside the doorway. His frown at the sight of her in a man's arms melted as he recognized their visitor.

"Red? Redmond Strait?" He looked Red over in astonishment. "You haven't changed a bit."

Red released Sarah and limped toward Michael, stopping a few feet away. His gaze flicked back and forth, and up and down, inspecting Michael's striking features and formidable frame.

"Who the hell are—?" Red came up with his own answer before the question was fully out of his mouth. "You're that *imposter*."

That, Sarah hadn't expected. She swiped at the moisture on her cheeks and hurried to Red's side. "Imposter? Uncle Red, what are you doing here?"

"Yer ma sent me t'see about you an' protect you from some varmint who showed up claimin' to be Arthur come back from the grave."

"He's—" She scowled in confusion. "How did she hear about him?"

"Somebody brought word ye were bein' held here and she stormed around like Pecos Bill on a twister. Frankie's baby is takin' his sweet time comin' and Lizzie's afraid to leave 'er, so she sent fer me." He looked her over, and she reddened under that inspection. The old prospector didn't miss much, and whatever he saw clearly caused him concern.

"You all right, Sarah?"

"I'm fine, Uncle Red, really." Her thoughts went straight to George Graham. What other *somebody* could it be? "I can—*we* can explain."

"*We*, is it now? You throwin' in with this tall drink o' water?" Red stepped right up to Michael, squinting to examine his face, his long hair, and muscular chest. He limped around Michael, looking him up and down with narrowing eyes. Completing that circuit, he faced the younger man and crossed his arms.

"Tell me somethin'," he commanded.

"What?" Michael braced as if he expected a fist to answer him.

"Somethin' you an' me would both remember."

"You mean . . . like . . . the time you danced in and out of a twirling rope, doing tricks, and impressed the hell out of our houseguests? If I remember properly, that night you roped a calf and a countess—in that very order. Whatever happened to her? The countess, not the calf." He glanced between Red and Sarah. "Lady Evelyn something."

"She come to a bad end, poor thing." Red flicked a look at Sarah before declaring, "She married me." He grinned at his own shop-worn joke. Briefly. "Answer me this," he went on, intent once again. "If yer really bug-happy Arthur come home, what's the name of that big butterfly Daisy wore on her dress at that first ball?"

"You remember that?" Michael realized Red was serious and rubbed his forehead, thinking. "I believe it was . . . a purple emperor. Yes, she had paired it with a yellow Cleopatra on her shoulder. But then, she had a *Parnassius apollo* in her hair. It was lovely. The butterfly, not her hair." He gave a start. "That's not to say her hair wasn't nice— I'm sure it was. It's just that the butterflies were such a pleasant surprise. At the time, that seemed more important than"—he slowed—"anything else."

In that moment Red must have made his decision. He laughed out loud at the rueful look on Michael's face.

"Those eyes . . . that stubborn jaw . . . he knows stuff . . . even talks like 'im." He turned to Sarah with visible relief. "This ain't no imposter—it's Artie. The duke Daize set her cap for some time back."

"Are you sure, Uncle Red? This is very important," she admonished.

"Sure as snow in January," Red crowed, grabbing Arthur's arm and pumping his hand. "Jesus, Mary and Joseph, boy, what happened to ye? Yer brown as a tater, hard as a brick wall, an' got hair like a girl."

Arthur cleared his throat. "I traveled and had some . . . adventures."

"Ye look like somebody took a knife to you an' whittled away everything you could live without. An' yer voice—I don't recall it soundin' like ye got a craw full of gravel."

"I suffered a little damage to my throat." He looked to Sarah with growing relief. "Your uncle knows me. He *recognizes* me." His squared shoulders relaxed as if some of the burden of doubt and mistrust had been lifted from them. "You were at the Earl of Albemarle's with Daisy when I went there to see his gardens," he told Red. "You fleeced the earl at billiards—got him so distracted by your cowboy stories, he couldn't concentrate on his shots."

"I did." Red nodded with shameless pleasure.

"And you were there at Beulah McNeal's when Ash and I beat the tar out of each other."

"What was that?" Sarah's bid for an explanation was ignored. Then she remembered the puffy eyes and fading bruises both men sported at Daisy's wedding. They had fought over Daisy? She was just a young girl at the time, but she remembered the looks the wedding guests exchanged and the whispers her mother and the countess tried to keep from her ears. Her throat tightened as her uncle nodded to confirm those recollections.

Arthur's relief at being believed, sent a stab of guilt through her. He had endured terrible hardships as he journeyed home, and when he finally arrived, he faced doubt and even more difficulty. However understandable and even sensible her handling of his claim was, it now seemed almost cruel. When he reached for her hands and squeezed them, she shrank inside.

With the sharing of a few tattered memories, Michael in truth had just become Arthur the former Duke of

Meridian. It didn't matter that she had privately come to believe him; having it established independently and openly meant they would have to deal with it.

"You really are Arthur," she said past the lump in her throat.

He was flushed and grinning, and she wanted so much to slide her arms around him and take part in his intense and long-awaited joy. But she knew that this revelation brought with it a whole new set of problems. Reluctantly, she chose *sensible* once again.

"Welcome home. Although calling you Arthur will take some getting used to. I rather liked Michael." She squeezed his hands and feared her eyes were saying a great deal more than they should. That fear was realized when he pulled her into his arms and hugged her so tightly she forgot to breathe.

"You can call me Michael . . . Arthur . . . whatever you like, Sarah."

She could feel Red's gaze taking in that embrace and groaned silently.

"Well"—Red cleared his throat, shuffling past them to the nearest chair and collapsing into it—"that's settled. Cow turds an' trail dust, I'm achin' somethin' awful. I rode more'n eight hours straight. My horse is plum tuckered out. You got any o' your liniment, Sarah girl? I reckon me an' ol' Renegade could both use some."

She broke away from Michael and tried not to blush. "Cow turds an' trail dust? *Really*, Uncle Red?"

"I been tryin' not to cuss so much," he said. "It sets Evie's teeth on edge. Especially when the parson comes to lunch." His expression turned downright pitiful and pleading. "Liniment? Please?"

* * *

Red's saddle-inflicted ailments were soon tended, after which he took a much-needed nap. Cook outdid herself with dinner later, and when she was called upstairs to the dining room for recognition, Arthur and Red vied to ply her with extravagant compliments that made the sturdy, sensible woman giddy with delight. After dinner, the three-some adjourned to the parlor, and talked for a good while over brandy and coffee. It was the most relaxed Sarah had seen Michael—*Arthur*—since he was carried unconscious through Betancourt's front doors.

Between Red and herself, they managed to fill him in on Red's and her sisters' marriages and astonished him with the news that Frankie had married Reynard Boulton and would soon give birth to their first child.

"The Fox? She married Reynard Boulton?" He looked dumbfounded. "Did a horse kick her in the head or some-thing?"

Red laughed so hard he nearly fell off his chair. "Aw, he's not so bad," he declared, sobering. "Got me an' the family out of a few scrapes. Now that he's the vi-count an' fixin' to be a pa . . . he's turned downright respectable."

"That I'll have to see with my own eyes." Arthur shook his head with a quiet chuckle. "The Fox all devoted and domestic."

"You may have to wait a while for that," Sarah chimed in. "Frankie had some difficulty at the start of the preg-nancy, and Reynard was frantic with worry. He hardly left her side for weeks. I can only imagine what he'll be like once the baby is here."

"Speakin' of scrapes," Red declared, steering the con-versation astray. "I want to hear about these varmints you got roamin' Betancourt."

She looked to Mic—Arthur, who grew serious and leaned forward to brace his elbows on his knees. "It's a small band, we think. They've struck the Crotons twice now—did a fair amount of damage this time. They took stock at two other farms, under cover of night. Odd thing is, they didn't enter the houses at those farms. They can't have gotten much of value—except livestock and chickens. At first, when there were just a few head missing, the farmers thought somebody was just stealing for food."

"But after today," Sarah continued, "it's clear they're after more than that. They beat Jess Croton and tore down fences . . . stole what they could carry and killed what they couldn't. And they shot at us as we were coming through the woods."

"Whadda they look like?" Red gingerly adjusted his seat on a pillow.

"It happened so fast . . ." Sarah shook her head and looked at Arthur.

"Nothing out of the ordinary," he said, thinking. "The two that came after us had kerchiefs over their faces." He frowned. "The horses looked to be plain saddle stock. One used a pistol and the other had a rifle, but neither was much of a shot. Either that or they didn't intend to hit us." He took a deep breath. "Can't say which, given how hard it is to hit a moving target from horseback."

"Damned straight it's hard," Red declared, studying Arthur. "So, you got rustlers and outlaws . . . yer farmers are sittin' ducks . . . an' the bastards have got Sarah's Fancy Boy." He rubbed his palms together and broke into a grin. "We got us a fight on our hands!"

"We?" Sarah's gaze slid from him to the pillow he rested on.

"Hell, yes." Red straightened on his seat, trying not to show his discomfort. "I ain't had any excitement in months and I'm a damned good shot. Ye think I'd let you go up against these varmints without me?"

She looked to Arthur with a sigh of resignation. "If he survives our varmints, Red's countess is going to kill him."

Chapter Twelve

Later that night, as the lamps were extinguished and the great house settled into darkness, Sarah made her customary rounds and stopped by the library at the rear of the house. There, a large window with a cozy window seat afforded a good view of the butterfly garden. Despite the moonless sky, there was enough light for her to see that Arthur hadn't made his usual night visit to the garden. She stood for a moment, taking in the serenity that Arthur found so absorbing, then she left the room in disappointment.

Returning through the darkened hallway, she spotted light coming from the study, paused to listen, and then nudged the door open. Arthur was braced over an unrolled map on the desktop. He was so engrossed that he didn't notice her until she spoke.

"What are you doing?"

He jumped—"You startled me"—then straightened and pulled two paperweights onto the map to hold it in place.

"I'm looking for what Red calls hideouts—out-of-the-way places these outlaws might go to store their booty and 'lay low.'" He gave her a wry look. "You know, your uncle's got a whole passel of terms for criminal endeavors. It makes a body wonder how he acquired them all."

"No mystery there. He's had a few run-ins with varmints

in his day. He was a prospector, after all. That's a rough trade . . . alone in the hills . . . searching for gold and silver. There were claim jumpers and thieves aplenty . . . too much whiskey around and not enough lawmen.

"He's a tough old bird. In a fight, you'd want him at your back," she continued. "Just ask Reynard. He and Reynard rescued Frankie from a kidnapping, you know. As you Brits would say, he acquitted himself most admirably." She came to stand near him and look over the map he'd been studying, aware that he was staring at her.

"What have you found?" she asked.

"That you Bumgartens are a dangerous lot," he said in that deep rumble he used when he was feeling something interesting.

"Red's not a Bumgarten, he's a Strait." She sensed that peculiar tingling in her skin that only occurred in close proximity to him.

"I am not referring to your uncle. You do realize that the first time I saw you, you were breaking a fellow's nose? After which you practically kicked another poor sod's wedding tackle into next week. The second time I saw you, you were packing pistols—one of which was pointed at me."

"Sakes." She produced a demure smile. "You make me sound like a harridan."

"More like a woman to be reckoned with."

She was standing too close to him, Heaven knew, but she refused to retreat. There were things in life that a woman had to experience to understand, and this surge of anticipation was one of them. Then he ran a finger down the side of her face, along her jaw, and across her lips.

"What are you doing?" she said, her nerves tingling along the path he'd blazed in her skin.

"Reckoning."

He leaned toward her slowly, as if giving her time to choose. It seemed like an age before his lips met hers and she responded with a soft moan that was as much relief as it was pleasure. *It's about bloody time.*

Her hands slid up his chest, traced his corded neck, and curled in his hair. It was thick and soft and twined around her fingers as if claiming them. She molded herself against him, marveling at the way her body heated where it was pressed against his. She wanted him closer, harder against her . . . wanted to explore all of the variations of caresses, embraces, and kisses . . . there must be hundreds—thousands—millions of them.

Boundaries she hadn't realized she lived within were suddenly gone. Possibility and experience became so much larger and grander than she'd ever imagined. How could kissing a man, mingling desire, pleasure, and purpose with a specific man—*Arthur*—make such a difference in her?

She felt lighter than air and suspended in time and space . . . she might simply float away if not anchored by his big, hard body. In her spiraling thoughts, she realized he not only held her close, he supported and grounded her. Her perception, her life, her very world was changing because of him.

She ran her hands up his broad back, stretching her hands, filling them with his hard muscles . . . exploring him the way she hadn't even allowed herself to imagine. Everything was suddenly possible in those deep, clinging kisses . . . traded breaths . . . tantalized senses.

His hands slid over her shoulders, back and waist, sending shivers of anticipation through her awakening body. She was sure he could feel her trembling against him, but didn't care if he knew how powerfully he affected her. It was enthralling, being with him like this.

Somehow they turned and she began to sink. The intensity of his kisses eased and when his embrace loosened, she found herself bent backwards over the map, with him braced above her. His breath was coming fast and his eyes shone in the lamplight.

"You are so beautiful, Sarah. So strong and determined. There is nothing you don't know or can't do." He stroked her face and let his fingertips trail down her throat and across one breast. A subtle change came over his face. "But . . . you're Daisy's sister . . . you're so much . . ." He shook his head, unable to find words. "And I'm . . . I've . . ."

In her mind she supplied them for him.

But *you're not Daisy,* you're Daisy's sister. You're so much *like her, but you'll never be her.* And I'm *still in love with her.* I've *traveled the world trying to get over her . . .*

As she sat up, he withdrew and watched her with an anxious look, clearly trying to gauge how she was taking his half-coherent rejection.

And how did he expect her to take the news that she wasn't her older sister's equal? That whatever pleasure and joy she brought him couldn't compare to what he had felt with Daisy? She slid from the desk and faced him for a moment, feeling a very different set of emotions rising in her . . . a stew of longings denied and pride scoured raw. How could she have been so stupidly gullible *again*?

She raised her chin, though she refused to meet his gaze. Her jaw clenched as she fought the humiliation settling over her like a shroud.

"Goodnight, *Arthur.*"

She walked calmly out the door.

By the time she reached her room and closed the door behind her, tears blurred her vision but she wouldn't let them fall. She was not going to crumble and moan over the loss of some imagined attachment. The cold truth was, she was a place-holder in his heart. If she had any doubt about that, his halting admission in the study had dispelled it.

She was *not* going to cry.

Oh, Lord, she was crying.

She had lost Fancy, that was enough of a blow. And now she had lost Arthur as well. Not that she'd ever really had him.

She gave in to a few sobs and some quieter tears, then took a deep breath and told herself sternly, *That is enough of that.*

She undressed and slipped into her nightgown, forcing herself to think about all the things she had neglected that day . . . overseeing the horses' training, planning much-needed renovations in the dairy, approving purchases from the village tradesmen, making certain Mazie and Deidre were inventorying the linen pantry. She had too much to do to get bogged down in absurd hopes and futile longings.

Through a night that seemed to stretch to eternity, she tossed and turned . . . lit a lamp and tried to read a book . . . wrote to her sisters Frankie and Cece . . . and then tried once again to make herself fall asleep. Staring at the canopy above her bed, she traced the vines printed on the fabric and thought of Frankie and the coming baby. A *baby*. She suddenly felt a powerful longing to see that little one, to hold him or her. To kiss those little cheeks . . . and touch that little nose . . .

She realized she was holding her arms as if a baby lay in them, and clamped them to her sides in dismay. She didn't want to think about the future, the prospect of many lonely years being "useful" to others. She had always joked to her sisters that she was the one who would be left unmarried, at home, taking care of their aging mother. It didn't seem quite so amusing now.

Her thoughts circled back to Frankie. Perhaps she could sneak back into London to see her sister when the baby came. She could use some sisterly care and advice, and Frankie had always been free with both.

But if she left Betancourt, would she ever come back? What was there here for her?

She had always known that the place she claimed here was temporary. At best she was Betancourt's caretaker, a substitute for her brother-in-law. She had expected she would have to give way to Ash when he came back to England. But she hadn't counted on coming to love it here . . . on growing attached to the house, the peculiar staff, the beautiful horses . . . to Arthur.

Tears rolled in earnest again. Was that to be her role in life? Healing and improving homes and hearts, only to have to hand them over to someone with a prior claim?

The kernel of anger banked under her hurt finally flared.

No—damn and blast it!—she deserved better. She was willing to work hard to see Betancourt restored, but not without recompense.

For the few days she tended Arthur, she wondered how Daisy could have chosen Ashton over him. He was so manly and knowledgeable and capable. He was even funny in a "what-did-I-say" kind of way. He wasn't at all what she had come to expect from her mother's and sisters' descriptions. Either their assessment of him had been appallingly off the mark, or he was a very changed man. And if he didn't want her, only saw her as her sister's replacement, then what the hell was he doing kissing her like she was the very desire of his heart?

Blast his infernal hide, he was deluding to himself if he thought he couldn't love anyone but—

Love?

If she hadn't been lying down, she would have dropped like a plank.

She was falling head over heels in love with Arthur Michael Randolph Graham.

* * *

Arthur's night was no more restful. He paced his room as his mind raced. He couldn't get Sarah out of his head. His entire life was in chaos and all he could think about was kissing her, touching her, making love to her. Even if she returned his feelings and they acted on that desire, where would they be? He could hardly expect a young woman of her age and status to consider a man whose future and fortune had been signed away and whose past was bizarre enough to send any respectable family into spasms.

In the library tonight he'd been a stammering idiot. What was it about him that made it hard to find words when words were the most important thing in the world?

"But, *you're so much younger than me and* you're Daisy's sister . . . you're so much *more than I deserve.*" He shook his head in chagrin. "And I'm *crazy about you. I've been all around the world searching for my heart and soul and I come back to find them right here at Betancourt.*"

Why the hell was that so hard to say?

As the sun was coming up, he bathed and shaved . . . during which he stared at himself in the mirror. Years of exploration and deprivation had carved any refinement he might have had out of his face and frame. In his usual garb, he could be mistaken for one of the outlaws plaguing Betancourt. Except for his "girlie hair." He had a flash of memory of Sarah curling her fingers in it and was tempted to—no, something had to be done with his hair.

Forced to dress once again in his rescued shirt, riding breeches, and boots, he thought about the clothes he'd left behind and headed down the hall to his old room. In his chest and wardrobe he found trousers—the waist was too big. And coats—his shoulders strained the seams. And shoes that fortunately still fit him. There were even some small clothes. But no shirts. With his stomach growling, he headed for the kitchen and the servants' hall.

He met Mazie in the upper hall and asked if there was a tailor in the village who might be able to take in his old trousers and see about his coats.

"Sikes." She paused to think, which must have been painful considering the way it screwed up her face. "Nary a shop, sarr. But Ol' Bertie were a seamstress back in the day. Still 'as eyes like an eagle. She's a wonder, she is."

He nodded, taking it under advisement.

Breakfast was underway in the servants' hall, but Old Edgar put down his napkin and rose unsteadily the minute Arthur entered their dining room. The old fellow glared at the servants who remained seated until they, too, rose in their master's presence.

Arthur was stunned. It took a moment for him to realize that word of Red's confirmation of his identity had spread through the staff. God bless them, they were responding as if he were still the duke. Instinctively, he nodded to recognize their gesture.

Then Edgar astonished him and everyone around the table with a half-mumbled, "Welcome back, Your Grace."

"Thank you, Edgar." His throat tightened. "It's good to be home."

A moment passed before Young Ned realized he had to step in. "We'll see to your breakfast straightaway, Your Grace." The underbutler ushered Arthur back out into the hall and hurried to the kitchen to inform Cook.

Arthur's breakfast was served minutes later, in the breakfast room. As the morning brightened and he fortified himself with eggs, sausages, scones, and coffee, Old Edgar's words rumbled around in his head until they penetrated every layer of his being.

Your Grace.

The old butler and even Young Ned addressed him—saw him—as the lord of Betancourt. They seemed pleased to have him back.

It struck him like a thunderbolt: Why wouldn't they? He had been their duke . . . and until Ashton showed his arse on the property, he still was their duke.

Betancourt needed a duke, damn it. Yesterday proved it. There were destructive forces about, and the estate needed someone to take the situation in hand. Sarah was determined and clever and had the gumption of three men. He wouldn't put it past her to go after the outlaws with six-guns blazing. But she had no regard for the odds in a fight—he'd seen her take on four men without blinking. And who knew how many they would face before that gang was rooted out and security was restored.

He, on the other hand, had judgment and fighting skills honed by experience. More importantly, he felt an obligation—no, a genuine love for his birthplace, his home. He owed it to Betancourt to step up and fulfill the responsibilities he was born to, no matter what the future might bring.

And he owed it to Sarah. He had handled that business last night with about as much grace as a water buffalo bollocks-deep in mud. He was so worried about making promises he couldn't keep and compromising her that he ended up making an arse of himself and embarrassing her.

Well, he had already made her a promise, a big one, about her horse. And he had to start fulfilling it straightaway. Fortunately, he had an idea of where to begin.

Betany was stirring as he rode into the village and stopped by the inn to learn where the prisoner was being kept. Bascom escorted him to Pankhurst's barn, where a brick storeroom was used by the county constables for detentions.

The padlock on the door was formidable and the

openings to the storeroom—the heavy oak door and one high window—were secured by iron bars. When Pankhurst turned the key and scuttled back, Arthur braced and opened the door.

Against the far wall of the small room, the man known as Steig was sprawled on a straw-stuffed mattress. His beard had grown, his hair was shaggy, and he was rumpled and irritable looking.

More than a week in such confinement had taken a toll on him. But he sat up, blinked at the light streaming in the door, and growled.

"You." He propped his arms on his upraised knees. "Whadda you want?"

"So much for introductions." Arthur stepped inside the room, settled his feet a shoulder's width apart and propped his fists on his waist. "You want out of here?"

"Does a hawk want to fly?" he answered. Then he studied Arthur for a moment. "It was just a friendly little dustup."

Arthur sighed. Negotiating already. This Steig knew the game well enough.

"I've got questions," he said. "If you've got answers, you might talk your way free."

Steig studied him with a scowl, clearly suspicious of that offer. "Where'd you learn to fight?" he asked.

"Shipboard under a captain as rotten as they come. Where'd you learn knife work?"

"Shipboard." Steig gave a rueful grin. "Royal Navy. 'Til I got tired o' rotten hardtack, pissed-in grog, and sweet navy discipline."

"And since then?"

"Tried a bit of bare-knuckle fightin' in London." He gave a humorless laugh. "Ended up back on the docks."

Arthur nodded, assessing the man and the information. "You want to take a swing at me?" he offered, testing the waters. "Free and clear, to square things up? I got a little help at our last encounter."

Steig sat straighter, eyes narrowing. "You gonna pay me for it?"

"Absolutely not."

Steig relaxed back. "Then I'll pass."

Arthur leaned back against the door behind him, crossing his ankles and tucking his arms over his chest.

"Who were those men you were with that night at the inn?" he asked.

The big man shrugged. "One calls hisself Gil, the other answers to Mace. I was in a tavern, keepin' the trade friendly for the barman, when they offered to buy me a drink and said they needed a head or two cracked. They offered me money and said there could be a tidy bit more."

"Did they say where or why?"

Steig gave a dark chuckle. "I didn't ask and they didn't say. Best not to know, in my experience."

Arthur nodded. He'd met a number of men with that same philosophy. Not bad men, per se; just survivors who did what they had to in order to get by. "That pair's not smart enough to plan anything on their own. You know who they work for?"

"Just signed on to get paid." He rose slowly, using the wall behind him for support. "That tavern fight was my first job. A man's gotta eat."

"Yeah, but a man needs more than food," Arthur said, catching Steig's gaze and probing it for the core of the man. He saw hard times, resilience, stubbornness, and no small bit of pride. Interestingly, the big sailor didn't flinch or attempt to evade this inspection. He stood as if before the mast, making his own assessment as he waited for Arthur's judgment.

It wasn't long in coming.

"If I let you out, I'll have to vouch for you to the magistrate. Since Bascom here and I are the principle witnesses against you, he'd have to take our word anyway." Arthur glanced back at Bascom, who gave him a shrug from the doorway. He turned back to Steig. "You willing to go to work?"

"Doin' what?"

"I need someone with judgment and experience . . . someone who doesn't mind bruising knuckles when the occasion calls for it, but also knows enough not to pick a fight for fighting's sake."

"What's it pay?" Then Steig cut a look at Bascom's earnest, law-abiding face. "Forget that—is the food any good? I ain't had a proper meal in three damned weeks."

Arthur glanced at Bascom and together they broke into grins.

"You'll be living at Betancourt, where the food and company are both better than you and I deserve. As for pay . . . we'll see what you're worth."

If there was any question in Arthur's mind about the course he had set, it was settled when Steig stepped forward and met his outstretched hand.

"I'm yer man, gov'nor."

"Nah, yer not," Bascom inserted as he watched them shake hands. "Yer the duchess's man now. She's the one what runs things up at the manor."

Chapter Thirteen

Dew was still on the grass when Sarah strode out to the stable that morning, dressed to ride . . . tall boots, split skirt, and a western hat. She was going to choose another horse and go after Fancy. Of the horses trained to saddle, Harley suggested a big, coal-black five-year-old that had shown both sense and speed. Midnight Mercury was clearly one of Dancer's direct offspring. She noticed Arthur's mare missing and the old stable man told her he had ridden out earlier in the direction of the village.

It was just as well, she thought. She wasn't ready to face him.

While they saddled Mercury for her, she went to check on Nero's and Nellie's puppies. Poor Nellie looked frazzled; she was besieged by seven hungry mouths. She welcomed Sarah with a wagging tail and didn't seem to mind when Sarah picked up one of the puppies. Sarah cooed and petted the little one and nuzzled her. All seven seemed eager to explore, so on impulse she enlisted Eddie to help her carry them out to the front lawn where they could feel grass for the first time and practice running. Nellie followed anxiously.

Her other dogs shot out the open front doors to join them. Sarah knelt to play with the puppies and introduce them to Gwenny, Lance, and Morgana. Nero appeared on the path from the stables and came running to see what was happening. He bounded over to nose his babies, and with him in the mix, Nellie's anxiety melted.

The parents crouched before the pups to tease and draw them first one way and then another, in a joyful game of keep-away. The little ones rolled and tumbled over each other as they followed their parents around the lawn. The other dogs grew bored with that game and came back to Sarah for attention. They settled on her lap and all around her.

She was so preoccupied that at first she didn't see the men walking a horse up the long drive. Play between parents and puppies halted as Nero spotted them and stationed himself protectively between them and his family.

Arthur paused a few steps from Sarah with a tentative smile.

"I see you've brought them out," he said, focused on her face.

"They need exercise," she answered, looking up, giving the hulking man beside him a critical eye. "Who is this?"

"Our new employee, Steig." He turned to the big man. "Meet the *duchess* of Betancourt. You'll want to stay on her good side."

"I can see that." Steig's gaze was glued to the guns on her hips.

Arthur followed Steig's stare to the same sight and his jaw dropped as she stood up.

Just then Red came limping from the house, calling, "There you be. Shoulda known I'd find ye in a pile of critters." He approached with a grin. "Those belong to that big beast of—whoa, Nellie." He stared at the revolvers she wore. "Those are my guns."

"They were," she answered, meeting Red's scrutiny with her own. "You left them in London. I thought they might come in handy, and it appears I was right. A woman has to look to her own protection these days."

"I'll do the protectin' around here," Red declared. "Hand 'em back."

"Come an' get 'em." She crossed her arms and glowered, daring him to try retrieving them.

"Sweet Jesus." Red looked to Arthur. "Don't get in her way, son. She's got a mood on, an' she does a mean quickdraw."

"I can imagine." Arthur tried to gauge the seriousness of the glint in her eyes. "I've seen her shoot." Then he crossed his arms and stepped closer to her. "Just what the hell are you doing, duchess?"

"I'm going after Fancy," she said with determination that registered in all three men's faces. "And don't call me *duchess*."

Arthur stiffened and an instant later risked life and limb to put an arm around her and pull her a distance away from the others. She stopped, wrenched free, and faced him with rising ire.

"Don't ever set hands to me like that again." Her tone was fierce.

"You can't strap on guns and go rampaging about the countryside." His arms twitched with the urge to do something she had just warned him not to attempt. "Much less, alone."

"I'm going to get Fancy back."

"No, *I'm* going to get Fancy back, as I promised. What do you think I hired Steig for?"

She looked at the hulking brute who was engaged in a stare-down with Nero, and then at her uncle, who was glowering at her. Just as she was about to loudly declare her independence from their blasted opinions, Arthur bent to catch her gaze in his and said the most disarming thing imaginable.

"I'll risk life and limb to bring him back to you. I know how much he means to you." His voice lowered and softened in a way that made his words unmistakably genuine. "I hope that's enough to convince you not to risk yourself unnecessarily, because that's all I've got."

"You can risk yourself, but I'm not allowed to?" she said, looking into his dove-gray eyes and feeling her anger fading.

"Risking myself for this place is my destiny, my reason for being born." He had the grace to look a little chagrinned. "It took six years and a lot of knocking around to get it through my thick head, but I've finally figured it out. Betancourt needs protection and that's what I was born to do. But protecting you is my *choice*. I don't want anything to happen to you . . . you're too . . . too . . . ."

"What?" She was not about to let him stammer his way out of telling her how he felt this time, for good or for ill. "I'm too *what*?"

"Precious."

Dear Lord. It was like a giant hand squeezed her chest. For a moment she couldn't get her breath. When she could draw air, her heart began racing and she felt prickles at the corners of her eyes. After a long minute, she delved into her skirt pocket, produced a hoof knife, and thrust the handle at him. She could see in his expression that he understood that she was handing over Fancy's welfare to him, including care of her handsome four-legger's injured hoof.

Without another word, she unbuckled the gun belt and headed for the house. As she passed Red, she thrust the guns into his hands.

* * *

Her shoulders were back, her head was high. The Queen of Egypt couldn't have looked more regal as she entered the house. Arthur's heart ached and his chest felt swollen; it was hard to draw a breath. He looked at Red and Steig.

"Don't know what you said to her, son," the old prospector said as he wrapped the gun belt around his revolvers. "But th' next time I have to meet with bankers, I'm takin' you with me."

He looked at Steig, who was still watching Nero closely.

"He gonna take my arm off if I touch one o' his pups?" the big man asked.

"Hard to say," Arthur said, watching the standoff. A ridge of hair on Nero's back was standing upright. "He's taken me to the ground before."

"Had me a dog when I was a kid. She had a litter—it's been a while since I saw pups." He looked up with a wry expression. "A bit soft on dogs."

Arthur and Red grinned at each other.

"You landed in the right place, old son." Red broke into a laugh.

Arthur put a hand on Steig's shoulder and urged him toward the side of the house and the kitchen door.

"Let's get you some food."

Arthur introduced Steig to Old Edgar, Young Ned, and Cook, who eagerly fulfilled Arthur's request that she feed the big man a good breakfast. News of the addition to Betancourt's staff spread quickly and the servants all found reason to return to the servants' hall to meet him.

He caused quite a stir, especially among the female staff. Cook was fascinated by the amount of food he could put away and Dolly couldn't stop staring at his big hands and broad shoulders. Mazie and Deidre argued over who would show him upstairs to his room and help him find the necessaries.

As it turned out, there was no time for such niceties.

As soon as Steig washed down his last bite with a gulp of coffee, Arthur had him on his feet and headed for the stable. Arthur's plan was to check several out-of-the-way places in the county that might serve as a hideout for the gang that attacked the Crotons' place.

As they were leaving the servants' hall, Young Ned rushed after him with a ribbon tape and wrapped it around his waist as he walked.

"What the devil?" Arthur paused, arms up, staring at the old underbutler, who stooped and squinted to read the numbers on the tape. A moment later, the old fellow laid the same tape across his shoulders and then shuffled off, murmuring numbers over and over so he wouldn't forget.

Arthur caught Steig's confused look and shrugged before leading him out to the stables.

Midnight Mercury, the big coal-black horse that had been saddled earlier for Sarah, turned out to be the best fit for Steig. The big man wasn't much of a rider, it turned out, but Arthur promised they would take it slow and give him a chance to learn. He saddled his own horse and took his new employee out on a ride to introduce him to Betancourt.

They stopped by a stream mid-afternoon, to water the horses and relieve and stretch their legs. Arthur found Steig staring at him, examining his every move. He faced the big man, wondering if there would be a repeat of their earlier match. Men like Steig took defeat seriously.

"We really just lookin' for a horse?" Steig said, his head tilted to a skeptical angle.

"We are." Arthur tucked his thumbs into his belt. "Not just any horse. *Her* horse. It was taken by some bandits in that forest we passed through some way back."

"There are plenty of other horses in yer stable."

"Not like this one. He's a prince among horses. And Sarah loves him."

"What if we run into the bandits what took him?"

"Then we'll do what needs doing." He broadened his stance. "I'd go to hell and back to return that horse to her."

Steig studied him for a long moment.

"You really a duke? Never heard of a duke servin' on a ship or fightin' in a tavern or chasing down bandits like a Bow Street runner."

Arthur thought on that for a moment. "If I've learned anything in life, it's that some things are worth fighting for." He met Steig's gaze full on. "Sarah Bumgarten and Betancourt are two of them."

Steig studied him, turning those words over in his mind. The duchess, they called her. A woman who wore guns and loved animals and made a tough, determined man like Arthur Graham want to do battle to rescue a horse. This "duke" had a soft spot inside that hard frame. Steig realized that if he wasn't careful, he just might come to like his employer.

"What on earth made him hire such a bruiser?" Sarah asked as she watched through the parlor window as they set off.

Red, ensconced in a chair with his feet on an ottoman, gave a huff of a laugh. "It's plain as the nose on yer face, girl. He's protection. Artie's makin' sure nothin' bad happens to Betancourt . . . and you."

"I can take care of myself, Uncle Red," she said, turning to him.

Red grinned. "Most times that's true. But these outlaws . . . we don't know how many there are or what they're after. Can't take chances."

* * *

Later that afternoon a rider arrived at Betancourt and was admitted to the house and shown to the parlor to await Miss Sarah. There, he found Red dozing in his chair with his stocking-clad feet propped on an ottoman.

Red awoke with a start to find a nattily clad young gent staring down at him with a disdainful look.

"Who the devil are you?" the man demanded as Red lowered his feet and struggled up to sit straighter in his chair.

"Redmond Strait. Who might you be—and who the hell let you in here without wakin' me up first?" He took in the smartly tailored clothes, impeccable grooming, and superior air. Instinctively, he knew this was not a man he would like.

"I am the duke's kinsman, and I'm here to see that in his absence, riff-raff do not invade these venerable precincts." His unpleasant expression left no doubt that he included Red in that category. "I was admitted by that half-wit Miss Bumgarten calls a butler. I am George Graham, Baron Beesock."

The name rumbled through Red and he ignored his awakening aches to shove to his feet. "You? I know old Beesock, son, and you ain't him."

"You must be referring to my father." The gent stepped back and made an adjustment to his riding coat. "He is deceased. I am now the Baron Beesock. And I ask again, who are you, sir?"

"This is my uncle, Redmond Strait," came Sarah's voice from the archway. Both men turned to look at her, and the young baron strode immediately to her and seized her unoffered hand. "He is here as a friend of Betancourt and"—she remembered his previous criticisms—"a chaperone."

"I am relieved to see you have taken my advice," George crooned, giving her hand more attention than was necessary. "I have come to see how you and Betancourt are doing. You look wonderful." He looked around and past her. "I take it your patient has been released into the wild once more."

"Who?" Red asked, jamming his feet into his boots and breathing hard as he yanked them on.

"My patient, *Arthur*." She looked at Red.

"Ohhh, the duke. You say you're Duke Arthur's kin?" Red came to stand beside Sarah. It took a moment for the baron to respond.

"You cannot mean . . . you truly believe that man is the Duke of Meridian?" He looked between Sarah and her uncle.

"I believe it because it's true," Red declared. "I spent time here with the duke, some years back. Come to think of it, with yer pa, too. You favor him." He tilted his head to a critical angle. "Maybe more'n you should."

"What is that supposed to mean?" Beesock's face clouded.

"It means . . . I know Arthur Graham when I see him. And this fella's proved he's the real deal. No question. Hell, all ye gotta do is look at him to see it." He scowled. "If you're really his kin, you should know that."

"I *am* his kin . . . but I have not seen him since he was a boy. And it is common knowledge that he is missing."

"Not any longer. He is home," Sarah said, watching the baron's reaction to their claims. "Though there are questions still to be answered, I am certain that when his brother arrives, all will be resolved."

The baron looked surprised. "Cousin Ashton is coming? Here?"

"We received a telegram last night saying he has taken the first ship out of New York. Weather permitting, he'll be here in a week or ten days."

Red watched Sarah studying Beesock and sensed now was not the time to ask the question.

"Where is this 'Arthur' now?" Beesock asked. "I would speak with him directly."

"He's out looking for my horse . . . it was stolen." She paused, grappling with a sudden surge of emotion. "A brilliant and priceless stallion and my beloved mount. We were set upon by some outlaws in the Meriton Woods. Fancy had picked up a stone and couldn't outrun them. They shot at us and we had to leave him. It is a great blow." She placed a hand over her heart as if assuaging pain. "He's a mix of Andalusian and Thoroughbred . . . dappled white with black mane and tail . . . with gaits as smooth as silk." Her voice cracked. "H-he's so spirited and so smart . . ."

"When was this?" The baron seemed truly alarmed as he reached for her hand again and held it tightly.

"A day ago. Arthur went out to search for him."

"Good God—forgive my language—but I am appalled. It appears that conditions on Betancourt are worse than reported. Armed bandits and outlaws roaming free, unopposed. Something must be done."

He straightened and raised his chin as if he were reciting on stage. "From this moment on, I shall devote myself to finding your beloved horse. Trust me in this—I shall find him, no matter what it takes."

Red retreated to his chair, but didn't sit as he watched Sarah escort Beesock into the hall, where Young Ned held the front door open with a scowl. He saw the way the old baron's offspring turned on the charm toward his

Sarah and, despite her retreat, pressed a kiss on her cheek. Damned peacock—takin' liberties with his little girl.

When the door closed behind Beesock and Sarah returned, he waved her to a seat and settled beside her on the settee.

"Arrogant arse. Throwin' his title around an' gettin' fresh with you. Who the hell does he think he is?"

Sarah told him about the baron's former visits . . . including the one that resulted in Arthur revealing his identity. She confessed her mixed feelings toward Arthur's revelations, and for the first time gave voice to her concern that accepting him as duke would somehow be disloyal to Ashton and Daisy.

Red smiled and patted her hands.

"I don't think you have to worry on that account. Daize was never much for titles, even when she was courtin' a duke. She went after a title to get you an' Frankie an' Cece into society. She was happy as a clam that she got Ash instead of Artie." He nodded for emphasis, but could tell it didn't reassure her as much as he hoped.

"And hey—when did that telegram come, sayin' Ash is on his way?"

She frowned, looked uncomfortable, then sheepish.

"There wasn't one. I made it up."

That was all the evidence he needed that Sarah had her head on straight. He began to laugh.

"Sarah, you're a gal after my own heart!"

"Damned fools!" George Graham used his crop viciously as he raced into the rolling hills just beyond Betancourt's boundaries. "What the bloody hell do they think they're doing? I told them to stay put and be invisible until I tell them when and where to go. Imbeciles!" He ground his teeth so hard that his jaw began to ache.

The sun was sinking as he kicked his weary mount up the rocky path to the cottage his hirelings were using as a base. He slowed as he entered the thick stand of trees. There should be lookouts posted to make certain no one stumbled onto their camp by accident, but no one stopped him and there was no signal to alert the men in the cottage.

As he broke into the clearing, it was deadly quiet and there were only three horses in the lean-to that served as their stable. There should have been a dozen or more. George rode right up to the cabin, no longer worried his hirelings might mistake him for an interloper.

The only resistance he encountered was the rickety front door. When he kicked it open, he found two men inside, neither of whom seemed properly concerned about his presence. They were preoccupied with their injuries. One had a bandaged head and an arm in a sling, and the other's ribs were bound and he was using a cut branch for a makeshift crutch.

"Where is everyone? What the bloody hell happened to you two?"

They both began to talk at once and between them he managed to put together an infuriating story. The ale and whiskey had run out, and the men had sobered up and gotten restless. One of the more intrepid dolts declared he was done waiting for orders, proclaimed himself leader, and roused the rest of the gang to follow him on a raid.

But once on Betancourt proper, they argued about which farm to attack first and the losing side sat out the raid at a camp in the woods. The others returned with nothing but some chickens, proving the winners hadn't chosen well. They quickly killed and cooked the birds, then, as they argued over what to do next, a man and a woman came riding through the forest not far away. They decided to recoup their lost opportunity and went after the pair.

The man and woman escaped, but they managed to capture a looker of a horse the couple had with them. At least, they thought they had. The beast reared and kicked and fought like a demon. A couple of the men wanted to shoot it, but cooler heads prevailed. The beast managed to inflict plenty of damage before they got it under control.

"Damn your eyes—that horse had better not have a scratch on it. Where is it now?" George demanded, knowing from Sarah's story that it was her horse. For the first time in hours, he drew a confident breath.

"In th' shed," the fellow with the injured ribs said, waving stiffly in that direction. "But ye'd do well to keep away from that devil."

George's smile twisted as he smacked his crop against his boot.

"There's not a horse born that I can't handle."

As he approached the shed he could see the beauty's luminous color and luxurious dark tail. They had tied it up away from the other horses and there was plenty of room and enough light to see it. George stood for a moment studying the beast, surprised to realize that Sarah Bumgarten's emotional description of her horse was literally true. Even an untrained eye could see what a magnificent animal he was . . . and, of course, George was no novice. He knew quality when he saw it, in horses and women. The beast didn't look any the worse for wear. His smile broadened as he thought of Sarah's gratitude when it was returned.

Yes, this beast was his ticket into Sarah's confidence and likely her affections. That thought was all the sweeter because Arthur was out searching for the same blasted prize, and he had no idea the contest existed or that it had already been won.

With his crop twitching, he walked straight up toward the horse's right side and—*wham!*—Found himself on his arse several feet away, blinking, then cursing as he grabbed his thigh and shuddered through a blinding wave of pain. He'd been kicked! Was his leg broken? As soon as he could breathe again he scuttled back and shoved to his feet. His leg bore his weight, but it hurt like every demon in Hell was jabbing it with white-hot pincers!

Anger exploded in him and he staggered to the front of the beast, slashing with his crop, heedless of possible damage. He wanted revenge.

He managed three slashing blows with his crop before the frantic horse reared and struck out with its front hooves and he went down again—not to awaken for some time.

Chapter Fourteen

By the end of their second day of searching for Sarah's horse, Arthur and Steig had covered all of Betancourt, met every tenant, and checked every potential hideout in half the county. Arthur spoke little as he and Steig entered the stables and handed over their horses to Eddie. Both were walking like every muscle in their bodies was on fire.

Red grinned at the sight of them approaching the house and called to Sarah. She ran out the front doors to greet them, but one look at their taut faces and tortured movement and she stopped.

"I've never spent so much time in a saddle," Arthur said, rubbing his lower back and wincing. "Every bone in my body has been jarred loose."

Red had a hard time suppressing amusement as they waddled, bow-legged, into the hall. "Aw, ye just need some of Sarah's liniment and a good night's sleep," he declared.

"Yeah?" Arthur looked ready to punch the old prospector—except that would require raising his arms.

"Uncle Red, really." Sarah took Arthur's arm to help him to the stairs and then looked at Steig, whose jaw was clamped shut, but whose eyes told the same story. "You come, too. I'm not sure you'll make it up three flights of stairs tonight. We'll put you in Arthur's old room."

There were several volunteers to apply liniment to Steig's aching frame, but in the end, stableman Eddie was drafted to the task—him being the most experienced at tending the aches of big muscular beasts. The servants were horrified by the thought of such personal duty with their duke, and he had no valet. That left Sarah to do the deed herself, with Red chaperoning from the open doorway.

Arthur's groans of relief and twitches betrayed an interesting dance between pleasure and pain . . . something Sarah had never experienced with a patient before. The feel of his warm, naked flesh beneath her hands as she kneaded his muscles was stimulating, to say the least. Her face reddened, her nerves came alive, and her body grew sensitive in places that she now associated with pleasure and *him*.

When she finished massaging liniment into his back and shoulders, she stood for a moment contemplating his sheet-covered derriere and the backs of his muscular legs. She carried the salve to Red, and thrust it in his hands.

"You'll have to carry on from here."

She couldn't meet her uncle's eyes as she hurried out the door, and his laughter followed her down the stairs.

The lights were already dimmed and the house was settling in for the night when there came a pounding on the front doors. Gas lights flared back to life and robe-clad servants scurried to see what was happening. Sarah was in her room, but hadn't yet begun to change into her nightclothes when she heard the distant thumping. She slipped her feet back into her shoes and headed for the front hall.

A disheveled George Graham staggered through the open front doors, looking like he might collapse. He ordered Ned, "Call your mistress—now!"

She appeared at the top of the stairs before Ned had a

chance to oblige. At the sight of the baron limping forward, she hurried to meet him at the bottom of the stairs.

"What's happened?"

"I found him, Miss Sarah," he said, his voice as strained as the rest of him looked. His beard was three or four days old, he wore only a shirt, riding breeches, and scuffed boots. He was covered with dust and his clothes bore spots that had a rusty, old-blood look. There was an ugly gash on his forehead that had crusted over. "Your horse."

"Fancy? You found my Fancy Boy?"

"I did. I promised you I would, and I did." He tossed a hand toward the door. "He's just outside. I brought him back to you."

"Is he all right? Is he hurt—did they—"

She collected herself and gestured for Ned to help her guide the baron to a seat in the darkened parlor. She ordered Mazie and Deidre to turn up the gas lamps and then bring her medicine bag. Ned was sent to the liquor cabinet for a decanter of brandy.

"Rest here, Baron," she ordered as he gulped the liquor and lay his head back against the chair. "I'll return shortly."

She rushed to the front door and down the steps calling Fancy's name. Her beloved horse stood in the moonlight, head down, looking exhausted and dispirited. At the sound of her voice he raised his head. She threw her arms around his neck and kissed his face as he sniffed and nuzzled her.

With tears running down her cheeks, she ran her hands over him, finding welts and slashes on his head and neck that spoke of an ordeal. He looked lean and hungry and was probably thirsty. He limped as she walked him slowly to the stable, where she checked his hoof. The imbedded stone had been dislodged—whether by human hand or by nature—but had left a wound that was going bad. She roused Eddie to help her put some bluestone on his hoof and wrap it. Then she mixed some salve for his scratches and instructed Eddie to see he was given water, a few oats, and all the hay he wanted.

Muttering a grateful prayer, she promised Fancy to return as soon as she could and went back to the house and her human patient.

The baron was sitting in the parlor letting the brandy take hold. She owed him a debt of gratitude, but couldn't help feeling uneasy around him. As she cleaned the cut on his head, his tale confirmed her earlier judgment that his head wound was at least two days old.

He had ridden all over Betancourt, he said, seeking word of a horse that matched Fancy's description. "I came across two men in an inn who said they'd been approached about buying a horse with special markings, but the price was too high and the details too sparse. The sellers found no interest and quickly moved on.

"I set out after them and located them in a woods well north of Betancourt," he continued. "I crept up on their camp and lay in wait, watching until there were only two men left in the camp. By this time I'd seen the horse they were trying to sell; clearly it was your Fancy. I tried to steal around the camp and untie him but they heard me. They caught me and knocked me senseless. I was stripped of valuables . . . even my coat. I awoke after a time, but played dead as they celebrated what they considered their good fortune.

"Whiskey made them careless. When they nodded off, I managed to rise and make it to their horse line. I untied your horse and led him away until it was safe to climb on his back and ride. The men roused and came after me, but I hid with your horse and my own, in a copse of trees. This morning I set off to the south, toward Betancourt. My leg injury made riding difficult, but all I could think of was your distress, Miss Sarah."

She listened intently and when he finished, said simply, "I am so grateful for your courage and selflessness, Baron. You must stay here tonight and allow us to tend your wounds—it's the least we can do."

She mixed him a draught for pain and had Ned and Mazie open a guest room. He was limping down the west hallway with Ned's help, when Red came rushing from the east wing in his suspenders and stocking feet.

"Fancy's back," Sarah told him quietly. "The baron brought him home. Wait for me in the parlor, Uncle Red . . . *please.*"

He looked at the plea in her eyes, nodded, and headed downstairs.

Once the baron was settled and nodding off, she stationed Mazie at his bedside and headed for the parlor.

As she recounted the baron's story to Red, it sounded even less credible than when he had told it to her. Red was silent when she finished, and he seized the brandy left on the tray and poured her a small glass.

Sarah sipped, shuddering at the fiery trail the drink left in her throat.

She pronounced her conclusion. "He's lying."

"Most likely," Red agreed.

"Fancy would never let anyone—even me—ride him bareback," she said. "He's quite adamant when it comes to having the proper tack between him and a human. I think he deems it a matter of respect." She took another sip. "It looks like he was treated roughly, but he was happy to see me." Then came the puzzling part. "But George truly was injured. His leg looks terrible and his head wound is too late for stitching. He'll have a beast of a scar."

"Well earned," Red said, frowning. "Still, I can't see

him thrashin' about in the woods, layin' in wait for hours, takin' on two toughs single-handed. He's damn near as fancy as yer horse."

"He is that," she agreed. "A bred-in-the-bone gent, for sure. So, how did he find Fancy so quickly and where did he get those injuries? There's a story behind it, but I have no idea what it could be."

"Well, what matters is yer horse is home." Red stood, pulled her to her feet, and gave her a hug. "You need to get to bed, girl. You need some rest."

"But I need to check on Fancy." Her protest was half-hearted.

"He'll be there in the mornin'. Like as not, he's tired as you and fast asleep, bein' back in his own stall." He corralled her with an arm.

For the moment, she was grateful to be ushered up the stairs and to feel cared for and watched over by her beloved uncle.

She honestly tried to sleep. But as the clock struck three, ushering in the longest hours of the night, she slipped into her robe and shoes and headed for the stable. Navigating by moonlight, she found Fancy still awake and was soon humming to and stroking him, putting them both at ease. When the horse finally lay down in the fresh straw, she spread a blanket beside him, curled up on it, and was soon fast asleep.

The next morning, Arthur was relieved to have at least most of his mobility back, thanks to Sarah's liniment and miracle powders, and a sound night's sleep. He made his way down the hall to check on Steig and found the man groaning as he struggled to dress himself. Arthur shook his head; they were both going to have difficulty climbing back on a horse today to continue the search for Fancy.

As they headed for the stairs, a door down the way opened and out stumbled a man in a shirt and riding breeches and stockings. He swayed as he turned to look down the hall toward the stairs and staggered, clearly shocked by the sight of Arthur and Steig.

Arthur's jaw dropped. George Graham had overnighted in one of their guest rooms? When in blazes did he arrive? And who gave the bounder a bed for the night? He took a couple of steps toward the baron, but stopped. The man looked like hell; a nasty head wound, a rumpled shirt, and stained riding breeches.

Red appeared a moment later, fully dressed and looking much-recovered from his own saddle-induced misery.

"What the hell is he doing here?" Arthur demanded, tossing a thumb over his shoulder at George. "Who admitted him to Betancourt?"

"My niece," Red replied. "Seemed reasonable to me, considerin' he delivered Fancy straight to her door."

"He what?" Arthur whirled on George, who bore a smug expression. "You found her horse? Where?"

George crossed his arms and steadied himself against his door frame. "In some woods to the north. At some risk to my health and safety, I might add. Thanks to me, Miss Bumgarten has her precious horse back."

"Hogwash," Arthur said, stalking closer to the baron.

"It's true," Red put in, wary of the tension rising between the men, and catching Arthur's arm. "I woke up last night at the commotion when he brought Fancy home. He's got a bum leg an' a nasty cut on his head. Sarah tended him."

Arthur was ready to put a fist through something, but there didn't seem to be an acceptable target at the moment.

"Where is Sarah?" he asked her uncle.

"I was awake after the clock struck three, havin' a cigar in the parlor, when I saw her slip out the door. I'm thinkin' she went to see Fancy. She was powerful worried about that four-legger."

Arthur clamped his jaw, then beckoned Steig to follow and headed down the stairs.

Sarah was indeed with her beloved horse. They found her sound asleep, sharing a blanket with the big horse. His head lay against her, and she was curled protectively around it. Arthur stood watching her for a long moment, feeling a flood of unsettling emotions. She looked so beautiful in the soft, early morning light, with her hair in a loose braid and her lovely features determined even in sleep. He wanted to touch her, hold her.

Steig mumbled something about needing food and ambled off toward the house and kitchen. When he could no longer hear Steig's passage, he stepped carefully across the cushion of fresh straw. She didn't stir when he sat down beside her, though Fancy lifted his head and sniffed.

"Go back to sleep, horse," Arthur muttered as he lay down beside Sarah and fitted his frame around hers. A minute later, Fancy raised his head higher and plopped it across them both. Arthur found himself stroking the beast's head, where he discovered welts and cuts that spoke of abuse. The bloody bastards. He felt a burning desire to deal the same to the sons-of-bitches responsible. "It's all right," he whispered, gentling his touch. "You're back with your Sarah."

She stirred at the sound of her name, though her eyes didn't open. "Just rest, sweetheart," he murmured against her ear.

As he held both Sarah and her horse, he had the palpable sense of something changing, something important happening to him and in him. He cared a great deal for this remarkable young woman. In the gray of early morning he swore on all he held sacred that he would protect her and his land and people with his last ounce of strength, his last drop of blood.

Betancourt was his home, his birthright, his responsibility. But he was coming to see that Sarah Bumgarten was far more than his passion; she was his destiny.

Sarah didn't want to wake, but she did . . . to the smells of horse and straw and the sound of a soft rumble that came from Arthur's chest. He lay curled around her, and Fancy was using her for a pillow. As she sat up and wiped sleep from her eyes, he murmured, "Good morning, sunshine."

She couldn't help but smile.

"What are you doing here?" she asked, looking around and nudging Fancy's head off her legs. The horse rolled upright and soon rocked to his feet. He stood, head lowered, watching them from the corner of his eye.

"I came out to see if you were all right and decided to keep watch for a while. There are dangerous elements in the neighborhood, you know." He sat up beside her, resting an arm on an upraised knee. "Better question: What are *you* doing here?"

"I couldn't sleep. I'm worried about Fancy. I've never seen him like this."

"He's got a few bumps and scrapes." He looked at the horse watching them, seeing more clearly the slashes on his face. "He might have a scar or two, but he's still handsome. I have no idea what horses find attractive in each other, but I doubt a scar or two will matter."

She took a deep breath, running her gaze over the horse.

"It's not his face I'm worried about, it's his spirit. He won't hold his head up and keeps closing his eyes as if expecting to be struck every time I touch him." She frowned and rolled up onto her knees to stroke Fancy's head and the horse flinched and turned away, just out of her reach. Her heart sank. "He should know by now that I'd never hurt him."

"Healing takes time, Sarah."

"I know. But, some animals—when they've been attacked or badly mistreated—never get over it. It breaks something inside them. I've seen it with carriage horses and dogs."

"You've said yourself, he's not an ordinary horse. And he's got you. He knows you care for him. He'll recover."

She bit her lip and looked down at him, seeing in his gaze a certainty born of personal experience that sent a wave of reassurance through her. He had been through harsh times and survived, even grown from them. There was a depth and a breadth to him that once again impressed her. Whole worlds of experience and hard-won wisdom lay at his core, waiting to be explored. She had never met such a man . . . worldly, wise, good-hearted, honest, handsome . . . and most surprisingly, humble.

"Don't underestimate him," he continued. "He's got what you Nevada folk call *grit*." His head tilted to that kissing angle she found so irresistible.

"I have to admit, you English have your share." Every nerve in her body was suddenly alive with expectation. It was time to make Arthur see her as something more than just Daisy's little sister. "Look at how you've come back from being shot."

She laid her hand against his wound. "The way you worked at the Crotons' that day. Then you spent days in the saddle looking for Fancy. You've worked through pain and limitations . . ."

"Yeah, well, I had a good doctor."

"So you did." She grinned at his admission. "But you

still have a way to go. There is one more thing I need to prescribe. An exercise."

"Oh?" His mouth quirked at the corner. "And what's that?"

"You extend your arm . . ." She raised his left arm and wrapped it around her waist. "And you contract your muscles, pulling toward you."

"And?" His smile was utterly seductive. She found herself falling toward him and braced with her hands on his shoulders.

"Repeat with the other arm." She reached for his right arm and he let her slide it around her, too.

"Like this?" He pulled her against him so his face was just below hers.

She shivered, looking down into the desire lighting in his eyes. Her heart began beating like a rabbit's on the run.

"Exactly like this," she said, now breathless. "It's important that both arms and shoulders receive equal attention."

"Any other instructions?" he said as she lowered her lips toward his.

"Just one. Repeat as desired," she whispered as she closed her eyes.

He met her lips with his and her whole body experienced a surge of raw pleasure as he sank back onto the blanket, carrying her with him. She lay atop his chest, feeling a curious sense of freedom, a sensual power at being in control of that kiss. She fitted her mouth to his, exploring the tastes and textures of him, and venturing away to trace the plane of his cheek and the curve of his jaw with her lips. When she opened her eyes, his were closed and there was a fierce look of pleasure on his face.

"Repeat," he whispered, adding, "please."

She obliged with all of the longing and need she possessed, and it ignited a firestorm between them. She ran her hands over his shoulders, his back, his neck . . . then buried her hands in his hair. He was hard and warm and responded to her as if he knew exactly what she wanted. Every curve, every angle . . . every hungry demand, every gentle persuasion . . . he met her in a delicious dance of sensation and response for which there was no pattern except that which was written in their very blood and sinew.

He traced her shape, learning with his hands the sweet body he had long since memorized with his eyes. By touch, he found her unboned curves firmer and sturdier than he expected . . . not that he had actually anticipated . . . except in late-night thoughts. But he had come to think of her as soft and curvy. It was something of a shock to have her meet his embrace with equal strength and a firm but supple response.

Her hips were firm and full, her waist lean and muscular, and her breasts soft and generous. She nibbled his lips in ways that ignited his nerves and when her tongue stroked his—sweet Jesus—he was suddenly hard and ready to—

He rolled and pulled her beneath him, unwittingly trapping her robe beneath his knee so that it slid open as she settled under him. Only a thin layer of lawn separated her intriguing body from his. He ran his hands over her, appreciating the provocative resistance of her musculature and the erotic yielding of her softer curves.

"Heaven's breath . . . you're . . . you're . . ."

"What?" She lifted her head to gaze at him with eyes shimmering.

"So . . ." Her expression was so mesmerizing he almost forgot what he wanted to say. "So . . . strong."

She gave a deep, throaty laugh that raised gooseflesh on his arms and shoulders.

"I ride. I wrangle horses. I tend big animals' ills. And I run an estate. I can't afford to be soft." There was an edge of apology to her words that caught him back for a moment.

"I didn't mean . . . oh, Sarah, I love the way you're made. And much as you'd like to think otherwise, you *are* soft," he said with a lump in his throat, "where it really counts." He put a hand on her half-bared chest, just above her heart. "Here. You have a big and loving heart, Sarah Bumgarten. It's what makes you so . . . very . . . precious."

Those words seemed to surprise her. She searched his face with a look of wonder and put her fingers to his lips, touching them gently, tracing them. He responded to that invitation by lowering himself against her . . . bracing to bear much of his own weight . . . then kissing the bare skin he'd touched above her heart. She responded with a soft gasp and he kissed a trail up her throat to her mouth and absorbed her responsive sigh into his kiss.

Time seemed to pause around them as that kiss continued and their faces grew hot and hands grew bold. There was so much steam in his senses that it took at least two repetitions of their names to register.

"Your Grace? Duchess?"

He lifted his head and went still, recognizing stableman Eddie's voice.

In an instant, he was up and away from her exposed form and pulling her up with him. She looked a little dazed, but recognized who was calling them and quickly retied her robe and picked straw out of her hair. When he pointed to the corner of the box stall and made a lowering gesture, she darted there and stooped, clutching her robe tightly around her bare legs.

Moments later, Eddie paused at the stall door.

"Yer Grace? You seen th' duchess? She got a visitor up at the house."

Arthur, who stood facing Fancy with his back to the

door, turned partway and cleared his throat. "What? No. She was here earlier, but she went back to the house. Say, where is that salve she put on these cuts? Looks like they need another round."

While Eddie ran to the tack room for the jar of salve, Arthur opened the door, checked that the alley was clear, and motioned her out of the stall. Her face was flushed and her eyes were glowing as she slipped by him and ran for the stable door.

Chapter Fifteen

Sarah's buoyant mood evaporated as she spotted a black coach-and-four by the front doors and a driver and footman unstrapping baggage from the rear of it. Lord, from the volume of luggage, someone expected to be entertained for quite a while. Dread started to pool in her stomach.

When she reached the kitchen, she found the staff in a tizzy. Cook was bustling in and out of the pantry, taking stock and worrying over both luncheon and dinner menus, while Ned was issuing orders to open a guest room and admonishing the servants to move faster. Listening to and acknowledging their sensible plans with nods, she soon sailed past them and raced up the servants' stairs to the upper hall.

There was a commotion in the main hall below, voices and the sound of boots tramping across the venerable marble and onto the stairs. Red's western twang billowed up to her, clearly under duress.

"I was busy sortin' things out, Lizzie, fer God's sake. An' you didn't send word to me about Frankie's baby."

The other voice belonged to her mother. "Redmond, you knew I was worried sick—how could you not write or send me a message about what is going on?"

Mama. Upset and demanding to see her . . . demanding an accounting of Red's mission . . .

Frankie's baby must have been born or she wouldn't have left London. Now she was here to sort out her daughter's situation and unmask this "imposter" who threatened her son-in-law's title and estates. It occurred to Sarah that not once in all her dealings with Arthur had he asserted a claim to the title. In fact, he'd been hesitant to admit to anything besides being born at Betancourt and being Ashton's brother.

This was going to take some explaining.

She slipped past footmen lugging trunks and bags, and kept Mazie and Dolly between her and the stair railing so she wouldn't be seen. The bathing room nearest her bedchamber was empty, and she quickly washed and then slipped back to her room to dress. She donned a presentable cotton day dress and had barely finished buttoning the cornflower-blue bodice when there was a series of sharp raps on her door. She called out "Just a moment" as she began to gather her hair into a sedate chignon, but the door flew open.

There in the hallway stood Elizabeth Bumgarten in her silk traveling clothes, wearing a stylish high-crowned toque and a grim expression.

"My poor girl!" She hurried across the room to embrace Sarah in a crushing hug that conveyed both worry and determination. "Are you all right? What has that beast done to you?" She thrust Sarah back to arm's length and inspected her thoroughly.

"What beast?" Sarah slipped out of her mother's grip and seized her hands to keep them from repeating that frantic hold. "Mama, I'm perfectly fine. Didn't Uncle Red tell you what's happened? How Arthur has returned?"

"Redmond is hardly a reliable source, even when

he's not drinking," Elizabeth declared. "Are you certain you're well?"

"Yes, I'm healthy and all is well at Betancourt. You should see the changes I've made. I cannot wait to show you around." She put on a cheery face, pulled her mother to a seat on the chaise by the window, and resorted to a tactic she had long since adopted to deflect her mother's curiosity. Questions—lots of them—ones Elizabeth wouldn't be able to resist answering. "But first, tell me all about Frankie's baby. Boy or girl? When was it born—why didn't you send word? We've been frantic with worry. How much did the baby weigh? What did they name it? Is Frankie all right?"

Elizabeth blinked under that barrage, but quickly reoriented. She unpinned and removed her hat, set it aside, and began with, "A boy. So there is now an heir. Born five days ago. Fairly big—eight pounds even—with a head of dark hair, just like his father's. Frances is doing well . . . refused a wet nurse and insists on doing the business herself." She sniffed as she removed her gloves. "Personally, I think she's overdoing it. I mean, I nursed you girls, but that was a case of needs must."

"What is he like?" Sarah asked, truly interested. "Is he cute as a button?"

"Don't be ridiculous." Elizabeth dismissed the possibility with a royal wave. "Newborns all look like little old men . . . red and squalling, the lot of them . . . Oliver included. But give them three or four weeks and they turn pink and cute on you. Merciful Heaven, you should hear the viscount go on about how exceptional he is."

Elizabeth paused for a breath, then realized she had just been diverted from her primary concern. "Back to this miscreant who claims to be Arthur."

"I think you should meet him straightaway and judge

for yourself," Sarah said, rising and helping her mother up. "Or perhaps you'd like to freshen up first, after your long carriage ride?"

Earlier, in the other wing, George heard the commotion outside and went to the window of his room, overlooking the entry court. A coach-and-four. A ton of baggage. As he watched the aged butler shuffle out to greet the occupants of the coach, his scowl deepened. The woman who exited the vehicle was not only familiar to him, she was the last person on earth he wanted to see at the moment.

Elizabeth Bumgarten had met Arthur previously, and if she confirmed what the old man said—that the wretch was truly Arthur—his plan to be named conservator of Betancourt could be set back months, even years. He had to find a way to undermine that identification.

After freshening and a change of garments, Elizabeth insisted on meeting "that imposter" straightaway. The fact that her daughter and her brother both vouched for his identity meant little when held against the fact that her dear son-in-law now enjoyed what was once the man's title. She declared that she had information from "a most exemplary source" that this "would-be-Arthur" was a conscienceless wretch bent on beguiling Sarah and enriching himself at Betancourt's and Ashton's expense.

As it happened, that "exemplary source" was standing in the parlor when she and Sarah came downstairs. George Graham wore no coat, his freshened clothes bore faint stains, and his boots—though newly polished—had abrasions that marred the leather. His hair was combed so that it fell over his head wound, and he stood straighter and smiled at the sight of Sarah's mother.

"Mrs. Bumgarten. What a relief to see you here." He limped across the parlor to take her hand and make a bow over it. "I have been so concerned. And Miss Sarah"—he took Sarah's hand, though it wasn't offered—"I must thank you for your hospitality. I was so exhausted last night, I fear I would have fallen off my horse before making it to an inn."

"It was the least I could do, George," Sarah said, watching the play of recognition between her mother and the slippery baron.

"George?" Elizabeth bristled at her use of the baron's given name. "Really, Sarah, I had no idea you and the baron were so *familiar.*"

George answered for her. "I have visited with your lovely daughter several times. When I learned that her horse had been stolen, I devoted myself to recovering it. I brought it back to her last night, and I fear I was in something of a state. She graciously insisted on tending my injuries." He lifted his hair to reveal the shocking cut on his forehead.

"Sweet Heaven!" Elizabeth gasped. "Are you all right, Baron?"

"I sustained minor wounds while recovering Sarah's Fancy from that beastly gang of thieves." George lowered his gaze as if too modest to recount his own heroism. "But with Sarah's care, I am recovering. And seeing you, my dear Mrs. Bumgarten, lifts my spirits immeasurably. Now that you are here, matters will be sorted quickly."

He drew Elizabeth's hand into the crook of his arm and led her toward one of the pair of settees that flanked the fireplace. Sarah was left to trail behind, watching George's charm find a target in her mother's eagerness.

"And how do you know the baron, Mama?" she asked, as if she didn't already know. The question was ignored as Elizabeth took in his limp and grimace of pain as he lowered himself to the settee beside her.

"Are you certain you should be up and about?" Elizabeth asked George, genuinely concerned.

"How like your daughter you are, ma'am, so full of compassion." He patted her hand. "We Grahams are of hardy stock, and I find I cannot lie abed while there are foul forces afoot at Betancourt."

"Foul forces?" Sarah inserted. "Which are those, George?"

"These villainous thieves and outlaws, Miss Sarah." He smiled at her as if he knew her challenge. "Though there are other threats, closer to home."

"Heavens!" Elizabeth looked to Sarah with alarm. "I've heard nothing of thieves and outlaws abroad here. Why haven't you called the authorities?"

"The authorities know, Mama. The constables are spread thinly in the county and are doing their best to prevent further loss and destruction." She rose, drawing impeccably mannered George to his feet. "Meanwhile, Arthur has employed additional security for Betancourt and is seeing to the problem personally."

George's face tightened around a humorless smile aimed at her.

"I find it hard to credit that the duke could have much success, since he is deceased . . . lying unmarked and unmourned on some heathen shore."

"Deceased? I believe reports of my death are wishful thinking," came a deep voice from the doorway. Arthur stepped into the arched doorway and stood with his feet planted shoulder's width apart and a steely glint in his eyes.

"Cousin George. As always, hanging crepe where none is needed."

He shifted his gaze to Sarah, then to Elizabeth. "Mrs. Bumgarten. How good to see you *again*."

Sarah's heartbeat quickened at the sight of him.

"You remember him, Mama. How could you not? He was betrothed to Daisy." She went to take Arthur's arm and draw him toward her mother.

Elizabeth rose stiffly and stared at Arthur as if trying to reconcile his current appearance with the man she had known years ago.

"I fear Sarah has been drawn under this man's influence," George declared, stepping to Elizabeth's side. "Surely you, who knew the duke well, must see that this man could not possibly be the Duke of Meridian."

"I . . . I . . . cannot tell." She stepped closer, then closer still, pulling spectacles from her pocket and donning them. She looked him up and down. "I can see similarities. But he looks so different."

"I am different, Mrs. Bumgarten," Arthur said, reaching for her hand. She extended it and he gave her a warm and purposeful smile. "And yet, I am the same."

"Yes, that expression . . ." Her eyes widened. "It certainly resembles Arthur's." She tilted her head one way, then another, examining him at close range. "I believe it may indeed *be* Arthur."

Sarah could have jumped for joy. "Of course he is." She threw her arms around her mother and Elizabeth, in shock, forgot to scold her for it.

"Good God!" George looked ready to burst. "The man is an imposter who must be rooted out." He looked from Elizabeth to Sarah to Arthur. "And if none of you have the wit or the will to do what must be done to save Betancourt . . ." He limped to the doorway, grimacing, and then paused to finish his threat. "I shall see you in the courts."

* * *

"I have questions," Elizabeth declared when the doors stopped trembling behind the baron's angry exit.

"Of course, you have," Arthur said evenly. "And I have answers."

After what could only be called a thorough interrogation, Elizabeth retired to her room for a rest and insisted that Sarah accompany her. As the door closed behind them, Sarah knew she was in for a dose of her mother's opinion.

"I've seen the looks he gives you. He watches you with what can only be called 'manly interest.'" She seized Sarah's hand and pulled her to a seat on the chaise. "I insist you tell me, right now, if the baron's charge of impropriety toward your person is founded in truth."

"Impropriety?" Sarah blushed in spite of her best efforts to forestall it.

"You know very well what I mean." Elizabeth scowled. "Advances."

"Oh. Goodness." Sarah told herself her advances toward him didn't count. "No."

"Sarrrrah." That maternal scowl deepened. It was as close to a truth serum as humankind had ever known.

"Truly, Mama, he's been a perfect gentleman. He may seem quite different from the Arthur you knew, but his character and conduct have been exemplary."

"*Uhm-hmm*." Elizabeth scoured her heated face and found something that roused her suspicion. "And you, young lady, has your behavior been as circumspect?"

"Of course, Mama. I have behaved with the utmost decorum."

"I am well acquainted with your version of decorum, young lady," Elizabeth declared. "And I know too well the trouble it has caused. Ripping off your skirt to shimmy down a drainpipe in trousers, the spectacle you caused over that cab driver whipping his horse, that time you visited an orphanage and the matron banned you from ever going back . . ."

"Those children needed to learn to sing." Sarah folded her arms.

"Dance hall ditties? Really, Sarah, you knew better." Elizabeth glowered. "Don't think I didn't see how you rushed to take his arm at the first opportunity." She wagged a finger. "You've developed a tendre for him. And I will tell you, it won't end well. He is—*was*—a duke. A damaged one, with a checkered past and a dubious future. He's already the talk of London—just ask the viscount." She paused and her eyes widened. "And his return means . . . Dear Lord . . . Ashton may no longer be a duke." The shock of that thought drained her face. "Surely not. What a cruel fate for Daisy and her husband . . . to have a dukedom snatched from them just when they've begun to enjoy it."

"But Uncle Red said—"

"Your uncle, bless his heart, is full of bullfeathers. As a duchess, Daisy is the toast of New York society." She looked off into the distance for a moment, imagining her daughter's social success. "I just wish I had been there to see that Astor woman eat crow."

There, Sarah realized, was the key to Mama's objection to Arthur. Her mother hadn't a clue what Daisy or Ashton thought of Arthur's return to the land of the living, she only knew it threatened her own long-distance triumph over New York's snobbish "400." As much as she loved her mother, she was not about to let Elizabeth Bumgarten's pride control her life. What she felt for Arthur Michael Graham was rare and wonderful, and she intended to follow her heart wherever it led.

* * *

Following her heart, however, proved to be significantly harder with her mother constantly on her heels. For the next three days, Elizabeth didn't let Sarah out of her sight. Under the guise of learning what Sarah had done with the money she had insisted on pouring into Betancourt, Elizabeth haunted her steps and second-guessed every decision she had made about the house, grounds, and working farm . . . including Sarah's insistence on personally working with the horses as part of their training.

"You simply cannot be out in the sun all afternoon with these beasts," Elizabeth declared, pulling her own wide-brimmed straw hat lower to shade her eyes. She stood at the fence of the training paddock, watching Sarah sending a yearling around in a broad circle to get him used to a halter. "Just look what it has done to your skin. You have *freckles*."

"Some people think freckles are charming," Sarah responded.

"Don't be ridiculous. No one likes freckles. Certainly no gentleman."

A masculine voice from over her shoulder startled Elizabeth.

"I fear you're not allowing for the wide range of tastes found in today's young gentlemen." Arthur came to lean on the fence beside her. "They're an opinionated bunch, not given to abiding by dictates of fashion. They like to make up their own minds about what is and isn't attractive."

"Speaking for yourself, of course," Elizabeth said with a hint of pique.

"Me? Heavens no. I had the 'gentleman' drubbed out of me somewhere south of the Suez. I'm just a son-of-a-duke now." He didn't bother to hide his admiration for Sarah as he watched her fighting down a grin. "Personally, I find certain freckles adorable."

With a broad smile, he nodded to Sarah, who nodded back before turning again to her yearling. Then he tipped an imaginary hat to Elizabeth and struck off for the stables.

"Infuriating man," Elizabeth grumbled, then dabbed moisture from her face with a handkerchief. "I should have brought my parasol. I'm going inside for some of that lemonade your cook concocts." She glanced toward the stables, where Arthur was disappearing into a doorway. "Have your stableman put the horse away when you're finished, and come join me for some refreshment."

Sarah knew exactly what was behind that last command. From the corner of her eye she had seen Arthur enter the stable. Her mother didn't want her alone with Arthur in the stable. She smiled to herself. Her mother's intuition was more right than she knew. A tryst wasn't exactly out of the realm of possibility. In fact . . .

When she had finished putting the yearling through his paces and allowed him to walk and cool down, she led him to the stable herself and grabbed a brush to get him used to grooming. But she hadn't gotten far when she heard a low voice from down the alley and paused to listen. She could have sworn it was Arthur. After a few more strokes, she set the brush aside and ducked out of the stall.

She approached quietly and slowed to a stop as she made out what he was saying.

"You're handsome, true, but that's not all there is to you, you know. You're strong and clever—oh, yeah, I've seen how you nudge up the latch on your stall door. Eddie complains about how he finds you standing in the alley most mornings. He thinks the stable boy forgets to drop the latch. But I saw you do it this morning."

She crept to the edge of the box stall and peered around it to find Arthur brushing Fancy. When he paused for a moment, Fancy turned to him and shoved his shoulder. Sarah blinked. She'd never seen Fancy do such a thing. He was insisting Arthur continue brushing him.

Arthur laughed softly and did just that.

"Why would you want out? You've got it good here. Sarah is crazy about you—hell, she came out here to sleep with you that first night you were back. Wish I had gotten that treatment when I was hurt." Fancy turned his head to Arthur and gave a snort that made Arthur bark a laugh. He paused pointedly in his brushing and Fancy heaved what sounded like a sigh and nudged his shoulder again.

All was quiet as Arthur continued to brush Fancy, but after a few minutes, the brush raked a tender cut on Fancy's neck and he lurched away. "Whoa. Sorry, fella." Arthur approached slowly with his hands at his sides. The horse's eyes were wide and wary. "I didn't know it was that tender. I'll be more careful, I promise." After a moment he tossed the brush away and held up his hands.

"I'll just use my hands. No more brush."

He approached inch by careful inch, and Fancy stood braced and uncertain. Then abruptly, the horse lowered his head and turned away.

It was all Sarah could do to remain silent and out of sight. Fancy was hurting and she wanted to go to him. But she also wanted—needed—to see what Arthur would do.

"I know, I know," Arthur said in low tones that accented the rasp in his voice. "You've been hurt. They hit you and whipped you . . . put a rope around your neck and dragged you off. I know what that's like . . . having a collar on your neck, being jerked back and forth. But that's behind you now."

He touched Fancy's neck gently, then began to stroke him. Gradually, Fancy turned his head back. Arthur got down on one knee in front of Fancy and cradled the horse's lowered head in his hands.

"You're tougher than you know. You'll get through this. Each day it will get a little better, and soon you'll be out in the pasture, kicking up your heels and making all the mares want to be your girl." He touched the cuts and welts on Fancy's face, then stroked him gently.

Tears pricked the corners of Sarah's eyes as she watched.

"Sometimes the bad things that happen to us, make us grow stronger and better. You were handsome before, but now you'll be strong and wise and a lot more dangerous. If bad men ever try to take you or your mares or foals, you'll fight that much harder. And you know what? You'll win."

When he rose, Fancy's head came up with him. For a long moment they stood face to face. Then Fancy lowered his head and pressed it against Arthur's chest. It was as close to a hug as a horse could get.

Sarah realized, as she watched with tears rolling down her cheeks, that Arthur had just revealed to Fancy something he had probably never told another human being. He had been taken and held in a collar. That scar around his neck, the one she had touched that first day, was from a shackle . . . a permanent reminder of a time he was powerless and beaten down. But he had endured and ultimately escaped. Coming home, she realized, was critical in his healing and recovering who he had been and who he was meant to be.

Now he drew on his own experience of healing to help her beloved horse move beyond pain and brokenness.

She had no idea how long she stood watching them or what broke the spell it cast over her. But the energy of the encounter changed, and Arthur asked Fancy if he wanted to get some air. The horse danced a few steps, as if he understood exactly what Arthur had said. His hoof was healing well; he was ready for some exercise. Soon they were walking, then jogging down the alley and out into the beautiful afternoon.

Sarah ran to the door to watch as they set off across the lawn, down the drive, and into an empty pasture. Fancy's head rose and his tail swished as Arthur kept pace, trotting alongside him. There was a familiar and reassuring rhythm to Fancy's gait as they began to gambol and jump and race . . . first one way and then another. When Arthur couldn't keep up any longer, Fancy ran on without him . . . sometimes at a full gallop, sometimes moving slowly, with fluid, dance-like steps. Every so often, he returned to nudge Arthur as if inviting him to play.

It took more than an hour for Fancy to tire, while Arthur had to bend over several times to catch his breath. Sarah watched from the shadow of the stables, and when they both stopped to rest she began to walk toward the pasture. By the time she reached them, Fancy was nibbling some tender grass while Arthur stroked him and talked to him. She could have sworn both he and the horse were smiling.

Fancy spotted her and came to greet her. She hugged him and carefully petted his head and neck. To her surprise, he planted his head on her chest, demonstrating his newest accomplishment, the horse hug.

Arthur joined them, and she hugged him too. He lifted her by the waist and whirled her around, laughing. She was breathless and dizzy by the time he put her down. They stood with their arms loosely about each other until Fancy intruded, demanding his share of affection.

Fancy trotted ahead of them as they made their way back along the lane to the stable, hand in hand. He was a different horse from the hurt and dispirited animal returned to Sarah four days before.

Arthur looked at her with a soft light in his eyes. She reached out to stroke his cheek, willing all the love in her heart into her smile.

"Thank you."

Later, as they walked to the house together, she slipped

her hand into his again and felt as if everything in her world was finally right.

Elizabeth stood at the side of the large parlor window, watching them holding hands as they walked slowly back from the stables. She closed her eyes, realizing it was already too late. Her daughter was too far gone. First a slippery earl and now a damaged and de-titled duke. She felt Red settle beside her, and opened her eyes.

"Come on, Lizzie, give 'em a break. At least one of those Graham boys is gonna be a duke. Ain't that what you always wanted for your girls?"

"Not anymore. I would much prefer a bank director . . . a high justice would be nice . . . or a commerce tycoon. Anyone but a duke."

She glared when Red doubled over with laughter.

Chapter Sixteen

On orders from Arthur, Steig had spent his days scouting the northern reaches of Betancourt, checking on the tenant farmers and watching for signs of the outlaws' activities. All seemed calm and orderly within the borders of the estate, which Steig both appreciated and distrusted. Still, he was being paid a fair wage and the food was good and plentiful. Cook even packed him a lunch most days. He was left to find his own drink, however . . . which was how he came to be in a roadside tavern in the foothills just north of Betancourt when two familiar faces appeared.

"Oy—Steig!" Gil spotted him at the back of the small tavern and dragged Mace over with him. "Yer a sight fer sore eyes. How'd ye get out?"

"Ain't a barn built that can hold me." Steig huffed a laugh and waved them into chairs at his table. "What are you two doin' up this way?"

"Got us a job," Mace said, waving the barman over with some ale. "Nothin' to break yer back. You lookin' fer work?"

Steig studied the two as he sopped the stew he'd ordered with a hunk of bread. "Could be. I'm eatin' the last of my coin right now."

"We can put in a word wi' our boss," Gil said, grinning,

showing his yellowed and gapped teeth. "He's comin' from London tonight."

"We're supposed to meet the rest o' the gang here, come sunset." Mace leaned forward with a boyish grin and lowered his voice. "They're bringin' the kerosene."

Gil and Mace looked at each other and snickered.

Kerosene. Steig reached for his stein and washed down a mouthful of food, thinking. Something was going to *burn*.

He appraised their eagerness and thought for a moment. These two had a knack for finding trouble and trouble was exactly what he was looking for. He needed to meet this "boss" and find out exactly what he planned.

"I'm in."

Chapter Seventeen

That evening after dinner, they collected in the parlor, where Sarah told the story of how she acquired Fancy and nearly gave her mother the vapors when she described how she sneaked out of the house each day to spend time training and bonding with him. Red chimed in to complete the telling, then went on to relate stories of Sarah's escapades as a young girl . . . her scientific experiments in the attic, her penchant for dragging home stray animals, her passion for museums and books, and even her dogged attempts to learn to ride a bicycle.

They prodded Arthur into telling a story of his travels. He was just in the middle of describing the great pyramids of Egypt when a pony trap was spotted coming up the drive, headed for Betancourt's front doors.

"Sir William Drexel." Ned announced their visitor with a shrug.

"Oh!" Sarah bounded up and explained to the others, "He is the Graham family solicitor. I wrote him when I learned of Arthur's return, asking his advice on the status of . . . things."

The gentleman who paused in the doorway was tall, graying, and distinguished looking, as befit a man whose legal reputation was widely known and whose clients included many prominent British families.

"Good evening." Sir William gave a nod to all present.

"Sir William, how good of you to come in person," Sarah said, offering her hand as hostess. He accepted it graciously, and greeted the others warmly as they were introduced. He lingered over Elizabeth's hand, murmuring that he recalled meeting her some years before, and Sarah could have sworn her mother's cheeks pinked.

"I apologize for arriving so late," he said to all and sundry. "There was a problem on the tracks and the train was delayed. I would have telegraphed ahead, but . . . stuck between stops, as we were . . . it was impossible." His gaze went straight to Arthur. "But, here I am." He crossed the room to stand before the younger man, searching his face.

"Arthur Graham. Upon my honor, I can see now why there was some uncertainty about your identity, Your Grace. Your travels have certainly changed you, at least in appearance." He waited for Arthur to respond.

"Forgive me," Arthur said, jolting back to the moment. "Seeing you again . . . you have changed so little . . . I feel like I am reliving events from years ago." He offered his hand and the lawyer took it with genuine pleasure.

"I am delighted to see you in good health, Your Grace. When the deadline for your return passed, I confess I grieved at having to put into motion the instructions you left in my care."

Silence fell over the parlor as every person present— except possibly Sir William—was thinking the same question. Arthur, however, was the only one entitled to ask it. Sarah and the others looked to him expectantly, but he simply smiled and motioned Sir William to a seat.

"No one knows better than I how taxing travel can be. We'll have the staff prepare a room for you." He motioned to Ned by the door and the underbutler nodded and left to execute the order. "Have you had supper, Sir William? Would you care for a bite of food and some coffee—a brandy?"

"I am not especially hungry, having lunched late, but I would gratefully accept a bracer."

They settled into a tense sociability during which Sir William, Red, and Arthur shared a brandy and Elizabeth and Sarah sipped a bit of sherry. Sir William quizzed Arthur about his travels, and Arthur had questions about the current government and the state of economic affairs.

Sarah looked to her mother in surprise; she had no idea Arthur was interested in London politics and the workings of commerce. But her mother was gazing intently at Sir William and listening to every word he said. It seemed even stranger to Sarah that her mother found talk of elections, cabinet appointments, and import tariffs so absorbing.

In fact, the talk was so mundane and lulling that when the question was finally asked, they almost missed it.

"So, what is my status?" Arthur asked calmly. "Am I alive or dead?"

Sir William cleared his throat loudly, reached for the decanter and poured himself another drink. Red's head snapped up from the back of his chair, Elizabeth's eyes widened, and Sarah's heart skipped beats as they waited for the lawyer's response.

"You may not like the answer I provide." Sir William looked quite unsettled. "You must remember that I counseled you to think carefully about the time requirement you set forth in your last will and testament. The five years you insisted upon is not what the courts generally accept as grounds for a declaration of . . . the sort you instructed me to seek."

"So, have the legalities been performed or not?" Arthur sat forward.

Sir William winced. "I fear I have failed to execute your

wishes fully, Your Grace. But in my defense, I consulted with some of the most nimble legal minds in the kingdom. To a man, they were of the opinion that if the will were to be probated and brought to Chancery, it would become a legal muddle that would lie unresolved for years, producing work for chambers of barristers until your estate was smothered by liens and drained dry."

"Which means?" Arthur said, frowning at Sir William's non-answer.

"It appears that, legally, you are still alive, Your Grace. My heartfelt apology."

"Alive." Arthur struggled to parse the ramifications. "I was never dead?"

"I could not proceed on a course I felt to be in conflict with the best interests of yourself, your brother, and your estates." The lawyer set his glass down and came to the edge of his seat, looking miserable. "I will understand if you wish to have another chamber take over your affairs."

The impact finally hit.

"Don't be ridiculous, man." Arthur shoved to his feet, causing Sir William to rise with him. "You had an idiot for a client and kept him from making an even greater mess of his life and holdings than he already had."

He looked to Sarah, then Red, then Elizabeth, and back to Sarah . . . all of whom got to their feet.

"I was never dead." He inhaled, his hands clamped on his chest and stomach. "Does that mean"—he looked to the lawyer—"I am still the duke?"

"You are, indeed." Sir William seemed relieved. "Under English law and custom, hereditary titles may only pass to another when the title holder is deceased. Since there was no body to certify and no declaration by a court . . ."

Arthur looked even more sober. "Have you contacted my brother?"

"I sent the required notice of the date you set, seeking his wishes in the matter, but have had no reply."

"No reply? At all? To the news that I was presumed dead and he was now the duke?" Arthur felt a flush of irritation that was quickly diverted by concern. "And have you contacted him since?"

"I have sent correspondence, including a telegram, but have had no response."

News that his brother hadn't bothered to respond to his presumed death was bad enough, but to ignore inheriting a centuries-old title and his obligation to their familial estates was unthinkable. Arthur stood for a moment staring at his boots, trying to make sense of it. Sir William's revelations were a lot to take in; they changed the way he looked at events and his part in them.

He looked at Sarah for a long moment, then turned and strode out.

She followed and saw him climbing the stairs.

"Where are you going?" she called from the doorway.

But he passed the ducal chambers and headed into the west wing.

He didn't respond because he didn't know what to say. He needed to clear his head and there was only one place where that could happen. He had to have a wall . . . a rooftop . . .

Questions flew thick and fast in the parlor behind her as she stood in the doorway. Red demanded to know details about what Sir William hadn't done, while Elizabeth insisted Sir William clarify Ashton's status . . . and her eldest daughter's. The answers she received made her slump onto the settee in dismay.

"I knew it. I just knew it would end badly for poor

Daisy," Elizabeth muttered. "He's not a duke, then he *is* a duke, then he's not a duke again . . . it's as if the Bumgarten girls are under some sort of ducal curse."

It was either follow Arthur or give her mother a good shaking. She chose the former. She climbed the stairs, trying not to think about what she would say to him. What could she say? That she was happy he was still the Duke of Meridian? That now he could assume his rightful place among Britain's nobility and take care of his home and people as he believed he should have?

It occurred to her as she climbed the stairs to the nursery floor and then to the servants' floor, that he was more willing and far better prepared to meet his responsibilities than he had been six years ago. Whether he realized it or not, his experiences abroad—good and bad—had prepared him for the life he now wanted.

At the end of the narrow uppermost hallway, a door stood open and she encountered yet another set of stairs that led to a half ladder that led to a hatch opening onto the roof itself. She lifted her skirts and climbed that short ladder to find Arthur standing at the edge of the roof, overlooking Betancourt.

His pale shirt was outlined against the darkness as he stood in much the same pose he had adopted in the butterfly garden. He seemed to be listening and watching, soaking in the night. She simply observed for a few moments, then softly called his name.

He didn't respond at first, but after a moment, he swiped his face and turned.

She stepped out onto the slate rooftop and brushed the dust from her hands and clothes. Drawn to the strong emotion she sensed in him, she walked to him and opened her arms.

When he entered her embrace and enfolded her in his

arms, her senses somehow connected to his. She felt what he felt, saw what he saw. She had never experienced such a thing before, this closeness, this sort of oneness.

They stood for some time, wrapped in each other's arms, content to share a moment that defined a change between them.

"I'm glad it's you," she said softly. "You're the perfect duke."

"I'm not so sure about that. Perfect is a hard standard. I've already fallen far short of it. Sir William was strong enough and wise enough to withstand the orders of a callow, ignorant young man. Let's hope I'm wise enough and strong enough to fulfill the faith in me that shaped his decisions."

She looked up at him with luminous eyes.

"You are."

He kissed her softly, then turned her slowly to show her the view that never failed to both inspire and ground him. "Look at it. Betancourt."

Lights in nearby cottages twinkled like stars, and the landscape had become a deep, velvety palette of dark blues and grays.

"It's beautiful. So, is this where you are when we can't find you?" she said, leaning her head against his shoulder.

"A habit from my youth." He rested his cheek on the top of her head. "When things became too much for me, I walked the tops of the brick walls or escaped to the roof. It always seemed to put things in perspective."

As they turned slowly to take in the panorama, they both spotted a bloom of light in the distance.

"What is that?" she asked, knowing from the way he lifted his head that he was studying it, too. "It isn't west, it's north . . . along the river."

"That's where the mill sits. Near Thomas Wrenn's farm."

The light grew and took on an orange and yellow hue that sent a dark sooty spiral skyward above it. Arthur released her and moved closer to the edge of the roof, staring at that light with growing comprehension.

"Arthur?" She sensed it, too. "Is that fire?"

"The mill," he declared through clamped jaws. "It's burning."

He grabbed her hand and pulled her to the stairs. He went first, to help her down, and together they hurried through the servants' quarters to the rear stairs. They were running by the time they reached the stairs in the entry hall.

"Ned!" he called, then, "Red!"

"What's goin' on?" Red appeared in the parlor doorway, followed closely by Sir William and Elizabeth.

"The mill is on fire. Get your guns and meet me at the stable." Then Arthur turned to Ned. "Where's Steig?"

"Not home yet, Yer Grace," Ned declared.

"Damn it. Fine. Send someone out to the cottages to gather the men . . . tell them the mill is on fire and we'll need buckets and shovels. Hurry!"

Ned nodded and moved faster than anyone had seen in years.

As Red raced up to his room, Sarah passed him on the stairs.

"Oh, no you don't—those are my guns!" Red bellowed.

"I'm not going for your blasted guns!" she shouted as she rushed down the hall. "If there's fire, someone could be hurt. Tell Arthur to wait for me!"

Arthur wasn't pleased to hear Sarah intended to come, but he had Eddie saddle her horse while he and some of the other men hitched a wagon and lit some lamps. She appeared in the stable yard a short while later, wearing a riding skirt, shirt, and boots. Mazie and Deidre were right behind her with her medicine chest, a crate of pots and bottles, and a carpet bag bulging with bandages and boiled linen.

"Wellington could have used you at Waterloo," he said as he stacked her supplies in the wagon at the men's feet, and gave her a terse smile.

She climbed aboard Fancy and noticed that Arthur and a couple of the dairymen carried long guns from Betancourt's hunting gear. They looked like they were going to war, themselves.

It occurred to her that Arthur thought the fire might not be an accident. A stone mill built on a river . . . the water wheel . . . the great stones turning inside . . . how could it catch fire? And the Millers' house lay nearby. She thought of sturdy Johnny Miller, whose ancestors had taken their name from their occupation. Would he have tried to put out the fire himself? He and his wife, Helen, had several children . . .

The four mile trek seemed to take forever. They collected a few additional men as nearby farmers caught sight of the blaze and joined them on horseback and in carts. The heat from the heavy timbers burning inside the mill and the wooden roof was intense as they approached. The nearby roof of the Millers' home had just caught fire from blowing sparks and Arthur and the men set up a bucket line from the millpond to the house, hoping to save it. It was clear to everyone that the mill was too far gone.

Shouting—a woman's voice—drew Sarah around the house to a weedy area beyond the kitchen garden. The miller's wife, Helen, was calling for help for her husband and son. Sarah dismounted in a rush, pulled Fancy out of the way, and tied him to the wagon. The woman knelt between the inert forms of her husband and eldest son. She was crying and her other children were wailing that their pa and brother were dying.

Sarah fell to her knees beside Johnny, rolled him onto

his back, and felt his neck for a heartbeat. He and his son both had a pulse, though they struggled to breathe and their faces were ominously red beneath a layer of soot. At first glance, it looked like they had burns, cuts, and possibly broken bones.

"They're not dead. Quiet down so I can listen!" She brought out her stethoscope to listen to their hearts and lungs.

"Water—I need clean water," she declared, shoving a bucket at the sobbing woman. "You have to help me help them. Go!" Helen gasped a breath as the sense of it got through to her. She pushed to her feet and ran for the well.

Sarah spent some time listening to their chests and washing away the soot to check for burns. Most of their cuts weren't bad enough to stitch, but Johnny's left forearm was broken. She sent the children to look for some straight sticks that would make splints, and had Helen help with the setting and binding of his arm. As they worked, she noticed that the woman had some bruises herself and asked what happened to her.

"I seen what they done to my Johnny—he fought 'em—those men. I ran to help, but they pushed me around an' one picked me up over his shoulder and carried me to the edge of the woods. He dumped me on the ground and I kicked an' screamed—I thought he meant to take me there an' then. But he told me to keep my mouth shut, and he'd send my kids out. He left me there. When my kids come running, they were scared and shakin'. I gathered 'em to me, an' I kept callin' out for Johnny. Martin dragged his pa out here, then collapsed. I didn't know what to do for 'em."

When Sarah and Helen began to work on Martin, he roused and, between coughing fits, told Sarah what had taken place. She felt as much as saw Arthur's presence when he came to squat beside them and asked if anyone was hurt badly.

"Cuts and bruises, broken ribs and broken arm—no serious burns. It could have been a lot worse," she reported.

"We saved the house," he said to Helen Miller. "Things will smell like smoke for a while, but at least you'll have a roof over your heads."

The woman started to cry again and Sarah put her arms around her.

Martin's story was exactly what Arthur and Sarah had feared. A group of men on horseback rode in just after dark. They went straight to the mill like they knew what they were about and started to toss kerosene over every bit of wood they could reach. Johnny rushed out to stop them and they beat him until he didn't get up again. Martin tried to help, but he got hit, too, and the men shoved Helen around, making crude jokes until one of them—a big man—picked her up and carried her off toward the woods. Martin tried to go after them but got knocked to the ground and kicked in the ribs. The men left as quickly as they came. Martin reached his father and pulled him out of the way of the heat and flames. He heard his mother calling and managed to drag his father to her before he, too, collapsed.

The story sent a wave of uneasiness through the men who had saved the Millers' house and now gathered around to see how the family fared.

Arthur took the men aside and spoke to their concerns for their own farms and families. This was not only destructive, it was intentional. Taken together with the wanton destruction at the Crotons' a week before, it was alarming. Someone was bent on wreaking destruction on Betancourt, and all present now realized that no farm, no property, or tenant was safe.

Arthur promised them a new mill, a better mill. They would rebuild. But until then, they had to stand watch, keep their stock corralled or in barns, and send a rider to Betancourt House with word of any suspicious strangers seen in the area.

It was past dawn when Arthur, Sarah, and the bulk of the rescue party returned to Betancourt House, having left the mill a pile of wheezing cinders and the Millers in the care of their closest neighbors. All of the rescue workers were sooty and exhausted from the heat.

Elizabeth and the house staff rushed out to meet them, asking questions and offering water, coffee, and cider. They all smelled like smoke and plans were made to have the men disrobe and wash outside, so their clothes could be cleaned before they returned to their homes. Sarah, however, was taken upstairs to bathe and was so grateful to be clean and shown to bed that she barely heard her mother's chastisements.

"Ladies don't go galivanting all over in the dead of night when thieves and outlaws are rampaging through the countryside," Elizabeth said irritably as she drew the drapes closed and tucked Sarah in. "I don't care if you are the only medical help in a hundred miles, you simply must know enough to stay home and let the men handle these things."

"I tended burns and broken ribs, and I set a broken arm," Sara muttered as she surrendered to exhaustion.

Elizabeth stayed by Sarah's bed as she sank into oblivion, and gently brushed her damp hair back from her face.

Her daughter was such a remarkable young woman, so learned, so compassionate, so determined to take on the world and reshape it into a better place.

"Why are you so reckless with your life, Sarah Bumgarten?" Elizabeth said with tears in her eyes. "Don't you know I would die myself if something happened to you?"

When Sarah was sound asleep, Elizabeth crept out of the room and closed the door carefully behind her. Her throat was tight and tears blurred her vision. She staggered and leaned against a console table in the hallway with her face in her hands. In the grip of powerful emotion, she didn't hear him approach.

"Mrs. Bumgarten? Are you quite all right?" Sir William stood with his arms dangling before him, as if he were about to reach out to her. "Is there anything I can do?"

Elizabeth looked up through a sheen of tears and the sight of him, so manly and strong, offering comfort, broke through her defenses. She nodded and he came to put an arm around her shoulders and led her to the stairs. She soon found herself on the window seat in the library with Sir William offering her a glass of water and apologizing that it wasn't something stronger.

He sat beside her, offered her his handkerchief, and held her hand until her tears ended and she straightened. When she looked up at him, his eyes were warm and filled with concern.

"Thank you, Sir William. I don't know what's come over me. I'm unstrung by all this danger, by all these changes. My Sarah is all I have left and I fear she is headed down a path to heartbreak."

"Do you mean her fondness for His Grace?" When she nodded he squeezed her hand. "I don't think you have much to worry about on that account. The duke is a good man and honorable to a fault."

"But my daughter is sometimes willful and too tender-hearted for her own good. She cannot always see the faults in people until it is too late."

"It is my experience, dear Elizabeth, that we must sometimes let the young ones make mistakes that they will learn from."

"As you did, William? With the duke?"

He sighed. "You have me there. But in my defense, I consulted with others on the matter, and I did have his best interests at heart."

"I know you did," she said with a sigh, laying her hand over his. "I don't mean to be difficult. I just don't know what to do. Sarah and Daisy, Arthur and Ashton . . . these hideous outlaws . . . everything seems so . . . tangled."

William surprised her by reaching up to touch her cheek.

"Things will *untangle* in their own good time, Elizabeth. Have a little faith."

Chapter Eighteen

It was the next afternoon when a horse and rider came charging up the drive to Betancourt's front doors. A stable boy took the man's horse and Ned admitted the handsomely dressed fellow to the house and started up the stairs to see if the duke or duchess were receiving callers. Before he reached the top, the man passed him, headed straight for the duke's chambers. Ned's wheezing protest fell at his back as he threw open the doors and strode into the room.

"Good God, still abed? Some duke you are! Get up, Supposedly Arthur, and let me have a look. At. You." Reynard Boulton, Viscount Tannehill, stopped dead as the man bolted from the bed and faced him in a defensive crouch. He looked like a wild creature . . . long hair, wildly tousled . . . tanned and muscular body, mostly naked . . . on his shoulder a *tattoo*. Reynard's jaw dropped.

"What the hell—Reynard?" The man's voice was deep and had a hint of a rasp to it. But when he straightened and brushed back his mass of dark hair, Reynard struggled to make out the features of a face he had known since his days at school.

* * *

Arthur stared back at his old school friend and produced a slow smile.

"Reynard Boulton. You old Fox, you!" Arthur bounded across the room and seized the stunned viscount in a bearish hug. Then he released Reynard and laughed at the disbelief on his face.

"It is you, isn't it." Reynard grasped Arthur's shoulders and gave them a shake, as if testing that he was real. "Lord, you're a different man. I'd have passed you on the street without a hint of recognition."

"I hear that a lot these days. But it's me. Want proof?"

"Will you be too insulted if I say yes?"

Arthur paused and thought a moment, his hands propped on his waist. He saw Reynard looking him over in amazement and realized it had to be something only Reynard would recall. Something very personal.

"You didn't piss in George Rector's bed that night at school. It was George himself. He cried and you took pity on him and said it was you."

"How did—how could you—" Reynard's whole frame reacted.

"I was in the corner of the dormitory, trying to get some sleep. Never slept in my bed, it made me too tempting a target. I saw the whole thing." He smiled. "That was when I started to like you."

"But, but you never said . . ."

"Your secret's safe with me," Arthur said, with genuine warmth. "It always has been."

Reynard, renowned keeper of society's secrets, was torn between being deeply moved and laughing at the irony of it. Laughter won out and Arthur joined him.

"It's so good to see you, Fox. It's like seeing a brother."

Moments later, Arthur donned his shirt and boots and led Reynard down the stairs to the breakfast room, where he ordered coffee and whatever Cook could put together on short notice. They were just tucking into the food when Red appeared in the doorway, looking like he'd run for the first time in years.

"I heard . . . I figured . . . it was you," he panted out, then as Reynard rose, hurried to give him a hearty handshake. "How's Frankie? And Little Oliver?"

"Both fine. Healthy enough to kick me out of the house and tell me to come and check out this 'phony Arthur' I've been worrying about."

Red looked at Arthur. "So he's come to toss ye out, eh?" He grinned at Reynard. "Ye'll have to go through me and his lawyer . . . and *Sarah* . . . if that's yer plan."

"Well, if you want this slug-a-bed for a duke, who am I to object?"

"For your information," Arthur declared between bites of eggs and toast, "I had reason to be sleeping so late. I was up all night battling a fire."

"A fire?" Reynard looked to Red, who nodded with uncharacteristic gravity.

"Sit down, son." Red waved him into his chair. "We got trouble."

Sarah found Arthur and Red in the breakfast room, telling Reynard Boulton—Frankie's beloved viscount— about their recent problems. Reynard was on his feet in a heartbeat, holding her hands and giving her a kiss on each cheek.

"You look wonderful, Sarah." He held her arms out to look her over. "I was concerned when I learned you came to Betancourt to rusticate after . . . but you've blossomed in the country air."

"You should see what she's done with the stables and the house," Arthur said with no little pride. "Daisy and

Ashton may have started it, but Sarah has put substance into the place and has polished it like a gem."

"I noticed that things looked different from my last visit. Granted, that was quite a while ago. Daisy's and Ashton's wedding, I believe." Reynard noticed Arthur's gaze lingering on Sarah and saw that she couldn't help blushing under his warm regard.

Reynard looked quizzically at Red, who was watching, too, and raised an eloquent eyebrow.

"It's remarkable," Sarah said, pouring herself a cup of coffee at the sideboard, "what a pile of money and some determination can do. I just hope it isn't all for naught. I assume they've told you about our difficulties."

"They have," Reynard said as she settled at the table with them. "And it's clear to me that this is an organized campaign. I can't imagine why anyone would terrorize the countryside like this, unless it was to gain something. But it doesn't appear they've taken anything of value." He paused for a moment. "We're going to need help. I have a friend in London who knows his way around dangerous situations. I'll send a telegram."

Later that evening, Arthur learned that Steig had returned and was taking a late supper in the servants' hall. He excused himself from company to see him and find out what he had learned.

"There you are." He sat down across the long table from the bruiser, who didn't bother to rise in his presence, as virtually everyone else on the estate did. "Where have you been?"

"Ridin' circuit, like you said." Steig looked up briefly, then turned his attention back to his heaping plate. "Why?"

"There was a fire at the mill. It burned to the ground

last night." Arthur watched Steig's surprise with a careful eye. "You didn't know?"

"Not a word." Steig toyed with his fork. "At the mill we saw . . . up north?"

Arthur nodded, watching Steig's eyes as he considered that news.

"I was south of Betany. It was dark as pitch in the woods. I feared Mercury breakin' a leg, so I put up in the Hopwells' barn for the night." He gave a half smile. "I do like that horse."

Arthur nodded, then related the details of the fire and the story the Millers told. He paused afterward, watching Steig's reaction.

"So, the miller's family . . . they're all right?"

"Coughing up soot, but they have a roof over their heads. They'll recover."

"Good." It was a firm declaration and seemed heartfelt.

"I want you in the north range tomorrow. We have to know what's going on up there. There were only four of them at the Crotons', now there are at least eight. One of whom was a big fellow." He let his gaze rest on Steig for a moment before rising. "The Viscount Tannehill has come for a stay. He's a crack shot and a demon with a blade. He's sent for some help from London. We've got to catch these bastards before they kill someone."

He rounded the table and grasped Steig's shoulder before heading back to his company. Pausing at the stairs, he looked over his shoulder at the big man tilting a stein of ale. He wasn't sure if the man was telling the truth. He prayed he hadn't made a mistake in seeing possibilities in Steig and hiring him.

The next evening, Reynard's friend from London arrived just after sunset. He was a burly fellow in a ready-made suit, who walked with a roll to his gait and a tension to his shoulders that said he was ready to punch a hole in the world if it became necessary. But when he smiled, his face lighted with wry humor, and his dark eyes hinted at a dead-on appraisal of every human being in sight.

Reynard introduced him in the parlor, where he shifted feet and seemed uncomfortable, especially under Elizabeth's scalpel-like regard. He blushed at Sarah's warm greeting, and seemed oddly awed by Arthur's stature and bearing. They talked and took refreshments, making plans for the next day. Then Red arrived from the stables wearing western boots and a vest, and carrying a lariat on his shoulder.

"Grycel Manse." Red rushed to grab his hand and engulf him in a rough-and-tumble hug. "You're a sight for sore eyes! Reynard said you might be too busy to come, but here you are!"

Grycel gave as good as he got from the old prospector, grinning as he half crushed Red's hand. "Redmond Strait!" He turned to Reynard. "If you'd told me Red was here, I'd have been here yesterday."

"You bring yer club?" Red asked, dropping his rope.

Grycel patted a bulge under his coat. "You bring your guns?"

"Never go anywhere without 'em." Red puffed up his chest.

Sarah shook her head at her uncle's claim, and Reynard rolled his eyes at their exaggerated display of camaraderie. But it wasn't long before Arthur, Red, Reynard, and Grycel adjourned to the study with a decanter of brandy and a box of cigars. Sir William was the lone male left in the parlor.

Sarah looked at her mother and sighed. But Elizabeth was busy patting the settee beside her and smiling at Sir William, who quickly accepted that invitation. The two were so busy gazing at each other and talking politics that they didn't even notice as she exited the parlor. She had never seen her mother show an interest in such affairs.

Left to her own devices, she headed for the stables to check on Fancy. Since his return, it had become her nightly habit to bring her boy a carrot and spend a few minutes with him. The lights were dim in the alley and there was a feeling of calm from the horses in the stalls she passed. But when she reached Fancy's stall, he was standing alert and arching his neck, then began pawing the floor of his stall.

Something was wrong. She called to him and reached for the latch, just as a burlap bag smelling of grain dust descended over her head and her hands were pulled behind her back and quickly bound.

"Get your hands off me! What do you think you're— Eddie—Harley—help!" She twisted and cried out as her arms were wrenched higher and she was bent forward. She kicked forcefully at her attackers with the heel of her lady boot. Muffled grunts and swearing indicated her kicks made contact, but it wasn't enough to stop them from wrestling her to the ground and binding her ankles securely.

From their strength and the sound of their voices, her captors were rough men, but they laughed like nervous children and kept repeating "We done it!" and "Wait'll his lordship sees what we got!"

"*Nero! Nellie!*" A hand clamped over her mouth and she was hoisted up and carried like an unwieldy log. She bucked and thrashed, loosening their grasp—just as something barreled into her captors, knocking them—and her— to the ground.

She lay stunned, recovering her breath, then struggled to sit up as growls, scuffling and cries of "Git off—aghhhh!" and "Mace—help!" mixed on two fronts around her. Nero and Nellie had heard her and come! With her hands and feet bound, all she could do was roll onto her aching side and inch away from the fight . . . praying that her dogs carried the day.

The attack lasted only a few minutes, but it seemed like an eternity. The scrambling and the barking receded as Nero and Nellie pursued her retreating kidnappers. She lay listening, hoping the wretches had lost an arm or a leg in the struggle—at least a few fingers. Before she knew it, her dogs were back, nosing her and giving high-pitched yelps of concern.

With a flash of insight, she pressed her still covered head to the ground and made whimpering noises like a hurt puppy, praying Nellie's motherly instincts would take over. The borderland collie did exactly what Sarah hoped . . . pawed at her head until the bag came off.

"Thank God." She took a deep breath of fresh air and struggled to sit up. The dogs nosed and licked her frantically, but she endured, feeling grateful for every sniff and sloppy dog kiss that came her way. Eventually, she caught Nero's eye.

"I need you to go for help, boy. Get Arthur—or Uncle Red."

He came alert as she repeated it, and then he started away. At the stable opening, he turned to look back at her.

"Get Arthur! *Go!*"

He took off at a determined run, but Nellie stayed by her side, alert and watchful as she tried to free her bound hands. It wasn't long before Nellie's puppies caught their mother's scent and spilled out onto the dirt track that led into the pasture. They climbed Sarah and licked and jumped on her until she was overwhelmed. "Come on," she groaned, "give me some room. I've just had a rough time."

If a dog could look sympathetic, Nellie did. She took charge and lay down carefully across Sarah's legs to keep her babies at bay.

"Ohhh, Nellie," she moaned as she realized what the dog had done, "do you have any idea how much I love you?"

In the study, serious talk about strategies for protecting Betancourt had given way to recollections of other fights and one-upmanship in recounting adventures. Brandy flowed and the laughter was almost loud enough to drown out the barking. It was distant at first, but grew steadily louder. Arthur glanced at the door with a frown, wondering where Ned and the servants were. It sounded like Nero was ready to take someone's arm off.

It was probably Steig coming back, he told himself. The big man was known to Nero and the dog would soon settle down. Instead, the barking grew even louder—downright frantic. Then the focus of it changed and it sounded like it was coming from outside the study's leaded glass window.

"Just a minute," Arthur said, placing his empty glass to hold open the map they'd been perusing on the desk. Outside, in the light coming from the study, he saw Nero. And the dog saw him. The big wolfhound lunged through the shrubs to slam paws against the window, barking furiously.

"Somethin's not right with that beast," Red said with a glower, rising.

It hit Arthur: Something *really* wasn't right.

"Red," he said, "you better get those guns of yours." And he headed for the front doors.

Nero met him as he stepped outside and the dog whirled around like a dervish for a moment, then headed for the stable. Every few yards he paused to bark at Arthur as if demanding he follow.

Arthur heard more than saw his companions exiting the house behind him and following. A hundred things went through his mind. Would the gang dare to move against the manor itself? Why hadn't he kept guns at the ready? Was the livestock corralled or locked up in the barns? What would they attack first?

He entered the stable and slowed in the alley between the box stalls, his senses sharp and his body taut with expectation. All seemed calm until he reached Fancy, who was pacing and tossing his head and snorting anxiously. More barking from Nero drew him to the cross alley, where the big doors to the pasture stood wide open. Something lay on the ground, just outside the range of light from the stable lanterns.

Nero rushed outside and Arthur saw Nellie run to greet him. As he stepped out of the stable, he heard Sarah's voice and it struck him like a lightning bolt. She was lying on her side on the ground, surrounded by Nellie's puppies.

"Thank God you came!" She struggled to sit upright. "They tied my hands and feet so tight, I'm losing circulation."

He was beside her in a heartbeat, on one knee, working at the rope that bound her hands at her back. It was a demon of a knot.

"Anybody got a—"

Grycel appeared and thrust a knife handle into Arthur's hand, and then he and Red rushed out into the pasture to look for her attackers. Apparently Reynard wasn't exaggerating when he said Grycel was always prepared for dangerous situations. Arthur freed Sarah's hands, rubbed them gently, and then cut the rope binding her ankles.

"Are you all right?" he asked, his heart pounding as he lifted her chin to search her face. Her eyes were big and dark-centered, there was dirt on her face, and her hair looked like it had been clawed five different directions. But he'd never seen her look more wonderful.

His heart paused, gave a powerful thump, and then settled back into a quick and steady rhythm.

"What did they do to you?" he demanded.

She took a deep breath and pulled her knees up so she could reach an ankle and began to rub it. He boldly took her other foot in hand and rubbed her ankle and lower leg. His touch was such a relief she almost groaned.

"I was about to slip into Fancy's stall, when they came up behind me, put a bag over my head, and all but wrenched my arms out of their sockets. I didn't get a look at them, but I heard them say they were going to take me to somebody they called 'his lordship.'" She flexed her ankles and turned her feet in circles. "That could be a nickname, I suppose, like the way people call me 'the duchess.' But then, they could have meant a man with an actual title." He helped her to her feet and it seemed perfectly natural to pull her into his arms. She sighed with relief and melted against him.

A moment later, he looked up to find Reynard leaning a shoulder against the frame of the stable doors, watching them. He was glad the light was poor; his face heated and had to be red as the devil.

"I checked out the stable . . . nothing amiss in here . . . in case you're interested," the viscount said dryly. "It could be they didn't have time to do any damage." He focused on Sarah. "Or it could be they came just for *her*."

Before she realized what was happening, Arthur had lifted her off her feet and was striding through the stable.

"This is nice," she said, sliding her arms around his neck and shoulders. "Not strictly necessary, but lovely, all the same."

"I'm not taking any chances with you," he said sternly.

"Because I'm so precious?" She looked up with pointed innocence.

"Because you could have . . . internal injuries."

"Ooooooh. Sounds serious."

"Potentially."

"Are you going to examine me?"

"Very likely."

"I can hardly wait," she said. "I should warn you, however, that my mother will probably take a dim view of you making free with my person. She's a bit old-fashioned."

"I'll handle her."

"Yes? How?"

"I'm a duke. I'll pull rank."

"Just so you know, she's not impressed with dukes. She thinks they're bad luck for us Bumgartens."

"Horsefeathers. The truth is, Bumgartens are great luck for dukes."

"We are?" She grinned.

"You in particular. You're a gold mine of industry and possibility."

"What kind of possibility?" With her hand on his neck she could feel the heat creeping up out of his collar.

"This kind," he said, stopping dead, a few feet from the front doors, and covering her lips with his.

Pleasure surged through her body in a hot, tingling wave. He let her feet slide to the ground while holding on to her waist, and she turned to press herself against him with all of the eagerness she had tried to deny.

The partly open door swung wide and there was a gasp of horror that could only have come from her mother. A moment later Sir William edged past Elizabeth onto the step, and when he saw what caused her reaction, pulled her back inside and closed the door with a resounding thud.

"My mother's not going to be happy about this," she murmured against his lips. He kissed her again as if he meant to make her remember it for the next hundred years. Her toes curled inside her lady boots, and she suddenly wanted to rub every part of him with . . . every part of her.

"Ye gods"—he paused a moment with a wry look—
"you don't think she'll do something drastic, like demand
I make an honest woman of you?"

A moment later his knees buckled from the force of a
huge dog slamming into them from behind. They both
staggered and held on to each other as they regained their
footing. He turned to look at Nero and could have sworn
there was a grin on the dog's maw.

"You—you—just when I was starting to like you."

The darkness and the abundance of hoofprints in the
pasture made tracking the kidnappers an exercise in futility.
Red and Grycel headed back to the stable and found Sarah
and Arthur gone and Reynard strolling the alley admiring
the collection of horses that had been born on Betancourt.
They reported that their search had yielded nothing, and
Reynard sighed and turned back to the horses. "They're
pretty enough. Any of them fast?"

"Oh, yeah," came a voice from down the alley. A big
man was leading a large coal-black horse to an empty box
stall near the stable entrance. "They got all the speed you
could want. Mercury, here, loves to run. And he can clear
a fence or a ditch like a bloody deer."

Grycel straightened and squinted at the man, then
strode down the alley, drawing Red and Reynard with him.
The man studied Grycel as he approached, watching his
powerful carriage and movement.

"Manse? Grycel Manse?"

"I'll be damned. Steig Osmussen!" Grycel gave the big
man a punch in the shoulder that would have sent most
men staggering. "What the hell are you doin' here?"

They clasped hands and shook hands ferociously until
it became clear that neither one would surrender. By mutual
consent, they dropped hands and laughed heartily.

"You know this big ox?" Red stepped up, looking almost petite in company with the two tall, heavily muscled men.

"I do," Grycel said, grinning. "We did some bare knuckle work at Mahaney's in London, some time ago." He looked at Reynard and gestured to Steig. "He was a brute in th' ring. Damn near took my head off a couple of times." He turned back to his former opponent. "I figured you for big time bouts. What happened?"

Steig expelled a heavy breath. "Got a little too rough. Decided it wasn't for me anymore." He clasped Grycel's shoulder warmly. "But you look like fightin's treated you well."

"Nah, I haven't been in a ring in five years. Got other business now."

"Yeah? Like what?" The horse grew restless, so Steig opened the stall and began to unsaddle him.

"This an' that. I help the Fox, here, sometimes." Grycel tossed a thumb over his shoulder at Reynard. "There's trouble on Betancourt land—gettin' closer every day. Tonight somebody tried to take Miss Sarah."

"What?" Steig wheeled, genuinely shocked. "Here? Tonight?"

"In these very stables," Reynard said, glancing around. "It went bad—they didn't get her—but the bastards escaped."

"Is the duchess all right?" Steig asked, looking like a thundercloud.

"She's okay," Red answered, putting a hand on the big fighter's arm. "But this trouble—it's getting outta hand. We gotta do something."

"So, you work for the duke now?" Grycel asked.

"Tryin' to keep the peace." Steig gave a huff of disgust. "I was riding the north border, like the duke wanted. Never occurred to me—or him, I reckon—that they'd strike here."

"It was a stupid move on their part," Reynard said. "Or desperate."

Grycel nodded agreement. "Well, I'm damn glad we're on the same side." He glanced at the others. "I'd hate to have to fight this big lug in a life-or-death contest."

Steig's smile faltered for a fraction of a second as he hefted the saddle and pad onto a rack outside the stall. He made sure the horse had hay and water, then turned to Grycel and the others.

"I'm half starved, but I need to hear more about this attack." Steig's camaraderie was firmly back in place.

As the four headed for the kitchen, Red sidled close to Grycel.

"Ossssmusssssen?"

Grycel answered out of the side of his mouth. "Now you know why he goes by just one name."

Chapter Nineteen

Sarah was starting to like the fiery taste of brandy, she just wished it didn't always come attached to a trauma of some sort. She dodged her mother's martyred looks and concentrated on recalling the details of the attack while tracing the bottom of her glass with her fingertips.

Mazie and Dolly had been waiting to take her straight upstairs when she entered the house earlier, and the women drew her a bath and laid out clean clothes. Sarah was surprised that her mother hadn't bustled in, taken charge, and insisted she go straight to bed. Instead, when she was dressed properly, Deidre brought word that the duke and her family were waiting for her in the parlor.

When she arrived, she found not just family, but also Grycel Manse, Sir William, and Steig gathered to hear her version of the failed kidnapping. As soon as she entered, Steig approached her with a grave expression and told her he was furious when the others told him what happened to her.

"The duke an' me talked, and from now on, I'll be sticking closer to home and checkin' on you regular, to make sure yer safe."

"Thank you, Steig," she said, touching his arm. "But I can't imagine they would try such a thing again."

"Who knows what the bastards'll try," Red grumbled.

Arthur led her to a seat and she explained again what had happened to her, ending with, "It happened so fast, I was caught totally unaware."

All present went quiet for a moment.

"Think hard. Can you remember anything else that might help identify them?" Arthur asked, leaning toward her. "Anything at all? When they spoke, did they have accents or call each other by name?"

"They just sounded like most country folk, hereabouts," she said, wetting her lips. "Sorry. Nothing unusual."

He took her hand and there was a not-so-subtle intake of breath from the vicinity of her mother.

Her gaze narrowed as she reached back into her memory to scour those events once again. "Wait." Events unspooled in her mind and her attention snagged on a detail she hadn't recalled previously. "There may be one thing. When the dogs attacked, the men were yelling and—" She halted, on the razor's edge of recall. "I could swear one said, 'Help me . . . M-Mace.' I think that's what it was. Mace. Is that a name?"

"Yes, and one I've heard before." Arthur released her hand and sat back, looking to Steig.

"One of the men who hired me to come to the Iron Penny the night we . . . met," Steig said, meeting Arthur's gaze. He frowned. "That pair called themselves Gil and *Mace*."

"Then, they've been around for a while," Arthur mused. "And someone—likely this 'lordship' fellow—is paying the bill."

Sarah looked from one pensive face to another, wondering if they were thinking what she was thinking. Apparently no one wanted to say it.

"Arthur was never summoned with a writ and seated in the House of Lords, and he didn't participate in local or

London society. What 'lordship' would hate Betancourt, or Arthur, enough to pay thieves and bullies to disrupt and destroy them?"

"There is only one I can think of," Arthur said. "He's not strictly a lord, but I can imagine he might style himself as one."

"George," Red declared, nodding.

"I don't know why I should be surprised." Arthur shook his head. "His father was as vicious and corrupt as they come. When he tried to ruin Daisy and I tossed him out of Betancourt, he hired some thugs to kill Ash, and damn near succeeded."

Sir William came to the edge of his seat and turned to Elizabeth.

"Didn't you say this George fellow mentioned going to the courts?"

"Well, yes." Elizabeth caught his train of thought. "But why would he be going to the courts?"

"The law is full of quirks and odd precedents. Most actions of the civil courts are taken because of a suit one party brings against another."

"You think he means to sue me or Betancourt?" Arthur looked baffled. "What for? What have I ever done to him?"

"I have no idea," Sir William said, rising. "But I should get back to London and ask a few questions. There is a late train . . . I'll go now and send word as soon as I learn something."

Elizabeth rose with him and followed him out. Steig mentioned he had calls to make at several tenant farms and left. Reynard and Grycel asked Red to take them to the destroyed mill so they could look around. Soon Sarah and Arthur were alone in the parlor.

"You really believe George is behind all this?" she asked.

"I can't afford to ignore the possibility."

"But he found Fancy and brought him home to me. Why would he do that if he was trying to ruin Betancourt?"

"There is no way he could ever claim the Meridian title; he's too distant now. I don't have children yet, but Ash does. As it stands, if something should happen to me, the succession would go on through them." He took on a look of flint striking steel. "If he's set on becoming a duke, he's in the wrong family."

Steig rode hard into the north edge of Betancourt, following the rutted track that led to the tavern where he'd met Gil and Mace. When he entered the taproom he felt a charge in the air that prickled the hair on the back of his neck. The barman jerked a nod over his shoulder toward the back. Steig followed a short hallway to a storeroom filled with barrels, crates, and familiar faces. The men he'd met two nights before still bore traces of soot in their craggy faces. When they looked up, they quickly looked down again.

Mace was bruised and bore bloody bandages on his hands as he sprawled on the floor against a barrel. Behind him a pair of legs that belonged to his unconscious partner were visible.

"Where the hell have you been?" His lordship was in a foul mood, and dealing out bruises.

"At the manor, where somebody tried to kidnap Sarah Bumgarten," Steig said. "The place was in an uproar. I couldn't leave—I was hired to make the place *secure*."

George gave Mace a savage kick that made him howl with pain. "It was these two imbeciles. After the mill fire, I told all of you to do nothing and stay out of sight. Then these two go charging into the manor itself and try to kidnap the one person on all Betancourt that I need to keep on my side."

"She deserved it . . . broke Gil's nose, she did," Mace said, gasping but not repentant. "We swore she'd get hers."

Another kick and a slash of that crop made Mace curl into a ball of misery. The baron paced back and forth smacking his leg, his narrowed eyes flitting over a scene none but he could see. "I need her to testify." He looked to Steig. "Is she hurt?"

"Shook up bad. And scared."

That registered with "his lordship," Baron Beesock. "She's scared?"

"She nearly got taken right out of her own bed," Steig said. "Hell yeah, she's scared. You should've seen her shakin' and cryin.'" He narrowed his eyes, looking troubled. "Almost had me in tears . . . poor sweet thing." The men grinned back, admiring his audacious duplicity. The smile he returned was yet another lie. He was not particularly proud of his performance or his presence here.

George studied that news. "That might actually be a good thing. The whole basis for my case is that the estates are in peril and no one is safe."

Steig picked an apple out of the barrel next to him and took a bite as he sat down on a nearby crate. Behind his apparent geniality, he was conflicted. Why hadn't he told Arthur what he'd learned during the mill raid? He'd managed to keep them from firing the miller's house and got the woman and her kids away to safety. Why was he back here, listening to this arrogant peacock? Because he felt comfortable in this company? Because he might have more to gain with them than with the duke and Miss Sarah?

Truth be told, he didn't know why Arthur had decided to release him. For his fighting skills? Because he felt some kinship with Steig's story? He could imagine Arthur as part of a rough ship's crew more than he could see him as an elegant, entitled nobleman. Despite riding beside him for two long days, learning about his ideas and concern for his people and estate, Steig had a hard time believing that goodness was real. Or that he deserved to be part of it.

Shaking off his doubts, he took a deep breath.

He had to know what this arse of a baron planned.

"What next, yer lordship?"

Two constables arrived at Betancourt the next morning to quiz Sarah on her ordeal. Her wrists, shoulder, and hip were sore, but otherwise she was healthy and felt almost embarrassed to be reporting that she was abducted all of thirty or forty yards, for a total of less than ten minutes. Her mother reminded her that if not for timely intervention, her situation could have been disastrous. She sat through the same questions she'd answered several times now, but was rewarded by the news that the county would be assigning additional men to police the area.

After the constables left, Sarah was desperate for something productive to do. She took Arthur by the hand and headed for the study.

"You need to learn the estate accounts," she said, and scowled at his groan. "This is part of your obligation . . . knowing and guiding the finances of Betancourt. You have a large house that takes a good bit of upkeep. Then there is the staff . . . we're actually short-staffed. Other houses this size have twice the number of servants and three times the groundskeepers."

"We have groundskeepers?" Arthur looked surprised. "Who?"

"We only have two, Carl Morgan and his son David. They used to farm, but Carl's leg was damaged in an accident and he had to give up farming. Betancourt needed someone to tend the grounds and oversee the seed storage and 'starts' for each season's planting. He was perfect for it—he's the one who suggested the additional plants for the butterfly garden."

"How long did it take you to learn all of this?" he asked.

"Eight or nine months . . . I've lost track. It's not as hard as it may seem."

"Not when you're a marvel of nature," he muttered, eyeing her.

She retrieved ledgers from the desk and joined him on the sofa to explain the bookkeeping. Included were lists of merchants and tradesmen that supplied Betancourt. They were long lists and each vendor had a story that Arthur needed to understand in order to handle the account properly.

She looked up to find him breathing in the scent of her hair.

"Are you listening?" she said, more pleased than annoyed. He was staring at her lips as if they were the object of a lifelong quest.

"Of course. I can adore your hair and listen at the same time. I'm really quite good at it. I've had plenty of practice lately."

Elizabeth entered the study at that moment, bearing a flat box wrapped in blue paper and tied with a yellow ribbon that had seen better days. Without a word she set the box down on Sarah's lap, and then sailed out of the study.

Sarah looked at the box in disbelief that slowly changed to horror—as if she expected it to sprout fangs and rattles. She shoved it off her lap, and when it hit the floor the tinkle of broken glass was unmistakable.

"What is that?" he asked, surprised by her action. "Did you just break it?"

"No." She stared at it, remembering when she'd last

seen it and her humiliation at the way the earl's bride sneered at it.

"Aren't you going to open it?"

"It's not for me," she said, feeling anger rising beneath that potent memory. She rose, crossed the entry hall, and walked straight out the front doors. Through the blood pounding in her head she heard his confusion as he called after her.

"Then who is it for?"

She kept walking, only half aware of her location and direction. She was shaken and *hurt*. The blue paper, the perky yellow ribbon she had carefully worked into a bow . . . where had her mother gotten that gift? She had thrown it on the floor that night and had heard the glass break. Her mother had to have picked it up. Why? Why would she do that and keep it all of these months?

More importantly, why would she give it to her now, in front of Arthur? The exertion of walking kept her focused. As long as she could think and examine her thoughts, she could keep tears and devastating emotions at bay.

A reminder, she realized. It was meant to be a reminder of what she'd experienced at the hands of a callous and duplicitous young nobleman. If so, it was also meant as a warning that it could happen again . . . with the duke her mother distrusted. And feared. For that was the basis of her distrust—fear. She was afraid her youngest daughter would put her heart and soul into Betancourt and its master, only to be spurned again.

The longer she walked, the more quickly she walked. Her hands were clenched at her sides and her heart pounded as she waded through tall grass, kicked weeds aside, and made gravel crunch underfoot.

"How dare she?" With each footfall she repeated it until the house loomed before her, and she realized the path she had walked was taking her right back to Betancourt and a confrontation with her mother.

Arthur sat staring at the gift in his hand, trying to make sense of Sarah's reaction and finding no starting point that might lead to an explanation. He was missing too many pieces of the puzzle. After several moments, he realized that in his hand lay the most important clue.

Carefully, he unwrapped the package . . . the yellow ribbon, the bright blue paper so carefully trimmed and tucked . . . and uncovered a sturdy pasteboard box. Inside lay a simple black frame with tiny gilt beading and broken glass. He carefully lifted out the glass to reveal a big blue butterfly—an Adonis blue that had been perfectly pre-served and framed for display. The broken glass had marred its luminous wings in two places and he couldn't help thinking it was a shame that such a fine specimen had been damaged by whatever accident broke the glass.

A butterfly. The sight of that painstakingly wrapped butterfly . . . or perhaps the fact that it was broken . . . had a devastating impact on her. He needed to find out why.

He waited, watching the front doors, growing steadily more concerned. Just a day ago she'd almost been ab-ducted out from under their very noses. If their stables weren't safe, who knew what might be lurking in other parts of the estate. She was out there . . .

He set the mounted butterfly on the desk and started for the doors.

She stepped into the entry hall before he could exit, and the set of her face alarmed him. This was not the capable, endearing woman he knew and loved.

Loved.

He hadn't allowed himself to think that before now, but he knew it to be true. Even angry, hurt, or disappointed, she was still the key that opened his heart and freed his passions. He loved her. With everything in him.

Whatever had upset her about that beautiful, damaged butterfly was important, and he needed to know what it was.

"Come with me," he said, snagging her hand to pull her into the study. She planted her feet and wrested free.

"Right now I have to see my mother." She opted for the stairs.

"This won't take long and it's important." He grasped her wrist this time and was prepared for resistance. He clamped an arm around her waist and—in a move she'd once warned him against—tried to pull her with him.

She stomped on his foot and broke free, glowering at him.

He looked up in disbelief. "You're furious and I don't understand why . . . except that it has to do with that damned butterfly. You don't owe me an explanation, but I sure as hell could use one right now." He looked down and flexed his booted foot. "That *hurt*."

Sarah put a hand to her mouth, staring at the confusion in Arthur's face. She had just stomped on his foot because she was angry at someone else. It was a measure of how out of control she was, and a reminder that being in pain or distress didn't give her the right to hurt someone else. Especially not the man she cared so much for. Was confronting her mother more important than her relationship with Arthur?

She gave in to her better angels and went to him, reaching tentatively for his hand. The fact that he let her take it said volumes about his heart.

"I'm sorry. I am angry at Mama and not thinking straight."

"Then maybe you'd better come into the study with me

and talk it over before you do something you'll regret." His voice was deep and had that rasp she knew meant his emotions were running high.

She entered the study with him, pausing to close the doors behind them. As he took a seat on the leather sofa and patted the seat beside him, she spotted the discarded paper and ribbon on the floor and the open box on the desk. She went to look at the butterfly.

Interestingly, the first thing to come to mind was that it wasn't nearly as beautiful as the ones in Arthur's collection. The memory of placing it in the box and wrapping it carefully produced only sadness, not the wave of loss and humiliation she expected.

"Who was it intended for?" he asked, watching her reaction, waiting for her answer in her own time.

"The young earl I thought would be my . . . future. It was his birthday, the night of that ball I told you about. We had often talked about and looked at butterflies and I bought this one to give him. He had said blue was his favorite color, and I expected this would remind him of . . ."

She took a deep breath and turned away to join Arthur on the sofa. He took her hand, threading his fingers through hers.

"How did it get broken?" he asked.

"I threw it on the floor in front of him . . . after his bride called me a 'sweet child' in her native tongue . . . which apparently is a dialect of Nastiness known as Sarcasm. I heard the glass break. I wanted him to hear it, too."

She placed her hand over their joined hands, amazed by the way he listened and by the way talking to him always lowered her tension. "It's strange, but I don't think I'm angry at him anymore. Seeing the butterfly again just made me a little sad. I learned from that betrayal, and it brought me to Betancourt." She took a deep breath. "You know where my interest in butterflies started?"

He shook his head.

"Here. I was fascinated by your collection, and started to read about them when we came to Daisy's wedding." She had connected to his passion for nature even then, and couldn't help thinking it had been with her all along . . . guiding her, protecting her . . . until it had drawn her back to him. "Maybe I should be grateful for that awful scene."

"Not quite grateful . . . yet . . . but it seems you've put it behind you."

"I believe I have. I haven't even thought of him for months. Not until I told you about what happened. And even then, I didn't feel any desire to see or even remember him." She realized what he said to Fancy applied to her as well. "A wise man I know once said that the bad things that happen to us can make us stronger, if we learn from them and grow beyond them."

"Really?" He gave a huff of surprise. "Who is this paragon of wisdom? I think I need to meet him."

"You."

He blinked.

"You've taught me a number of things, Arthur Michael Graham. Not the least of which is the depth and resilience of my own heart. Your example has not been lost on me. You're what Betancourt needs." She paused, then realized she had to say it. "You're what *I* need."

She lay her hand against his cheek, realizing why she was so angry at her mother. It had nothing to do with that stupid present or a failed flirtation; it had everything to do with her mother's lack of trust in her and stubborn lack of regard for Arthur. It was time she remedied that.

"You're the heart of my heart," she said, pressing a soft kiss on his lips. "Don't ever forget that. I surely won't."

He sat there, stunned by the change in her, as she stood and took a deep breath. "Now I'm ready to talk to my mother."

She found Elizabeth in her room, resting on the chaise near the open window. She closed the door softly, but her mother heard her enter and sat up, looking wary.

"We need to talk," Sarah said.

Elizabeth nodded and waved her to the chair near the fireplace. Sarah ignored the gesture and took a seat beside her mother on the chaise.

"I was furious with you," she said with a calm that amazed her. "I came back into the house ready for a shouting match—to tell you to go back to London and mind your own business. How dare you bring that awful reminder of that night and stick it under my nose?"

"I thought you needed—"

"A reminder of my past failures? My youthful indiscretions? My gullibility in thinking someone might actually love me?"

Elizabeth looked genuinely horrified. "*No*. Not that—not any of that."

"What then?" Sarah demanded. "What was your purpose in planting that present on my lap, in front of Arthur?"

Her mother looked down, thinking, chastened by Sarah's words. "I wanted you to remember that things—situations and people—are not always what they seem. Arthur has been through a great deal, and it has changed him. God knows if it is for better or for worse."

"Well, God surely knows—because I certainly do—it is definitely for the better. He's experienced pain and injustice and learned from it. He's been held against his will and even imprisoned, but he endured. His love for his brother and Betancourt gave him the strength to overcome tremendous obstacles and return to his home. I've seen him with his tenants, with animals, and with tradesmen . . . watched him organize men to fix fences and barns, fight a fire, treat injuries, and yet he's humble enough to weed a garden with his own hands. I know his heart, and that is what matters to me."

"But Sarah—"

"No, Mama. No buts or what-ifs. He's not perfect, I suppose, but he's perfect for me. And that's what matters. I'm not perfect either. I'm headstrong and independent and too proud of my learning to listen to others sometimes. But I've made a place for myself here at Betancourt—"

"For now," her mother warned softly and with regret. "That is what worries me most. You've put your heart into this place and into that man. But what happens when . . . if . . . Will it last or will he decide to abandon it all again because it is too complicated or difficult?"

"I don't know what the future holds, Mama. None of us do. But I do know I'll be here with him as long as he needs me."

Sarah's statement was meant to reassure her mother, but even as Elizabeth opened her arms to her daughter and held her close, she realized that there were so many variables in the situation that her daughter was not counting. Danger, difficulty, legal challenges on the horizon, family struggles and contention . . . it would not be an easy path for them. And while Arthur seemed smitten with Sarah, as she was with him, there was no guarantee that he meant to give her the title that her love and dedication to him had already earned. That of *wife*.

Chapter Twenty

That afternoon two additional constables arrived with Officer Jolly at Betancourt, were introduced and taken into the study to peruse maps of the estate. Arthur, Red, Reynard, and Grycel met with them and Arthur issued them shotguns usually intended for ducks and pheasants.

None of the constables were comfortable with firearms, so Red took them out behind the coach house for some practice. Their performance was not impressive until Sarah appeared, borrowed one of the guns, and cleared all of the targets off the wall.

Shortly, the constables were shooting with more determination and considerably better accuracy.

Evening was coming on when Steig returned to Betancourt and sought out Arthur for a word.

"What did you find?" Arthur asked, studying the man's closed and unreadable demeanor.

Steig responded with news that was at odds with his grim demeanor. "Nothin' in particular. But there's a feel out there. Something's brewin'."

"It's been a week since the fire . . . three days since their attempt on Sarah," Arthur recounted. "You think they're planning something else?"

"Whatever they're aimin' to do, it ain't done yet," Steig said.

Arthur nodded.

"Any sign of Gil or Mace?"

"Nah. Probably layin' low. Stupid bastards . . . goin' after the duchess like that."

Arthur nodded. "Well, Reynard and I are going to ride out and take a look around. I'd like you to stay here and keep Sarah safe."

"Understood," Steig answered, straightening.

"She's in the house now, but God knows where she'll be in ten minutes."

Steig nodded and headed for the house. He breezed through the kitchen, giving Dolly a playful wink as he snatched a fresh roll and a slice of the beef she was cutting.

He munched as he made his way upstairs to the entry hall where Ned was dithering over the dirt the men's boots had left on the black and white marble. He asked the underbutler where Miss Sarah could be found and got a preoccupied shrug. He peered into the parlor, which was empty, and then the study, where Red was enjoying a nap. Mazie came down the main stairs carrying a basket of linen and paused to glower at the crumbs he was dropping.

"Eatin' in the hall, Mister Steig—wot's got into ye? Shoo—get on wi' ye!" Just before she bustled him outside, he managed to ask after Miss Sarah. "Now where else would ye 'spect to find the duchess? Wi' some critter, somewheres."

He was pushed out the door. Shrugging, he stuffed the rest of his snack in his mouth and headed for the stables. But she wasn't there. Eddie and Old Harley were brushing down the young horses fresh from training, and said they hadn't seen her. They pointed him to the dairy, where the dairy maids mentioned they'd seen her down by the cottages.

He started for the cottages, beginning to worry, when he spotted her in the doorway of one of the small houses speaking to a couple of women. He strode purposefully to her, intending to tell her she should stick closer to the main house and let him know if she needed to venture out so he could accompany her.

But she turned to him with such a mischievous smile that he was taken aback for a moment.

"Just the man I was hoping to see," she said, beckoning him inside. He ducked through the doorway, but was surprised to find there was plenty of room to stand upright inside. It was a tidy cottage—two rooms that smelled not of whitewash, but actual paint. The sunny cream color took on a golden hue in the early evening light that made the main room cheery. Two stuffed chairs sat before a cozy fireplace, and there were a table and chairs for eating beside a small cooking stove and sink. Someone had even provided a couple of pictures for the walls.

"What do you think?" Sarah asked, watching his puzzlement at being ordered inside.

"It's real . . . clean," was all he said.

She nodded to the women with aprons, mobcaps, and brooms and they gave awkward curtsies and hurried out the door.

"I know you're not comfortable in the servants' quarters. You're not used to living cheek by jowl with so many nosy women." She smiled when he gave a start. He also wasn't used to being observed or talking about his personal preferences. "So I thought since there was an empty cottage, you might prefer making your lodging out here."

He looked around, eyes wide. "You want I should stay out here? I haven't done nothin' to anybody, I swear—"

"That's not what I mean at all, Steig. You're part of Betancourt now. You keep unusual hours, and if I read you right, you like your privacy. Here, you'll have it."

"This . . . it's for me?" He was having a hard time making sense of it.

"It is." She pointed to the smaller room. "That's the bedroom. It's small, but the bed should fit. And there are quilts and pillows. You can still take your meals at the manor with us. You won't have to cook."

He stuck his head into the other room and stared at the bed and lamp and the cupboard meant for clothes. Pulling back, he seemed a little dazed.

"Look around a bit, get the feel of it," she said, heading for the door. "I'll be in the stable when you've decided."

She stepped out into the golden evening and he heard her greeting people from the other cottages as she headed to the stables. He wobbled over to one of the stuffed chairs and sank into it. It actually fit his big frame. He looked around and his gaze fell on the open door. Use that door now . . . or . . . commit to the duke and Betancourt. And Miss Sarah's safety.

She had just offered him a place to be and a sense of belonging he hadn't felt in years. God knew he didn't deserve it . . . but . . .

He had a decision to make.

A short while later, he stalked past the barns, outbuildings, cottages, and the old blacksmith's forge, which was now a toolshed. Some people skirted him on the path, others were brave enough to smile or give him a nod of greeting. He'd been here long enough to become a familiar face to some of Betancourt's folk, but his size and tough demeanor kept most of them at a distance.

When he entered the stable, Old Harley pointed to the cross alley and tack room, where he found Sarah on her knees beside a large wooden box full of puppies. They were climbing and sniffing her and licking at her fingers. She looked up at him with a smile and said, "Pick one. They're not ready to leave Nellie yet—it'll be a couple of weeks. But you get first pick."

He was stunned. "A pup? You'd give me one of yer dog's pups?"

"If you want one. The duke said you had a dog once and you have a soft spot for them. You may need some company in your new home."

He sank to his knees, staring at the box of squirming, yipping puppies and slowly began to smile.

To Sarah it looked like he was having to crack parts of his face to get them to move. But finally he reached out to one of the puppies and gave it a pet. He glanced at Sarah and she smiled.

He picked up two different pups, holding them up, letting them chew on his fingers, looking them in the face. The third he chose was a fuzzy, short-eared gray puppy with copper-penny eyes. It didn't nip, it licked him and stared back at him as if it recognized its new master. He pulled it close to his chest and the pup nestled against him. He stroked the soft coat and ears gently and looked at Sarah with a wonder that was almost painful to behold.

"I'll take 'em both—the house an' the pup." His voice sounded thick with emotion. "I'm yer man, duchess."

Sarah grinned as she pulled out a red ribbon and tied it around the puppy's neck, indicating he was taken. And for the first time since she came to Betancourt, she forgot to correct someone for calling her *duchess*.

* * *

The next afternoon was quiet and increasingly overcast. The oldsters among the house staff started to complain of lumbago and pain in their knees and shoulders, declaring their symptoms a sure sign of coming rain. But not a drop had fallen by the time a coach-and-four turned into the drive and headed for the doors of the main house.

"There's visitors . . . Miss Sarah." Mazie panted, looking like she might collapse from running up the stairs. "Ned sent me . . . to fetch ye." Sarah stood in the hallway, having just knocked on her mother's door to return a ladies' journal her mother had left in the parlor. Her mother called for her to enter and sat up quickly when Sarah handed her the journal and the news that they had a visitor.

"Is it Sir William? Has he come back?" Elizabeth asked.

Mazie was already down the hall, out of range of the question.

"Mazie would have said it was Sir William." She looked unsettled by a thought. "I just hope it isn't Cousin George with more unpleasantness."

It wasn't George.

As Sarah and her mother approached the top of the stairs, they heard a familiar voice call, "Come back here, you little devil. Don't you dare touch anything!" A moment later they spotted a young woman in a finely tailored suit charging down the entry hall after a very young child who was giggling and running full steam back through the hall.

Sarah halted, scarcely able to believe her eyes.

"Daisy?" Her mother grabbed the railing and charged down the steps. "God in Heaven—it's Daisy!" She squealed like a child on Christmas morning. "Daisy!" By the time she reached the bottom of the stairs, Daisy had caught her fractious two-year-old, scooped him up in her arms, and hauled him back to where her mother was in danger of exploding with joy.

Elizabeth threw her arms around Daisy and the little one, repeating Daisy's name over and over, rocking her from side to side. Sarah floated down the stairs, filled with conflicting emotions . . . happiness at seeing her beloved older sister and dread at what her presence here portended. By the time she reached them, Daisy was pulling away from her mother's embrace to introduce her young one: "This is William. He's two years old and, with good reason, we refer to him as Wild Bill."

"And where is Little Red?" Sarah asked, craning her neck for a peek out the front doors.

"Oh, he's here, too. With his father. They'll be in shortly— Sarah!" Daisy thrust Wild Bill into her mother's arms and lunged at her sister with open arms. "Ohmygod—look at you—you're beautiful!"

She hugged Sarah, set her back to look at her with true pleasure.

"When did you get to England?" Sarah asked when she was able to think again. "Why didn't you let us know you were coming?"

"We figured you'd expect us—after bombarding us with telegrams and letters. The first one we got was a bit of a puzzle, but the second one—from you—was clear enough. Wild horses couldn't have kept Ash from booking passage. And I was not about to let him come to England without me. It's been too damned long—" She clapped a hand over her mouth. "Too *blessed* long since I've seen my family. The boys needed to see their Grandma Lizzie, Uncle Red, and their newborn cousin! What did they name him?"

"Oliver." Elizabeth tried desperately to keep her grandson's hands off her hair, her broach, and the lace on her collar. "Heavens, he *is* a wild one."

"Where is Ashton?" Sarah hurried to the open door and

pulled it wider. The driver and footman were unloading piles of baggage that poor Ned eyed with dismay. A five-year-old boy was running all over the place, yelling, "Where's the ponies?"

That had to be her nephew, Redmond. Aptly named. He clearly had a streak of Uncle Red in him. She rushed out to see Ashton and found him watching his offspring's exuberant response to his boyhood home with pride and relief. When he spotted her coming toward him, he brightened— "Sarah!"—and met her with open arms and a whirl that ended in a hug.

He looked down at her with a tension that was fully explained by three short words. "Where is he?"

Sarah looked toward the stables and the barns and outbuildings.

"I'm not sure. Reynard's here and Uncle Red, and Reynard's friend Grycel Manse. Sir William Drexel was here for a bit, but had to get back to London. I'm sure if he had known you were on the way, he would have stayed."

She nibbled her lip, searching the side yard, coach house, and stables for a clue to where they'd gone. Just as she was about to suggest they go together to look for him, four figures appeared around the bend in the lane that ran through the working heart of Betancourt.

"Wait—that may be them now." She began to wave furiously.

Arthur and the others had been out checking the security of the barns and outbuildings, and looking over two newborn foals. Reynard was making a case for training some of Betancourt's horses for racing of one sort or another, when they came around a bend in the lane and spotted a coach at the front doors. Sarah was waving wildly, and beside her a tall man in a dark suit was rubbing the back of his neck as he strained to see them.

A bolt of lightning couldn't have had more impact on Arthur than the sight of the man beside Sarah. His shape, his posture, the way he rubbed his neck . . . even without a clear look at his face, Arthur knew his identity.

Dear God—he had come!

Arthur started to walk, then run, ignoring the questions and comments around him.

"Is that who I think it is?"

"It's about damned time that boy got here!"

"This oughta be good."

Each stride raised his heart rate until the pounding in his chest made it hard to breathe. He slowed as he neared his brother and came to a stop a few feet away, taking in every detail, every nuance of his brother's appearance.

The questions that lay between them—at the moment he couldn't remember a single one. All he could think was that his brother was home. All of the times he'd dreamed of this—seeing the one person in the world who had shared his life and knew him, cared for him—had been promises to himself that he would find a way home. It was this meeting that had kept him alive through pain, captivity, and deprivation. All of that came flooding back at once—he could hardly breathe.

"Ash," he managed to whisper.

He could tell his brother was feeling the same intense emotions. Ash's face . . . his features were stronger, more chiseled than Arthur recalled, and his body seemed thicker. He was dressed handsomely—had an air of confidence about him as he took in the details of his long-lost brother's appearance. His chest seemed to be swelling . . . his heart had to be pounding, too.

They locked gazes, looking into each other, searching, feeling their way back to each other after years of separation.

"Artie."

Emotions erupted.

Arthur lunged for Ashton with open arms and was met halfway by his brother's frantic embrace. They held each other so tightly that joy squeezed out of their eyes and ran down their faces. They rocked back and forth until they were unable to contain the intensity of feeling—it exploded from them as laughter. They hugged and laughed and nearly pulled each other off their feet as they celebrated seeing, hugging, loving each other.

Shouts of excitement came last, bleeding off the excess of emotion as they released each other. They kept hands on shoulders, afraid to let go completely, and swiped their eyes, grinning. Slowly, they came back to awareness of the people collected nearby.

Red, Reynard, and Grycel approached to a respectful distance. Daisy and Elizabeth stood on the steps behind Sarah, holding two young boys. The women's cheeks were wet and their faces were glowing as they absorbed and reacted to the reunion, each in her own way.

The tide of pleasure was so full in Arthur that there were no questions about voyage or absence or reasons in his mind. He just wanted to enjoy the moment and relish the presence of people he'd held in his heart for years.

"Daisy," he said, hurrying to meet her as she came off the steps to throw her arms around him. He picked her up and whirled her around, then set her down to gaze into her face.

"Careful—that's my wife," Ash said with a broad smile.

"Yeah, well, she was my betrothed before she was your

wife," Arthur said with a husky laugh. And he hugged her again.

"Look at you!" Daisy tugged on a lock of his long hair. "When did you get so tanned and so . . . so . . . wild looking?"

"A lot happens in six years," he said, smiling. The words worked like an incantation that began clearing the fog of euphoria in his head. "You . . . you're as lovely as ever, Daisy. Even more so." He chuckled. "Marriage to my wayward brother can't be all bad."

In short order he was introduced to his nephews, Redmond and William. The boys stared at him, until the one known as Wild Bill climbed anxiously up into his mother's arms and the one Daisy called "Red" studied him with a frown before asking, "Why's your hair like a girl's?"

"They're American, all right." He laughed and leaned down to face his nephew with sudden inspiration. "Because I'm like Samson, from the Bible. The longer my hair, the stronger I am."

Little Red's eyes widened and he looked to his mother, who gave a silent chuckle and nodded. As he watched the boy's reaction, it struck him that there might be some truth in what he'd said. His hair was a reminder of the strength it had taken to endure and overcome. And Sarah liked it. That alone was reason enough to let it stay the way it was.

When he looked around, he found her beside Ash, talking with the men. He strode out to them in time to hear Ash say, "Couldn't—wouldn't believe it until I got Sarah's telegram. A man who claimed to be my brother? I couldn't imagine why you lot couldn't tell if it was him or not."

Ashton turned to look at him as he approached, and the others looked at him, too.

"Now I see why. Good God—I couldn't have picked you out in a roomful of strangers. Well, not at first. What the hell happened to you?"

"That's a story," Arthur said, feeling a new tension climbing up his spine. "A whole bag of stories."

"Yeah? Like what?" Ashton said with a tone that was a little too flippant to sit well on Arthur's ears. "Having too much fun to think about the folks back home?"

Arthur's mood changed so quickly it was a shock to even him.

"Like being held captive in India by a maharaja," Arthur said, each successive word packing more of a punch. "Like almost a year in a Cairo prison. Like going without food for days and sleeping on the deck of a ship because below decks smelled like rot and piss. Like knowing that the rest of the world considers you *dead*."

Ash turned slowly to face him, matching his rising hostility.

"Not a word. You didn't bother to write or send a message. Six damned years, we waited. *Six. Years*. Thinking you were dead."

"Six years of deprivation and captivity," Arthur declared. "Six years of counting on you to manage and protect Betancourt. Six years of trusting you to honor your word." Arthur's eyes burned.

The questions, the anger, the injustice of it all came roiling back.

"You knew I had promised Daisy time in New York," Ash said. "And you were too busy exploring the world to think about anyone else."

"You didn't just spend some time in New York, you left England and didn't look back. You abandoned Betancourt and your responsibilities to it—even after Sir William wrote you."

Ashton glanced around with a look of disdain. "It doesn't exactly look like the place suffered."

Arthur felt it rising, the anger, the need to lash out and make his brother answer for his rejection of the role he'd been born to . . . heir to the heir. His muscles tensed, his fists clenched. When the burst of fury hit, his fist shot out and connected with Ashton's face.

Sarah cried out as Ashton staggered aside and grabbed his jaw.

"What the—" Ash staggered in disbelief. "You bastard."

"You git—you know I was born true—and *first*," Arthur snarled and landed another blow, this time in Ash's middle.

Ashton managed to pull his midsection back enough to blunt the impact. All that second punch had done was make him angry. In a flash he let his own fists fly, and suddenly it was an all-out fight.

Elizabeth's frantic voice rang out: "Red, Reynard—do something!"

Red saw Sarah start to move and rushed to restrain her.

"Ain't nothing to be done," Red declared, grappling with Sarah and settling the matter for all onlookers. "It's between them. Gotta let 'em get it outta their blood."

By that decree, no one would be allowed to interfere in this bout—it was between brothers who had scores to settle. They were so intent on the fight, they didn't notice when the big man on horseback arrived, dismounted, and rushed to join Reynard and Grycel.

"What the hell's goin' on?" Steig demanded.

Reynard folded his arms and tilted his head toward the big man. "Brotherly differences. They're working it out."

Steig frowned, but then relaxed enough to critique their fighting styles. "The duke would've made a good bareknuckler. Look how he keeps his fists up and tight. The way he throws from his legs doubles his power."

After several pounding blows, Ash and Arthur paused and stared at each other, panting and bleeding. Ash ripped off his coat and vest, while Arthur unbuttoned his shirt and tossed it aside, explaining, "This is the only decent shirt I have. Don't want your blood muckin' it up."

Ash's response to the sight of Arthur's naked chest and muscular frame was one word: "Shit!"

Red turned Sarah bodily and shoved her stubborn form toward the front doors. They collected Daisy and the children on the way. Elizabeth realized what he was doing and pulled her daughters by the arms into the house. She closed the door firmly and stationed Ned to see that no one escaped.

Sarah rushed into the parlor and stood at the big window, watching the mayhem unfold between Arthur and Ashton. Her heart was in her throat as they traded blows and sometimes wrestled, pushing, each trying to sweep the other's feet or knock him down.

"We have to stop this," she groaned as Daisy settled beside her.

"They're big boys," Daisy said, sounding more annoyed than worried. "They'll stop when they've had enough." Apparently the sight of her husband and his brother bashing each other senseless didn't alarm her.

But then, Sarah recalled, her sister had seen them fight before . . . over *her*.

How dare Daisy stand there watching this without so much as a twitch of concern?

"You realize this is your fault," Sarah declared, turning to her sister.

"My fault?"

"You broke his heart and made him leave home. He spent years knocking around and being knocked around because you chose Ashton."

Daisy's jaw dropped. "No one made him do anything. It was his decision to leave Betancourt because he wanted to see the world, to explore and discover . . . the way he had never had a chance to do. He'd been practically imprisoned here by his nasty uncles and coldblooded aunt."

Sarah stared at her sister. "Is that what you tell yourself so you can sleep at night?"

"Really, Sarah!" Elizabeth stepped in. "Is that any way to talk to your sister after she's come halfway around the world to see you?"

"She came to see you," Sarah said, glaring at her mother. "And Red. And most likely to check on her children's inheritance. It had nothing to do with me." She looked back at Daisy. "I'm afraid you're in for a disappointment, *Mrs.* Graham. Arthur is not only alive, he still holds the title. You're not a duchess, after all."

Daisy shrank back, stung by Sarah's words.

Sarah realized Daisy's shock was genuine and knew she'd overstepped her bounds. But she believed every word she'd spoken and she did not intend to suffer her mother's rebuke or demand for an apology.

Trembling with anxiety and anger, she turned on her heel and strode for the stairs. She had to see what was going on outside. Blood had been drawn. Sooner or later, someone was going to need medical care.

Daisy put Wild Bill down and sent her boys out of the parlor, telling them not to touch anything, before turning to her mother.

"What in blazes was that all about?"

"I told her getting involved with Arthur was just asking for trouble . . . and here it is. I'm so sorry, Daisy." She reached for her daughter's hands. "I know you had your heart set on being a duchess. I know when you go back to New York as a plain Mrs. it will be embarrassing, but I'm sure we can find a way to explain it that will calm the gossip."

Daisy yanked her hands away and stared at her mother in disbelief. "You told her I had my heart set on being a duchess?"

"You *did.*" Then Elizabeth wavered. "Well, maybe not at the end, but you did have a difficult time deciding between the duke and Ashton."

It took all of Daisy's restraint to keep from pinching her mother. It was true that she had wanted to marry a duke, but not for any of the reasons her mother probably conjured.

"Worse yet, she's developed a disastrous attachment to Arthur," her mother continued. "I tried to tell her he will never be a proper duke. He went through trials in his travels and came back changed . . . *odd.* You only have to look at him to know he'll never be accepted in proper circles."

Daisy never failed to be astonished by the extent of her mother's narrow-mindedness. How could the woman have lived this long and still measure people by such pitiful standards? Daisy had no idea what her brother-in-law had been through in his travels, but he had come back anything *but* odd. He was strong and charismatic and handsome in a way that suggested exotic depths. In short, he was a stunning specimen.

"You've been steeped in pinky-up London society so long," Daisy declared, "you've forgotten what real men look like. Why on earth would he want to be stuck in London's suffocating and judgmental society?"

"He's a duke. He has societal responsibilities." Elizabeth stiffened. "You know better than anyone how unforgiving society can be."

"I also know—better than anyone—how unforgiving *you* can be." It was a hard thing to say, but Daisy knew that nothing less would penetrate her mother's headstrong pride. "It took a long time for you to forgive me for being me. I came to England and nearly sacrificed my life to make you happy." She saw Elizabeth's shoulders round slightly and almost felt guilty. Almost. Her mother was a hard nut to crack.

"So, Sarah has taken a fancy to Arthur," she said, musing on that.

"I'd say it's past the 'fancy' stage," Elizabeth said. "He kisses her and touches her whenever she is near. In plain sight of everyone. It's . . . it's . . ."

"Mutual," Daisy supplied with sudden understanding. "That explains a lot." She looked toward the window, thinking of Arthur's manly allure and her sister's fervent defense of him. She took Elizabeth's elbow and drew her to a settee. "What I want to know is, why was she at Betancourt when he came home?"

Elizabeth was still stinging from Daisy's words and lifted her chin. "I'm not sure she would wish me to tell that story."

"Bollocks," Daisy said, glowering. "I'm her Nevada-bred sister, not some London gossip. Start talking."

Chapter Twenty-One

Arthur's hands hurt like hell, his lip was split, and his left eye was swelling. His only consolation was that his brother looked just as bad.

"You abandoned the place. Just walked off and left it." He took another swing, but just clipped his brother's jaw. His arms were about as responsive as hanging sides of beef.

"No more than you did, *brother*." Ash swung back but only connected with Arthur's upraised arm. "You knew I wanted nothing to do with the title. I had other plans."

"You agreed to be my heir."

"Only because you wanted it. I had no idea you'd actually *die*."

"It's not like I didn't want to come home. I couldn't."

"How the hell would I know that? All I knew was you were cold and dead in some godforsaken—I didn't even get to see your body and mourn you. God—I hated you for dropping the stinkin' title and all of Betancourt's demands . . . on . . . my . . . head . . ."

Ash swayed and fell forward, straight into Arthur, who just managed to keep from falling over. In a moment they were both on their knees, hanging onto each other to stay upright.

"I hated you for not coming home to take my place.

Betancourt needed work and guidance and protection—and you weren't here."

"Looks like it didn't do so bad," Ash said through swelling lips.

"Thanks to Sarah," Arthur snapped. "She was here when I came back . . . brought Betancourt and me both back to life." Pronouncing all those "b's" through split and swollen lips was downright painful.

Neither was ready to give up, though their blows were pathetic. They were exhausted. A couple of more punches and—

A bundle of fury burst through the ring of men watching the bout.

"Out of the way," Sarah growled as she charged the stubborn pair. "That's enough! You're through—both of you!" She pulled Arthur back enough to put her arms between them and push them apart.

"Listen to me, you overgrown louts," she ordered as they fell backward and stared at her. "It's time you stop bashing each other like schoolboys and at least *pretend* to be mature, responsible adults."

She said to Ash, "Your brother went through hell. It was never his choice to stay away from Betancourt. He spent years trying to get back here, and when he couldn't it broke his heart. He came back thinking you might never want to see him again."

She turned on Arthur with equal heat. "And you—your brother couldn't bear to come back here and take your place, because to do so would mean accepting you were dead. He loved you too much to give up on you. If you can't see that, take my word for it until your vision clears."

She paused to let that sink in and could see from the way Arthur and Ashton were looking at each other that she might have gotten through.

"Somebody's trying to tear Betancourt apart, and if you

keep this up, you'll do the job for them." She took one and then the other by the ear, pinching hard enough to make them complain—"Ow!" "What the hell?"—but comply. They scrambled to their feet, bent over to accommodate her fierce grip, and lumbered along with her toward the doors.

Behind them, Red, Reynard, and Grycel glanced at each other and shook their heads. Women—those looks agreed—just did not understand.

But the bout was mostly over, and the threatening storm was sending down big fat drops of rain as warning. They shrugged and headed inside, too.

Steig paused to pick up Arthur's discarded shirt and looked thoughtful. "Did you see that ink on th' duke's shoulder?" he asked Grycel.

"Yeah. A tattoo," Grycel answered. "Never seen one like that."

Steig gave a half smile. "I have. It's tribal. And it's an honor."

Thunder rolled and the sky opened up to pour buckets down on Betancourt. The summer storm had the rough men collected in the Meriton Woods drenched and ill-tempered . . . glaring at each other and at the treacherous sky. Worse yet, *his lordship* hadn't arrived, and the longer they waited in the wet, the less chance they had to execute his plan successfully.

Their pitch-soaked torches were wet, the cloths in the necks of the kerosene bottles were waterlogged enough to boil for tea, and the chances of keeping a match alight in this downpour were nil. Nothing was going to burn tonight. They turned around and headed back to their cabin, only to meet his lordship's coach on the north edge of the estate.

The hire coach's wheels were stuck in mud and their employer was shouting threats at the coachman and footman as they tried to push it into a less boggy rut in the road. The appearance of his retreating gang was enough to put his lordship into a full fury.

Hanging back in the coach doorway to avoid the downpour, he ordered his minions to dismount and help the driver right the vehicle. Their moment of hesitation brought him to the edge of sanity. He produced a gun and fired . . . right above their heads, making their horses nervous.

In short order, several of the men dismounted and waded into the sucking mud to add their shoulders to the effort. His lordship felt the coach move and resumed his seat in the vehicle, failing to see the angry looks his hirelings exchanged.

He'd held out the promise of hard coin in payment, but so far, they'd had only bitter ale, watered whiskey, and his lordship's high-handed abuse. The farms he'd ordered them to raid had yielded next to nothing because he'd ordered them to leave the houses alone and the barns standing. He'd said he didn't intend to take over a devastated and empty estate.

All of that changed when he got kicked by that demon horse and lay hurt for a day or two. He took the beast off to Betancourt, and when he came back, he was angry and didn't seem to care anymore about leaving the place standing. He bought more kerosene and made plans to burn a path to the heart of the estate when he returned from London.

But his business in London took longer than expected. They had been ready for days and were tired of waiting.

Now that he was back, nature had thrown a wet blanket—literally—on their plans. Fortune didn't seem to be favoring his lordship's quest for control of Betancourt.

The men had grumbled before, but now they began to make plans of their own.

The great house shuddered and the window panes shook under ear-splitting peals of thunder. The servants lighted the gas lamps and looked anxiously at the windows while opening guest rooms and planning for a larger than expected dinner. As the thunder receded, leaving simple, steady rain in its wake, there was an air of relief about the house. It seemed as if the storm had broken the last of the tension among its inhabitants.

Elizabeth had shooed the children to their rooms for stories and naps, while the men finished their brandy in the study and trailed Daisy and Red to the breakfast room to check on the brothers. Sarah had already examined the combatants for cracked or broken ribs and had bound areas on each that seemed to qualify.

"You're a mess," Ash said with a grin that clearly pained him.

"You look like a half-gnawed bone," Arthur countered.

"Boys," Sarah said in a dangerous tone.

They looked at each other with similar glints of defiance.

"Who's the duke?" Arthur said, knowing he was treading on thin ice.

Ash laughed, holding his injured lip. "You are, you bastard."

"Damned right I am." Arthur laughed, too, then grabbed his ribs and groaned.

Sarah stared at the pair of them, shaking her head. *Men.*
When Daisy appeared, Sarah handed her sister a wet

cloth for cleaning Ashton's split lip and bloody knuckles, while she tended similar injuries on Arthur.

Red laid Ashton's coat and vest over the back of a nearby chair, while Steig handed Arthur's shirt to him and leaned close to study his tattoo.

"Nice work. Where'd you get it?" Steig asked, viewing from several directions the circular pattern that capped Arthur's shoulder.

"An island. The East Indies."

"What'd you do?" The big man planted his hands on his waist and looked like he wasn't moving until he heard the story.

"A bit of swimming." Arthur looked uncomfortable with the topic.

"Come on, guv. You don't get honored just fer swimmin'— not in a place where folk are all practically born in the water."

Sarah stepped back and narrowed her eyes. "What did you do? I think it's time you told that story, since it left such a distinctive mark on you."

Arthur shifted on his chair and glanced at his brother. Daisy abandoned tending her husband for a moment to see what they were talking about. Sarah didn't especially like the admiration Daisy showed for Arthur's tattoo . . . and possibly his muscular shoulders . . . and chest . . . and legs . . .

"I swam into some fish and pulled a kid to shore." Arthur shrugged. "Turned out, it was the chief's kid and he was grateful. They 'honored' me by pounding some ink into my skin." He paused and gestured to his tattoo in a dismissive way. "It's supposed to tell what I did, but . . . I can't read it."

Steig frowned. "What kind of fish?"

"Fish is fish." Arthur flexed his hands to see if they were still bleeding.

"Not to those folk," Steig persisted. "What kind of fish did you swim into?"

"I think I was drunk at the time," Arthur said, trying to steer away from the subject. "They make a fermented coconut drink that can really—"

"What kind of fish?" Sarah sat down on a chair facing him, with a look that was straight out of Elizabeth's interrogational repertoire.

Arthur studied her resolve, sighed, and gave up the answer.

"Sharks. It was a group of sharks."

Sarah sat back with widened eyes. Steig hooted a laugh and gave him a slap on the back that made him wince with pain.

"I heard tell, that mark alone will get ye into Heaven, no matter what yer sins. Congratulations, guv, yer a saint—guaranteed."

The look on Arthur's face was priceless: a combination of uncertainty, embarrassment, and relief. "I never talked about it," he said, rubbing his thighs as if they hurt. "I figured nobody would believe me."

"Well, it helps that Steig here vouched for ye," Red said with a grin. "But with what I've seen you do, I'd believe it."

"Me too," Sarah spoke up. When he looked at her she was smiling with a pride in her eyes that made him almost forget the aches in his body.

"Not only do you come back looking like a Greek god, you come back a certified hero—with a decoration for bravery inked into your skin," Ash declared with amazement. "I hope you'll put in a few more details when you tell that story to Little Red. I want him to hear all about his uncle's adventures."

There was a moment of congenial laughter.

"Stick around, Ash, and you may have your share of

tales to tell," Reynard said from his perch on a nearby sideboard.

"What do you mean?" Ash looked from his brother to Reynard and Red. Troubled looks gradually replaced their easy mood. "What's happened?"

"Betancourt's been struck by a gang of outlaws," Reynard said. "Several times. Thieving, harassing the farmers, and recently they've taken to using fire—they burned down the old mill."

"Our old mill? The one our great-great-great-grandfather built?"

"The very one," Arthur said, watching Ash's dismay. "And we believe they aren't finished. We've been working on plans to stop them."

Ashton focused on Arthur with dawning comprehension.

"There really *is* danger, then. I thought you were just poking my conscience."

"Finally," Arthur said with what looked like a wink, but might have been just a twitch of his swollen eye. "If I remember correctly, you were never one to miss out on a good fight."

Ashton tried to grin, but grabbed his cracked lip with a wince.

"These days I make it a practice to inform my wife before I bash someone senseless. . . most of the time." He looked at Daisy with what could only be called adoration. She rolled her eyes, and he looked back at Arthur. "Count me in, big brother."

Dinner that evening was a bit chaotic, since Daisy insisted on having the children at table with the adults. The servants regarded Little Red with a jaundiced eye when he insisted on sitting by his "Unca Art-tur" and pestered the duke with question after question that all began with the word *why*.

Arthur was the soul of patience and promised they'd find a pony among the riding stock for Little Red to practice his horsemanship. Elizabeth asked Daisy pointedly where the children's nanny was. According to Daisy, the woman was terrified of boats and water and after some discussion, they decided to leave her in New York and manage on their own. Westerners excelled at self-sufficiency, after all. Elizabeth tsk-tsked in disapproval but said nothing more.

Later, in the parlor, Ash and Daisy talked Arthur into telling a story or two of his travels to the boys, to all of them. After some thought, he talked of seeing herds of zebras and antelopes and elephants that filled the horizon in Africa . . . being chased by a rhinoceros . . . sleeping in trees to avoid being eaten . . . butterflies so big they looked like birds. The children were awed and begged for more.

When he obliged, Sarah found herself imagining him on the African plains, the wind blowing his hair, his face alight with the joy of discovery. She loved the music in his voice as he told of his experiences and she wished she had asked him more questions about his travels before now.

After Daisy's boys were ushered off to bed, he told one last story . . . of being abducted from his hotel and sold to a caliph in need of a man to read and write English. Unfortunately, while confined to the palace, he resorted to his old habit of walking walls to find some peace. One of the walls he chose happened to surround the caliph's harem. He was spotted, arrested, and thrown into a dungeon.

After three months he escaped with the help of a love-sick jailor who agreed to help him if he composed poems to a lady the jailor wished to court.

"Fortunately, I recalled a few poems from English literature's finest. The work I gave him, alas, was not original with me. In my defense I did have a pang of guilt over passing them off as mine. Literacy is a valuable skill in most parts of the world, but a dangerous knowledge to possess in a few."

Later that night, as Sarah was making her final rounds, she saw Daisy leave her room and move a bit too quietly down the west wing hallway. Concerned, she followed and was soon trailing her sister up two flights of stairs to a familiar door. As Daisy entered the attic, Sarah hung back, trying to calm her racing heart and think rationally about what was happening. But there was only one reason Daisy would be climbing into the attic on such a wet and inhospitable night.

After a few minutes, she entered the attic herself and paused to let her eyes adjust. The hatch that opened onto the roof was thrown back, admitting enough light for her to navigate to the steps. She crept up them, listening, and finally peered out the opening to locate the source of the voices.

Her stomach felt like it dropped to her knees.

Arthur stood silhouetted against the night sky holding Daisy's hand. Their words were mostly carried away on the breeze, but she caught snatches here and there. "Worried", "happiness", and "regret" came through clearly enough. He turned Daisy to point out landmarks to her, and the memory of him holding her in his arms, pointing out Betancourt's features the same way, was so sharp in Sarah that she gasped and clamped a hand over her mouth. Drawing back into the shadows, she closed her eyes for a moment. She couldn't resist one last peek before making her way back downstairs.

It was a mistake.

He was facing Daisy, taking her by the shoulders . . . leaning closer . . . It was a gentle, intimate moment, filled with such . . . oh, God . . . *regret*. She turned and felt her way to the door.

Later, she wasn't sure how she had gotten to her room. She must have flown down the stairs. When the door was locked behind her, she stood for a moment while her body decided how to react to such a devastating blow. But there was nothing, no rage, no ache of betrayal, no tears or trembling.

She felt utterly empty.

The fear she harbored had been given form and substance before her eyes. He really did love Daisy. And that meant that in every touch, every caress, every kiss between them, she had stood as proxy for her sister.

Daisy was his first love and the reason he left Betancourt to see the world. While he was too honorable to try to compromise his brother's wife, his heart was clearly hers.

Dearest Heaven. What was she to do? Leave Betancourt? Pretend she hadn't seen that tender moment and go on as if nothing had happened? Neither seemed possible, since both required more strength and courage than she possessed at that moment.

She had believed when he called her *precious*, that he meant it. She sank onto the bench at the foot of the bed. How could she have let herself fall again into the very situation that she came to Betancourt to escape? Giving her heart and hopes to a man who would only . . .

No.

Some newly grounded part of her raised a fierce objection. She wasn't the same bookish, impressionable young girl who mistook flattery for true regard. She had learned a great deal about people and purpose and reading the soul-traces visible in a person's eyes. She had taken her fate into her own hands and come to Betancourt to do something good with her life.

Her knowledge of Arthur and her own stubborn sense of

fairness refused to let her equate him with the self-absorbed young earl who had used her for his amusement. Arthur, she had to admit, was not driven by wealth or rank or status. He was not a man who treated people like pleasant trifles or disposable curiosities. She called up memory after memory, resurrected pleasures and confidences and feelings she had shared with him.

She was honest enough to reach past her own hurt to see the larger reality. His responses and words weren't false or faithless. He truly did enjoy her company and the pleasure they had shared . . . which only made it that much harder to deal with. How could she ever separate his true feelings for her from the specter of his lingering feelings for Daisy?

It was a long time before she succumbed to sleep that night, and her dreams were almost as disturbing as the heartfelt conflict she experienced awake. She rose the next morning feeling tired and unsettled. But by the time her nephews banged on her door, begging her to show them the puppies she had mentioned, she had regained most of her self-possession.

Daisy stood a few steps away, watching, and followed them as she took the boys by the hands and led them out to the stable to see Nellie and her puppies. Sarah didn't have much to say, except to caution the boys about handling Nellie's babies gently. Little Red and Wild Bill glowed with excitement at the sight of the curious, bright-eyed puppies climbing out of the box to greet them.

The boys tried to pick them up, but the puppies were already quick at escape and enjoyed running. Sarah found herself smiling and then laughing at their antics and looked up to find Daisy's eyes alight. It was hard, in the presence of all of that youthful joy and innocence, to hold on to hard feelings toward her sister. Being lovable was not something a body could control.

Clearly the puppies needed exercise, and at six weeks,

they didn't have to be carried out to the front lawn. Sarah led the parade and soon the boys were laughing and chasing the puppies all over an acre of grass still soggy from the previous day's storm. Mud and water flew.

"They're going to be filthy." Daisy crossed her arms, but with a smile. "Mama is probably glued to a window somewhere, having a heart attack."

"We have bathing rooms and hot water." Sarah came to stand by her sister. "Boys and puppies are both washable."

"Thank God." Daisy chuckled.

"I just wish harsh words were as easy to wash away," Sarah said.

Daisy turned her head to look at Sarah.

"He really didn't leave because of me." Daisy paused. "In fact, it was Arthur that convinced Ashton to marry me. Ash was determined to sacrifice his love for me so I could have what he thought I wanted. He knew I wanted to marry a duke and he knew why. You. And Frankie. And Cece. I was determined to make up for my mistakes and get you an entrance into society.

"The night that Arthur and Ash had it out . . . Uncle Red and I arrived just in time to hear Ash and Arthur each demanding that the other marry me. 'You marry her'— 'No, YOU marry her.' Talk about humiliating. Arthur made it clear he had places to go and discoveries to make . . . that he didn't want to marry . . . and certainly not me." She gave a wry laugh. "He knew I loved Ash and that Ash was being a splendidly selfless ass."

She turned to Sarah. "You were younger and I don't know how much you overheard—Mama was frantic to avoid gossip. But surely you remember how they looked on our wedding day. Black eyes, swollen lips, bruises everywhere. It was a pure scandal. Arthur, we learned that week, had a lot more gumption than anyone guessed. And a wicked right hook."

"Apparently, he still has," Sarah said, sensing the earnestness in Daisy's revelations. Why hadn't she listened to Uncle Red? "I'm sorry for blaming you and acting like an idiot about the fight. It wasn't your fault. I guess brothers have a different way of dealing with each other."

"Yes. We sisters are so much more civilized," Daisy said dryly.

Sarah opened her arms and Daisy walked into them. They hugged each other, and let the tension of the last day drain away. They didn't even notice when three big dogs joined the fun, racing the puppies and boys and tossing up mud and grass. It was only when Nero and Nellie and Lancelot came to jump on them to get them to play that they realized what a mess the dogs and boys had made.

Elizabeth met them later in the entry hall with towel-wielding servants and a glare that could have cut steel girders.

"You and your dirty animals!" she declared, staring at them and the muddy streaks, paw prints, and handprints on their skirts and faces.

Sarah looked at Daisy, whose Wild Bill was joyfully patting her on the face with hands caked with mud. Little Red stood between them wet and covered with mud—holding tightly a wet, dirty puppy that was streaming what everyone hoped was water onto the floor.

Daisy looked at Sarah, who was holding wet and mud-spattered Nero and long-haired Nellie back by the collars . . . while they shook vigorously. Drops of water and mud were flying all over the entry hall.

Sarah's eyes widened and she said out of the corner of her mouth, "Which one of us you think she's talkin' to?"

Chapter Twenty-Two

Evening was coming on—the sun had finally fought its way through the clouds to paint a glorious tapestry of color all over the western sky. Tea had been served earlier in the parlor and there was time before supper for a walk out to see the horses in the pasture. Ashton and Arthur led the way and Daisy, her boys, and Sarah followed. They stopped by the pasture fence and Sarah called the foals over for carrots the boys held, while Ashton and Daisy climbed the fence for a closer look at Dancer's progeny.

"They're beautiful!" Daisy called, approaching one black beauty that wore a halter. "Easy girl, easy. I'm your granddaddy's best human friend." Soon she was petting the young filly and running her hands over a perfect, near-Thoroughbred form.

"Twelve of them," Arthur said as he strode out to join her and Ash. "Twelve coal-black ones. Sarah says that Dancer's offspring breeds true."

"I've kept Dancer for riding, mostly—haven't ever used him for stud. He covered several of Betancourt's mares when we were here," Daisy said.

"I seem to recall," Arthur said with a wry grin.

Daisy looked at Ashton. "Maybe when we get home, we ought to find a few good mares and see what he produces."

The boys ran to their parents across the pasture, enjoying the freedom they were allowed. Sarah followed, making sure they didn't get too close to the horses and directing them around the occasional horse pile.

Daisy picked up Wild Bill and Ash picked up Little Red so they could pet the horse, while Arthur settled beside Sarah and put his arm around her.

She looked up at him and found him gazing at her with pleasure that was heart-melting. She smiled back and leaned a fraction of an inch closer to him, appreciating his heat and maleness with every part of her. Her heartbeat quickened and for a moment she thought she was hearing . . .

A bell? Arthur tore his gaze from hers and looked off across the pasture and trees, toward Betany.

"Is that a church bell?" Daisy asked.

"It can't be," Sarah said, listening. "It's ringing too fast . . . and a single tone." She had heard Betany's church bells each week for the last seven months. There were three bells in the tower, pulled in different sequences by practiced ringers. They always played in a melodic order . . . never just one bell and never so *frantic*. She grabbed Arthur's arm.

"Something is—"

"Wrong." He not only finished her thought, he interpreted it. "It's an alarm. I've never heard it rung before, but I remember hearing talk about it."

"Let's go," Ashton said, heading for the fence. "Back to the house."

Arthur grabbed Sarah's hand and they headed back. "Today is Saturday. Do they still hold market in Betany each week?"

"Yes," she answered, sharing his growing concern as they reached the fence and he helped her over. "Farmers and tradesmen set up stalls. It's a local market . . . mostly garden produce, leather goods, and soap made in farm kitchens. A tinsmith sets up, there's a hardware man to repair equipment, and sometimes a scissors grinder."

Arthur took Little Red out of Ash's arms so his brother could help Daisy across the fence. Meanwhile, the bell continued to ring frantically, joined by odd pops and bangs that, under other circumstances, might have been mistaken for Christmas crackers. Sarah froze, listening. She looked to Arthur, who met her gaze with his assessment.

"Gunfire."

A shiver went through her. There was trouble in the village. Bascom said the ruffians had caused problems there before, wrecking stalls and ruining market goods, breaking house and shop windows, terrorizing the villagers. If they had brought guns this time . . .

He handed Little Red back to Ash, and then turned to Sarah and pulled her into his arms for a moment.

"Get to the house and get your medical supplies ready." Regret filled his eyes . . . as if he had much to say and no time left to say it. "There may be injuries. I'll send for you when it's safe."

"No, you won't," she said with a stubborn tilt to her chin, "because I'm going with you."

"Sarah—"

"No arguments," she said, slipping out of his arms. "I'm going. If people are hurt, the sooner they get treatment, the better."

He grabbed her hand and pulled her to a halt. With a bittersweet smile, he gave her a short, fervent hug and then took off at a run.

By the time they reached the house, Arthur was issuing orders like a general. They blew through the front doors and shortly Red, Reynard, and Grycel were mobilized and heading for their assignments. Eddie and Old Harley started saddling horses and hitching up a wagon for the duchess. A stable boy ran to the cottages to round up men and bring them to the stables, where Arthur would meet them. Families of the workers were sent to the manor house as a precaution, and the servant hall, breakfast room, and dining room were soon overflowing with anxious women and excited children.

The men on the estate collected at the stables, as previously arranged. The strategy they had settled on—borrowed from the events in the American West—was simple: make the outlaws focus on a force of men confronting them, while a second force came in from behind. Arthur and Red would lead one contingent, Ash and Grycel would lead the other. Reynard, an expert marksman, would go with the local constables to the rooftops to deliver fire from above. Steig was assigned to the wagon, to keep Sarah safe and just possibly to keep her from doing something reckless.

Soon they were racing down the drive and turning toward Betany. Sarah and Steig brought up the rear with the wagon full of workers and medical supplies.

Sarah wished she had at least one of Uncle Red's guns. Steig was a reasonable substitute, but she determined there and then that she would purchase her own gun as soon as possible. As they neared the village, Steig slowed the wagon to watch the mounted party sweep down the lane ahead of them. Sarah gripped the edge of the seat with white hands, waiting for gunshots or worse.

They heard shouts and banging and the whinnying of anxious horses, then all went quiet.

"Let's go," she ordered, giving Steig a tap on the arm.

He slapped the reins, and moments later they rolled along the lane past the Iron Penny and into the center of the village. The small green was littered with broken stalls draped with ripped canvas. Goods and equipment had been dragged off into the lane that circled the green and it was clear that the glass in the few shop windows that faced the green had suffered another assault. Arthur and Red had dismounted and were moving among the stalls, checking on people and asking questions.

Sarah took a deep breath. It wasn't as bad as she expected. Steig pulled the wagon up to the damage and the men in the back jumped out to begin searching for injured. Soon Sarah had a number of patients, mostly with bruises, small cuts, and the occasional black eye or broken finger. The local constable, Officer Jolly, was among the injured and he told Arthur and Ash what happened while Sarah treated a gash on the side of his head.

A group of four men had come at the end of the market day, and they rode through the stalls wielding clubs. They bashed everything they could reach, laughing and clubbing anyone who tried to intervene. They harassed men and women alike and nearly trampled a few children. The vicar was present and ran to the church to sound the old alarm. Angered, one of the gang produced a gun and fired shots at the local shop windows. When Bascom arrived with his gun and fired at them, the wretches rode off, yelling that they would be back to finish the job.

"Did you recognize any of them?" Arthur asked Bascom, who shook his head.

"Never saw any of that lot before."

Arthur frowned. "Then they've brought in additional men."

Arthur, Ash, and the workers from Betancourt helped clear some of the shattered stalls and stack whatever goods remained intact so they could be retrieved. When all the patients had been treated, Arthur sought out Sarah and the rest of the Betancourt contingent.

"I don't get it," he said, looking around. "It looked bad at first, but in reality, there was more commotion than damage. Nothing was even taken."

Reynard leaned his rifle on the wagon wheel, annoyed that he hadn't gotten to shoot. "You think they could find a better way to get attention."

The others looked at him and then each other with realization dawning.

"It was a diversion," Arthur said, snapping straight. "Good God—and we fell for it."

"That means," Red said, looking at Reynard and Grycel, "they're—"

"Somewhere else." Sarah looked down the village lane toward Betancourt. Her knees went weak at the thought of what and who they had left behind.

"Mount up!" Arthur called, heading for the horses tied at the side of the green.

Steig helped Sarah into the wagon and she waved Betancourt's workers into the back. In moments they were passing the Iron Penny and giving the horses their head on the road to Betancourt's gates.

The lights in Betancourt's windows were a welcome and reassuring sight. All was quiet in the front court, the stable yard, and as far as they could see toward the barns. Dusk had settled and the eastern sky was mostly dark, but there still was enough light from the west to provide contrast to a billow of smoke rising to the north.

Ash spotted it first and grabbed Arthur's arm, pointing.

Arthur uttered a curse and called to the others. "It looks like—"

"Fire!" Red shouted, pointing to the northwest.

Arthur whirled and, sure enough, there was a second plume of smoke.

"Damn and double damn," he muttered, scowling, thinking fast.

A second later he began giving orders, splitting up their force into two groups and speaking to each. He issued cautions and set priorities: people first, animals second, houses and barns after that. If a structure was more than a quarter engulfed, let it go and concentrate on higher priorities. They could rebuild houses and barns; they couldn't replace lives.

Sarah watched him calling for shovels, buckets, and blankets, taking it all in hand. He stood with his feet planted, looking strong and confident and her heart seemed to swell in her chest. He was indeed born for this: leading, guiding, and protecting. He hadn't been able to stop this attack from happening, but he was determined to end it and see those responsible punished.

She was coming from the house with arms full of rolled bandages and wooden splints, when Arthur caught her.

"Where are you going?"

"With you," she said. "Where there's fire, there will be injuries."

"We need you here." He pointed to one fire, then another . . . then spotted something that made him run to the front steps of the house. Frustrated by his lack of view, he looked over his shoulder at the house and was soon climbing up a drain pipe.

"What are you doing?" Sarah called, running after him. "These drains are old—you'll get hurt!"

He stopped three-quarters of the way up and looked back over his shoulder. His gaze fixed on something to the direct west of Betancourt House. A moment later he scrambled down the pipe and landed heavily.

"A third fire just started," he told her. "It looks like Arnett's place . . . Thomas Wrenn's and now Elias Ender's. Each one closer to the heart of Betancourt." He took her by the shoulders, and she grasped his waist. "I have to go and help them, Sarah. But I need to know you're taking care of things here. And that you're safe."

He kissed her and then buried his face in her hair, inhaling its scent.

"Because I'm so precious?" she said with tears rising. It felt like he was saying goodbye.

When she looked up, his eyes seemed dark, almost haunted.

"Because I love you with all my heart."

Before she could respond, he turned away and headed for his horse.

"Steig is here to help you," he called to her from horseback. "Give him back the big knife that's in my desk. If there's trouble, send Eddie on a fast horse to Arnett's—that's where I'll start."

In a moment they were gone and an eerie quiet descended on the court and house. Daisy and the other women and children who had come out to say farewell to their husbands and fathers stood in silence, some wiping away tears. Sarah straightened and squared her shoulders. She had work to do.

"They're off and Godspeed to them," she called out. "Now let's get inside and do some planning of our own." She ushered them inside, then sought out Steig and led him to the study and the desk Arthur referenced.

When she opened the drawer and drew out a long, wickedly sharp blade, Steig's eyes widened and he began to smile.

"The duke wants you to have this," she said, handing it to him.

He held it, running his finger down the large blade, and nodded.

"He's a good man, your duke," he said.

She realized the knife being returned meant a great deal to him.

"He sure as hell is."

Elizabeth was astounded by the way the house was inundated by dairy maids, goose girls, mothers with small babies, and matrons with work-toughened hands and fierce eyes. But when she learned what was happening, she had to agree with Sarah that it was necessary.

Soon there were buckets of water in each main-floor room and blankets for wetting in case of a fire. Children were put under the goose girls' authority and set to practicing evacuating single file and running to the farthest edge of the front lawn. The servants checked windows, locked up valuables, and brought up stores from the cellar so Cook and her helpers could feed the group when the time came.

Sarah caught Old Edgar wheezing up the stairs with a pile of pristine folded shirts in his hands. "What is that, Edgar?"

"Shirts, ma'am."

"Whose shirts?"

"His Grace's."

She frowned, confused. "Where have they been all this time?"

"Butler's pantry, ma'am," he replied as though it were the most sensible thing in the world, "with the silver." And he trudged doggedly on up the steps to deliver them to the duke's chamber.

As the house settled into the night, Sarah headed for the roof to assess the state of the fires. Daisy followed her up the stairs and they stood side by side, watching the flickering glow of flames robbed of their menace by distance.

Daisy put an arm around Sarah's shoulders, giving her a squeeze.

"They'll be all right."

"I pray so. I'm not sure what I'd do if . . ." Sarah halted, unable to say it.

"I know," Daisy said. "I feel the same. Ash is the heart of my heart."

They stood together, praying that there would be no additional flashes of light or blooming spirals of smoke. Heaven only knew what the men were facing out there in the heat and terror of the night.

Arthur led his contingent into a maelstrom of fire and destruction. Arnett's place was the first farm set ablaze and the barns and sheds were roaring infernos, beyond help by the time they arrived. They must have fired the house last; it had just started to burn heavily.

He caught sight of a couple of men climbing out of a side window, carrying bags of loot. He shouted above the roar of the flames for Red and the others to look for the Arnetts, and spurred his horse after the two. He ran them down before they reached the horses stashed in the lea of a stone fence. They dodged his horse, but he jumped and landed on one before he could get away. The wretch smacked the ground hard beneath him, but scrambled to his feet as soon as Arthur did and swung the cloth bag he held like a weapon. The other man attacked from behind, knocking Arthur to the ground. Arthur rolled to dislodge the man, and was on his feet in a crouch in seconds. From their movements and clumsy blows, they were not skilled fighters; it was only a matter of time before they went down.

Then out came a knife. A pitiful four-inch weapon, but in the right hands even a small knife could do damage. Arthur pivoted and went after the unarmed outlaw first, parrying the man's hard, bony fists while landing quick, sharp punches. He had to move quickly to keep the other man in his sights as well. Then came a perfect opening for his potent uppercut and the first barn burner lay senseless on the ground.

Then he wheeled on the knife fighter and narrowly avoided being cut as the man swung furiously at him. They circled each other and Arthur used his feet, making contact with the second man's legs, but never hard enough to unbalance him. The arcs of the knife became wider and oddly predictable, betraying the man's inexperience. Every swing took his arm too far across his body and left him vulnerable for a valuable second or two. Arthur assessed his motion, then caught him with a punch before his backswing gained momentum. The man struggled to regain his balance while stabbing frantically at Arthur.

Seizing the opportunity, Arthur blocked a blow, ducked, and used the power in his legs to explode upward, catching the man's chin and snapping his head backward. The wretch and his knife went flying in different directions.

He dove at the man and landed on top of him. They wrestled, but after a few well-placed punches, his opponent went slack beneath him. Arthur was pulled up and away from his battered opponent.

"That's enough, son," Red declared, panting from having run after him. "He's done. You got 'im."

By the time the red drained from Arthur's vision, the wretches were bound hand and foot. Red told him the Arnetts had fled toward a neighboring farm and were found in a nearby hay field. They had helped Old Bec, Young Bec, and the children to reach Ralston's place, while Samuel returned with Red to make sure the fire didn't spread to his harvest-ready fields or nearby stands of cherry and walnut trees.

Sparks from popping timbers and collapsing rafters

blew into grass that was dry enough to catch fire. They grabbed blankets, wetted them, and ran to beat out the spreading flames. It was the better part of another hour before the fire had consumed most of the barn and outbuildings and settled into seething coals and red-centered blackened spikes. The men coughed and staggered off to an unburned patch of ground and collapsed.

"My whole life," Arnett said when he could speak without coughing. "They just burned my whole life." The enormity of it hit him and he swayed, looking like he might be sick. Then he spotted the two men who lay bound at the edge of his burning farm—the men responsible for destroying a lifetime's worth of work. With a cry that came out of the deep wound they had inflicted on him, he bolted up and rushed to vent his pain and fury on them. He got in several savage kicks before Arthur and Red managed to subdue and restrain him. They dragged him away and held him until he was calmer.

One of the Betancourt men approached, carrying two cloth bags, and set them down by Arnett's feet. "We found the things they took."

Arnett's shoulders drooped and he looked like there might be tears in his eyes. He looked inside one of the bags and drew out a silver plate that clearly meant something to him. He clutched it to his chest and when he looked up, Arthur saw the light from the man's burning house reflected in his eyes. "My ma . . . the last duchess give it to her before she died. For her service."

No one spoke for a few moments, respecting Arnett's grief.

"The others?" he asked, looking up. "They got away?"

"What others?" Arthur and Red exchanged looks.

"There was four of 'em. I swear it. An' the one what give orders to fire my barn and house . . . he was dressed like a fancy gent."

Chapter Twenty-Three

Betancourt House vibrated with tension as the female contingent of Betancourt tried to settle in for the night. The women spoke in quiet tones and tried to distract themselves with talk of stitchery, quilting, and preserving the harvest of their gardens. The children packed into the breakfast room grew restless in their unfamiliar surroundings.

Elizabeth recalled seeing some books in the library that she thought might have stories to divert the older children. Daisy helped her pick out a few books and they gathered half a dozen older children in the library for Elizabeth to read to them. Daisy and Sarah found some colored picture books for the younger ones, and Daisy organized the mothers to hold their young children while she showed them the books and told them Wild West stories for each letter of the alphabet.

For the few children who could not sit still for stories, Sarah found some dominoes and encouraged them to build things on a tabletop. A couple of enterprising older girls located some slates and chalk for other children to draw.

Through it all, riding Sarah's thoughts were the memories of the mill fire and the dangers Arthur and Red and the others would face in battling both flames and outlaws.

She paced and checked again and again with the servants about the placement of the rain barrels in strategic locations around the exterior of the house and the ladders they had stationed near windows to help with evacuation in case the doors were blocked.

The expectation of danger was as exhausting as the danger itself.

She fetched a shawl and stepped outside for a breath of fresh air. However, truly fresh air was in short supply. A light wind had carried the smoke from three different fires to Betancourt's doors. As she stood on the steps, the breeze carried more than noxious smoke, it brought the sounds of anxious and frightened horses. Alarmed, she headed for the stable. Horses had sensitive noses, and apparently closing and latching the stable doors wasn't enough to keep the smoke from them.

She found the center door standing open and stepped into the center alley. Nellie's box was empty and so was the chair where Old Harley passed many evenings with a concertina he used to serenade his charges. The smell of smoke was almost worse in the stable than outside. She quickly realized why: The big doors that opened onto the pasture stood wide open. The sound of horses whinnying and thudding against the sides of their stalls echoed down both wings of the stable. Where was Harley? Eddie knew better than to leave these doors open—she had told him they needed to keep them closed and he said he'd already latched them. Why were they open? And where was Eddie?

A bad feeling crept up her spine as she turned toward Fancy's stall and heard him neighing frantically and pawing the floor. She began to run.

"There you are." George Graham stood just inside Fancy's stall, crop in hand, with an icy smile on his face. Behind him, Fancy had backed into the far corner of the stall with his ears back and his eyes wide and anxious. "I wondered how long it would take for you to come and check on your beloved horse."

"What are you doing here?" Sarah said, instinctively keeping her voice calm and level.

"I thought perhaps I should check on Betancourt's precious horseflesh. It cannot have escaped your notice that these animals are worth a pretty penny." His eyes were dark and strangely emotionless. They sent a chill down her spine. "And you may have noticed—there are bad things happening on Betancourt tonight. It would be a shame for your stables to catch fire, trapping these fine animals . . . destroying a significant part of Betancourt's burgeoning wealth."

"Where is Eddie?" She looked around, knowing now that his absence was no accident. "What's happened to him?"

"Oh, he's around here somewhere," George said, glancing around with a hint of amusement that made her wonder if he'd been drinking.

"And my dogs . . . where are they?" She only now realized that Nero and Nellie—the puppies—were missing.

"They bark, you know, and we can't have that tonight. A couple of fellows who came with me are not overly fond of dogs. In fact, they've met your big dog before. They're renewing their acquaintance as we speak."

"What have you done with him?" Sarah was losing the battle to control her reaction. He had brought men with him and they'd done something with Eddie and Harley—now had Nero and Nellie. God knew what they would do to dogs that had gotten them into trouble before.

"I came to protect you, dear Sarah." His face warmed a degree or two. "I feel a responsibility to make certain that the vicious band of outlaws plaguing Betancourt doesn't harm you or the stately heart of my family seat. At least that is my plan."

"Protecting Betancourt?"

"Of course. That's been my plan all along . . . becoming the conservator—the guardian, if you will—of Betancourt. But I learned three days ago that my petition to the courts has been rejected. They will not even give my evidence and arguments a hearing since word has spread of the duke's 'resurrection.'" He stepped out of the stall to confront her. "Most unfair. What has happened to English jurisprudence, that a gentleman of consequence cannot even get a hearing before a magistrate?"

"You wanted to be appointed conservator of Betancourt?" she said, seeing pieces of the puzzle dropping into place. "Like your father was."

"Not like my father." A flicker of anger appeared in his otherwise cool demeanor. "He was greedy and foolish and he paid for it—I paid for it. He drained what he could from Betancourt, but gambled and frittered it away. At the end, he had nothing to show for his years of legal larceny." He advanced on Sarah with a new light in his eyes.

"I, however, know that the secret to wealth is to create, not destroy. I will be a true guardian to Betancourt. With my care it will flourish and provide wealth for generations yet unborn."

"*Your* generations," she charged, wishing she could take it back as soon as she said it.

He only smiled.

"That goes without saying. With the one duke dead and the other never present, someone had to take over Betancourt. That someone should have been me." His expression changed so quickly, becoming a slate of anger, that she took an involuntary step backward. "But then you came along . . . barged in to the estate and started changing things, improving things. How was I to make a case for neglect when you were so damnably competent and attentive to Betancourt's needs?"

"You honestly thought you could take over Betancourt? But you'd never be the duke . . . there were already successors . . . Ashton's children."

"Who needs a title, sweetest, when you hold the reins and purse strings? My old father had that part right. He raised a duke who knew nothing and did nothing. And I could have done the same . . . I still can." He backed her against the opposite stall. "Fires are so capricious in their destructive force. It wouldn't be the first time a pair of brothers were orphaned at a tender age and given into the hands of an attentive relative."

"You're mad." Her heart pounded with anger spawned by fear. He knew about Daisy's boys! Those fires were meant to draw Arthur and Ash out into the countryside and into danger—to make their deaths a plausible accident. "You intend to kill Arthur and Ashton?"

He pulled out his watch and smiled at what it said.

"It's probably already done. The question, my luscious little chatelaine, is whether you are smart enough to join me and become a mother to your two orphaned nephews."

"They're not orphans. They have their mother, Daisy."

"Not for long."

Dear God, was he so warped and inhuman that he thought that she might join his quest for power over the dead bodies of her family? Never in her life had she felt such revulsion, such gathering hatred toward another human being. She had to do something—had to stop him somehow.

He read the change in her face.

"No? A pity. You're a tempting slip of muslin." He reached into his coat and pulled out a pistol. As he cocked it, he leveled it at her face. "We would have made splendid partners."

"Nah," came a deep voice from down the alley. "She's not yer type, yer lordship."

Sarah went weak with relief at the sight of Steig standing a few yards away, his back against a box stall. His arms were at his sides and his feet were crossed at the ankles.

"You." George glared at him. "Where the hell have you been? I've been waiting for you—I have a special job for you tonight."

"I work here, you know," Steig said, pulling out the large knife she had returned to him only hours before and using its tip to clean his fingernails. "Have to make it look like I'm the duke's man." He gave a dark chuckle. "When I really am . . ."

"Mine," George claimed, lowering the gun a bit. "Well, here is your next job." He turned to her with chilling anticipation.

Sarah looked between them, stunned, unable to credit that they knew each other . . . were working together. The treachery of it gripped her throat, denying her a protest. Steig . . . their Steig . . . was working with George?

"Miss Bumgarten won't be joining us in our new regime," George continued with elegant malice. "Unfortunately, that means she will have to suffer the same fate as her precious horse." He threw back the tarp on a wooden case of bottles that had rags stuffed in their necks. A faint odor of kerosene wafted out.

Sarah gasped, realizing what he planned. "No . . . nooooo . . ."

"You're a cold man, yer lordship," Steig said, shaking his head.

"A clever man," George said, grabbing her as she tried to dodge him and run for the door. "No, no, *duchess*." He smirked as she twisted in his grip, and when she freed herself unexpectedly, he lashed out with the pistol and struck her viciously.

She staggered and fell back against the stall, holding the side of her head. Her vision swam and she could barely get her breath. She tried to force herself upright, determined not to cower, but sank to her knees instead. A strange dark cloud started to close around her consciousness. She looked at her hand, having the feeling that it belonged to somebody else.

"You should have shown me more respect," George snarled. "But you liked playing the almighty duchess too much. When that muscle-bound buffoon appeared, you decided he was a better *get* than a mere baron."

As George raised his pistol to strike her again, there was an odd whoosh of air above her head. The gun clattered on the concrete floor and a slow-building cry of pain and disbelief welled out of George. She looked up, sensing Steig rushing toward them and saw George holding his bleeding arm and gasping in horror. The big knife lay across the alley on the floor.

"I may not be the duke's man," Steig said with disgust, "but I'm sure as hell not yours." He stooped beside Sarah, who shrank from him until the sense of what he said got through to her. "I'm the duchess's man."

"Stupid, double-dealing bastard! You'll pay for this!" George snarled, cradling his damaged arm and staggering backward toward the stable doors. "You too, you worthless whore! I'll see you dead this night or die trying." Then he turned and ran.

Steig pulled her to her feet and looked at her head, growling at what he saw. "Gotta get you someplace safe." He picked her up in his arms and she was too busy fighting down a wave of nausea to resist.

He carried her out into the night as she sank into darkness.

* * *

George stumbled and cursed and wrapped his arm in his handkerchief, cursing even more when the handkerchief soon was soaked with blood, too. He headed for the row of cottages behind Betancourt's barns that he had designated as the meeting place for his men. If they had finished their task as human torches, there would be twelve of them . . . an unholy discipleship of destruction that George had shaped into a force ready to execute his orders without question. The night called for men with no morals or misgivings to trouble their consciences.

He spotted the group of men in shirtsleeves well before he reached the cottages. He halted, scowling, and thrust his wounded arm behind him. There could be no sign of weakness in the leader of this pack of wild dogs.

He planted himself in the middle of the path and knew they saw him. That brute, Shackleton, was in front, stalking hard and fast, his fists clenched around a massive cudgel. They approached in a phalanx bristling with weapons, and they showed no sign of stopping. What the bloody hell was going on?

"Where the hell is the kerosene?" he demanded with a ferocity that had always brought them to heel. But they came on.

"Don' know, don' care," Shackleton said, slowing only slightly as he passed. The others separated to flow around George and then closed ranks again as soon as they were past. Furious at the slight to his leadership, he charged after them and grabbed Shackleton by the back of the shirt, dragging the man to a halt.

"What the hell do you think you're doing?" he snarled. "We have to have that kerosene. Barns and stables won't burn without it, you idiot."

Shackleton's soulless gaze settled on his bloody arm and he could see pleasure dawning in the man's bloated face. "There'll be time for burnin' after we're done."

"Done with what?" The pain in his arm fueled his fury. "You there—Gil, Mace—go to the stable and get the crate I left there." They looked to Shackleton and then back at him, but didn't move. "Are you deaf?" He smacked Mace across the mouth so hard that his hand went numb.

"We got us a new plan," Shackleton said with chilling malice. "We're gonna get paid." He pointed with his cudgel at the great house. "An' that's our paymaster's strongbox."

Their intention was suddenly clear. They intended to breach the house and loot it. The animals were going to despoil his future home!

"Imbeciles. You have to stick to the plan—you set the fires and when they go running to deal with the fires, I go in and grab the brats. That's all I want—those boys. The rest—the horses, the women—they're yours. Take them, kill them—I don't care. But you will not loot my house."

"Your house?" Shackleton gave a nasty laugh. "We'll do what we damned well want. And what we want is everything in that fancy house." Shackleton gave him a shove that nearly sent him sprawling in the dirt. He caught himself and drew himself up squarely.

"How dare you?" If he'd had his gun, the brute would be dead.

"We dare because we've got these." Shackleton brandished his club and the others roared agreement and raised their weapons.

George rushed through them to the front doors of Betancourt, desperate to keep them from stealing him blind. He planted his back against the doors, but they shoved him aside as if he were nothing. That wretched Mace gave him a shove that sent him flying down the front steps. He found himself on his butt in the gravel, dizzy, with his heart pounding strangely. As he struggled to his feet he realized his fine coat and trousers were both red with blood. The fools would ruin everything he had worked for. There was still time—but he would have to do it himself. Damn Steig for turning on him! He staggered back toward the stable once more, just as the women began to scream.

Arthur was never so glad to see his brother as when they met at Elias Ender's burning farm. Ashton's contingent had arrived before him, and after half an hour of fighting to contain the blaze, were sweaty and tired and spoiling for a fight. But, as they soon learned, there was no one to battle. The bastards had ransacked Ender's modest house, set the place ablaze, and absconded before they arrived.

"You didn't catch anyone?" Arthur asked, wiping sweat and soot from his brow.

Ash shook his head. "At Wrenn's place they were gone by the time we got there. The same here." He growled. "I just want to get my hands on one of them."

"We caught two stragglers at Arnett's farm, but they don't seem to know much. New hires, apparently." Arthur looked around and spotted the aging Elias holding his sobbing wife, Emma. "Why would they bother with this? They can't have gotten much of value. It was just . . . a . . ."

"Distraction," Reynard declared, meeting Arthur's eyes.

"Damn it." Arthur turned away grinding his teeth. "A second time!" As he turned back, his stomach knotted and he could see Ash, Red, and Reynard reaching the same conclusion: George's goal was Betancourt itself.

He selected a couple of local men to stay with Elias and Emma, then ordered everyone else to mount up. Soon they were riding hellbent for Betancourt House.

The sight of the barns, stables, and house still intact was a relief as they approached on the lane that ran through the heart of the estate. But as they neared, screams and crashes coming from the house made them spur the horses and draw weapons. They abandoned their mounts to rush the front doors and found the entry hall in chaos.

The hall table was overturned and the vases that always held the season's flowers lay in shards on the marble floor. The sound of thumping and cries of pain came from the parlor and they rushed in to find Elizabeth and two dairy maids with fireplace tools whacking away at two men protesting and trying to scuttle out of reach on the floor. Elizabeth's hair was hanging, her dress was torn and her face was flushed with fury.

"Don't you dare move!" she snarled at the men, holding a poker poised for another strike.

"What the hell, Lizzie?" Red rushed to her and she glowered at him.

"How dare they come into this house and threaten my family and our people?" she declared, simmering. One of the gang held out his hand, toward Red, begging him to intervene.

"She's crazy! Don't let her kill us!"

Red smiled with wicked glee. "Give 'im another one, Lizzie. Don't think he's learned his lesson yet."

Elizabeth gave him a whack on the leg that set him howling.

"Where's Daisy?" Ash asked.

"Upstairs with the boys, I think." She was practically panting. "These animals are all over the house—mangy dogs!"

Ash took off and Red drew his guns and followed, drawn by the combined yells of angry women and hard-pressed men. In the dining room, chairs were overturned, the chandelier was hanging askew, and dishes were shattered all over the floor. One portly matron was sitting on her attacker, rearranging his face with powerful punches while he tried in vain to seize her hands or roll her off his chest. Another invader was writhing on the floor and covering his head from blows from a cudgel he had once carried. Battle cries, the banging of metal pots, and the crash of crockery wafted up from the kitchen, indicating Cook was stoutly defending her domain. Everywhere they looked, Betancourt's women were defending themselves, their children, and the great house from the heathen invaders.

In the library, books had been ripped from the shelves and the furniture had been overturned during a search for valuables. Several children hid behind curtains and in corners while a robust matron kept a heavy foot on an invader's neck while flailing him with a rug beater, daring him to move.

The only place they found invaders still upright and dangerous was the study. Led by a big muscular brute, a group of three was ransacking the desk, cabinets, and shelves, looking for valuables. Papers and folios were strewn everywhere—paintings had been wrenched off the walls and tossed aside.

Arthur peered quietly around the door for a moment, zeroing in on the ringleader. Then he charged the man and Reynard and Grycel went after the other two. Arthur grappled and wrestled and finally managed a throat punch that sent the brute to his knees, where a knee to the face snapped his head back and finished it.

"Where is he?" he demanded, shaking the thug by the shirt.

"Who?" The man was only half conscious, but half should do.

"George Graham—your employer."

"In . . . hell . . . I hope . . ." With that, his mind slid out of Arthur's reach.

They dragged the threesome into the center hall and Red volunteered to keep watch—with a gun in each hand.

Everywhere they went the women were subduing their attackers with a vengeance unique to mothers protecting their homes. Fireplace pokers, bed warmers, rug beaters, ladles, bread paddles, not to mention a host of kitchen knives . . . who knew there were so many potential weapons in a great house? The men stood watching in awe and no small bit of discomfort. After all, they were supposed to be the rescuers. They had come prepared to fight for their wives and families and found their rescue . . . not needed.

Ashton came to the top of the stairs and called for help. When Arthur and Reynard bounded up the stairs they found four men sprawled in the upstairs hallway, two of whom were bleeding from head wounds. Daisy was hefting an iron poker and dancing around like a mad woman. "Give me another one! Let 'em just try touching my babies!" She wanted a few more attackers to bash. Ash looked bewildered.

"This wasn't all her," he said, eyeing Daisy and then the battered men on the floor. "Mazie and Deidre had a hand in it, too."

"Wouldn' let nothin' happen to Yer Grace's rooms," Mazie said to Arthur with a big smile, patting the handle of a smashed bed warmer.

"Where's Sarah?" Arthur rushed to her room to look and came back with a scowl. "Have you seen her?"

That made Daisy calm a bit. "No." She frowned, thinking. "I saw her take a shawl and step out for a bit of air. It was kind of crowded in the house and a bit crazy . . . even before these fools charged in."

"I'll look for her," Arthur said, knowing Sarah's penchant for being in the middle of the action and thinking she was probably somewhere standing over a vanquished foe like an Amazon warrior. "She's here somewhere."

They dragged the invaders down the steps and began

to search the rest of the guest rooms. Over the next quarter hour, they collected the gang members from all over the house and brought them to the entry hall. Cook provided roasting twine to bind their hands. When they were trussed up like Christmas geese, and counted, there were ten of them . . . none of whom answered to the name George Graham.

Arthur and Reynard questioned the men and learned that "his lordship" had indeed been present, but he didn't join their raid on the house. He insisted on burning some barns instead.

Chapter Twenty-Four

S arah awoke slowly with a crashing pain in the left side of her head. She couldn't make sense of her location at first, or of the fact that she couldn't move. It was dark and something was wrapped around her. She blinked to clear her vision and realized she was in a bed—a very large and comfortable bed. She turned her head and recognized the smell of the linen—Arthur. She was in Arthur's bed? How did she get here?

"Miss Sarah?" It was housemaid Dolly's voice. "Are you all right?"

She clutched her throbbing head and tried to think. George. The stable. Steig. It was a jumble in her head, but something drove her to fight her way out of her cocoon. There was chaos outside in the hall . . . voices and thumping and shrieks of rage.

"Careful, miss. Ye had a bad knock to the head." Dolly was sitting in the stuffed chair by the bed and rose to wet a cloth and dab her face.

"What's going on?" she managed to say, wishing she had some headache powders.

"Those blasted outlaws—they charged in lookin' fer spoils—that's what they said. Started pushing Miz Elizabeth an' others around. She picked up a poker and let one have it. Then all hell—heck broke loose."

"Mama? Hit somebody with a poker?" The knock on the head must have scrambled their brains. She couldn't imagine . . .

She slid off the bed and Dolly was quick to support her. There were men's voices outside and more thumping, like something being dragged down the stairs. Dolly helped her to the bathing room, where she splashed water on her face and examined her head wound in the mirror. There had been some bleeding, but at least none of the blood was on her clothes. The longer she was upright, the more secure she felt on her feet.

"So, who is fighting out there?"

Dolly shrugged. "I been in here with you ever since Steig brought you in. He said he needed you somewhere safe and couldn't think of a safer place for the duchess than the duke's bed."

She might have chuckled if her head hadn't hurt so much.

There were more voices outside the duke's door. Was that Daisy? Then a faraway bell rang and it took her a minute to realize it was the alarm they had established for "fire."

George had kerosene—he was burning things!

Her first thought was the stables—the horses—Fancy!

She stepped into her boots and pulled them on, against Dolly's advice. Moments later, she was out on the balcony overlooking the hall. There were a dozen or so men trussed up like turkeys on the hall floor. Several women, including her mother and Daisy, stood over them with weapons poised. Daisy looked up at her as she came down the stairs.

"Where have you been? Arthur was looking for you." She paused at the look on Sarah's face and came toward her.

"What's burning?" Sarah asked. "I heard the bell."

"Someone spotted a fire at one of the barns and the men took off."

Sarah kept walking and was soon on the steps, staring in growing horror at tendrils of smoke curling out of the stables.

"The horses!" She took off running. With every step she battled back the pounding that she feared was a sign of something worse than a mere headache. She refused to think about herself as she pulled open the stable door and was hit with a blast of hot, smoky air and the cries of panicking horses. Galvanized, she ran down the alley and stopped dead at the sight of George Graham entering Fancy's stall with something in his hand. Her Fancy screamed with fear or possibly rage.

"Get out of there!" she cried, rushing forward, coughing in the smoke. Farther down the alley she spotted flames.

"Bastard!" George was unsteady on his feet, but lurched toward Fancy, swinging his riding crop wildly. "You'll pay for what you did to me."

"George, stop!" she cried, watching Fancy begin to jump and rear. His eyes were wide and panicked; she had to get him out of there. She looked around for something to defend Fancy and herself with. Down the way she spotted George's gun on the floor, wedged against a stall, and rushed for it.

When she turned back George was lashing Fancy with his crop and she cocked the gun, praying it was still loaded and functional. Would she really shoot George?

"I said stop!" Every breath tested her resolve. "I'll shoot!"

George turned on her and he looked pale and gaunt—his clothes were bloody down his right side and she realized he was wielding the crop with his left hand.

"You!" he snarled, though with less force than she would have expected. He had lost a lot of blood, was limping, and his right arm was dangling uselessly. "I'm gonna kill your horse—kill it and leave it to burn!" His eyes were black, bottomless pits. "Maybeee . . . I'll kill you first!"

He came at her with his crop raised and she fired the gun, aiming for his shoulder. He staggered backward—right into Fancy's path. The horse reared and struck with his hooves.

George gave a cry of panic and pain as Fancy came down with his hooves again and he was knocked to the floor. Even in the chaos, Sarah heard bones crunch as Fancy reared and pounded him again. With a final gurgle, George lay still.

Sarah hung onto the open stall door and coughed. Her head was reeling, she wanted nothing more than to escape and breathe fresh air. But she had come to rescue Fancy and the others and couldn't quit now. She stumbled forward and grabbed Fancy's halter, pulling him out of the stall and giving his rump a slap that sent him running for the open door.

She turned back, drawn by the cries of horses and foals panicked by the smoke. Ripping a piece from her petticoat, she tied it over her nose and mouth, and pulled herself along the stalls, opening one door after another, leading the horses down the alley toward fresh air and safety.

Smoke now filled much of the stable and flames were roaring in the cross alley and tack room. Shielding her face with her arm, she bent low and ran past the searing flames to the other wing. There were more horses to release . . . more flames and smoke. Her lungs felt raw and she was growing dizzy as she staggered to the door at the end of that alley and pounded and kicked it until it opened. When she turned she spotted Nero and Nellie lying near the door. She knelt and shook Nero, yelling to him until he roused. She pointed to the door and he rose shakily and staggered toward the fresh air. She spent a moment trying to rouse Nellie, but had to go back for the horses.

She led the frantic horses through the smoke, guided by the floor alone. She was flagging by the time she got to the last stall . . . where she found Eddie and Harley slumped against the wall.

Choked with panic as much as smoke, she called to Eddie and Harley, but they were too groggy to understand. She fell to her knees, shaking them, trying to get them to wake up. It was useless. Then she crawled and dragged herself outside the stall, hoping to summon help. Nero and Nellie were both gone and she couldn't send them for help. Already on her knees, she collapsed, feeling darkness overtaking her again. If only she could have one more good breath . . . one more glimpse of Arthur's face . . .

Arthur carried her out of the burning stables and laid her on the ground outside. Frantically, he listened for her heartbeat and tried to rouse her. She was alive, but unconscious and her breathing was tortured. Her face was red but didn't look burned. She looked like she'd been through hell itself.

He carried her into the house and up the stairs—straight into his own chambers. He was barely aware of the women crowding into the room, of Daisy and Elizabeth, Dolly and Mazie and even Cook offering to help. He soon had basins of cool water, toweling, and Sarah's own medicine chest at his disposal.

No one objected when he rolled her onto her side and worked the fastenings of her dress; in fact, Daisy quickly realized what he intended and began to help.

"She needs to breathe," Arthur said, ripping her corset laces.

He tried to rouse her to give her water, but she didn't respond. He sat on the edge of the bed beside her, feeling as if life was draining out of him.

"Come on, Sarah, breathe. Fight for breath," he said, praying she somehow heard him. "You've got too much to live for to quit on us now. We need you." His voice dropped to an emotional whisper. "I need you."

For the first time in years, he was truly frightened. He focused on bathing her face and exposed skin and stepped back to let Daisy and Elizabeth remove her clothes and replace them with a light nightgown. He looked over her medicines, but there was nothing in them to treat damage to the lungs. He asked for weak tea and lemon water to give her whenever she roused and bathed her face to cool her, desperate to do something more.

The constables brought barred wagons to haul away the prisoners and the house was gradually righted. Betancourt's families were reunited and returned to their homes. One barn had suffered significant damage before they could put out the flames, and the stables were a total loss. It seemed George was most intent on doing damage that carried an emotional toll for Sarah and Arthur . . . which meant destroying the stables with their most promising horses still inside. George, they discovered, had met his end with little blood in his body, a hole in his shoulder, and broken bones inflicted by the very horse he had tried to burn.

They sent a telegram to Sir William Drexel, detailing Sarah's plight and George's demise, asking for Sir William to notify his next of kin.

The house grew strangely quiet as Arthur, Elizabeth, and Daisy kept a vigil by Sarah's bed. No one felt like talking. Red, Ash, and Reynard tiptoed into the room to see Sarah, and Red's eyes filled with tears as he stroked her hair. Grycel and Steig stayed by the door, watching, their faces downcast and big shoulders slumped under the weight of worry.

After Steig brought Sarah to the duke's bed and set Dolly to watch over her, he had gone out to the barns to find George and stop him from setting fires. He managed to stop all but one fire by grabbing an axe and chopping away boards in the path of the flames. Grycel and Reynard joined him and took over to evacuate animals when word came that Sarah had been trapped in the burning stables. Nero had staggered out and located Arthur, who followed the dog back to the little-used far door of the stable. There he discovered Sarah, Eddie, and Harley. Steig arrived in time to carry Old Harley and Eddie to safety and then battled through the smoke and flames to find Nellie's puppies. They had crawled into an overturned tack chest that had protected them long enough for them to be discovered. He worked over the little dogs to bring them around, and all but two of them survived . . . including Steig's own puppy.

Arthur sat by Sarah the entire next day and night, stroking her hand, moistening her lips, offering her water and weak tea whenever she stirred. He talked to her, telling her stories he had learned in his travels and promising her he would take her to some of his favorite places . . . when she recovered. By the second morning, the wheezing in her chest seemed to lessen and she rested better, but they still had a long way to go.

The following morning, the pony trap from the rail station came jostling up the drive and Sir William and the driver rushed inside, struggling to carry a good-sized crate.

They insisted on taking it straight up to Sarah, and when they began to unpack the thing, there were glass bottles and dials and tubes that Sir William told them would produce oxygen.

Sir William had clients in the medical field who used oxygen therapy for their patients with lung deficiencies. When he received their telegram he contacted one of the doctors straightaway and arranged to bring some of their oxygen equipment to her.

But he had trouble understanding the instructions. Arthur took the paper, read the diagram, and before long had the apparatus assembled and working. He tried it on himself first and was surprised by the fresh spurt of energy it gave him. He held the tubing to Sarah's nose and cajoled and entreated her to breathe deeply.

As they watched, her color seemed to improve and she seemed to draw deeper, hungrier breaths. After the treatment, Arthur threw his arms around Sir William and for the first time in two days felt a spark of hope.

But it was another full day and several additional oxygen treatments later that she finally showed signs of rousing. Arthur was still by her bedside that evening when her eyes began to flutter.

"Sarah . . . precious . . . love . . . wake up." He groaned, afraid to hope. "God, please wake her up . . . please." He called to her, holding her hands and then stroking her face.

The urgent tenderness of his touch and the emotion of his voice finally penetrated the darkness that engulfed her and she began to struggle toward consciousness. She was aware of discomfort—her chest hurt and her head felt like it was in a vise. It would be so easy to sink back into that comforting darkness, but Arthur was calling her and she was desperate to respond.

She tried to open her eyes but they were so heavy, and when she tried to speak, she began coughing so hard it hurt her entire body. She tried to turn, and someone helped her roll to her side and thumped her on the back. She opened her eyes to the sight of Arthur's frantic face near hers.

"It . . . hurts . . . to breathe," she said, surprised by how raspy her voice was. It hurt to talk, too. She reached out to touch him, but her arm fell short. It looked like tears were rolling down his face when he grabbed her hand, kissed it and pressed it against his face. Arthur was crying?

She heard other voices and was given a tube and told to inhale as deeply as she could. It hurt to inhale but she did her best, and moments later she did feel better. When they gave her the tube later, she understood what they were saying, took it between her lips, and breathed in deeply. Oxygen, they said—they were giving her oxygen. It made sense, even though she had no idea how they had worked such a miracle for her.

Another day passed before she was fully alert and able to sit up. She had a million questions.

"Nero and Nellie? Eddie and Harley?" she rasped out. "Fancy and the other horses—oh, the puppies! Where are the puppies?"

"Steig found the puppies and brought them out," he told her, smiling at her concern for her animals. "Nero got to be a hero—*again*. He managed to find me and barked until I followed and found you. Eddie and Harley are lodging upstairs while they recover—getting the best treatment of their lives. We only lost a handful of animals—though the main barn is heavily damaged."

She took a deep breath that made her cough. Arthur plumped her pillows, hoisted her up against them, and then got her a drink of water.

"I'm in your bed?" she asked as she spotted her

mother settling a tray on the bedside table. "And Mama allowed it?"

"It was the nearest bed. Plus, you've had quite a few visitors; we couldn't get them all in any other room. And there is this equipment William brought—this oxygen apparatus."

"You need nourishment." Elizabeth elbowed Arthur aside to sit on the bed with a bowl of soup. She proceeded to spoon the broth into Sarah, who felt a bit ridiculous being fed like a baby bird.

"Here, give it to me," she said, taking the bowl and drinking it down.

"Really, Sarah." Elizabeth was aghast.

"I think I need some real food," she said hoarsely, looking past her mother to Arthur. "A slab of beef, some potatoes . . . and cake . . . or a trifle . . . Oooh, some raspberry trifle . . ." She practically melted at the thought of it.

The longing in her face convinced Arthur. He laughed.

"Whatever you want, sweetheart."

"You can't eat such things, your system is too delicate." Elizabeth glowered at the empty bowl in her hands. "You need something soft and bland to—"

"My system's about as delicate as a bronc rider's," she said, frowning back at her mother. "I just shot a man, rescued horses from a burning stable, and survived nearly being burned alive. I don't think some pudding and cream and raspberry preserves are going to do me any harm."

Elizabeth pulled her chin back and blinked.

Arthur laughed even harder and sent Mazie running to the kitchen to tell Cook to find some raspberries and start the cake and pudding *fast*.

That evening Sarah had fresh raspberry trifle for dinner, which she shared with Little Red and Wild Bill, who came

o visit her. Wild Bill brought a picture book with him and
limbed up beside her to "read" her a story. It was quite
maginative . . . full of cowboys and big boats and baby
logs . . . also known as puppies, he informed her. Little
Red listened as long as he could bear it, then snatched the
ook to read the "real words," surprising his mother, his
grandmother, and his uncle Arthur.

Sarah laughed until she had a coughing fit, and the
hildren were ushered out so she could have an oxygen
reatment.

"Thank God," Arthur said as she inhaled, exhaled, and
ought the urge to cough. "I thought they'd never leave.
You realize, this is the first time we've been alone for . . .
lays and days . . . I've lost count of how many."

She smiled. "True. I've been hoping we'd have a few
moments without an audience." She handed him the
breathing tube and he set it aside and gave her his hand. "I
want to thank you for saving my life."

"It was purely selfish on my part," he said. "I'm not
ure I would have wanted to go on living if something happened to you. I can't imagine Betancourt without you."

She smiled and made a soft whistling sound. "That's a
big claim. So you think of me as part of Betancourt?"

"Absolutely."

"Like the dumbwaiter, the marble floor in the entry hall,
or the indoor plumbing?"

"No." He looked astonished that she would take his
words so literally. "What I mean is, everything I see reminds
me of you. Everywhere I look I see something you've
ouched or changed or improved in some way."

"So, you're saying I've been useful?"

"Of course not. I mean, more than useful. You've been an inspiration."

"My life's goal. Being an inspiration. Be sure to tell Parliament I want white marble for my pedestal."

He studied her for a moment, seeming at a loss until he caught the twinkle in her eye.

"Vixen. You aren't the easiest woman in the world to compliment, you know." He reached for her other hand and sat on the bed beside her.

"You do have a way of talking all round what you really mean."

"And what do you think I really mean to say?"

"Something a bit more personal."

He sighed and looked thoughtful for a moment. She was right. "So I guess this is where I tell you that I love you with all my heart."

"So, tell me that." Her expectation was clear.

His jaw dropped, but a moment later he collected himself. "Sarah Bumgarten"—this wasn't so hard, after all—"I love you with my whole heart. With all that I am. With everything in me."

Those were the exact words she needed to hear. She collected them into her heart, feeling their warmth and sincerity find a home in the love and connection she felt for him. And while he was being so cooperative . . .

"With all of your heart?" she said, smiling, searching his eyes. "I don't have to share it with, say . . . Daisy?"

"Daisy? Why on earth would you—" He halted, searching her eyes and seeing in them a vulnerability he didn't expect. Ah. She wanted to know if he still had feelings for Daisy. He understood that, and he would be totally honest with her. "A part of me will always love Daisy for the part she played in awakening me to life. But if you're asking if I love her as a woman, a lover, a mate—no. The only woman I want in that way is you, Sarah Bumgarten. You're extraordinary. So loving. So beautiful, inside as well as out. And animals love you at first sight. Or sniff."

"Animals?" She looked incredulous. "First sniff?"

"Me included," he said. "You make my blood pound and my bones ache and my loins . . ." He stopped and reddened. "Well, you get the idea."

"Indeed I do." She grinned and patted the bed beside her. "Come and tell me more."

"In your sickbed?" He feigned being scandalized. It wasn't like it hadn't crossed his mind a few hundred times since she awakened.

"I know I'm not much to look at right now, but you don't have to ravish me, just hold me. Consider it therapeutic."

He looked at her pale face, thanked God Almighty, and smiled. "You're the most ravish-worthy woman I've ever seen, Sarah Bumgarten."

"I suspect you may need spectacles soon, Arthur Graham," she said with the start of tears in her eyes. "But I'll cherish every word you just said until my dying day."

Someday he would tell her how he had felt as he searched frantically for her through flames and smoke . . . how his heart nearly broke as he carried her limp form out of the stables . . . how his entire world seemed to be dying with her. He had never prayed so hard or so passionately in his life.

For the day and a half that she lay on the cusp of life and death, struggling to breathe, he felt like his own life was suspended with her. He couldn't eat or sleep or leave her side. And when the oxygen came, he could have sworn he saw wings on Sir William's shoulders. The lawyer was truly the answer to prayers.

Someday he would tell her all of that. But right now, she only needed this from him . . . to be held and comforted and loved by the man who would adore her forever and keep her in his heart.

He did precisely what she suggested and climbed up into the big bed beside her and pulled her into his arms. She felt soft and curvy yet somehow strong in his arms. She was all that was good and passionate and caring in humanity, and he wanted to be joined to her fully, completely. But in the back of his mind he heard her telling him clearly that she wanted to be *anyone but a duchess*.

He kissed her on the top of the head, listened gratefully to the whispery mews her breathing made against his chest, and postponed that tricky bit of negotiation as he gradually joined her in sleep.

"It's awfully quiet in there," Elizabeth said to the group gathered with her outside the doors to the ducal bedchamber. Red and Ashton, Daisy and Reynard also had their ears to the crack between the doors, listening. "I still don't think this is a good idea, leaving them alone like this."

"Mama!" Daisy stage whispered. "She's sick. And they have to work it out between themselves."

"I don't know how," Ash said. "Artie can be damned indecisive."

"Heh." Red gave a salacious laugh. "Ain't nothin' indecisive about the way that boy's been watchin' Sarah."

"Watching and doing are entirely different things," Reynard said, straightening from the door knob as if he'd been pricked. "You realize, I have been accused for years of listening at keyholes, but this is the first time I have ever actually *done* it. And there's nothing to hear."

"We should give them more time," Daisy said. "She could be napping, or she might have needed a breathing treatment."

Elizabeth scowled with determination. "All right, we'll give him more time. But if he hasn't settled it by tomorrow morning, he'll answer to me."

"These Graham boys." Red shook his head as he grabbed Reynard's sleeve and headed downstairs, leaving Elizabeth, Daisy, and Ashton to monitor the door. "Practically had to pound Ash to a pulp to get him to the altar with one o' my girls. God knows what it'll take to make Artie knuckle under."

Chapter Twenty-Five

L ate the next morning, a contingent headed by Elizabeth and Red forged into the duke's chambers on a mission they all agreed—however reluctantly—was necessary. Daisy, Ashton, and Reynard accompanied the family elders and behind them Sir William provided moral support.

Sarah was sitting up in bed, freshly bathed and clothed in a frilly bed jacket. Dolly had slipped into the room earlier to help her prepare for the day and had even brushed her hair and put it up for her. Beside her, Arthur was still drowsing, luxuriating in the fresh air streaming in the open windows and the fact that Sarah was feeling much better and was . . . in his bed. It was something of a rude awakening to have the doors thrown open and have the entire family invade his personal bedchamber.

"What the devil is this?" He sat up, raking his fingers through his hair.

"We've come to have a word, Your Grace," Elizabeth said in her most imperious tone.

He looked from her to Red's serious expression, then at Ashton's and Daisy's faces. Reynard wasn't wearing his usual sardonic half smile and—good Lord—Sir William looked like he was attending an execution.

"What's going on?" Sarah said, her breath coming faster, her wheezing louder. "Mama? Daisy?"

"Shush, Sarah." Elizabeth waved her response away. "This is between Arthur and us."

"What is?" Arthur said, feeling awkward suddenly at being in his own bed . . . with Sarah. He rolled to the side of the bed, straightened his breeches, and tucked in his shirt. His feet were bare but he was not about to go searching for boots or shoes just now. He drew a bracing breath and strode around the end of the bed to face them. "What do you want?"

"To put things right," Red said, glancing meaningfully toward Sarah. "Seems you've put our girl in somethin' of a pickle."

"You have it wrong, there, Red," Arthur said irritably. "There was nothing between us last night."

"Exactly," Red said with narrowed eyes.

He turned to look at Sarah and found her just as shocked as he was.

"I mean nothing happened between us," he declared.

"That's not true," Daisy said, frowning at him.

"And if it is, it's a pity," Ash put in with a superior sniff. "We Grahams have a reputation to maintain."

"As do we Bumgartens." Elizabeth crossed her arms, glaring at Ash.

"All of which is not getting us to the point." Reynard stepped forward, his hands clasped behind his back. "It's simply this, old man. We've seen the way you and our dear little sister look at each other and defend each other and obviously care for each other. And we think it's about time you did something about it."

Arthur knew he might be considered a bit thick in romantic matters, but a wholesale intervention by both families *and* legal representation was completely beyond the pale.

"What happens or doesn't between Sarah and me is none of your business," he declared, jamming his fists on his waist.

"Mama . . . Uncle Red . . . this is . . . humiliating," Sarah said, pulling the covers higher.

"It certainly is," Daisy said, stepping forward. "So end it, Arthur. Don't you have something to say to Sarah? Something of great importance?"

"I've already said it." He threw his arms up in frustration.

"You proposed?" Daisy said, her face lighting.

Sarah groaned and hid her face in the sheet. "You're all going to pay for this. I swear it."

"I declared undying love for her, to her. And . . . though it might have been the lingering effects of the oxygen, making her giddy . . . she seemed to take it well."

Ash stared at his brother. "And?"

"And what?"

"Did you or did you not propose marriage?"

"That is, I repeat, none of your business."

"You're missing the point, old boy." Reynard gestured between himself and the others. "We are making Sarah's happiness . . . and yours . . . our business. God knows how long it will take you two to get around to it, left to your own devices. And Ash and Daisy will have to head back to New York in a couple of months."

Daisy smiled and patted her stomach. "Number three on the way."

"Really?" Elizabeth broke into a squeal of delight that was quickly damped as she remembered the business at hand. "We simply want you to . . . do the right thing."

"And what if I ask her and she says no? What then?"

"What makes you think she'll say no?" Red asked, looking confused.

"Only the fact that she's stated in no uncertain terms

that she does not want to be a duchess. And every time someone has called her that, she has corrected them."

"Not entirely true," came a deep voice from near the door. Everyone turned to find Steig and Grycel leaning against the door frame, listening. Steig stepped forward with a gray puppy in his arms, petting the creature as he said, "I called her *duchess* jus' the other day, and she smiled."

"An' I called her *duchess* just this mornin' as I helped her bathe, and she smiled at me, too," Dolly said, stepping to the edge of the group.

"Good God," Arthur said in disbelief. "Anyone else want to comment? There must be a goatherd or goose girl somewhere on Betancourt whose opinion hasn't been heard!"

At the back they heard a giggle. It was Mazie.

"Arghhh!" Whatever pride he had left was writhing. He would have asked her ten times already to be his duchess . . . if he weren't so . . . what? Afraid she would say no? He had faced imprisonment, the threat of beheading, wild beasts, and crazed pirates with more confidence. She had already told him she loved him in a dozen different ways. What good would waiting do?

"Fine!" He stalked around the bed to where she was sitting with her eyes squeezed shut and her face aflame. He pried her hands off the coverlet and said her name softly. She opened one eye and then the other, and he saw in them a strange mixture of humiliation and hope. He pulled her around so that her bare feet dangled off the bed, and he knelt in front of her.

"This is not how I would have done it. I'd have gotten you flowers for your hair and champagne and a ring for your finger. I'd have taken you out into the butterfly garden at night and pointed out navigational stars and constellations to you. I'd have told you how lovely you are and how you make my life complete in ways I could never imagine. I'd have kissed you tenderly and held you against my heart."

"There's still time for all of that," she said in a whisper that drew her family and the household staff forward to catch her response. "I'm not going anywhere."

"Well, there is one place I do want you to go. With me." He swallowed hard. "To Betany's church, to say vows before God and the rest of the county." When she opened her mouth to speak, he pressed his fingers against it. "Wait. Before you answer . . . I know you don't want to be a duchess. It's a lot of responsibility and a lot of constraints and I'm not the richest duke in the realm . . . so you wouldn't exactly live in the lap of luxury. Hell, I barely have one shirt to my name. But, I love you so much it hurts, and I promise to respect you and care for you always. I pray that's enough. Marry me, Sarah. And everything I have, everything I am will be yours for the rest of my days."

Sarah felt his need, his hope, his promises of love and devotion reaching into her soul and searching out the same in her. It didn't matter that it was half coerced—she knew it would have happened sooner or later. It didn't matter that her family and his and half of Betancourt were now crowded into the bedchamber, gawking at what should have been a tender and private—

She was suddenly so full of love and joy and pleasure that she could have shouted it from the rooftop for all of Betancourt—all of the world—to hear. The hell with *private*!

"I don't want to be *a* duchess, it's true," she said, placing her hands on the sides of his face. "But I very much want to be *your* duchess, Arthur Michael Randolph Graham. I want to marry you and live with you and make babies with you . . . and raise horses and cows and goats with you . . . and see Betancourt flourish and become the best place to live in the entire kingdom." She lowered her face toward his, praying the intensity, the depths of her love for him were visible in her eyes, the way his love for her was in his.

"I love you with all my heart, with everything in me. I couldn't be prouder to call you husband and share my life with you."

He burst into a huge grin and threw his arms around her, kissing her with all the love and passion her accept-ance created in him. She slid to her feet and he picked her up carefully, ignoring whatever proprieties he might be violating in this passionate display with his bride-to-be.

There was hugging and smiling and hand-shaking . . . a little crying . . . some puppy barking . . . all over the room. The chaos, the excitement, finally got through to Sarah and she took a couple of deep breaths, and pushed back so Arthur would put her down.

"Stay," she said with a smoky rasp that said she meant business, and she turned to the group. "All right, everybody out!" She waved her arms, feeling a little light-headed, but determined.

Her mother managed to drag her into a teary-eyed hug on the way out. Red did the same, and of course Daisy had to have one. Reynard pulled Ash away, telling him he'd have to wait for a more appropriate time for a brotherly buss. She closed the door firmly behind them and turned the key in the lock.

"I want some time with you, Your Grace," she said. "And another of those kisses you just gave me. Where on earth did you learn to kiss like that?"

Chapter Twenty-Six

Banns, a wedding dress, a trousseau, a proper celebration . . . there were a thousand and one details to planning a wedding in only a month. Fortunately, Red's beloved countess, Evelyn, arrived quickly and was overjoyed to finally help marry a Bumgarten and a duke. She and Elizabeth soon had matters in hand. Daisy's wedding dress was still at Betancourt and with some alterations was made to fit Sarah nicely. Arthur was reunited with his long-lost shirts, and his trousers and jackets had been altered perfectly by the eagle-eyed seamstress who had retired to Betany. The same vicar who presided over Daisy's and Ashton's unusual nuptials eagerly agreed to finally perform the Duke of Meridian's true wedding, and Bascom agreed to furnish tables and ale aplenty for the celebration of the duke's marriage.

Daisy and Frankie would be their little sister's attendants and Ash and Reynard would stand up with Arthur. Sir William made a quick trip to London to check on his clients' cases and came back just before the wedding with a ring set with a beautiful ruby ringed with diamonds. It had been Arthur's mother's ring and was one of the few pieces of jewelry that escaped his uncles' larceny . . . primarily because Sir William separated them from the rest of Betancourt's treasure at the request of Arthur's and Ashton's father. Sir William told them that, even gravely ill, the former duke had tried to see to his beloved sons' futures.

By her wedding day, Sarah was fully recovered from her ordeal; good food and fresh air had put color in her cheeks again. Her hair was a splendid mass of curls flowing down her back and her white satin gown was augmented with flowers of blush pink and white. Daisy asked if she was nervous and Sarah laughed.

"Not a bit. I can't wait to see Arthur in his ducal best. And if he's cut his hair, I'll have to tie him up and hold him captive until it grows again." She grinned at Daisy's wicked laugh. "I don't think he'll complain."

Arthur looked every inch the duke in his best morning clothes, and to Sarah's relief, his long hair was full and flowing, just as she wanted it to be. From that day on, it would be his signature in society, though when he arrived in the House of Lords, he would likely have to wear it in a queue. With his broad shoulders, tanned skin, and smiling eyes, he was a walking dream for every young woman in attendance. And some not so young.

He burst into an exuberant smile when she and Red appeared at the rear of the sanctuary. *That*, guests whispered to each other, *was a man in love*.

For the life of them, neither Arthur or Sarah would remember later exactly what words they exchanged in the little church. It went so quickly and so smoothly that it had a surreal quality . . . out of time and place . . . just the two of them . . . already joined in their hearts and now joining in a way that would proclaim to the world their loving bond.

Soon they were exiting the little stone church to hugs and handshakes and not a few tears. Everyone was there: Frankie and Reynard, Daisy and Ashton, and even Cece and her husband Julian, who came all the way from Paris to see her wedded and to provide music that left hardly a dry eye in the little church.

Many of Betancourt's tenants and Betany's village folk attended the nuptials: Bascom and his wife, the Arnetts, the Crotons, the Millers, and Thomas Wrenn's family. Of course Eddie, their newly appointed stable master, was there in his first-ever suit. Of special interest to the family was Sir William Drexel's presence and his prominent seat next to the mother of the bride.

After greetings and well wishes, Sarah and Arthur ran through a shower of rice to their flower-draped carriage and climbed in for the ride back to Betancourt. They gazed at each other and held hands, filled with such joy they could only laugh and hug and beam with pleasure.

It was a beautiful summer day and the front lawn was set with tables and benches, and food was trundled out on handcarts and set up. Cece and Julian joined with local musicians in providing wonderful music for the fête, while Red presided in his booming voice and welcomed one and all. Food was plentiful, wine and ale flowed, and when the dancing began, all were surprised to see Duke Arthur take the first turn on the lawn with his duchess.

He was quite a good dancer, it seemed, with Sarah in his arms and in his heart. He led her into a waltz that Cece and Julian played just for them, and kissed her so lustily afterward that the men in the crowd raised a roar of approval and the women all laughed slyly and clapped. Afterward everyone danced and drank and made merry.

The party would go on for hours, but without the happy couple. They slipped out of the crowd, ran to the makeshift barn that now held their horses, where Eddie had Fancy saddled and waiting for them. Arthur removed his coat and she pinned up her train into a bustle. They climbed aboard Fancy and rode out into the countryside to walk hand in hand through wheat fields and cherry orchards, beside streams and alongside pastures filled with sheep. This was their home, their duty, and their deep and mutual joy. Their vow, on this day of days, was that they would tend it and care for it together, making the land prosperous and the people safe.

They removed their shoes and slipped out of stockings to wade in a creek and lie out on a large rock afterward to dry off. While they stared up at the sky through the swaying branches, a butterfly landed nearby and as they watched, it came to investigate the flowers on her bodice.

"It's a sign," she said softly.

"A blessing," he agreed, threading his fingers through hers.

They watched until it flew away, then he rose onto an elbow and kissed her. His lips were as gentle as the stroke of a butterfly's wings as he showered unbearably light kisses down her chest to the rim of her bodice. By the time he reached her breast she was aching inside, hungry for the pleasure she knew could be hers with him now.

She pulled him back up to face her.

"Now," she said. "Here."

"I am not a man to take a nuptial outing unprepared," he said with a wicked laugh. "Wait here."

He returned with a blanket, spread it out in some soft grass, and escorted her to it. The row of tiny satin-covered buttons down her back was an unexpected challenge.

"Your mother planned this dress, didn't she?" Arthur said with a groan. "So damned many buttons."

Sarah laughed. "It was Daisy's wedding dress first—I suspect that if she did it on purpose, it was to annoy Ashton. He was not exactly her first choice for a son-in-law."

"No." He chuckled. "I was."

"And she finally landed you. With my help, of course."

She glanced over her shoulder. "I should have asked Daisy for the secret to getting out of this dress quickly."

He groaned, said, "Brace yourself," and there was a terrific rending sound.

"Oh my gosh—what did you—oh. Ohhh." She was all but freed from the heavy satin. He had ripped the lower part of the button closure apart, which was no small feat considering the number of buttons and the strength of the satin and taping. She shimmied out of her gown and turned to him in corset and petticoats. "I love your vest, it's quite elegant. But it has to go." She attacked his buttons and soon he was shedding both vest and shirt.

Her petticoats came next and then her laces.

He traced the slope of her back and stroked the breadth of her shoulders as her corset slipped away. His lips replaced his hands and she sank back against him, holding her breath. This pleasure, this access to his body was hers from now on, as hers was his. She turned in his arms and he kissed her deeply, evoking a response that had been building in her for weeks, months. She rocked up onto her toes, sank her fingers into his hair and pulled him down into a kiss so fierce it took his breath and hers.

He staggered as she pressed her body hungrily against him and in a moment they were on the blanket, in a sea of frothy lace and gleaming satin, shedding the last of their clothes. She ran her hands over his shoulders, his back, and his chest as he tantalized her breasts with his palm and then filled his hands with her buttocks, her thighs.

"You are so beautiful. I am such a lucky man."

"Ummmm," she murmured against his lips. "Such a good man." She raked the side of his neck with her teeth and he shivered. "With such tasty kisses."

"As good as raspberry trifle?" he murmured, kissing and nibbling his way down to her breasts. Taking her nipple in his mouth, he pulled invisible cords of sensation in her that reached all the way to her sex. Her body responded, tightening, preparing, moving against him.

"Better. Oh, Arthur . . . much, much better."

He paused for a moment and pushed up to absorb the sight of her nestled in a tangle of lace and shimmering satin. "Tell me you won't regret that the first time isn't in our bed."

"I won't. There will be plenty of other times in that bed, I promise you." Her gaze softened as she studied his handsome body and beloved face. He was hers, to love, to pleasure, to care for. It was pure grace that had brought them together. "What better place to complete our loving than here, on the land we love . . . in the shade of these gracious trees . . . to the music of nearby water. I will always remember this, my sweet Arthur, with joy."

He smiled and lowered himself to her kiss. Together they sank deeper, deeper into unexplored desires. Their hands moved at the urging of impatient hearts and rising passions. By the time he nibbled his way down her stomach and back up to her other breast, she was open to him completely, nothing held back. He covered her with his body and the sheer physicality of that contact was breathtaking. She undulated against him in ways that she had never imagined herself moving, stimulating a hunger in her skin that seeped through her muscles and sinews, all the way to her very bones. She welcomed him between her legs and discovered even sharper, more focused pleasure as they began to move against each other together.

By the time he joined their bodies, she received him eagerly, relishing every delicious sensation of fullness and completion. He paused to kiss her tenderly, reading her response and letting it guide his movement and his own response.

He moved slowly at first, giving her time to adjust and himself time to maintain control. But before long, she was moving in counterpoint to him and felt herself tensing, moving more forcefully, pushing beyond the limits of her experience to a realm of pure discovery. Her boundaries began to melt and mingle with his so that she sensed they shared feelings, even as she experienced wave after wave of luscious new sensations.

She rode a mounting spiral of pleasure, sensing something building in her, a voluptuous bloom of heat and urgency that made her moan and wrap her legs around him, taking him deeper, holding him tighter. Then reality erupted all around and within her in a brilliant, shuddering climax that broke bounds of time and place. She held him tightly as she sank back into her time and place . . . back into a body that had just amazed her with its wisdom and daring.

He nuzzled her ear and kissed her hair and blew across her overheated skin. "Are you all right?" he whispered with that seductive rasp to his voice.

"I am wonderful," she said, not sure why she suddenly felt like crying. Tears rolled back from her eyes into her hair and he kissed those, too. "I'm not sure why there are tears. I'm so happy." But still the tears came and he laughed softly and shifted to lie beside her and pull her into his arms.

"It's no small thing, marrying and discovering pleasure with the one you love." There was an odd huskiness to his voice that made her look up. There were prisms of tears in his eyes, too, even though he was smiling. "When you're this full, something has to overflow."

"Happy tears," she said with unabashed wonder. "I thought they were an old wives' tale." She wiped her tears and stared at her damp fingers.

He gathered her against him and they lay together for a while, drowsy and luxuriating in the closeness their loving had created between them.

"I don't want to go back," she said. "I just want to stay here all evening, all night."

"You do have a romantic streak in you." He touched her nose playfully. "But about two in the morning, I think you'd be wishing you were in a comfortable bed. And it just happens that I know one that is empty."

"Oooh. Is it a big bed?"

"It is."

"And is it soft?"

"As a cloud."

"What are we waiting for?"

They kissed between garments, and tickled and laughed. It took a long time to make themselves presentable. And they were going to have to make up a story about the buttons on her dress . . . which no one in their right mind would believe. But it wouldn't matter. Such things were winked at for newly married couples on their wedding night.

As they rode Fancy back to Betancourt House, they resigned themselves to making rounds of their guests and delaying their retreat to the big, comfortable bed in Arthur's chambers. But by the time they reached the celebration on the lawn, everyone was tipsy and spouses were canoodling and young people were getting frisky. Someone had inadvertently let Sarah's dogs out of the house and they were running all around and snitching food from abandoned plates and stealing shoes that had been shed for dancing.

In short, no one really expected the happy couple to spend the rest of the evening with them. And if anyone noticed the significant hole in the back of her gown, they didn't mention it. Not even Elizabeth, who apparently had imbibed quite a bit of wine and was giggling with Sir William over . . . who knew what.

So, as the sun set and lanterns were lighted, they hugged those who had to be hugged and thanked those who had to be thanked, and disappeared up the main stairs of Betancourt House.

For luck he carried her across the threshold of their bed-chamber and deposited her on the bed. She stretched like a cat caught in a sunbeam, reveling in the vibrant joy of being alive and in love. Dolly had opened the windows to cool the room for them and the bed had been freshened with clean linen. Flowers from the garden outside and from bouquets inside the bedchamber perfumed the air. It couldn't have been more perfect.

He came to the bed and stood looking down at her with such love, such pleasure visible in his face that she sighed in utter contentment.

"Now it's time for your wedding gift," he said.

She bolted upright on the bed.

"What wedding gift? I didn't know you were . . . Were we supposed to get each other gifts?"

"I've chosen something I know you've wanted for a long time." He stepped back into the moonlight streaming through the open window, took a deep breath and began to sing.

"Oh my darlin' . . . oh my darlin' . . . oh my darlin' Clementine . . . you are lost and gone forever . . . dreadful sorry, Clementine."

She went from a grin to a laugh as he sang—surprised by how full and pleasant his voice was. But it was his choice of song that filled her heart with joy. It was not only the duck-calming song that he'd finally learned, it was a nod to her American heritage.

She started to go to him, but he held out his hand to stop her.

"Wait! I learned all the verses, just for you." He contin-ued: *"In a cavern, in a canyon, excavating for a mine . . . dwelt a miner, forty-niner, and his daughter Clementine. Oh my darlin', oh my darlin', oh my darlin' Clementine . . ."*

By the time he reached the part about Clementine's sandals being "boxes without topses," her face hurt from grinning, but she couldn't stop.

He put in a few dramatic flourishes: clasping his chest and lifting his chin to a ridiculous height. From outside the doors came the strains of violins in accompaniment. He had recruited Cece and Julian? She laughed even harder.

By the time Clementine "hit her foot against a splinter" and "fell into the foaming brine," she was weak with laughter and had to lean on the pillows for support.

But the real climax was something not even Arthur could have predicted. When Clementine's ruby lips were "blowing bubbles, soft and fine" a terrible howl arose outside the window. Arthur stopped singing and rushed to see what was happening. On the darkened lawn below the window sat Nero, Nellie, Lance, and Gwenny . . . their muzzles pointed skyward as they howled in concert with his singing.

Refusing to be bested, Arthur stalked back to his spot in the moonlight and continued to sing . . . about how he missed his Clementine. And the dogs took up howling again. This time he continued to the end, where he "kissed her little sister," then "I forgot my Clementine."

From outside the door, voices joined him and the howling dogs in a final chorus . . . that soon dissolved into hysterical laughter.

Sarah was weak as she slid from the bed and rushed to him with open arms.

"You crazy, wonderful man!" She hugged him wildly, kissed him deeply, and succeeded in drawing him into her mirth. Soon they were lying on the bed, trying to quit laughing and having a devil of a time doing it. They finally drew deep breaths and settled together, arms entwined and legs tangled together.

He gave one last chuckle. "So did you like your gift?"

"It was magnificent." She smiled. "But you know what this means."

"Not really." He had no idea what was in her head. She never failed to surprise him. "What does it mean?"

"If we have a little girl, we have to name her Clementine."

His head fell back on the pillow.

"Oh, God."

Epilogue

Ascot, five years later

The sky was a rare, pristine blue, the temperature was balmy, and the grounds were manicured to perfection . . . it was a gorgeous day for the Gold Cup at Royal Ascot. Everyone who was anyone was in attendance and decked out in finery unique in the social season. Gentlemen wore their best gray or black morning clothes and top hats, and ladies wore light summer dresses in a rainbow of colors and hats that strained the skill and imagination of the best milliners on the Continent. A year's wages was the starting price of many of the fanciful silk chiffon and feather-trimmed creations on display.

Even among such rarified company, the Duke and Duchess of Meridian caused conversation to cease for a moment as they and their friends, the Tannehills, passed by. He was tall and tanned and she was curvy and delicate. She wore a pale blue dress and a hat that was elegant, but with a hint of whimsy that matched the light in her eyes. Few would have guessed that she had given birth to their second child, a daughter they had named Cassandra, mere months before.

Old rumors stirred. He had disappeared for a while, captured by pirates . . . he saved a chieftain's son . . . he had been lost in the desert for days . . . and most amusing to the duke himself, he had been shipwrecked on an exotic island and found a great treasure. What else could explain the resurgence of his estate and the stables that were gradually becoming the talk of the racing world?

He had indeed found a treasure, he was wont to say. She filled his arms and his heart and never failed to surprise him with her goodness and uncanny insight into horses and people. Both were drawn to her in ways that he would never fully understand, only appreciate. Thus it was no surprise when a couple . . . a pasty middle-aged-looking fellow and his overdressed, overfed wife . . . nudged and elbowed their way through the crowd to make their acquaintance.

"Kelling," the man said, offering the duke his name and hand in a total breach of etiquette. "I've been told you're quite the horseman. Have a stable on the rise." The whiff of strong liquor that reached them explained at least some of his behavior. "Do you have a filly in this cup?"

"Meridian," Arthur said, as he took the man's hand and tipped his hat to the woman standing half a step behind her husband, eyeing him over her husband's shoulder with insulting thoroughness. "And no, I do not. Betancourt horses are bred for the National Hunt."

Just then, Sarah turned from speaking with her sister to find herself facing a man she knew but was shocked to barely recognize. Terrence Tyrell, Earl of Kelling, had once been the desire of her girlish heart. Looking at him now—his sallow skin, dark-circled eyes behind a pair of spectacles, and paunchy middle—she had to wonder why.

He greeted her with more propriety than he had shown Arthur, waiting until she extended her hand to reach for it.

"Have we met before?" he said, slow to recognize her. "No, surely I would recall meeting such a . . ." He stopped as recognition dawned. "Oh. Well. It was lovely to . . . um . . . meet you," he babbled. "Heard so much about you." He turned and ran into his wife as she stepped forward, squinting at Sarah.

"We know each otha?" she said in heavily accented English, extending a limp hand that Sarah judiciously ignored. "Ima sure you meet me somewhere. Canna recall it. But then, one meets so manny, manny people. Ohhh . . . I have a hat just like that." Her lidded eyes were full of unpleasantness.

"We have to be going." Terrence gave his countess a nudge that was perilously close to being a shove. But he couldn't resist one last glance at Sarah. "So good to see you . . . doing well."

As he trundled his wife off into the crowd, Sarah looked up at Arthur and found his eyes had that steely glint that betrayed strong emotion.

Reynard leaned over her shoulder to mutter, "I would have told you what happened to him, but I suspected it would be more satisfying for you to see for yourself someday."

She glanced up at Reynard's sympathetic smile and turned to her sister Frankie, whose loving and supportive expression made her grateful all over again for being born a Bumgarten.

As she took Arthur's arm and they continued down the stands to find their seats, she looked up at him.

"You do know who that was?" she asked.

"I do." His arm tightened under her hand, but he gave her that deliciously devious smile she loved. "I swore to flatten him if we ever came face-to-face. I hope you're not too disappointed."

She laughed and gave his arm a loving stroke. "Not really. In fact, I admire your restraint."

"Well, he was wearing spectacles, after all, and I got a good look at his wife." He chuckled. "I expect he's been punished enough."

AUTHOR'S NOTE

There you have it. The third and final installment of my Sin and Sensibility series. I confess, it was hard letting these characters head off into their happily-ever-after without me to chronicle their further exploits. But they deserve some fun and—I think you'll agree—some privacy.

Sarah and Arthur are among my favorite characters ever. Their growing love and its impact on their families and community are an example of how love can spiral outward from two people and make the world a better place. That's my firm belief and my hope for the world.

Though this book doesn't center around one specific historical happening, it still required a good bit of research . . . some of which you may find interesting, too.

Thermometers and stethoscopes? In a story set in the 1890s? Yep, they had 'em. I do admit that some of the stethoscopes looked different from current day models, but they were coming into common use in Sarah's day and provided information so necessary that it makes me wonder why they weren't invented sooner.

Sarah did indeed treat man and beast, though some of her knowledge came from books. One piece that did not, was the use of "bluestone" to treat infections in horses' hooves. It was the early version of copper sulfate, which is still used today by big animal vets to treat infections in horse and cow hooves. Thanks, Dr. Pol, for starting me on that train of research.

Honey on a wound, however, was known as a home

cure for generations before Sarah tried it. And the germ theory was indeed becoming the predominant theory of illness in England and across the world. However, word of it was slow getting out to many places and the necessity of hand-washing was considered a bit too fastidious and unproven for some time after Sarah's adoption of it.

And while we're on the subject of historical medical practice, you may be shocked to learn (as I was) that oxygen was known as the agent of respiration from 1800 onward. By the mid-nineteenth century, oxygen treatments were being given to select patients in larger medical centers. By Sarah's day near the turn of the century, it was used as therapy for a variety of lung complaints . . . including smoke inhalation. I confess, I was desperate to help Sarah survive, and when I learned the equipment was available in her day, I had to see she got that help.

As for the legal mess Arthur started when he charged off to see the world—Sir William was right in saying that a hereditary title could only be passed to another through the death of the title holder, and seven years absent/missing has long been the standard waiting time before declaring someone dead. This was a sticky wicket for me and I was grateful to Sir William for making it clear.

So much for the American dollar princesses and their happily-ever-afters.

I must add that HEAs, as they're known among romance readers, are not limited to gorgeous young women with buckets of money. Mothers and mothers-in-law—especially those who have paid their dues—deserve some love, too. I'd like to think that after Sarah's wedding, her mother, Elizabeth, kept company with Sir William, who was a widower. He became much loved by the family and—who knows?—there might have been yet another Bumgarten wedding. You can decide.

Thanks so much for joining me on this journey. I'd love to hear from you! Stop by BetinaKrahn.com for a look at what's happening now and what's yet to come! Drop a comment or a picture to be added to my list.

Grace and Peace,
          Betina

When she abruptly ends their engagement, he thinks himself well rid of a tempestuous and unpredictable female . . . until he reads the *Times* two days later.
It seems there was a reporter on the river that day who witnessed Lauren's rescue of the two women and decided it would make a juicy story.
When her father is besieged by reporters insisting on details about why his daughter's engagement has been broken, he realizes Lauren is in trouble. Her behavior is considered laudable by some and scandalous by others. Her reputation hangs in the balance. And Rafe has been labeled as "less than a hero."
There is only one option.
Lauren and Rafe must temporarily put aside their differences and appear in public together to put down all the rumors.
What could possibly go wrong?